EMILIA ARES

SERA
PRESS

ALSO BY EMILIA ARES

Love and Other Sins

THE LOVE AND OTHER SINS SERIES

LOVE
and Other
CAGES

EMILIA ARES

SERA
PRESS

Love and Other Cages

Copyright © 2024 Emilia Ares

Published by

SERA
PRESS

Hardcover: 979-8-9903839-2-0
Paperback: 979-8-9903839-1-3
eISBN: 979-8-9903839-0-6
Audiobook: 979-8-9903839-3-7

Cover Design: Miblart
Copyediting: Elizabeth Cody Kimmel
Proofreading: Mike Waitz

LOVE AND OTHER CAGES
EMILIA ARES

SERA
PRESS

In Loving Memory
Arkadiy, Zhorik, Sergey, Gevorik, Emma, and Sophia

"The most beautiful people are those who have known defeat, known suffering, known struggle, known loss, and have found their way out of the depths. These persons have an appreciation, a sensitivity, and an understanding of life that fills them with compassion, gentleness, and a deep loving concern. Beautiful people do not just happen."

— ELISABETH KÜBLER-ROSS

This is for the beautiful people.

ADVANCE REVIEW COPY

FOR IMMEDIATE RELEASE
CONTACT: SERA PRESS
INFO@SERA.PRESS

PUB DATE: OCTOBER 15, 2024

LOVE AND OTHER CAGES
BY EMILIA ARES

THE NEXT BIG SUSPENSEFUL ROMANTIC THRILLER SWEEPS READERS UP IN AN EMOTIONAL RIGHT PERSON-WRONG TIME TALE WHERE FAMILY DRAMA AND VIOLENCE CLASH IN CONTEMPORARY L.A.

AVAILABLE WORLDWIDE
WHERE YOU CAN LEAVE A REVIEW ASAP:

GOODREADS
STORYGRAPH
FABLE
BOOKMORY
LIBRARY THING

B&N
INDIEBOUND
AUDIBLE
SCRIBD
LIBRO

SET REMINDER TO LEAVE A REVIEW ON OCT 15:

AMAZON

TRADE REVIEWS

"Ares' prose is both lyrical and evocative, immersing readers in the emotional depths of the story. Love and Other Cages is a compelling and poignant exploration of relationships under strain, and I would certainly recommend it to fans of suspenseful romantic thrillers everywhere."
—*Readers' Favorite*

Book Title: Love and Other Cages
Author: Emilia Ares
Publisher: SERA Press
Page Count: 448
Pub Date: October 15, 2024

Paperback: 979-8-9903839-1-3
Paperback Price: $16.95

Hardcover: 979-8-9903839-2-0
Hardcover Price: $29.95

ebook: 979-8-9903839-0-6
eBook Price: $4.99

Audiobook: 979-8-9903839-3-7
Audiobook Price: $14.95

SERA
PRESS

🌐 www.emiliaares.com

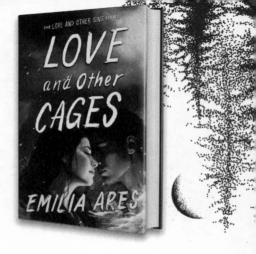

Get exclusive access to letters between Oliver and Remi —the librarian who saved Oliver's life— when you sign up for:

EMILIA ARES' VIP READERS CLUB
emiliaares.com/vipreaders

Get first glance at series content, release information, and updates.

Join the
**EMILIA ARES'
READING TRIBE**
on *Facebook Groups*
or the
**LOVE AND OTHER SINS
bookclub**
on *Fable*
where we can chat about Oliver, Mina, Nyah, Xavi, make predictions and more.

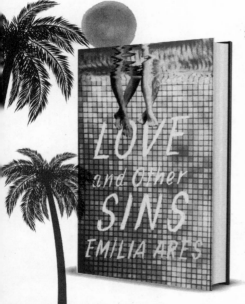

PLEASE REVIEW MY BOOK

I sincerely hope you enjoy this reading experience. If you do, I would greatly appreciate a short review on Goodreads, Amazon, or your favorite book website. Reviews are crucial for any author, and even just a line or two can make a huge difference.

WHERE YOU CAN LEAVE A REVIEW:
GOODREADS
STORYGRAPH
FABLE
BOOKMORY
LIBRARY THING
B&N
INDIEBOUND
AUDIBLE
SCRIBD
LIBRO
AMAZON (AFTER OCT 15)
AND MORE...

CHAPTER 1

OLIVER

Oliver Mondell and Oliver Rosales were two different people, and I was both of them.

Oliver Rosales woke up every day wishing he hadn't. Oliver didn't have dreams; all he had was his harsh reality and the nightmares it spawned. He barely slept at all, but that was all right because sleep was a privilege he couldn't afford to risk his life on.

Oliver Mondell slept worse than most but it had nothing on Oliver Rosales' insomnia. The night Oliver Mondell slept in Mina Arkova's room for the first and only time was the best night of sleep he'd had in his miserable life. It was of little consequence that the bed was far too small to fit them both comfortably, or that his left arm had gone entirely numb halfway through the night. They'd been glued together in the same position for so long, both equally reluctant to let go of the bond crystalizing between them. It didn't matter that it was entirely too hot in that house and that he had shed what seemed like a fourth of his body weight in sweat throughout the night.

Because all that mattered to him was that he was with her. When he woke up, Mina Arkova was in his arms—their limbs entwined like the roots of two trees. Despite an especially tumultuous trial of friendship, Mina had made him feel like a whole person in a way he never had before. She had this uncanny way of shining light on all his best parts. He'd revealed the darkest, most repulsive pieces of his past to her—the pieces he kept hidden from the world—and in turn, she'd embraced them with openness and an unconditional love he'd never felt before.

Oliver Rosales didn't have a Mina Arkova in his life. Oliver Rosales didn't even know a Mina Arkova could exist—a person so free of judgment and so full of love that she had the capacity to extend her heart to someone who had been as unfortunate as he had been, and still see hope for him. The only person who'd ever given a damn about Oliver Rosales was a kind and intuitive librarian named Remi, who didn't ignore the warning signs. Remi didn't just throw a life raft to a drowning boy, she jumped into predatory waters and fought beside him to pull him away from harm. Oliver Rosales thought she'd done it out of pity, and pity wasn't love. Pity didn't heal wounds the way love did. And pity didn't make a boy into a man—only self-love could do that.

Oliver Rosales did not love himself. He didn't know how to. When the old librarian's compassion had grown into love, Oliver Rosales still couldn't bring himself to acknowledge it as more than mere commiseration. So, he said goodbye to Oliver Rosales of Santa Clarita, goodbye to Remi, goodbye to every reminder of his old life. He shed that skin and became Oliver Mondell of Los Angeles—the blank slate, the entrepreneur, the hopeful one.

In Los Angeles, Oliver Mondell slowly began to weave a web in his brain that bridged mere survival to self-acceptance to self-love. Every successful business interaction, every rent check paid on time, every purchase made, every good grade, every smile from Mina Arkova contributed to that bridge.

Last night, that bridge was brought to near completion because each time he cut open his chest to reveal the oozing tar inside and spoke of his abuse aloud to Mina, she continued to smile that healing smile at him. Only now, it was with deeper understanding of all he'd endured. The bridge grew thick, and its supports more intricate.

One day, Oliver Mondell would come to terms with the fact that Oliver Rosales deserved to be loved—by others and himself. But for now, he was far too pleased, waking up with his arms around the most perfect girl he'd ever known. A girl who'd gotten a glimpse of the festering wounds beneath his well-camouflaged bandages and loved him for them, not despite them. A girl whose delicate, slender fingers draped across his chest, effortlessly elegant even in sleep. A girl whose powerful thigh rested heavily over the center of his body, grounding him under the weight of her potential energy. A girl whose round, parted lips funneled a gentle caress of breath against the skin of his neck. His girl.

This moment couldn't exist in Oliver Rosales' wildest dreams. This moment would never be possible again in Oliver Mondell's worst nightmares.

CHAPTER 2

MINA

Yesterday, I hit bedrock. Today, I was soaring for the stratosphere.

I recalled the nearly indiscernible flicker of fear that flashed in Oliver's eyes as he finally revealed his heart-breaking secret to me last night. When someone you fall for unlocks their Fort Knox of a chest, pulls out their own beating heart, and places it into your open palms, you're supposed to handle it gently. Especially when that someone is as guarded as Oliver. *Don't crush me*, Oliver's gaze seemed to plead as he bestowed his trust on me.

I had run down to the kitchen to distract my mother, hugging her tightly so she wouldn't turn and see what I saw through the window—Oliver jumping lightly from the tree onto the ground. I continued clinging to Mama, stubbornly holding her face against mine as the beautiful dark angel who had crept silently from my bedroom window made his escape.

I watched Oliver disappear safely, my heart in my throat. As Mama pulled back, she cupped my face between her palms and furrowed her brows, sensing something was off. A thick coat of guilt oozed over me, sticky and unwelcome.

I promised myself this would be the last time I kept something from her. No more lies between us. No more half-truths or secrets. I needed things to get back to normal.

"We are okay, *babychka. Minachka*, nothing can ever changing our bond. Loving you, always, no matter the what," Mama reassured, pressing her lips against my forehead before pulling me back into a tight embrace.

"Your pronunciation is getting so good, *Mamachka*! Remember how you used to say 'alvays' instead of always and 'no matter the vaat' instead of what? You can drop the 'the' by the way," I suggested.

"Huh?" She knitted her brows.

"Never mind, it's perfect. You're perfect." I nestled into her, wishing I could sink further into the cocoon of her love. She always did know my every thought without me having to verbalize it. From now on, I would tell her everything. The way I always had. The way she deserved. We would be okay—we had to be. We were the only family we had around here.

Reparations would not likely go as smoothly with Nyah. My hands were itching to call my best friend—to grovel, apologize, beg for forgiveness even though I already did that last night. But one more time wouldn't hurt, just to be sure she knew how sorry I was. It was the least she deserved after what I put her through at that stupid party.

I was upstairs when I heard it—the sound that turned my entire world off-kilter.

Thunk. I jumped, startled by the sound of muffled reports and a loud crash. *What the hell was that?*

Instinctively, I crouched as I rushed over to my window and

peered outside. My throat tightened in horror as I saw it—a huge, shiny black SUV in our driveway, blocking in Mama's car. *Who are they? What do they want?* I heard a sound that made my blood run cold. Muffled male voices, coming from the room directly below mine. The kitchen. *My God, they're INSIDE the house*, I thought in a panic. Cell phone, I told myself, trying to control the wave of panic rising in my throat. I raced to the bed and pulled off the covers, feeling around for my phone. The male voices were coming from another room now. There was a violent clatter. I froze—petrified. The walls rotated around me as my breathing became shallower and shallower. My feet turned to lead. I needed to do something—hide, find a weapon, *anything*.

Loving you, always. Mama's voice echoed through my head. Inching my way carefully to the door, I dialed 911 with one hand and braced against the doorframe with the other as I checked the stairwell to make sure it was clear. I dashed into Mama's room as quietly as I could. She needed me, fast, that much I knew. But running downstairs without a weapon or any backup would be stupid.

"911. What is your emergency?" I could barely make out the operator through the pounding in my ears.

"There are men here...we're being attacked in our house," I hissed through my teeth. "I think they have guns and they're here to hurt us. Please hurry," I urged.

"Okay, honey, I'm gonna get help out to you right now. Stay on the line while I pull up your location." I heard her keyboard clacking furiously. "What's your name, hon? You said the men are still in your house?"

"My name is Mina," I whispered, straining to make out the voices downstairs. "Yes, they're downstairs in the kitchen." Did they have Mama? Or had she hidden?

"And you said they had guns? Do you know how many weapons there are?"

"No, I mean—at least one. Probably more. They're downstairs in the kitchen—I think they might have my mother."

"And where in the house are you? Is it somewhere you can stay hidden?" I knew she was trained to stay calm, but the lack of urgency in her voice made me want to scream.

"In my mother's room," I murmured.

"Okay, good. Stay hidden. Do not make any noise. You're doing great, Mina. Help will arrive shortly, I promise you. Remember. Stay hidden. You said your mom was downstairs?"

"Yes." I heard an explosion of voices then, men's voices shouting, and another voice—Mama's, barking back at them. I felt a wave of nausea hit my stomach. They had her. I stood up shakily, steeling myself to go down and fight for her.

"They have my mother," I said, my voice rising with panic. "I have to do something...they're going to hurt her!"

"Mina, stay with me, okay? Don't move. Stay where you are and hide until help arrives. I'll stay on the line with you, just hold on..."

I crept deeper into Mama's room, almost tripping over the open suitcase and the piles of clothes scattered around the floor. I located the pocketknife she kept in her purse on the nightstand. I palmed it, and pressed the button that released the blade. *There's a crowbar in her closet*, I remembered. *"For keeping the creeps humble,"* Mama would always say, laughing. As I quietly rummaged through the closet, I glanced back at the door, but the sounds of struggle continued. Mama was putting up one hell of a fight, the image of which made my hands shake violently. My heart was hammering in my chest and sweat coated my palms, but I managed to wrap my fingers around the crowbar. Still shaking, I dashed back to my room on the tips of my socked toes.

If they caught me on the stairs, it would be over. *Head-to-head, brute strength would win.* The only way out of this was to take them by surprise. I knew I only had one option. I dangled a leg out of my window, reaching for the closest branch of the tree. *This is it*. With trembling hands, I gripped the largest branch of the tree for dear life as I shifted my full weight over and mapped my descent. I had to be quick, or they'd spot me. The crowbar was tucked into the back of my shorts and scraped a painful path along my skin as I hung down and stretched my leg out, feeling for the next step, but couldn't land on anything solid.

Instead, I hung, suspended in the air, aiming for the branch below. I let go, landing with a violent crack. The crowbar fell out of its tuck and landed in the grass with a heavy thud. I scooted in toward the trunk of the tree, inch by inch until my legs found footing on another branch below. I kept descending until finally I was all the way down. I felt around for the crowbar and ran for the front of the house.

I saw no driver in the SUV, so I gambled my luck on everyone being inside. Our front door was standing wide open. I crouched and crawled up to the front steps, making sure to stay low.

"I told you there's no one else here! Why are you dragging me up the stairs?" I heard Mama scream. I knew that she was screaming not in an automatic terror response, but to communicate her position to me. Taking a deep, ragged breath, I crept through the open door and stepped behind a planter, squinting as my eyes adjusted to the scene in front of me. Two men were dragging my mother up the stairs. One had her around the waist, and the other was struggling to keep hold of her legs, which kept bucking and kicking him. Neither of them had spotted me yet. She almost broke loose for a moment, and when I caught sight of blood smeared across her face, a hot, pulsing anger exploded in my chest. I choked back an animalistic growl and lunged, waving the crowbar high over my head.

A scream tore through my vocal cords as I connected with the back of the first man's skull, a heavy *thwack* sounding in the air. He lurched off-balance then catapulted toward me, hitting me at hip-level and taking me down the stairs with him. Pain erupted through my body as I hit the floor and felt him land on top of me. I braced myself for his attack, but quickly realized his body was limp. A warm, sticky moisture coated my hands and face. Blood. I bellowed and grunted as I shoved his unmoving body off of me and staggered back to Mama and the second man, who held her in a chokehold at the top of the stairs.

"*Bizhi*, Mina!" she barked out hoarsely. *But I can't run, Mama, I can hardly see.* I must have hit my head when the oversized creep knocked me down. I blinked over and over, but everything was a blur of burning red. I couldn't hear past the ringing in my skull. I felt around me frantically, half deaf and partially blind. I put my hands up and grabbed the banister to steady me. The whole house felt like it was spinning and only the staircase was holding me up. "Mina," Mama croaked, her voice breaking this time.

She sounded so weak; her voice was all wrong. *I have to get to her.* Pulling myself upright by the banister, I nudged the limp mammoth of a man with my foot to make sure he was still unconscious.

"Mina," Mama tried again, her eyes focusing on the floor to my left. "*Ya pnula yego pistolet.*" *His gun!* She'd kicked away his gun. I spotted something metallic at the foot of the stairs, and when I looked back at her, she gave me a nearly imperceptible nod before kicking and punching her captor with all her might. I took the opportunity and reached down, fingers wrapping around the metal.

Thunk. I stilled at the sickening crack. I forced my head up just in time to watch the cretin smash Mama into the stairwell wall again. A sob tore through me as she went limp and silent. Blood began to pool on the stairs from an ugly gaping wound on her head.

I stood shakily, training the gun on the man crouching over

her. I squinted, fighting to focus on the bulk of him as he hid like a coward behind Mama's limp body. Would I be able to shoot the bastard without hitting Mama?

"Please," I hissed through my teeth. "Just let her go. You can take whatever you want—just let her go."

The man made an ugly laughing sound, then grabbed Mama's hair and dragged her back toward him, positioning her more securely as a shield in front of him.

"Stop!" I screamed.

"You better drop that gun, little girl," he said, flashing a menacing grin. He had a sharp chin, a nose like a hook, and salt and pepper hair. As he dragged her up the stairs, she let out a cry of pain, and her hands shot up to grab his wrists.

"Stop it!" I bellowed. Fury boiled deep in my belly. "I'll kill you. I swear it." I stood up on shaking legs, ignoring the sharp pain cutting through my ankle. I fired a warning shot into the ceiling to let him know I meant business, then aimed the gun back down at him, unflinching.

My blood had turned to ice. My whole body felt like it was shrinking. I couldn't feel my legs beneath me, and I was beginning to hyperventilate, desperate for the room to stop spinning.

"Calm down, bitch!" he barked.

The command was so ridiculous I almost laughed.

"You're telling me to calm down? You have my mother's life in your hands, you piece of shit. And if you hadn't noticed, I have a gun pointed at your head. I'll kill you and I won't bat an eye! Now, let...her go." I clenched my teeth, my heart racing so fast that my chest throbbed in pain. Just as I focused my sights on his head and he tried to crouch behind her, the sound of sirens blared through the streets behind me, growing louder and closer by the second. The man's eyes frantically darted between the gun and the door.

"Screw this," he spat, using the distraction of the sirens to release Mama, lifting and practically throwing her down the stairs at me, as he turned to make his escape. I dropped the gun and launched my body forward, desperate to break her fall, but her head cracked against the stairway wall before I could catch her. She landed in my arms as limp as a rag doll. From the corner of my vision, I could see her attacker racing into my room, but my only thoughts now were for my mother.

As I held Mama and tried to figure out where the blood was coming from to stop it, a booming voice cut through the sirens. "LAPD. Everybody on the ground!"

Ignoring them, I kept my gaze trained on her. "I'm here, Mama, I'm here. I'm here," I chanted to her in a whisper.

"Hands in the air!" the same voice bellowed.

"Stay with me, Mama. Stay with me. Stay with me. I love you. Stay with me." I cried out in a prayer to God because she wasn't drifting anymore; her eyes were closed. Her chest was still, no longer rising and falling.

She was gone.

CHAPTER 3

OLIVER

"What do you mean Led Zeppelin's the greatest band of all time? Ever heard of the...Beatles?" I argued, pinned under Xavi as the six-minute buzzer went off, marking the end of our jiu-jitsu round. I was seriously regretting coming into the dojo today. I was having trouble focusing on anything other than the invading memory of Mina's thighs wrapped around my waist in her room this morning. After I snuck across her yard and back to my van, I drove to work but couldn't focus on a damn thing, so I rode my motorcycle over here, hoping to expend my pent-up energy.

Xavi released his hold and stood from his mount, offering me a hand up. We shook hands and separated, catching our breath before assuming sparring stances across from each other on the mats, preparing for the next round. I'd lost the last three rounds. It wasn't even close. I was panting like a pug but a stupid smile kept creeping up the corners of my mouth.

"That was an easy nine points, third time in a row...where's your head at, Oli? Also, the Beatles? Really? Of all the bands? I didn't take you for a Beatles fan...ah!" The buzzer went off and Xavi cried out as I went for the takedown. He managed to stay on his feet. I took him down with a sweep to the back of his leg that he didn't see coming.

Xavi was a tall Filipino-Brazilian-American seemingly built of pure steel, with jiu-jitsu superiority clearly running in his veins. He didn't mess around. This guy was usually top of the class unless a more experienced brown belt happened to be visiting. He'd been training since he was a kid. We were of similar build, but he was much more skilled and had clocked more hours on the mat than I could ever rack up, even with the way I'd been tripling my time commitment at the dojo lately.

I positioned myself over him quickly, locking his arms and legs in a bind. "Nice! Y-you w-weasel," he hissed through gritted teeth as he tried to maintain his composure. I knew he was hurting because binding him this way was especially taxing on my own forearms and shins. After some struggle, he had me off-balance with a powerful hip thrust and used the momentum to flip me. He was in the dominant position now. I racked my brain for my next maneuver, but he was anticipating all my moves and blocking them so well that I couldn't help but let out a chuckle at my hopelessness. Amusement was a welcome change of emotions; it granted a flexibility that anger could never allow. My grin grew wider as a calm spread through me— a balm for the jagged ridges of maneuvers mapping paths through my mind.

"You feeling okay? You're usually pissed when I have you pinned on your back," Xavi teased.

"That's cuz you don't stink as much as usual," I managed to grumble, all the while working to slip my elbow out from under his bind. "So, my mind's not fogging over from the reek. Maybe you've lost your edge, Xavi," I fired back, shifting my weight to my right side and sliding out from under him. As soon as I was out, I wrapped my legs and arms around his back while he was still on all fours.

Xavi faltered for a moment but flipped me off his back and onto the mat seconds later. He reasserted his dominance. "Lost my edge? That's rich from the guy who can't stay out from under me."

"Can't I?" I groaned and tried once more to slip from under him, but his pin was airtight now, inescapable. I thrust my hips up to shift him off me just as the reset buzzer went off again.

"Shit," I muttered, defeated. Xavi had already lightened his bind, but we both lay there a few moments longer, panting like dogs in the heat. Instead of torturing myself mentally and considering the other strategies I could've tried like I usually did when he defeated me, it was the memory of Mina's profile as she rested her cheek against my chest that came to my mind like a prophecy and a prayer. I was almost overcome with the feeling I'd had when I awoke this morning with her in my arms. The soft skin of her shoulder pressed into the nook of my underarm, the curve of her waist beneath my fingertips, the smell of her temple ingrained in my memory, filling me up like the feeling of home.

Xavi hopped off me, holding out his hand and chuckling. "What are you so happy about? You just had your ass handed to you. You're lying there like a princess with some goofy smile on your face. You high right now?"

"Naw." I took his hand and stood, hoping I wasn't blushing red. I followed Xavi toward the bleachers, where we both plopped down. "I'm high on life."

"High on life? Someone give you a rusty trombone last night?"

"Do I even want to know what that is?"

"Use your imagination." Xavi waggled his brows suggestively and I shoved him.

"Don't be nasty," I joked, shaking my head. But after a

moment, the urge to share something about Mina became even stronger. Every sense in my body was on overload, like my entire system was quivering. If I didn't tell somebody *something* about her soon, I might actually explode right here in this dojo. *Slow your roll,* I cautioned myself. *You're not the guy who vomits his feelings—that's just not you, man.*

I shook my head clear, ignoring the warning and nudging Xavi with my right foot. "Hey, so remember that girl I was telling you about?"

"The one who friend-zoned you? The dancer?" Xavi asked.

I chuckled, remembering opening up to him about that when Mina and I were going through the thick of it a few weeks back. "Yeah, her," I said, grinning wider than I meant to.

His smile grew too as he raised his eyebrows. "Nooooo!" Xavi's grin matched mine. "Dog, you hit that?"

"Naw, not like that. It's just that…I mean, we kind of made it official. We're like, boyfriend/girlfriend. She's my girl now," I confirmed, almost more to convince myself it was really true. *She's my girl.*

"For real? Congrats, my man. I'm happy for you," Xavi said, gripping my shoulder with a massive hand.

"Thanks." I shrugged him off casually.

"Yo, lemme see a pic." Xavi gestured to my phone.

"A pic?"

"Of your girl, what's her name?"

"Uh, Mina. A pic…" I exhaled, looking through my phone for photos, scanning image after image of what was mostly electronics for work and screenshots of receipts. "I guess I don't really have any pictures of her."

"What's her handle?" Xavi asked, pulling out his phone.

"I don't know," I replied, genuinely unsure. "I actually don't have a profile."

"Don't tell me you're one of those anti-social media people," he said.

"No, it's nothing like that. I just never really bothered with it, I guess." The truth was the lawyers warned us about our digital footprint, and how the opposing counsel could use information gathered about us in our case.

"Seriously? That's rare these days."

"Is it? Oh here—" I scrolled to a picture I took of Mina jumping midair the day she invited me to watch her dance at the studio. I hesitated showing him, but figured *What the hell?* Sharing something precious to me...that had to be part of my growth. Right? I rotated the screen out to him. He took it from me and brought it closer to his face.

"Holy shit. She's hot."

"Yeah, she is."

I grabbed the phone back just before he tried to zoom in.

"Nice try. Wipe the drool," I joked, cramming the phone into my pocket.

"Easy there, tiger." Xavi grinned.

"Can't help it."

"Having seen that pic, I can't say I blame you. So, what's up? Gonna go see her now?" Xavi asked.

I ran a hand over the back of my head, contemplating. I was dying to see her, but I knew I should give her some space. She needed bonding time with her mom to make up for running away from home again yesterday.

"I wanna, but I dunno what her plans are. What about you? Doing anything today? Wanna grab a quick bite?" I asked him.

Xavi paused, then said, "My man, I'd love to. But I'm sorta tight on cash right now."

"I'll spot you, no worries," I insisted.

"Naw, I couldn't let you do that. I gotta work anyway."

"Where do you work? You need a ride?" I offered.

"Naw, thanks anyway. I work here."

"For real? I didn't know that."

"Yeah, Master Rig's the man. He hooked it up for me. He lets me train for free and in exchange, I help him out here and there," he explained.

"Nice." My eyes traced down to his duffle bag. It was big, too big for just his training gear. I realized what it could mean. I knew what it looked like when someone's whole life was in one bag. Xavi might not have a permanent living situation, I realized, and the thought gutted me. I recalled my stupid comment from earlier when we were sparring, and I felt a pang of regret. "Ey, I'm sorry about that joke I made."

"What joke? No worries, shit I don't even remember what you said."

He followed my gaze, shooting a glance toward his bag. He shook his head. "Oh, no. It's just temporary."

"If you ever need a place to crash, let me know," I offered.

"Thank you for the offer, Oliver. I appreciate that. I'm staying at a homey's place right now actually, but yeah...no. I'll, umm...I've got a better job lined up—just hard to get hired without references and shit."

"I'm serious, Xavi. Here, I'll text you my address. If you ever need to crash, just come by, okay? Anytime. There's plenty of room," I insisted. "I've been there. You just gotta be smarter than me and accept the help. If you need some extra cash, uh, I can...I uh, I deal with electronics resale. I could actually use some help from time to time."

Xavi's shoulders perked up at the offer. I nodded, mirroring his excitement at the prospect of working together.

"Electronics resale? What's that mean?" he asked.

"Like a hustle. Buying and selling," I explained.

Xavi's eyebrows drew together and he quickly shook his head. "Oh, nah. I don't wanna do nothin' illegal. Thanks for looking out though." He raised his palms.

"Not illegal. I buy from Craigslist and sell to exporters. But lately, I've been expanding to sales online, and I got some direct accounts set up with the retailers. You any good on a computer?"

Xavi laughed suddenly. "For real? I am, actually. I taught myself to code. Plus, I'm a video game junkie." He lit up.

"Well, see—that's perfect. I need something way simpler. Just responding to customers, answering questions, keeping prices on listings competitive, posting product pics, listing SKUs...just basic stuff, packing and shipping," I explained, hoping I wasn't getting ahead of myself. I hadn't fully thought this through. *Am I ready to bring someone else on board?* The only thing I cared about right then was helping him.

"Umm, I dunno what to say, man. That sounds perfect. You sure?" he asked, his eyes bright.

"Hell yeah, I'm sure. You'd be helping me out."

"How much you paying?" Xavi asked.

"Ugh." I laughed, uncertain how to answer. I hadn't thought that far ahead. "We can check online for comparable positions at other tech companies. I'll match the going rate."

He laughed too, rubbing the top of his head like he was still trying to process his unexpected good luck. "This is crazy...I'm excited."

"Yeah, me too," I said.

"When do I start?"

"Lemme see what Mina has planned today. Either way, we'll figure it out. I'll hit you up. Maybe you can come by after you're finished here? I'll show you around and order pizza or whatever you're feeling like," I offered.

"Sounds perfect, man." He shook his head, and I thought I heard a mumbled "Wow" as he walked away.

After I toweled off and changed, I grabbed my bag and headed for the door. Xavi was still in the practice area, mopping the floors.

"All right." I patted his back. "See you later, man."

"Later, brother," he said. There were relief and joy in his voice. My heart squeezed at the sound of that. *Brother.*

As I walked out of the dojo, still sporting my shit-eating grin, my phone buzzed. My smile stretched even wider when I saw the name on my screen. *MINA.* I answered almost immediately.

"Hey, baby. I was just going to call y—"

"Oli," she breathed. Voice weak, broken. My grin drained from my face.

"Mina? What is it? What's wrong?" I pressed the phone harder against my ear, trying to gauge every microscopic sound she produced.

"The men. Th-they came back."

CHAPTER 4

MINA

The sterile smells of hospital and copper mingled in the air every time I inhaled—there was just no escaping it. A sticky residue coated my clothing and parts of skin that I couldn't wash off well enough. I felt as if I'd bathed in blood—it was inside my ears and deep under my fingernails. The police had let me wash up in the sink after they took the samples of what they needed from me, but I couldn't stand long enough to wash thoroughly.

The waiting room was quiet today. People came and went every minute or two, delayed a few seconds by the police at the doors who were screening all visitors because of what had happened to Mama and me.

I dislodged a gunky ball of congealed blood from my fingernail. Nausea roiled in my belly at the sight of it, but a sound distracted my attention—the sound of feet pounding down the hallway. I lifted my eyes, filling with hope before he even reached the doorway. *Oliver*.

He hung momentarily in the entrance until his gaze fell on

me. The sight of him sent a bolt of strength through my body and I stood up to rush to him, but the floor felt unsteady beneath my feet. I swayed, and he reached me before I fully lost my balance.

He pulled me into his arms, pressing his palm against my back, and crushed me against his chest. His fingers tangled in my hair without hesitation, the clumps sticky and knotted against my scalp. He pressed his lips against my forehead, and I shut my eyes, inhaling his scent and burrowing against his hot skin, forgetting the sickness in my gut for a heartbeat. Oliver's presence soothed the tension coiled in every one of my nerve endings. He took a step back and held me by the shoulders.

His eyes raked over me, scanning for signs of injury. "Are you hurt?" His gaze landed on my bandage. "Mina...your arm—"

I shook my head. "It's fine. It's not that bad, just a scratch. My ankle got the brunt of it," I rasped, leaving out the bit about my bruised ribs. I shuddered, forcing the image of the man landing on top of me from my mind.

"What happ—where's your mom?" he asked, his eyes searching my own.

"Mama was supposed to fly out tomorrow..." I trailed off.

"Fly where?"

"To get my—my grandfather the medication that he needs for the cough he's been dealing with—"

Oliver glanced toward the double doors of the waiting room.

"Is she in there? In the Trauma Center?" he asked, his voice so quietly compassionate it brought tears to my eyes.

I couldn't bring myself to say the words, so I nodded.

"But she's okay, right?"

Hot tears burned my eyes, and I shook my head, gripping on to Oliver to stay upright. Oliver's hold tightened as my head lolled and rested against his chest. My shoulders shook from my restrained sobs. I felt him sigh and his hand stroke my hair. He brushed his thumb against my cheek while his other arm supported my body. His fingers were warm.

"Mina, look at me. Look at me." He held my chin between his fingers and tilted my face up toward him. I could see the outline of my dark shadow reflected in his eyes, pools of molten steel that were warmer and more open than I'd ever seen them.

"Your mom is going to be fine," he asserted. "Okay?" He scanned my face carefully. I dropped my head on his shoulder and clung to him, my safe harbor amidst an unyielding storm.

"I don't know," I whispered. My voice was raspy, and it hurt to speak. "They took her from me and wouldn't let me go farther. They took some samples." I gestured to the blood. "And brought me here to wait."

"That's not...I mean, is that your mother's blood?" he asked, hesitantly.

I nodded, then shook my head then shrugged because I honestly didn't know. "Probably...maybe the guy's blood too. I think...I don't think he, uh, I think he didn't...he wasn't breathing I don't think. The other one ran upstairs so I—it got kind of messy." I forced out the words as my chest spasmed and I struggled not to cry. Oliver rubbed my arms, trying to soothe the fit of anxiety that was starting to grip me again.

"Here," he said, shrugging off his hoodie and placing it over my head. I inhaled the scent of him, my nerves settling slightly from the familiar essence of bergamot and white ginger enveloping my senses. I lifted my shoulders higher, greedily taking pleasure in this small comfort. "How badly is Lily injured—"

"They're operating, but it's gonna be okay. It has to be okay," I interjected, more to myself than anything.

"What happened?" Oliver asked.

"They shot her." I winced involuntarily as I said it. "I don't know how many times she got hit—damn it, that's right, I need to find out what the medication was called. The one grandpa needed. I have to get my hands on it somehow and get it to him. I think she was gonna buy it in Canada 'cause you don't need a prescription for it there, and then she was gonna fly it to him. I think that was the plan, so I gotta go home and look—" I began to shuffle toward the door, but he stopped me, placing a hand lightly on my wrist.

"Mina," he said, a tenderness in his voice I'd never heard before. "You can't go back there, it isn't safe. Not right now. You have to stay here. I get that you're worried about your grandfather's meds, but let's just take this one step at a time. You need your energy—don't use it up on designing a contingency plan you don't even know you're gonna need."

Everything he said sounded right, but when I got anxious, I argued. And I was very anxious.

"But what am I supposed to do? How am I supposed to help him? I can't just—I need to at least call them," I urged, fumbling for my phone. It wasn't in my pocket; I didn't have pockets. Not on the seats behind me, either. I checked the tables nearby, but then recalled the moment I dropped the crowbar. "Shit, it probably fell out when I climbed down the tree," I mumbled to myself.

"You called me, Mina, remember? You called me from here. So, it has to be somewhere." Oliver looked around, then knelt by the chairs. He stood with my phone in his fingers.

"Here," he said, placing it in my open palm. Oliver brought his fingers to my cheek where the scar from the alley attack had almost completely disappeared. I still winced instinctively. He dropped his hand down to my fingers, concern furrowing his brows. "Maybe you should wait?" he suggested, softly. "Don't call them now. You're not in the right headspace to tell them any of this." I opened my mouth to argue, but he went on. "If their health isn't good, the stress from this news will only make it worse. And you know they'll worry. And we don't have answers yet. You need time to calm down from this, let the adrenaline settle. We need to focus on Lily. Right? It's all about your mom right now. Once we have some more information on how she's doing, it'll be easier to give them some peace of mind."

I heard his words, but it took time to register them. After processing his suggestion thoroughly, I realized he was completely right. About everything.

"That's true," I admitted. My legs suddenly felt like jelly. I turned to sit in one of the waiting room chairs before I collapsed right there in the middle of the room. Oliver joined me in the chair beside mine. We sat in silence for a few minutes.

He rubbed the back of my hand with his thumb over and over. The sensation was almost hypnotic. I focused on the rhythmic, circular motion his fingers made along my skin, and I blocked out everything else. I felt as if I could sit there forever, Oliver stroking my hand, still in the moment when my mother might be all right. But that brief comfort fled when I saw two police officers enter the waiting room. As I'd both hoped and feared, they came directly to us. The tall, bearded one spoke to me first.

"Miss Arkova, we need to ask you a few more questions. Come with us, please." I vaguely recognized him. I was pretty sure he was the one who restrained me when I tried to follow Mama into the OR. The same one who lifted me from the floor and escorted me to this chair after promising he'd make sure she was safe. At least, I thought it was him...everything was a blur. The second officer was an older, Asian-American man with short black hair. He looked familiar, too. He might have been the one who took the DNA samples.

"How is she?" I stood, Oliver right there with me, not letting go of my hand.

"The doctor can tell you more about that when they finish operating," the officer said.

"I can't leave until I talk to the doctor. They told me to wait here."

"They're still operating. As soon as she's stable, the doctor will come and speak with you. For now, come with us."

I took a step backward, and almost fell over the chair. Oliver caught my arm and steadied me.

"I have to stay here," I insisted, shaking my head. "You should go back in and make sure she's safe. They could come back for her—she's a witness! You should go back," I repeated firmly. A heavy panic set in as I considered her vulnerability. This hospital was big. There must have been other entrances, other waiting rooms. I looked at the faces surrounding me. Many of them couldn't help but stare at the scene unfolding. My body grew tense from their attention, but no one seemed to be a threat.

"She's very safe," the bearded officer with tired eyes insisted, and my gaze returned to his. "We have additional officers stationed at the entrance as a precaution. We need to take your statement for our report. Normally, we'd take you back to the station for a statement, but we've been given orders to do it here," he explained, gesturing for me to follow him. I didn't budge.

The bearded officer sighed, rubbing his earlobe for a moment, then tilted his head toward me. "Think about it like this," he said. "The sooner you answer our questions, the sooner we can get the investigation underway and gauge the threat against you and your mother," the officer reasoned, speaking slowly like he was talking to a small child.

I was taken aback by the genuine concern I detected under an otherwise monotonal timbre.

"We aren't taking you anywhere far. We're just going some-place more private so you can talk to us freely." Both officers glanced over at Oliver several times throughout the speech.

I considered Oliver's position in this mess. He was technically a witness to my assault in the alley—an assault executed by an oversized thug whose face still haunted my nightmares. The purpose? To send some sort of message, a warning, to my father from an underground Russian organization. Which one specifically, I still did not know. But the thug had made his message clear: If my father failed to fulfill his task, their organization would retaliate with violence. And they had.

Despite Papa's assurances that he had sorted his affairs, it was clear that he'd failed to appease these people. They'd sent these henchmen to our home today to fulfill their promise of violence, and instead I killed one of them. I imagined they'd be coming for me next. There was only one thing I knew for certain, though...I didn't want Oliver mired in this mess any more deeply than he already was.

"I'll come," I told the officer, glancing around the room a final time.

"Great. There's a breakroom right through this hallway. They've cleared it for our use."

I looked back at Oliver. He nodded at me and squeezed my hand. "Don't worry. I'll keep an ear out for the doctor and I'll come get you right away if there's news," he reassured.

"No need," said the second officer. "I'll let the waiting-room guard know where they can find us." The second officer left to speak with the guard.

More at ease, I nodded back at Oliver. I released his hand, reluctantly. For a moment, I feared I'd float away without his touch to ground me. I followed the bearded officer toward the exit, but as we approached, I heard my name called from across the room.

"Miss Arkova, wait!"

I turned, eyes searching for the source of the voice. A dark-skinned woman with long black hair, dressed in a form-fitting gray suit, and a leather laptop satchel strapped across her chest strode toward us. She presented the bearded officer with the documents. He didn't look at them. Instead, he took the documents from her and used them to gesture to her, up and down.

"What's this?" he asked.

"Why don't you try and read it?" she questioned him, face scrunching with incredulity. Who was this woman? Why did she know my name? Clearly, the officers outside let her through.

The bearded officer looked down at the documents with furrowed brows. His face remained unchanged as he gave them a once-over then handed them to the second officer, who had returned from speaking with the guard. The second officer took more time with the papers than the first. He looked back at the woman, who was scrutinizing me with an indecipherable expression.

"You got ID?" the second officer asked the woman, who reached into the zipper pocket of her satchel without breaking eye contact with them and presented the officers with a small, laminated card. The second officer examined it with curiosity.

She didn't wait for him to return it. She pulled the card out of his hand and asked him, "Have you secured a room inside? I need some time alone with my client."

Client?

"Client?" the bearded officer asked, echoing my thoughts.

"That's what we're saying," she answered quickly.

"I'm sorry," I interrupted. "What exactly is happening right now?"

"Should we remove the units covering the entrance?" the second officer asked.

"No. We've coordinated with your chief. He's sending units to cover the back and side entrances as well," the woman explained.

"What can you tell us about this?" the bearded officer asked her.

"Nothing," said the woman, face unreadable. The bearded officer nodded and directed us through the doors.

The woman proceeded; the officers clearly having conceded that she was running the show now.

Who the hell is she? I followed quickly, eager to place distance between Oliver and this investigation, eager to learn more about this woman and her part in all this. I glanced back to find Oliver standing where we left him in the waiting room, a troubled expression haunting his face. He nodded again. *I'm here.* I turned away from him, the crack in my heart growing into a deep chasm and hope flickering out in me like a flame fighting a hurricane.

CHAPTER 5

OLIVER

A s soon as Mina and the police officers disappeared into the hospital hallway behind the large metal security doors, I felt a restlessness spread through my limbs. I began to pace the perimeter of the rectangular waiting room. After about a minute or two, the guard started eyeing me suspiciously. At last, he spoke up, "Hey. Sir. I'm gonna have to ask you to take a seat."

"Huh?" I replied automatically. "Oh, yeah. Okay. Sorry."

I took a seat along the left wall so that I could keep an eye on both the entrance and the hallway. I knew I promised Mina I'd stay put and keep an ear out for the doctor, but I felt a vital impulse to be by her side through this. She needed someone, she needed me more than she realized. When I was holding her in my arms, I had been carrying most of her weight. She was collapsing, exhausted—the adrenaline from the attack must have been wearing off because she could barely stand.

I didn't like the worry on her face when that woman in the business suit blazed in out of nowhere, flashing papers around. I needed to find out who the hell she was. I was itching to talk to the cops who let her through, but I wouldn't leave this room. I promised Mina.

I took the farthest seat away from the other people in the waiting room, anxious to be alone with my thoughts. When Mina had called me, I'd raced here faster than I had ever ridden a motorcycle in my life.

My phone buzzed, and a new message from Xavi came through.

> Yo finishing up around here whas the plan?

I tapped my thumb on the screen. *Shit, Xavi.* I forgot about him.

> yo some shit came up with Mina...i don't mean to flake on you but it's kind of an emergency. u know wat? imma actually have u start without me if u don't mind. imma send u my address just call me when ur there n I'll tell you where the keys r n walk you through some stuff.

His response came almost immediately.

> ey...u sure ??? we can just do a raincheck if u want?

I looked around, making sure no one was looking for Mina, then typed.

> no i can really use the help. i need to list some stuff n i need to get pics of certain items. i don't remember them off the top of my head...
> there's a list. We'll talk wen u get there i'll order you some food meanwhile wat u in the mood 4?

XAVI

i'm good with whatever bro

After about half an hour, I was growing restless, watching the double doors every twenty seconds, standing up and checking the entrance every minute despite the guard eyeing me with unwarranted suspicion. I needed to take a piss so badly, but I was afraid to miss the doctor, afraid to miss Mina. I could not risk letting her down—not today.

Another five minutes and I'll go, I told myself.

Ten minutes passed.

Another five minutes and I'll go, I told myself.

Those five minutes were almost up when the double doors opened wide and out came the woman in the business suit followed by Mina. I shot up to my feet and dashed across the waiting room. The woman marched wordlessly past me and headed out the exit.

Mina barely registered me at first. Her gaze followed the woman out the door, distress haunting her eyes. I tilted my head to catch Mina's gaze and reached out to rest my hand on her shoulder.

"Mina? What happened? Did you hear news about your mom?"

She blinked up at me and seemed to register my presence at last. She nodded weakly and set her features in an inscrutable mask, a mask that bothered me to my core.

What didn't she want me to know? What was she trying to spare me from? I was on her side no matter what. Didn't she know that? She had to know that.

"I love you," I assured quietly but her vacant expression remained unmoved by the words. "Mina?" I asked again.

"Hmm?"

"Is everything...I mean I know everything isn't *okay*, but did something else happen?"

"Has the doctor been out here?" she asked, suddenly panicked.

"Not yet. So, you haven't heard any news yet either?" I pressed.

"No," she confirmed, frustration lacing her tone.

"Not too much longer now, I'm sure."

She nodded. *Now what?* I gestured to the seats.

"I can't sit. I've been sitting for a while. I need to walk around," she said, moving away from me along the wall then pivoting back along the same path, frantically staring at the double doors. She paced like that for a minute. I stood nearby, racking my brain for a way to comfort her. The security guard who asked me to have a seat earlier was eyeing Mina irritably.

"He doesn't like us walking the room for some reason," I murmured to her.

"Why?" She searched for who I could be talking about and her eyes landed on the security guard behind the front desk.

"Beats me," I answered.

"Take a seat, ma'am," the guard ordered as though he heard us.

Mina strode to the counter and leaned forward, both hands on the security guard's desk. Her eyes bored into his.

"Yes?" he asked her, coldness staining his voice. I took Mina's hand and placed myself between them, my feeble attempt at protecting her from what was clearly going to be a negative interaction.

"I pace when I'm nervous, I need to pace. I can't sit right now."

"Pace outside," the guard said, avoiding her eyes, leaning back in his chair and sipping on a soda. "Please have a seat, ma'am or leave," the asshole continued to address her without looking at her.

Mina opened her mouth in disbelief. "Are you..." Her words dried up mid-sentence. I gave her a moment to speak through her outrage but as soon as it became clear that she had been rendered speechless, I stepped in, anger searing through me.

"Seems like if you're just a basically unsympathetic person, it's kind of weird to decide to work in a hospital ER." I led Mina away from the counter as I spoke, eager to put some distance between us and the guard. "People are fighting for their lives in there, and not all of them are going to make it," I stated over my shoulder, focusing all of the venom I could muster on him.

I turned back to Mina, who met my gaze, and my demeanor immediately softened. The worry tinging her eyes made me realize how insensitive my words had been. "I'm sorry, I didn't mean it like that. This is where they *save* lives, Mina. Everything's gonna be okay."

I pulled her against me and leaned over, burying my face in her hair. It was damp and smelled of soap but not the sweet smell of apricots that usually drifted from it. Instead, it was a sharp almost antiseptic kind of clean smell that felt foreign coming from her. She let me hold her but her body was rigid, guarded and she quivered slightly. *Baby, what happened in there?*

"Mina, who was that woman you went off with?" Mina lifted her eyes to me, her gaze darkening but she didn't offer an explanation. "That woman who came in here and shook up those officers. The one with the briefcase..." I went on as if we didn't both know exactly who I was referring to.

"My lawyer," she stated blankly.

"Your lawyer?" I questioned, trying to maintain a casual tone. "Okay, so that's—so you did know her? It's just that you seemed confused about her."

"No, I didn't know her," Mina said.

"Oh. Okay. Well, who hired her? Did they appoint her? Why do you need a lawyer?"

"I don't know," she answered, but there was more she wasn't telling me. I could sense it.

"Was it your father?" I pressed.

"Oliver, you can't—I just don't want to talk about it right now. I feel nauseated," she said quickly and went to slump in the nearest chair.

"Okay, no problem." I nodded and sat down next to her.

I sat in silence, reaching for her hand, absently rubbing her thumb with the pad of mine. She pulled her hand back to press her palms against her temples. She leaned forward and rested her elbows on her knees. A tear slid down along her inner forearm toward her leg.

"What is it, baby? Talk to me," I whispered.

"Miss Arkova," a voice came from across the room.

"Yes?" Mina sprang to her feet, but couldn't seem to take a step forward to meet the doctor, a dark-skinned woman in teal scrubs and a white coat holding a file over a clipboard. Her hair was pulled back under a bright band, the only color in a bland room. There was a solemn expression on her face.

I stood alongside Mina and helped her close the distance by supporting her back with one arm and grasping her other arm with my palm firmly. I continued offering her my support as we took a few steps across the room to meet the doctor, but as soon as we grew near enough, Mina abruptly pulled away from me entirely.

My hands didn't know what to do with themselves so I shoved them into my back pockets. The doctor faced Mina, as if she'd already determined I was a non-factor in the equation.

"Miss Arkova, we were able to retrieve several bullets. She also had a number of shrapnel wounds—it took longer than I would have liked to get it all out, but ultimately, we managed to get it all. Your sister is stable—"

"My-my mother," Mina corrected.

The doctor blinked a few times, almost as if she was going to argue about Mina's relationship to her patient, then she shook her head brusquely.

"I'm sorry. Your mother. We're keeping her in a medically

induced coma for now. She suffered a severe head injury during her fall and we did detect some moderate swelling in the brain. We want to keep her under until the swelling subsides significantly."

"Oh, my God," Mina exhaled sharply. I reached for her hand but she crossed her arms across her chest, keeping her focus on the doctor. I returned my hands to my back pockets. "For how long?" Mina asked.

"That depends on a number of factors. It could be a few days but shouldn't be more than a week. Her vitals are looking good and we're hopeful. We'll know more in time—"

"But she's going to be okay, right? Can I see her?"

"It's too early to tell how the concussion will affect her in the long term. We never know with head injuries. But to answer your question, you can see her now."

Mina's eyes suddenly blazed with hope.

"And can I stay the night? I don't mind sleeping in a chair— I'm just afraid that...I mean, I need to be with her."

The doctor looked down at her clipboard rather than meet Mina's pleading gaze.

"Unfortunately, that's not possible. Not until she's out of the Critical Care Tower. Right now, it's a fifteen-minute visitation window until she's out of the ICU." Mina's frown became a grimace.

"But I just—"

"I'm sorry, Ms. Arkova, it's hospital policy," the doctor interjected. "And only one visitor can be in the ICU at a time. And immediate family only. No exceptions." The doctor must have meant me because she looked at me apologetically before turning her attention back to Mina. "You can talk to your mom, and you can hold her hand. Some people swear that even in a coma, a patient knows when their loved one is with them."

"But you did say she's going to wake up, right?" Mina pressed, her voice quavering.

The doctor did her best to give Mina a reassuring smile, but she didn't answer the question. "I know it's overwhelming but just try your best to remain calm for your mom while you're with her," the doctor added before looking back toward the double doors. "I'm so sorry, but unless you have any questions, I really need to get back."

"Thank you, doctor," Mina pronounced.

"You're very welcome." The doctor smiled at Mina sympathetically. "The information desk on the third floor will direct you to the bridge that goes to the Critical Care Tower, and they'll give you her room number at the front desk there. The elevator is back through these doors, down the hallway, and on your right." The doctor turned and headed back inside, passing the two officers who'd questioned Mina earlier. The one with the beard nodded at Mina as they crossed the waiting room and exited through the main doors.

"I'll walk you up there," I insisted.

"No," she stated flatly. My mouth dropped open. *Why is she trying to run me off? She was just attacked, and on top of that, she was an eyewitness to her mother's attempted murder.*

"Mina, it isn't a good idea for you to be alone right—"

"Oliver, please. Just let me go see my mom," she interrupted.

I knew that look on her face. It meant that there was no point in trying to change her mind. "I'm sorry," I offered.

She shrugged. "You have nothing to be sorry for," she stated blankly. "You don't have to wait for me. I'll be okay."

Maybe I had done something wrong. Maybe I hadn't done enough. Maybe it wasn't about me at all. This was so much bigger than me, bigger than anything I could do in this moment besides just being here.

Or was it that lawyer lady? I wondered. At some point in the day, Mina's energy toward me had totally changed, like I'd suddenly become a stranger to her. Did it start before she talked to the lawyer? No. No, I was sure it hadn't. So, maybe the lawyer had said something to Mina—something that made her want to distance herself from me.

"I mean yeah, obviously you'll be fine," I said, choosing my words carefully. It's like there's one subject I shouldn't talk about, but I don't know what the subject is. "I'll just head outside for some fresh air while you see your mom. I might just hang out for a while."

Mina nodded without looking at me. "Okay—see you around."

Unsure of what else to do, I chose not to read into the hollow feeling of failure that her effective dismissal had left me with. Though it took every ounce of will I could muster to walk off and leave her there alone, my gut told me I had to do it, to avoid worsening whatever it was that had caused her to pull back from me.

I headed outside to sort out what was going on with the police, but there was no one there, not one patrol unit in sight. No one was guarding the entrance. No one was monitoring the sidewalk or the parking structure from what I could see. *What just happened?*

CHAPTER 6

MINA

A hospital volunteer with black, thinning hair offset by a brilliant smile checked her computer and told me that Mama was on the eighth floor of the North Tower. She took forever to explain how to get there, her eyes widening slightly as she took in the blood clumped in my hair and clinging stubbornly to the skin of my neck. This hospital was the largest in the city and finding the right wing had proven to be an undertaking, but I knew she would receive good care here and that thought put me at ease. I approached the gray-haired woman at the front desk of the Critical Care department.

"Can I help you?" she asked.

"Oh—um, yes, please. I'm here to see my mom."

"What's the patient's name?" asked the woman. She looked at me expectantly, as I took in her appearance. A short pixie cut that made her look like an art teacher, and the teal scrubs that it seemed like everyone in this section was wearing.

"Mina-I mean Lilia Arkova, l-i-l-i-a a-r-k-o-v-a. I'm Mina, her-her daughter," I rambled in one breath. She smiled at me and nodded, seemingly unbothered by the bloody clumps atop my head.

"Room 8346. Just be sure to keep your voice down as to not disturb the other patients, and keep the visit to no longer than fifteen minutes. That's all we're permitted to allow at this point. She's scheduled for an assessment in half an hour, so you may want to stick around for that. Also, can you please provide the best number to reach you in case any questions come up?"

"Yes! Of course! three-two-three—" I began but she placed a sticky note before me and handed me a pen. I wrote out my number as neatly as I could manage to make sure she had all the numbers right. I wrote my name under it as well and read the numbers out loud to her for confirmation.

"Please, call me as soon as you know anything...please," I urged. "Even if it's just to say that nothing has changed."

My eyes brimmed with tears that I'd been fighting to hold back because I knew if I'd succumb to the waves of pain, I'd drown. *She's going to wake up*, I told myself shakily. And they're going to find the guy who tried to kill her, and I will make him pay.

I reinforced my mental walls that held up the delusion that everything would turn out okay, feeling oddly refreshed by my own artificial bravado.

As I approached the hospital room, I didn't see any police officers outside, and that sent unease prickling through me. But no sooner than I had the thought, I spotted the officer a few yards away, patrolling the hallway and checking the doors. I sighed audibly in relief. The officer walked right past me, giving me a cursory nod as he passed. *Does he know I'm her daughter?* His gaze trailed from my sticky, matted hair, down to my blood-covered pants. I yanked Oliver's hoodie down lower around my hips.

I turned to watch him continue his patrol down the hall-way, back toward the reception desk. I turned again to face

Mama's door. Room 8346. I prepared myself for the worst. I knew it wasn't going to be pretty, but the doctor's reminder to stay calm for her was floating somewhere in the back of my subconscious and I held onto that reminder like a mantra.

As I pushed the door open and stepped inside, my eyes immediately fell upon her. Nothing, not a million years of preparation could have equipped me for the sight of my mother's motionless form. The woman who brought me into this world, the warrior, the beam of light in my life was now buried under a tangle of tubes. The tape that stretched from cheek to cheek across her upper lip to keep the weeds of tubes in place was like a polymer muzzle.

The largest of all the tubes was the one that protruded from her mouth, and the sight of it truly drove home the realization that her life was tethered to those machines. It sent an unsolicited jolt of terror straight to my gut so strong I stumbled backward.

Taking a deep breath, I reminded myself that I had to be calm for her. When my breathing finally slowed, I moved to her bedside, reached for her hand, then pulled back. An IV and tube were taped into place on the back of her hand, running up over her head to where the IV drip was hanging.

I made my way around the other side of the bed, where I could reach for her left hand, which was unencumbered by tubes and needles. She seemed so small and frail, drowning beneath blue and clear vines of polyurethane. I brushed her fingers lightly with my own, then enfolded her hand in mine like it was made of tissue paper. Her fingers were ice-cold against my sweaty palm. I sandwiched her hand between both of mine to warm her frozen skin as I raised my gaze to her heavy lids.

"Mama," I whispered, my breath hitching as it left my lungs in short riffs. As I spoke, I saw an almost imperceptible twitch of her eyelids. My heart did a somersault. *Can she sense me? Does she know I'm here?*

"*Mamachka?* Can you hear me?" I squeezed her hand gently, urging her to send me another sign. My gaze trailed the blue veins on her translucent lids, heavy and unmoving. My line of sight drifted down to the rise and fall of her chest and stayed there, the motion bringing me solace.

"I'm so proud of you," I whispered, leaning closer to her ear. "You fought those monsters off all by yourself...for so long. I thought—" My voice broke. I cleared my throat, resolving to tell her what I needed to say. "I'm sorry it took me so long to get down to you. I—I was looking for a weapon. I found your crowbar in the closet. You're so smart to have that—to always think ahead. To think about the what-ifs. You're always...you were right about everything, Mama. We should have left while we still could. I was dumb, selfish and I'm sorry, I'm so sorry. I got to you as fast as I could. I stopped him from hurting you. I didn't think about it. I just did it. I didn't mean to *kill*"—My voice broke on the word—"him. But...I'd do it again. I'd do it a thousand times for you. I'd do anything for you," I rasped.

My voice was shaking, my hands were trembling with rage and guilt and the frustration of all the things I couldn't control. I knew I needed to calm down. I bit my lower lip, inhaled deeply through my nose, and gave a gentle sigh.

"Mama. There was a woman downstairs, she—she says she can protect you...if I help her. But it means I have to do something that would—" I choked on the words, fighting to get them out as if the utterance might ease the terrible weight I felt pressing down on me from every direction.

"I made her promise me. I know I can't trust her fully but we don't have a whole lot of options right now. So, just know I'm here but...if, if you don't...I mean, just to tell you if you wake up and I'm not right here, don't worry. I didn't leave you. I would never leave you. It'll be temporary...I promise. Nothing can keep me from you." The lie tasted bitter on my tongue. I knew I couldn't promise her anything.

I wanted so much to believe she could hear me. But at the same time, my knees almost buckled in panic at the thought of just that—her hearing every word I was saying.

"But don't worry about me, Mama. You know it'll take a hell of a lot more than those assholes to crack me. And that's thanks to you, Mama." I pressed my lips to her hair. My tears smeared across her forehead.

"I'm sorry," I choked through the cry that escaped me, and I wiped the wetness from her brow with a tissue from the box on the table beside her bed.

I blew my nose and washed my hands before rejoining her bedside and taking her hand in mine again. I would stay with her until they forced me to leave. "Loving you," I whispered. *Loving you.* The phantom shadow of Mama's voice whispered back to me, echoing her unfaltering resolve to keep the word in the present tense. *Loving you.* But the silence that followed hurt the most.

My heart squeezed in my chest, aching to hear her say the words back to me.

Minutes passed and my legs began to tingle with numbness. I shifted my weight, bending my knees marginally to bring blood flow to them. I pulled the strands of hair away from her forehead and ran my fingers through her hair the way she would with mine to soothe me. Her fingers were still cold to the touch. I left her side reluctantly to find a nurse. A knock came from the direction of the open door just as I moved toward it and a nurse came in, rolling a piece of equipment along with her.

"Hello, miss, it's time for Ms. Arkova's assessment. Her visiting time is over for today. Sorry," the nurse informed, adjusting her thick-rimmed glasses on the bridge of her nose.

"I was just going to find someone to ask for a blanket—her hands are freezing."

"Oh, no problem. I can ask someone for you." She leaned her head back out into the hall and spoke to a man passing by. "Marlon, can you do me a favor and hunt down a blanket for 8346, please."

"Yeah, for sure, but you owe me," I heard Marlon reply, teasingly.

"Yeah, yeah, thank you," the nurse answered, rolling her eyes at him and moving past me into the room. Their light exchange reminded me of the rest of the world for a strange moment. These were people who dealt with trauma on a daily basis. They worked amidst suffering and death every day, and I knew they had to find lightness in these moments to survive the weight of it. My heart squeezed for them, appreciation filling me for their strength. It must take a lot of inner strength to work surrounded by the pain and fear of others day in and day out.

"Thank you." I smiled at the nurse but it didn't reach my eyes. It couldn't.

I continued to watch her as she jotted down numbers on her clipboard and entered information into the computer by Mama's bed. I spotted more dried blood residue stuck beneath my fingernails that I must have missed on the first wash.

I pulled down the sleeves of Oli's hoodie over my hands to hide them. His scent rose around me from the movement. I shut my eyes and imagined him here with me—the heat of his fingers laced through mine, his thumb tracing steady grooves, his warm hands like home, the way he would watch me unwaveringly, as though committing every gesture to memory so that he'd never forget. The tightness in my chest began to ease slightly.

The mechanical sound of the hospital bed being adjusted cut through the silence, startling me. The nurse's eyes darted in my direction for a brief moment before she peeled Mama's hospital gown open to examine the bandages low on Mama's hip, which was already bruising in various shades of blue and violet. White medical tape lined the gauze around her wounds, the contused skin luminous against the fluorescent light.

I was mentally blocking the memories of her being shot to make coping with her condition easier, but that was wrong on so many levels. I needed to be present—razor-sharp and focused. I needed to step the hell up and stop hiding from this like some spooked kid.

"How many bullets were removed?" I cleared my throat, willing strength into my voice. "I never umm...I was holding her but I only saw them try to stop the bleeding around her hip in the ambulance and I think her leg was bleeding, too..." I trailed off but the nurse didn't look up from her work on Mama's bandages.

"Yes, it looks like there were two hits to her lower hip. The bullet they removed from her lower leg was lodged in there pretty deep. Luckily, it looks like there was no fracture. Her chart doesn't say there was one at least."

"Can I see it?" I asked in a lowered voice, mustering up the mental walls I desperately needed to continue to suppress the sob lodged at the base of my throat. She returned my gaze and nodded slightly. I approached Mama's bed and watched the nurse peel back the thin white sheet over Mama's left side. She then pulled up Mama's hospital gown to reveal another square patch of gauze, taped to her lower leg. "Did they give her stitches?" I asked.

"Umm..."—She checked back with the notes on the computer and clicked on a few things before answering—"It looks like they used a dual-adhesive hydrogel. They usually use that if they're dealing with layers of muscle or an area of frequent movement."

"Will she...is there any reason to think she won't walk again?" I asked, my voice quavering.

"It looks like both her hip and lower leg weren't fractured, so the chances are good...but the doctor will speak with you more extensively about her recovery when she's conscious. There's definitely going to be a recovery period but I've seen patients walk after wounds like this. It's just hard to say for sure. Is she an active person?" she asked, offering a gentle smile.

I nodded. "Yeah, well...she used to be, but I guess her work's been getting in the way of that a lot lately."

"Well, she'll have to refocus on her health. And I'm sure she'll have a speedy recovery when she does."

As I watched my mother's frail, vulnerable form lying on the bed, the nurse's optimistic sentiment fell flat, leaving me feeling empty and unconvinced

"What else can I do for her?" I inquired, my tone tinged with a sense of urgency.

"Just be there for her," she answered like it was the simplest thing in the world. My eyes shut at that. Tears flowed out of me like magma, slow and unstoppable.

It killed me to think I wouldn't be able to give even that to Mama, to just be there for her. Those men could come soon and I'd have to go. That's what I had promised, and I keep my promises. It wasn't a matter of *if* but *when*. If I fought back this time or even attempted to evade them, the deal I made with Patricia downstairs would be compromised.

"What else?" I implored.

"I'm sorry, I'm not sure what you mean. Like what else can you do?" I nodded. "Maybe, you can talk to a therapist? You've both been through a traumatic home invasion. Finding someone to help you work through that trauma would probably help a lot after everything you've endured," she finished, vaguely, most likely from a lack of information about what exactly happened.

"Yeah." I nodded. She started on the bandage around Mama's lower leg next. I watched in silence as the nurse peeled off the tape with care and replaced the bloodied gauze with a fresh bandage.

The door opened, and Marlon came in with the blanket, which I took from him with thanks. "I can do it," I insisted. I moved toward Mama and covered her legs gently, checking to make sure the nurse was finished with her assessment. She nodded and I spread the thin, gray blanket over Mama as evenly as I could manage with my enervated fingers. When I was finished, I leaned over her cautiously.

"I love you, Mamachka. I'll fight like hell for us," I whispered as quietly as I could manage, hoping that the nurse couldn't hear. "I won't give up. I promise." I left a kiss on her forehead, imprinting her scent—the smell of warmth and home—to my memory.

"All right, let's let her rest," the nurse said gently.

"When can I come back?" I asked suddenly, falling to pieces.

"Tomorrow, visitation opens at 8:30 a.m. You can see her then—"

"And you'll call me if anything hap—"

"Yes, of course. If her condition changes or if there are any questions, you'll be the first to know." Then the nurse walked over and touched my elbow lightly. Her gaze danced from my knotted, bloody hair to my neck and blood-coated pants before flickering back up to my eyes, and she smiled sympathetically. "You should rest, maybe take this time to get cleaned up, grab a bite to eat if you can?"

My stomach flipped inside out at the thought of food. I nodded and took one last glance at Mama before turning to make good on my deal. The sooner I was taken, the sooner she'd be safe.

CHAPTER 7

OLIVER

"Mina? Where you at?" I asked into my phone, pressing the device harder against my ear to make out her words over the street noise.

"I left—I just—to apologize and let you know I was gonna go —care of some stuff—"

"Mina? Mina, your voice is breaking off. I can barely hear you. Tell me where you're at...which way did you exit? Why didn't I see you."

"I left through a differe—building," her voice was faint but the signal was getting better.

"Okay, tell me where you are and I'll pick you up—"

"No. It's okay. I'll be okay. I have a lot I need to do."

Something in my gut tightened. *What the hell? That guy could be looking for her right now!*

"Mina! You can't be alone right now. Just tell me where you are and wait for me. I'll come get you." There was a long silence. I lifted the phone away from my ear. She was still on the line. "Hello?"

"Oli, just—"

"Mina! This isn't a game. This is serious." My voice cut through harsher than I intended but I couldn't help it. I had to get her to listen to me. Why wouldn't she listen?

"I know this isn't a game, Oli. This is a choice. I choose to be alone. I need to be alone." Her voice came through the phone line this time, just as loud and clear as my own—a javelin straight to the gut. My brain scrambled to produce a response but my body was shutting down on me, momentarily stunned into silence. "I'm sorry," she whispered but it sounded too damn close to "goodbye." And I couldn't understand it. Why was she pushing me away?

"Mina...please, talk to me," I begged, unsure who needed whom more. Just keep her on the phone—keep her talking. At least do that much. "Mina?" The distance between us was making me physically sick.

There was another long silence and I had to check my phone again to make sure she was still on the line. Finally, she spoke. "You need to stay away from me—"

"Mina—"

"No, Oliver. You wanted me to talk, so just...please, just listen. Nothing good can come of this relationship...for you. It took me too long to realize that shitty ass truth but if you're honest with yourself, you know it just as well as I do. We both thought those thugs were gone. I thought my father handled his business and that this shit was over. Evidently, I was wrong about that. Very wrong. I don't know what happened but I know it's dangerous. It's dangerous to be around me right now. I can be reckless with my own life but I can't be reckless with yours. So please, Oliver, please just let me go and do what I need to do and live your life."

Live your life? Is she delusional? I let another moment pass to make sure she got out everything she planned on saying, but I couldn't keep my mouth shut a moment longer, terrified of the line going dead. Of losing our connection for good. "Mina, this is me you're talking to. If you think that I'd leave you to deal with this by yourself, you don't know me very well."

"That's right, we don't...know each other very well. That's even more reason why you shouldn't get sucked into my messed up disaster of a life. It's my mess, not yours. You need to stay the hell away from me. I'm serious right now. I can't handle something bad happening to you because of me, because of all this shit, Oli. Please, just..." Her voice broke and it tore into my heart the way she sobbed through those last words.

"You want to know who I really am, Mina? I'll tell you. I'm the guy who when someone I love is hurt, I do anything to stop their pain. I don't give up just because something is dangerous or hard. I don't turn my back and I don't walk away."

I heard a faint sigh on the other end of the phone—so soft it might have just been the breeze.

"This isn't some loyalty test, Oliver. This isn't hypothetical. This is real. I killed a man. That's a cold hard fact."

"In self-defense!" I cried. "My God, Mina, he was trying to murder your mother and he almost succeeded! There's no judge and jury in the world who wouldn't understand that. Mina, please. You saved her life."

"I don't even know that for sure, Oliver. She might not make it."

I opened my mouth to argue with her, desperate to keep her on the line, but her next words took the air clear out of my lungs. "Oliver, my mind is made up. What we need is a clean break."

"I need to be there with you! That's what I need and it's what you need." I ground my teeth in frustration. I had to get to her—to hold her—then everything would be okay. As long as we were together, everything would be okay. *A clean break? What the hell even was that?* "We barely even got started," I intoned.

"I know"—a deep sadness laced with exhaustion weighed her

words down—"God, Oliver, I know. This isn't fair. I'm sorry." With that, she was gone. The call ended. I dialed her back immediately, but the call went straight to voicemail.

I pulled my keys from my pocket and bolted for the parking lot, redialing her number as I ran. "Come on...come on...come on...pick up. Pick up." Voicemail again. She'd turned her phone off, I realized. *I've lost her.* I rounded the corner toward the wall where I had left my bike. Shoving the key into the ignition with one hand and my phone into my pocket with the other, I pressed the start button and the bike roared to life with a turn of my wrist.

The doctor said the Critical Care rooms were in a different tower so all I have to do, theoretically, is ride around the perimeter of the hospital and I'd be guaranteed to spot her somewhere along the sidewalk. Right? I had no other plan. I squeezed the brakes hard as a car cut me off. *What color was she wearing?* I thought back, but for the life of me, I couldn't remember. I remembered her arm was bandaged—she was cold. I had given her my black hoodie. The memory of that moment hit me suddenly.

After the fourth time around the hospital grounds scanning through pedestrians for a girl in a black hoodie, I pulled over and searched for Nyah in my contacts. I called her without thinking through exactly how much I was going to tell her.

"Hello?" Nyah's voice was amused and curious.

"Hello, Nyah? Did Mina reach out to you today?" I blurted in one breath.

"Holy crap, is this deja vu? Am I trippin' or did we already have this conversation yesterday?" She laughed.

"I'm not kidding, Nyah. Did she call you? Did she tell you where she's going?"

"What's wrong, Oliver?" Her voice lost its levity. "I thought you guys patched things up? Did you do something to upset her again?"

I hesitated for a moment but was left with no choice. "This isn't about us. Mina's mom is in the hospital."

"There's no way you're lying about something that serious, just to find a way to talk to Mina, is there? Because that would be insane. You get that, right?" Nyah warned.

"It's not a goddamn joke, okay? They were attacked in their home by two guys. I was with her at the hospital. I'm still here but after they let Mina go up and see her mom for visitation, instead of coming back out to me...she ran off. I don't know where she went. I called her and she just said it's safer if I stayed away from her, that she was dangerous. Now, she's not picking up. And it isn't safer, Nyah...it isn't safe for her to be alone. One of those guys is still after her. I need to find her, Nyah. Can you please, please call her. Do what you need to, say whatever you need to say but just get her to tell you where she is," I rambled, already feeling regret for betraying Mina's trust again by telling Nyah the things Mina clearly didn't want anyone to know. But I was out of options, and didn't know what else to do.

"What the hell? Holy crap—Lily is in a coma? How did this happen?...Okay. Give me a sec—okay...let me call Mina." The call ended.

I messaged Xavi to answer his questions about printing labels. I explained the process of packing orders and cross-referencing order numbers in way too much detail, but it was helping me stay distracted enough to keep my shit together until Nyah called me back. When my phone rang, I jumped so hard I almost dropped it.

"Me again. She's not picking up, Oli. I called her like a dozen times. I even called the neighbors but they said they're out of town. How's Lily? What the hell happened?"

"She's not good. They put her into a—a medically induced coma. She hit her head and they're waiting for the swelling to come down before they take her off the drugs. It also sounded like she got shot, but I think they got the bullets out."

"Oh, my God." Nyah's voice was the deepest I'd ever heard it. The normal bell-like quality to her tone had turned dull and flat.

"Yeah."

"And Mina? Was she hurt too? Who were they—was it like a random home invasion?"

"I don't know. She seemed physically okay, But I didn't have much time with her. Her arm was bandaged. She was pretty shaken up. Honestly, I don't know how she was keeping her shit together given what happened."

"What *did* happen?" Nyah pressed. "All you've said was it was two guys in a home invasion type thing. Why Mina and her mother? What did they want?"

"I don't know," I said, truthfully. "But I get the feeling Mina is blaming herself for it—and maybe that's why she went AWOL."

"Typical Mina," Nyah grumbled.

"You would know," I replied, unsure if it was typical of Mina to blame herself for things. She didn't seem overly self-depre-cating to me but I hadn't known her as well as Nyah had.

"Yeah, I would, normally. But she didn't call me, did she? She called you." There was a bitterness in her voice, hurt. "Whatever. I'll keep trying her," she added. "I'll let you know if I hear anything. I hope you do the same."

"I will," I promised and ended the call.

I pulled up to Mina's street and cut the engine. There was caution tape fencing off the perimeter of the house, but no one seemed to be around: no police, no detectives, no one.

The street was eerily quiet aside from the bark of the neigh-borhood dogs. I kicked open my kickstand, and stood the bike up in the driveway. I walked toward Mina's house, ducking as I approached the caution tape. *This is a crime scene now*, I told myself. I knew I shouldn't be here. She wouldn't be here but I didn't know where else to try.

I'd already tried the dance studio, as well as the few routes to her home from there. I texted Nyah to check the hookah place in the valley since she lived close by, while I rode over to check her house.

I approached the front door cautiously, aware that there could be CSI techs in the house still processing the scene. I reached for the door handle, then froze as I heard something inside the house. Footfalls? Light and delicate, like—

The door flew open and Mina stumbled out, one hand pressed to her chest, the other clutching her backpack, eyes wide and unfocused. I grabbed her gently by the shoulders, but she barely registered my presence.

"Mina, what is it?" I demanded, my eyes darting between her and the house. I checked the street again to make sure we were alone.

I felt a surge of adrenaline course through me, my fight or flight mechanism in full throttle. Mina just stood there, breathing raggedly, her eyes blank and her hands trembling, as if she were sleepwalking her way through a nightmare.

"Mina, I got you," I promised. She was panting wildly, wide-eyed. Her pupils dilated as she patted her chest with the palm of her hand, fighting for breath. The more she fought, the more it evaded her. "Breathe, Mina. Breathe, baby." I held onto her shoulders and ducked my head so that we were eye to eye.

"Is someone else in the house?"

Mina shook her head no. She was still struggling to calm her rapid, shallow breathing.

"I think you're having a panic attack. Yes?" I asked her, trying to will her to look into my eyes.

"Mina, listen. I need you to look at me. Focus on my eyes. Breath in. Out. Breathe with me." Mina's eyes were locked on my chest as she clung to my forearms—her fingers twitched and she released a slow gust of breath. "Good. In. Out. Just like that. Let's try a longer one now—count to four. In. Out." She sagged suddenly, leaning her full weight against me. "Let's sit on the stoop here," I suggested, but she shook her head in protest.

"I...can't...stay...here—" she gasped.

"I get it." I nodded. "You need me to go in and grab anything else for you before we go?"

"No!" She clutched my forearm to prevent me from moving, but she didn't need to; I wasn't going anywhere.

"I'm right here, Mina."

"Can we just walk?" she asked. "Away from here?"

"Of course we can, baby."

I wrapped my arms around her waist and pulled her close. The scent of her skin enveloping me and the relief of having her near soothed the tension coiled in my nerves.

Mina's breathing had slowed now, and she seemed to fully register my presence for the first time. I hugged her close, and as we began to walk, she wrapped one arm around my waist. We walked in silence until the road bent slightly, and her house was finally out of sight.

She stopped and slumped on the curb, resting her head between her knees.

I watched her back rise and fall from the slow heavy breaths.

I sat beside her, close enough to speak softly but far enough to give her the space she clearly wanted.

"Don't do that to me again, Mina. Please, don't run from me like that again. Please, baby, it—I can't handle it," I pleaded. She kept her head down, eyes hidden from me.

I looked around us again, brows creasing in disbelief. Where were the goddamn police? I didn't understand why they didn't have someone here.

"Why'd you come back here by yourself?" I asked her calmly, as casually as I could manage. She didn't answer, just kept her head buried in her lap. "What if they'd come back, Mina? What then?"

"Maybe that was the point," is what I heard her say, but that couldn't be right, could it?

"Maybe that was the *point*? Is that what you said?" She didn't respond.

Anger flooded through me and I felt swept away under the current. "You want them to come for you? Is that what you're saying? You got a death wish?" Now I was the one who needed to focus on my breathing. I sucked air into my lungs slowly and blew it out in a soft whistle.

Remember the training. Remember to breathe. This isn't about you or your feelings. It's about her. Focus on helping Mina.

"I've got no choice," she said flatly.

"Why would you say that? Of course, you have a choice. Don't give up, baby." My voice was calm again, reassuring. "Don't give up so easily. I know you're scared—hell, I'm scared, too. But I've got you, okay? I've got you." I'd be her hope, every time she lost it.

"Oliver, you don't understand," she snapped, finally looking up from her lap.

"Then, help me understand," I begged. She avoided my gaze and lifted her chin to the sky as though the answer were there. I looked up to the reddening hues with her, searching for understanding. *What am I missing here?* I glanced back at her.

"Talk to me," I urged.

"I want to, but I can't." She wiped a tear from her face and stood suddenly.

I jumped to my feet, as if just standing next to her would ensure she didn't run off again.

"What happened in the house just now?"

Mina shook her head as if she wasn't quite certain. "I had to find the name of that medication my grandpa needs—Mama had it written down in a journal in our kitchen and there were some things I wanted to get for Mama. I didn't know if I was allowed inside, so I waited for the crime techs to leave and I snuck right in. And I noticed it right away."

"Noticed what?"

"All the drawers were turned out, and some of the cabinets were standing open. Maybe the cops did it—I don't know. I-I had this stupid idea that I should get Mama's favorite pillow, so after I found the journal and my backpack, I started up the stairs..." Her voice faltered as she tugged at the neck of the hoodie that I'd given her. "I thought I'd be okay, but the stairs... the blood..."—A sob tore through her. "Oliver, you wouldn't have believed what she looked like in that hospital bed, that tube down her throat breathing for her...she was so weak. I've never seen—" I stepped toward her, wrapping my arms back around her, cradling her head with my hands, instinctively. She sobbed silently into my chest, choking down the sound and her body shuddering beneath my embrace. "I'm so-so goddamn useless I couldn't even do the s-simplest thing for her—one damn pillow. She would have turned the whole world inside out for me and I could barely handle being in that hospital room with her. Stupid...weak...piece of—"

"Shhh-stop it. Don't say that crap about yourself. You're a goddamn warrior, Mina. You *protected* her. You saved her life! You got her help. You fought, baby. They attacked, you fought back and you won, because you're both still here. You gotta take it easy right now and give yourself a break. This isn't normal shit you're going through. None of this is okay. But Lily is going to be okay. I know she is. I can feel it and that's thanks to you. And when she wakes up, she'll tell you the same thing." I cupped her face with my palms. "Listen, let's get the hell out of here. Please, baby, it isn't safe here. Please. Let's go somewhere else and talk. Or—or we can not talk, we can just rest...anything you want."

Mina looked around as if seeing her surroundings for the first time.

"I mean, I guess I could use a shower."

"Great idea. Let's go back to my place. You can take a nice hot shower. I'll make you some tea. You can rest—"

"No," she cut me off, panic blazing in her eyes. "No, we—I don't want to go to your place. There's a hotel across from the hospital. I'm gonna stay there. I'll drop off a hotel pillow and blanket for her. Yeah. That'll work," she said more to herself than me. She met my eyes briefly before looking back to the road. "Can you drop me off?"

"Drop you off?" Dropping off meant leaving her. Alone. The one thing I could not do. "Mina—"

"That's okay, you're—I can just get an Uber—"

"No. I'll take you. Come on." I gestured toward my motorcycle.

"I actually—I don't think I can handle a ride on it, Oliver. I'm feeling dizzy." I mentally kicked myself. I should have realized the danger. She'd been attacked only hours ago and here I was offering to hoist her onto my death mobile.

"I didn't think, I'm sorry," I confessed. "I'll order us a car and leave my bike here."

"No, it's okay. I'll order it." She pulled out her phone but barely held onto it in her trembling grip.

"Mina, just let me get you the ride at least," I ground out.

"Okay," she caved. "Thank you."

I pulled out my phone and swiped away the notifications about texts and calls. There were several from Xavi. I focused on finding the address to the hotel across from the hospital and ordered the car. There were a few drivers nearby.

"A Lux ride? No. Just get the regular option—"

"Just let me take care of you...please," I insisted.

She shrugged, shook her head, and sighed heavily. Her gaze bored into me then softened. She embraced me without warning, more a collision that morphed into a hug. I melted and molded into the feel of her against me. I traced my fingers along the line of her spine—up and down—inhaling the sweet citrus, woodsy, floral scent of her that had returned almost completely, now, as though emerging from somewhere deep within.

I held her like she was the last person on Earth because to me, she was. She was the only one who mattered. I held her like this was the last moment we'd share because for all I knew—the way the stars had cursed me—it just as well could have been.

CHAPTER 8

MINA

I jumped back from Oliver's embrace, breath hitching in my throat. Just past Oliver's shoulder, I caught sight of a black SUV moving closer to us by the second.

"What?" he cried in response to my palpable alarm. "Shit—the car," he realized. "I didn't think, I-sorry, here, let me cancel this guy and get a regular ride like you asked, hold on..." he rambled, bringing out his phone in a flash.

"No, don't. This is fine, thank you," I insisted. "What am I gonna do? Cry every time I see a black SUV?"

I started toward the car and reached for the handle but Oliver got there first. He held the door open for me and confirmed the driver's name.

The driver, a nice enough looking older gentleman in a wrinkled white dress shirt and glasses, had classical music playing softly and a rosary hanging from his rearview. The man's kind, crinkly eyes gave him a friendly sort of appearance.

I nodded reassuringly at Oliver before ducking into the

vehicle. He moved to get in with me, and every cell in my body gravitated toward him, wanting him there with me, needing the solidity of his physical presence, and the safety I felt when he was with me. *But I have to be strong now*, I told myself. I held my hand out to stop him from getting in the car.

"No"—The word stuck in my throat. I knew that the pain in my heart was an illusion, that it was some part of my brain registering the heartache I'd endured earlier today.

I hated that I was hurting Oliver. His heart was bleeding out in the shrinking, barbed cage of my love. But I had to go on alone—even if it meant ripping a hole into my own chest to do it. Because the longer I deluded myself that we had a chance together, the more likely he was going to get killed trying to save me. It would be my fault and I couldn't bear it. I had to dislodge the words, somehow. I cleared my throat and tried again, "I meant what I said before."

"Mina, I—"

"I meant it and you can't change my mind. You're not coming." I pushed him away farther and slammed the door as his mouth fell open. His arms went slack at his sides. The driver reversed until he was directly across from Oliver. "You riding up front with me?" the man asked him.

"No, man. Go ahead. Take her to that address," he answered in a low voice—a voice deprived of any emotion.

I can't do this. My fingers twitched to reach for the door handle. I had to. I balled my hands into fists. I couldn't let him put himself in danger for me again. My eyes filled with tears as I saw him moving away from the car, his expression blank and emotions impossible to discern. I blinked over and over, rubbing my eyes and bottling these final seconds together. I wanted to memorize every line and curve of his face.

Oliver stepped back onto the sidewalk as we drove off. I rotated in my seat to watch him grow smaller through the back window before the driver finally turned and he was gone from view.

My heart was lodged in my throat and my breath turned ragged once more. *In. Out.* His voice resonated from some deep corner of my mind.

My hands went numb. My chest squeezed in on itself. The soreness in my ribs from the earlier fall was throbbing more keenly now that the adrenaline had passed.

I pushed away the need—the need to be in the intoxicating warmth of his arms, especially now, as I felt I was being pulled apart into pieces. This morning seemed like another lifetime ago—awakening with him beside me made me feel cocooned—a plump little caterpillar in the midst of a transcendent, inevitable metamorphosis only to be prematurely torn from my sanctuary, flung onto the floor and crushed under a boot.

Oliver's vacant expression after he had masked his hurt kept flashing in my mind, as did the image of Mama in that hospital bed covered in tubes. I wished I had the clarity I needed to convince Oliver why things had to end this way between us, but I'd done what I needed to do, and that's what mattered.

I had once foolishly believed that the attack on me in the alley was a fluke, a scare tactic to get my father to put his affairs in order, and that it had worked on him and that was the end of it. I truly thought my father would do anything to ensure our safety because I couldn't imagine anything else. It's what I would have done. What I *had* done, that morning on the stairs.

I now knew only too well that what we were dealing with was much more serious than a paranoid manifestation of a nightmare. Patricia, the woman who had intervened in the police investigation at the hospital, had made it perfectly clear that I had to keep those I loved away from the situation at any cost.

"One of the largest and most interconnected crime syndicates in the greater Moscow region," were impactful words. And those were the exact words Patricia used in indicating precisely who and what I was up against. They weren't words someone forgets. So, even if I had to shoot Oliver down a trapdoor against his will to keep him safe, I'd have done it.

Oliver seemed to buy the idea that she was just another ambulance-chasing lawyer. Patricia had warned me not to speak with anyone about our conversation. She had explained that to do so, I'd be putting their lives at risk.

It felt like all that remained of my heart now was a pile of jagged little shards between my lungs. The last thing I wanted was to cause Oliver any more pain than he'd already endured, but I didn't see another choice. I was trying to shield him from something much more dangerous than simple heartbreak. That's right, I just had to keep reminding myself why this was necessary. There was no other way. I had considered every option.

The rosary dangling off the rearview swayed as the SUV slowed to a stop at a traffic light. I checked the cross streets—we were about five minutes from the hotel now. *I had considered every option.* I reran the scene through my mind. Patricia had those two policemen stand outside the door and guard the breakroom for us while she spoke with me in a voice so hushed, I had to lean in to hear her properly. I asked her who she was. She told me she worked with the CIA. She showed me her credentials, but how was I supposed to know if they were real? It wasn't like I looked at CIA badges every day. The police gave her access to me, so the badge must have been legitimate.

"They're going to try to take you, the men sent by this RBOC group—"

"RBOC?" I asked.

"Russian Based Organized Crime group. They're going to try and take you and you're going to let them," Patricia pronounced as though she were reading my fortune. I flinched.

"Why would I do that?" I challenged, outraged.

"Because we can protect your mother. And we can track you, you won't be alone—"

"Track me? I'm not...that's just-this is wrong, you're supposed to..." I stammered, at a loss for words. "Just help us! You're CIA! So, help us. Hide us. New identities...whatever it takes, we haven't done anything wrong. We deserve protection."

"Okay, we can do that," Patricia lilted, a slight tilt to her head.

Her expression was blank, impossible to read. It was too easy. Okay, *we can do that.* All I had to do was ask? A moment ago, she wanted to ship me off with those men to...to what? Gather intel for her? And now, she was cool with me asking for protection? But then I processed it, what it meant, to run, to hide.

"It would mean goodbye. Goodbye forever, to this life. Right?" I asked but I already knew the answer. Goodbye to my friends, everyone we ever cared about. No public success of any kind, nothing to catch the eye, no online presence, minimal career accomplishments, no newspaper coverage, no photos, no online job submissions, no press coverage. No online dating. We'd have to be meticulous, careful—looking over our shoulders for the rest of our lives. But we'd be alive.

She nodded, an almost imperceptible tinge of sadness in her eyes like seeing me discover the limitations of that life had jolted her steel facade in some way.

"And they could still find us," I went on. "No. Worse. My grandparents, my cousins in Russia would be exposed. Someone would still have to pay for my father's dealings. They'd make sure of it. They won't let this go, will they? So, if I choose to hide, I'm damning the rest of my family to the point that I might as well be putting the nails in their coffins myself. I don't really have a choice, do I?" My veins ran ice-cold at the realization.

"You're a smart girl," Patricia confirmed. "You're also very brave and strong." I waited for the "but." There was only silence.

She knew I'd come to this decision on my own. She knew it all along. She was a profiler, a good one.

"We don't have much time and there's still a lot to do. We have a few hours to prep and release you. Are you in?" Her eyes glistened but her mouth and brows remained level.

I don't really have a choice, do I? "I'm in," I said, but a louder instinct screamed for me to run.

She had promised that if I went with them willingly—the men of this RBOC—when they came for me, she'd ensure Mama's protection and they'd have foreign assets near my location at all times in case an emergency extraction was necessary. I didn't buy that, not completely.

I still had a feeling she couldn't guarantee my safety the way she was trying to sell me on her know-it-all demeanor. There was a desperation in her offer—I was their best shot at gathering inside information on this particular RBOC, at the moment.

Patricia—her cold eyes and expression devoid of any sign of human sympathy—briefed me on the delicate nature of the situation. She was willing to promise a lot in exchange for the coordinates my capture would provide—protection for Mama at a top of the line rehab facility, she even committed to sending a foreign asset to bring my grandfather the medication he needed. I promised to cooperate to the best of my ability.

There was no other way out of this. I'd do it—I'd let them take me. I'd report to my handler about everything I saw. I shook my head as I imagined what would happen to me if I surrendered myself to those men. Just the idea of doing that felt insane. It was hard to believe it would be anything other than suicide. But Mama would be safe. My family would be spared.

As the driver pulled up to the hotel, I pulled my backpack up from the floor and mindlessly pressed it against my abdomen, preparing to leave. I thanked the driver before stepping out and heading straight for the lobby, ignoring the question the bellboy had asked me.

I checked into my hotel room with Mama's ID and credit card. There was no sense in trying to hide the money trail—they'd find me anyway. Still, I kept glancing over my shoulder like someone could grab me at any moment. A creeping feeling in my gut told me I was being followed. I shook it off and took my room key from the cheery woman checking me in at reception. Brushing off my suspicions, I focused on finding my room and getting into the shower as fast as possible.

The hotel was newly renovated, with all the amenities a person could dream up. Even the regular room was spacious. The sumptuous bed called to me. I resisted, intent on washing this nightmare of a day down the shower drain.

My hands trembled as I lathered my hair. I scrubbed my hands raw with my fingernails then scraped under each nail, sending every drop of residual blood down the drain. Rosy scratch marks marred the skin of my hands and forearms from the thorough scrub, but I preferred the burning to the strange numbness that had been spreading through my body from my stomach since this morning.

After emerging from the shower and wrapping myself in the plush hotel robe, I brewed a cup of chamomile tea, hoping to steady my still-shaking hands. I redialed the number to the hospital, the fourth time since I'd left, and punched in the extension for the Critical Care reception.

"Mount Joseph Medical, Critical Care Department, this is Delilah, what is your name?"

"Hi Delilah, I'm Mina Arkova, I'm calling about Lilia Arkova, room 8346, I'm calling to see if there's been any change in her condition—"

"Miss Arkova, I'm afraid there have been no changes. We are still closely monitoring her and the swelling is going down gradually, but I'm afraid that's all I can tell you."

"When can I see her again? The nurse said first thing tomorrow but I want to bring by a blanket and pillow for her, so maybe I can come n—"

"I'm afraid Ms. Arkova's visitation allotment has been filled for today per our Critical Care unit guidelines and unfortunately, the doctors have advised against any outside pillows, blankets, scarves, shawls, or other personal items of this nature in the Critical Care unit. We have a policy against it, so..."

"Wait, why?"

"Why? Umm, well I'm not sure exactly, it's just the policy but it's most likely a safety issue to make sure the airways are always clear. The pillows have to be a certain way. Also, patients often share a room or get shuffled around, and some have allergies and if people have dogs or cats at home, the blankets might have hair—"

"We don't have dogs or cats—"

"I understand, I'm sorry, it's just policy. There's nothing I can do. But when she's moved into a regular room it's a bit more relaxed. I can ask them to send in an additional blanket if you'd like? I know the ones we have are really thin but we can ask the doctor or nurses for approval and send her more. I know they don't like to bundle the patients too much because it risks a fever."

"No, that's okay, she already has an extra blanket."

"Please rest assured, Miss Arkova. Your mother is under constant monitoring and I assure you she's in good hands."

"Thank you so much, Delilah. What's the earliest time I can come see her tomorrow?"

"Visitation begins at 8:30 a.m. tomorrow," Delilah said.

"If anything changes...if she wakes up or gets worse, please put it in the notes to call me right away—"

"Of course, we'll call you if there are any changes—"

"I'm right across the street so I can come by at a minute's notice."

"All right, Miss Arkova. It's in the notes here. No worries. We have your information," she assured. "Is there anything else I can help you with?"

"No, I guess...just pray for her, please," I begged, reluctant to end the call as it seemed my only connection, however tenuous, to my mother. I walked over to the floor-to-ceiling window and pressed my forehead to the glass. The hospital was right across the street. Mama's wing was in the southwest corner.

"I will," she answered kindly.

"Thank you," I whispered and ended the call. I shut my eyes and prayed for the first time since we'd lost my baby sister. I hadn't known what I was doing then and I didn't know what I was doing now. I just prayed for everything to turn out all right, whatever the hell that meant.

I was exhausted so I tried to get some sleep, but my stomach was in knots—I devised endless theories about my father and what he possibly could have done to piss these people off so badly, anything to keep my mind off Oliver and the gnawing pit in my stomach. I distracted myself long enough to fall asleep by watching a Spanish game show. I could hardly understand the concept, so it was a perfect cognitive timeout. Later, I flipped to the golf channel, another game I didn't follow very well. I became much more relaxed, but my mind was still having trouble settling.

During the news, an infomercial came on about a "life-changing" scrubber sponge shaped like a smiley face. It made me think about the time Mama and I were doing our spring cleaning and we had both bruised our wrists playing tennis the day before. We were suffering miserably trying to get the grime out of the kitchen tiles when Mama had this crazy idea. She said, "What if we figuring up a way to attach the scrubber or cleaning brush to end of the drill?"

We spent that whole day at the hardware store, scheming up ways to attach a cleaning brush to a drill bit, making bad drilling jokes, fantasizing about the creation of our very own home improvement empire, and ultimately, buying an assortment of superglues to Mickey Mouse the prototype.

Half the fun was how convinced we were that it was the most brilliant idea ever and that it would absolutely work. And, honestly, for a full two minutes, it did. We had the cleanest four by four square patch of kitchen tile on the block, but when the glue gave way and the rubber bands snapped, we lost our balance and head-butted each other. Our laughter filled the house that day, floor to ceiling.

Mama always had a way of making the most mundane things full of sparkle. She turned hardware stores into fantasy lands and cleaning chores into summer camp games. Later, and much to our delight, we found a company that manufactured cleaning brushes as drill accessories, and we laughed at our audacity to believe we were the first to think of the "revolutionary" idea.

I finally drifted off to sleep sometime after the local news did a feature on a new vegan doggie cafe in West Hollywood making a splash with their doggie lattes.

I dreamed that I was back in my house. The men were there again. But this time I couldn't see them. Each time I turned to find them, they'd be gone and reappeared somewhere else in the house, like ghosts. When I found a gun at the foot of the staircase, I picked it up and trained it on one of them who began running right at me, but when I squeezed the trigger, the man was gone.

Mama stood in the distance, smiling at me but there was blood in her mouth. I screamed her name but the dream changed and I was gone.

I was somewhere else now, and I couldn't remember what had just happened. Now, I was running through a strange house. I didn't know why I was running. I just knew I had to keep going. It was a familiar house yet eerily different than any place I remembered. Sort of like finding yourself in a place that you'd been to many years ago but everything was backwards, inside out, somehow. Each room I passed through was packed with people. No one acknowledged me or even looked my way as I ran past.

No one was chasing me but I felt frightened nonetheless. I knew that if I'd stop, I'd be in danger so I kept going. I was nearing a corridor when I tripped over something lumpy on the floor of a dark hallway and fell to my hands and knees. I looked back and saw it was a body. I tripped over someone who was sitting on the floor in the hallway, slumped against the wall.

"I'm sorry," I bit out. But the person didn't move. They didn't even respond. I looked closer and brushed the dark hair out of their eyes—their lifeless eyes. Their expression was vacant. I scrambled away from the body, crawling backward until I hit a wall.

I rushed to stand and all the faceless bodies around me turned toward me, pointing. I looked down to where they all pointed at the bloody knife in my tight grip and then back at the body on the floor.

I woke up gasping. Sweat lined my brow and my tank top was wet, sticking to my stomach and my back. I was dizzy, disoriented, out of breath, confused by the unfamiliarity of the room. As soon as I realized where I was and remembered why I was here, a suffocating melancholy weighed down on me.

I found myself calling Oliver's number before I even realized what I was doing. I ended the call quickly just as the first ring sounded on the line and sensible reasoning kicked in. *You can't call him. You need to leave him alone. It's the only way to keep him safe.*

My stomach rumbled and growled—a reminder that I hadn't had anything to eat all day. Room service prices were a rip-off so I ordered a Caesar salad, two sides of fries, and extra pita with hummus for delivery from a late night spot across town. I added water bottles to meet the delivery minimum. I temporarily satiated the growling with some chips from the convenience tray above the mini-fridge, another rip-off but I needed something right then.

I muted the television as a breaking news story was reporting another armed robbery, a home invasion. The robbers took the dog.

The same numbness from before was spreading through my body once again. It started at my stomach and worked its way down my arms through to my fingers. My ears felt like they were ringing, and hints of rising panic sparked in my gut.

I reminded myself—*one, two, three, four. In. Out.*—trying to regulate the increasingly frantic breaths. Those potato chips were an agent of chaos in my empty stomach. I rolled off the bed and onto the floor, releasing a thespian grunt of discomfort.

My phone chimed behind me with a notification. I reached for it with a moan to find a text from Oliver.

> hey you okay?

For a mindless moment, I thought it was sweet, like he could feel that something was wrong until I remembered that *he would have seen on his call log that I'd called and hung up.* He was just checking in on me, making sure I was okay.

> Yeah. You?

I wrote back to him. I thought I heard something just outside the door. I brushed the fear off but then there was a definite thump, like something had fallen on the carpet in the hallway. I froze. *What the hell was that?*

My phone chimed again and I jumped.

OLIVER

Need me to come up?

Come up? What the hell did that mean? I dialed Oliver's number. He picked up on the first ring. "Mina? Everything good?"

"What do you mean do I need you to come up? You're here... at the hotel?"

"Yeah, I'm in the lobby."

"Oliver—"

"Did something happen? Lily?" he quickly asked.

"What? No. I—I called you by accident," I fibbed.

"Oh," he sounded both relieved and dejected.

"Go home, Oliver," I begged, though it was the last thing I wanted him to do.

"I'm not leaving you alone here. Sorry."

"How long are you planning to stay down there? How long have you been here?"

"Don't worry about it," he said, like it had nothing to do with me. Reception would probably ask him to leave, eventually. What if they didn't? What if he stayed there all night?

"We need to talk. I'll come down and get you," I said and hung up.

I pulled my shoes on and headed for the door, smoothing my hair and rubbing the sleep from my eyes. My heart was pounding so hard the whole way down to the lobby that I could hardly hear anything besides the ringing in my ears.

The elevator doors opened and Oliver was there, leaning against a wall in the lobby, waiting for me, his phone in hand, his jaw set. I tilted my head and held the elevator door for him until he stepped inside.

"How long have you been here?" I questioned. It was close to midnight. I'd been asleep for at least a few hours now. My heart pounded through my chest as we rode up on the elevator, buzzing from our mere proximity. I wanted to lean into his body, rest my cheek against his chest, wrap my arms around his hips, and graze my hands up his back. He was leaning into the elevator wall with his shoulder, arms crossed, looking down at me with concern in his gaze, closer than he needed to be.

"A while," he answered, voice flat, eyes scanning me for answers I couldn't give.

"No one asked you what you were doing here so late?"

"I'm a guest." He shrugged.

The elevator doors opened at my floor and I led him to my room as I ironically told him, "You should go home, Oliver."

He raised his brow at me. "I can go back to the lobby if you want. You're the one who said we needed to talk."

"Obviously we do, because I wanted to explain more clearly why it's dangerous to be here, to be near me. I don't want you putting yourself at risk and it's obvious that you still don't understand. Otherwise, you wouldn't be here"—I looked around the hallway—"Okay, just...come in. Please, let's finish this inside."

"You're not gonna convince me to leave, so, save your breath," he argued.

"I can call security, you know," I bit back.

"You wouldn't do that," he asserted, his eyes boring into mine. *Yes, I would. Wouldn't I?*

"I will, if you hear me out and still don't go," I threatened and meant every word.

He opened his mouth to argue but a look of hurt overcame him. He stood before me, incredulity in his gaze, tight-lipped, an uncharacteristic scowl marring his effortlessly handsome features.

"Oliver, what exactly do you think you're going to do to stop these men? Do you have any idea how dangerous they are?"

"I'm not going to sit back and let them hurt you without a fight," he seethed, jaw clenched.

I shook my head, boiling with frustration, desperate to get him away from here, away from me but at the same time longing to bury myself in his arms and get lost in him.

It would be so easy to just take a step forward, to close the distance between us that was causing a chasm in my chest. It would feel so right to just press myself against him, click into place, my softest parts against his hardest parts. We had always fit together so perfectly, hadn't we? I needed something, anything to pull me out of the intoxicating, nearly gravitational pull he had on me.

"What was her name? Who was she?" I asked.

"Whose name?" He knitted his brows.

"The woman who left her lipstick on you the night you told me you loved me?"

His expression shifted from confusion to hurt and from hurt to anger. "That's what you choose to talk about? On this of all days?" he pronounced, taking a step back, darkness seeping into his tone.

"Well, isn't that what happened?" I went on, not missing a beat.

Oliver was quiet, possibly reining in his temper, before he finally spoke. "It soils it, when you say it like that. It soils a memory that, to me, is close to sacred. That night and every-thing that happened that night between us is sacred to me. I somehow thought you might feel the same."

I was speechless. I felt that way too, or at least, I thought I had. It surprised me how I could just shut those feelings off, push them aside to try to trivialize our connection.

"I know what you're trying to do," he accused. "You're

pushing me away. Can we at least go into the room to have this conversation?"

"No. I just want to know her name. I want to know what happened. We never got a chance to talk about it because I was upset but I'm not anymore," I explained.

"Nothing happened. I refused her. She was being inappropriate. She's no one to me. There's nothing to tell," Oliver stated resolutely.

"Tell me her name." My voice grew sharper, my neck flushing hot.

"It doesn't matter," he hissed.

"It matters to me."

"It shouldn't," Oliver promised, gently this time. He reached for my wrist, but I took a step back from him, determined to stay the course.

"What was her name, Oliver?"

"Kiran." The name on his tongue was like the bite of a blade across my chest. He had said their exchange hadn't mattered. Then, why did it still burn so keenly? Because I was forcing it to burn, that's why.

Something in Oliver's expression gave—a light flickered out in his eyes as he said her name, like he had disappointed himself.

"Kiran," I repeated, my heart splintering at the sound of those two syllables.

"Kiran Kaur. CJ's wife," he went on.

"CJ, the exper—exporter—" I stumbled on my words. This was news.

"Yes. CJ, the exporter, the one you met when I brought you along on my business deal meeting, downtown."

"His wife...wow." The shock of that rolled through me. This, I wasn't prepared for. It had been a grown woman. I had called her a woman, assuming but not knowing for certain who it was

—this was a confirmation. Concern and a protective instinct brought rise to outrage at this, at her.

"She and I haven't spoken since," he promised.

"I'm sure that helps CJ sleep at night," I declared, bitterly.

"CJ doesn't know. I doubt I'd be walking if he did," he admitted.

"Nice." My tone was glacial. I was riling myself up, goading myself into reliving that same storm of jealousy and possessiveness that had me in a chokehold the night I spotted the stains of lipstick on his skin, because I realized if I was going to drive Oliver off, I had better make it convincing.

I took another step away from him and crossed my arms, speaking verses with my body language as I ignored the resolve it must have required for a young man to refuse the advances of a grown woman. Instead, I tried to focus on what those advances must have looked like. I was going to cling to the memory of Kiran's lipstick on him that night until I was numb. Was she desirable? Was he attracted to her?

There was only one problem. It wasn't working. I didn't care, even if she was the most beautiful woman on Earth and even if he was drawn to her. He left her to find me, to make sure I was safe. He was right—whatever happened between him and Kiran didn't matter. I still wanted him. I would always want him. I swiped my keycard against the door, and pushed it open.

"Come in," I grumbled.

The corner of his lips turned up into a sad smile, almost imperceptible, like he'd won and lost something both at once. He didn't waste time before slipping past me into the room. I quickly followed, checking behind us one last time before shutting the door, bolting it, and chaining it.

"You feeling better?" he asked as he took a step toward me, reaching his long, elegant fingers out to brush against mine. I pretended his response wasn't a dig at my failed attempt to make myself mad at him.

"Yeah. A bit better. I can see her hospital window from here. I wanted to be close to her, I guess. I don't know what else I can do."

"Neither of you deserved this," he whispered. "I would do anything to take it away from you." There was so much tenderness in his gaze.

"It is what it is," I told him and turned to walk farther into the room. "They're still after me. It's not about if they catch up to me at this point—it's just come down to when. And I don't want you there when it happens." He held on to my hand and pulled me back to face him.

"I have to be alone," I said.

"I don't accept that," he pronounced, fingers tensing around mine.

"You have to accept it. When they come back, I'll have to go with them—" I regretted the words as soon as they left my mouth, but it was the truth and maybe if I told him the truth, or a part of the truth, he'd understand.

"What? The hell you will—"

"I'll have to. And if—if you're there, it'll be messy. I don't want you involved. I couldn't take it if..." I shook my head, unable to find the necessary words to convey my irreparable affliction. Opposing needs battled within me, two lions ripping each other apart for domination—my hopeless yearning for him to always be near me and my instinct to protect him by getting him as far away from me as possible.

As I mulled over what to do next, Oliver untangled his fingers from mine and brought his palms up to cup either side of my cheeks. He seemed to be savoring every inch of my face with a youthful wonder in his eyes, like a child holding a soap bubble in his palms for the first time.

He leaned in and lightly brushed his lips against mine. I didn't pull back. Instead, I opposed his every movement, mirroring the velutinous caress of his strokes. He was the paint-brush. I was the liquid canvas.

The rush of sweetness and longing was almost more than I could bear. *Just a kiss, just for a moment*, I thought. I let my eyelids drift shut and deepened our kiss. What could it hurt? A small kiss goodbye. But I was lost in my addiction to him—thoughtless, lustful, greedy.

He drank me in like I might disappear, fingers almost bruising as his tongue pushed into my mouth. I opened wider for him, savoring the taste of him and pulling him toward me so that our bodies were almost flush. I wanted to learn him, to memorize what he looked like when he kissed me this way. I opened my eyes. Oliver's expression was possessive, conquer-ing, a scorching adoration that I could feel in my soul.

Don't let this be the last time, I repeated like a prayer again and again as I ran my fingertips up and down his broad shoulders toward his neck.

My breasts raked against the smooth, hard surface of his chest. Even through the fabric, it sent an electric current over my skin. He moaned into my mouth, the sound reverberating lower toward my core, kindling a small fire that could burn down a whole forest given strong enough wind.

I reached up for his chest, stroking over the hard muscles through the cotton of his shirt with the pads of my fingers. He wrapped his long fingers around my wrists, stopping my gentle strokes against his chest and pausing our kiss. His lips were still pressed into mine, his breaths shallow, moving in and out of my parted mouth.

I had to concentrate to keep my hips from rolling against him, but I craved the contact desperately. He advanced on me, pressing me against the back of the closed door. The metal door handle jutted sharply against my bottom but the delicious fric-tion of his weight between my legs almost had me bending at the knees, melting toward the floor. He tugged on the collar of my t-shirt, exposing the skin of my shoulder. He bowed his head and grazed his teeth against the tender flesh at the base of my neck, and the sensation sent shockwaves straight to my core. Heat pooled at my center as he teased me with soft bites along my clavicle mixed with kisses and caresses of his tongue.

Oliver let out a euphoric exhalation against my skin that unleashed a guttural sound from my throat. With a display of strength I had never before experienced from him, he pressed into me as he lifted my thighs around his waist, pushing me harder still against the door. It was too late to stifle the moan that escaped through my lips.

He surrendered a smile of pure satisfaction, a gaze so domineering yet deeply affectionate, it was almost palpable. "That little sound you just made was music to my ears, sweetheart"— The whisper of his words tickled my lips, each word broken up by soft kisses—"More. Music." I gasped for air, arching my spine hungrily. His lips were on my neck in an instant. He took everything he could. I was ready to give him everything. I was ready to do anything to banish the loneliness—consumed by the emptiness within me.

He pulled us away from the wall, guiding me with little nudges toward the bed. I liked this lost feeling—this disorientation, this lunacy. I wanted to stay in this warm limbo forever, teetering on the edge of abandon. We were a tangle of love and limbs—a lambada of broken dreams and desperate longing.

The breath whooshed out of me as Oliver scooped me up and carried me across the short distance of the room, toppling onto the bed and over me. He braced himself on his elbows. I peered up at him, my head still spinning from the rushing blood coursing through my system at the speed of light. The mattress groaned as he pulled me farther onto it, one of his heavy thighs resting between my legs. He tenderly brushed the strands of hair from my eyes.

"Tell me why you really called me." His tone was husky and

low. His voice, a velvet caress against the dark matter of my mind, leaving the groove of a path only he could fill.

"I don't know," I breathed. His eyes darkened and lowered. *Come on, Mina,* they seemed to say.

"Mina. Why did you call?" he repeated, calmly, sternly.

Guilt. Guilt was the answer. My guilt consumed me and I was disgusted with myself. Oliver made me forget that. That's why I called. When I was with him, I forgot all of my shortcomings. He thought I was good and so, I was. I hungered for that feeling, but it wasn't just that. I was worried about him, felt guilty for how I'd left him in too vulnerable of a place. *Guilt.* "Because I needed you," I said.

I knew what those words would do to him. My desire would empower him. When he wrapped his hands tightly around my waist, I sighed with pleasure. Slipping his fingers beneath my tank top, he trailed them up to the base of my breasts, cupping them slowly, nearly circling them with the length of his fingers. Avoiding the peaks while kneading with a touch that was a delicious balance of rough and tender, he palmed them again and again as I arched to him. The pressure in my core felt like a taut coil, steadily tightening. Each stroke of his expert hands brought me closer to the edge, ascending higher and higher toward the cliff end.

We were fully clothed but the raw vulnerability of need in his gaze, in my guttural moans as we ground our bodies against each other, ensured my earlier coyness had been entirely abandoned. His thigh rolled up my core, my fingers ran down his back. He kept rolling and shifting his shoulders to get my hands off of him, flexing his jaw while reluctantly releasing his hold on my breasts to pin my hands down with his own.

A part of me wanted to submit to him, to give him the comfort of control so that he could relax. But I couldn't help wanting to return his caresses, to show him affection. It was instinctive for me. How did I think I'd be strong enough to resist this?

He was battling an instinct to stop me from touching him, to regain complete control over me. But he moved my hands away with such care—a slow, steady force—like he was fighting himself through the movement. He channeled the weight of his frustration into pinning me down, into every roll and grind of his hips and I was going to lose myself like this. I blinked up at him.

Then, Oliver's warning came to the foreground of my mind, sudden as a snowstorm. *I've slept with women who prefer when it's intense...sought out aggressively sexual women...exclusively physical... not emotional...*

He warned me that he couldn't give me the intimacy that I wanted. I froze beneath Oliver, reluctant to give away just how unsure I had been of my own ability to handle what was unfolding between us. And I was almost entirely certain he had been wrong—he was more capable of intimacy than anyone I'd ever met. He just needed time.

There wasn't enough time. We were supposed to learn each other, feel this through, slowly. It wasn't fair to either of us. The realization that this could be the last time we ever saw each other was closing in on me, and with it came the reminder of why I was staying in this hotel room in the first place. I shut my eyes, overwhelmed by guilt and shame.

Oliver stilled above me. Not yet entirely withdrawn but utterly motionless. "I'm sorry," he whispered.

"No. Don't be," I managed. The sound of his voice brought me to open my eyes. "I want this, it's just..." I compensated for my loss for words with a weak smile.

His gaze was filled with concern and a hint of fear. My hands shot to my face, making a sloppy attempt to wipe away the tears. A choked giggle burst from my lips. I covered my eyes with my hands and shook my head trying to calm myself. But regaining composure wasn't easy as my body shook with the relentless buzz of nervous energy.

He gently pried my hands from my face. As I looked up, my gaze was met by a warmth in his. Oliver's earlier frustration with losing control was now seemingly gone. The pad of his thumb smoothed my brow, soothing me with gentle strokes. "Let's stop, baby. We can stop," he offered.

"I wanted this, I promise," I quickly reaffirmed. Desperation broke through my voice. I reached for him, fingers brushing his biceps. "You're perfect, it's not you," I assured, voice shaky.

I needed him to know what he meant to me, that he was the best, most perfect thing that ever happened to me. That he was a gift, he deserved to be cherished and loved. He deserved more than this. I needed to tell him, but the words wouldn't form. "You're perfect," I repeated, barely more than a whisper.

The weight of him bearing down on me was such a warm, welcome relief. It would've been enough, just this feeling of safety alone. I could've stayed like this for ages. But of course, there was more and Oliver was searching for it. He was restless, relentless in his pursuit to comfort, to please, to give pleasure. Even now, his arm found the gap between my spine and the mattress to fill it, support it.

I drank in the sight of Oli's face, inches from mine, his luminous, ardent gaze, his angular jaw, his rich ochre skin like the fire-gold glow of evening twilight, his disheveled dark curls, the slight crook on the bridge of his nose that I never noticed before now.

"You're so beautiful," I murmured, realizing I'd verbalized the thought. "It takes my breath away sometimes," I confessed. He smiled and shook his head incredulously, as though it was the most ridiculous thing he'd ever heard.

"There's something else, Mina. Tell me," he rasped, thumb moving across my brow again in gentle strokes, silent promises.

"It's too much." I shook my head.

"Let me help you carry it. Please."

I shook my head but this time, I tried, despite the urge to clam up. "It's shameful," I whispered, heat rushing to my cheeks. "It's sinful. Me, here with you, while she's right over there, fighting for her life. I should go to hell for this...amongst other reasons," I murmured, voice small and clipped and bitter.

He didn't speak right away. He hardly moved a muscle and his thumb stilled on my brow. For a moment, I regretted saying the words. But then, he dropped his forehead down to press it against mine. He exhaled slowly and I filled my lungs with the sweet, minty scent of him. We were utterly still, breathing each other in. There was something potent in our combined scents, something heady and magnetizing.

Intoxicated by it, I brushed the tip of my nose against the bridge of his in a long, gentle stroke. Then, I did it again, against the stubble of his cheek this time. Our lips brushed and I arched into him, caving to the impulses my body was demanding. His fingers ran along the base of my throat and stopped there. Our breaths were short and ragged now. My fingers tightened around his powerful biceps and his hold on my throat tightened reflexively for only a moment but it was enough. The taut tension of my restraint snapped, and I gave over.

I bunched Oliver's shirt in my fists and crashed my mouth into his. He gasped, taken by surprise, mouth open, breath hitching. He was tentative at first, but my body was telling me that I wanted this more than I'd ever wanted anything and his body was clearly listening.

Our skin was heating up again. Every place we touched seemed to be on fire. I stroked his tongue with mine, tangling my fingers in his hair, wrapping my legs around his hips and pulling him closer. I needed him to fill me until I couldn't think or see. I wanted to be consumed by him.

He moved away the damp strands of hair that had fallen across my eyes. The tips of his fingers caressed my cheek, trailing down the side of my face toward my jaw, lower toward my neck until he reached my collarbone and traced a straight line along my shoulder and down along my side to my lower back.

He hardened as his hand splayed across my backside, squeezing and pulling me up and into him. We were locked, now, hip to hip. He resumed the trace of his fingertips, back up my side, my collarbone, my neck.

I moaned in frustration, desperate for more friction. I was sure I would spontaneously combust if I was kept in this state of suspension, right on the edge. He leaned forward, lowering over me until his mouth brushed my ear, his voice gravelly.

"It isn't sinful, Mina. This isn't sin. This is love."

CHAPTER 9

OLIVER

S ome gifts are curses.

The blare of sirens awoke me, the sound, a sobering reminder that we were sleeping across the street from a hospital. There'd probably been sirens throughout the night but this was the one that finally jolted me out of a deep, dreamless rest. Even before I opened my eyes, I could sense something was wrong. The air around me felt too still. The reassuring sound of Mina's breath somewhere nearby, missing. The warm solace from curling my chest around her spine, of holding her, wrapped in my arms, displaced.

I stretched my leg out diagonally, resolved not to panic, searching for Mina's icicle toes. My leg reached the edge of the bed, still nothing. When I rolled over, I found more nothingness, just an empty place, a vacant pillow and next to it, on the bedside table, a note. "Mhmm, no..." I muttered as I scampered up to reach for it.

Last night was a gift, thank you and I'm sorry. I won't hurt you anymore. I won't call. You're the best person I've ever met. I hope that one day you'll forget about this. I hope the pain of this moment won't be forever. I hope, one day, it won't even be a dot on the canvas of your life. Live well. I love you.

I jumped out of bed, flipping the sheets inside out looking for the rest of my clothes, crawling around the floor for my socks and shoes. I threw them on before running toward the door.

I grabbed my backpack as well and pulled my phone out of my pocket. The time said 8:56 a.m. My phone's battery life was in the red. I dialed Mina on the way out the door. It went straight to voicemail. I dialed her up two more times before trying Nyah. She wasn't picking up either. I waited for the elevator. I texted Mina.

> Call me.

I pulled up my texts with Nyah and typed out a message for her.

> Mina bounced again. i ended up staying in her room @ that hotel i followed her to across frm the hospital. i woke up she was gone. left me a note...says she's staying away frm me and frm everyone to keep us safe. i'm gonna try the hospital n keep u posted. plz lmk if she hits u up

There was a message from Xavi.

> Yo gonna start packing the last few orders in 10, gonna grab a coffee u want one?

I rode the elevator down as I shot him a quick text back.

> thnx na i'm good. ill b there latr today…keep me posted on how it goes

Nyah replied.

> Got it. k I'll let u know if anything but I doubt she'll tell me shit. GL…lmk if she's @ hospital. I'll try to call her.

I was across the street and running into the main entrance of the hospital when Nyah sent another text.

> shes not answering.

I lied to the security guard about who I was and told him I was family, so he let me up. The receptionist in the Critical Care unit wasn't as chill. She narrowed her eyes at me.

"Ms. Arkova's daily visitation limit has been filled today. Her daughter didn't mention any additional family coming. The police were clear, no one was to be allowed in but the daughter, they didn't say anything about—"

"So, she was here? She already left?" I blurted.

"We can't give out that kind of information."

"Sorry, I get it. I'm just…I wanted to see Lily and Mina doesn't know I'm in town yet and I wanted to catch up with her and she wasn't picking up her phone. Can you please just tell me how long ago she left?" I asked, trying to sound hopeful but not desperate. I offered a sincere smile. She returned it and nodded slightly, leaning in.

"You just missed her. We gave her a little extra time with Ms. Arkova. That's another reason I can't let you visit. Ms. Arkova needs to be undisturbed so she can focus on recovering."

"I completely understand. Well, I'm going to leave my number here with you. If you don't mind, keep me in the loop about Lily's recovery if you have trouble reaching Mina at any point," I said as I jotted down my name and number on a Post-it, handed it to her with as calm and warm a smile as I could muster before power walking back to the elevators.

My phone buzzed urgently. I clicked the elevator button repetitively while answering.

"Ey Xavi man, I'm sorry, I was checking on my girl, her mom's in the hospital...what's—"

"Oliver! I don't know what to tell you but it looks like some kind of raid is happening at your storage unit, man. I'm here and they're saying you need to get your ass down here too...ASAP."

"Raid?" The word was hardly more than a whisper. *What fresh hell is this?* A part of me had feared, and in many ways, anticipated this moment ever since Kiran—the wife of the exporter I sell to—had unexpectedly warned me that I was being watched by the police and maybe even the feds.

"I told them I'd try and get you on the phone but listen, man, they said if you don't get down here like...now, they're comin' after you. Trust me, man, that doesn't sound good...so, just get your ass here while it's still...you know, voluntary."

"Is it the feds or the cops?"

"I don't know, man, they're not wearing name tags, brother. But it's a whole ass unit up in here, let me tell you that."

"I'm on my way." I ended the call and immediately dialed Nyah. She picked up on the second ring.

"Oli?"

"Nyah, I need your help—deja vu—I know." I caught Nyah up about Mina and visitation. "Nyah, I want to look for Mina but the police are at my storage unit and they're saying I need to get my ass down there, now."

"Storage unit? What do you mean police? Police-police?—"

"Yea—I don't—"

"Why? What're you storing in there? Dead bodies?" She

laughed uncomfortably, as though she actually believed that it was a damn possibility.

"I'm not one hundred percent sure what exactly is going on or why they're there...that's what I'm going to find out."

"What do you need from me, then? You want me to hide the chainsaw for you?" She laughed.

"Nyah—"

"Oh, Lord. What if they heard that? What if they're buggin' your phone and heard me say that? All right, I want to be one hun-duurrr-red percent clear that I. Will. Not. Hide anything for this shady ass lil' Daniel—"

"Nyah, please, just listen to me. Mina wrote me a goodbye note. I've got a bad feeling if we don't find Mina soon—I'd ignore this BS and go look for her myself but Xavi's at my storage unit and I don't want them messing with him or thinking he's responsible for anything so—"

"Who's Xavi?"

"He's a buddy of mine. We train together. He's working with me on my busine—doesn't matter. Point is, I have a feeling she might've gone back to her house, because she made it sound like she actually wants those men to find her and when they come for her, she's planning on going with them—"

"Whoa, wait what? That makes no sense...why would they come for her again? Why would she go with them? What is happening?" Nyah's voice went shrill.

"It's too complicated to explain and we're running out of time. I'm sorry to ask this of you...she just—she can't be alone but...it's not exactly safe for you to be with her either. So, is there anyone you can ask to go there with you, to her place to at least check if she really is there?"

"My dad's at work right now, but my cousin's in town. I'll see where he's at and ask him to come with me."

"All right. Thank you! If anything happens, call the police. I'll deal with my stuff as fast as I can and I'll meet you after. In the meantime, try to—"

"I'll find her and I won't let her ditch me."

"Thank you, Nyah."

"Hold on...it's Mina! She sent me something," Nyah said, her voice growing farther from the phone.

"What? What's it say?" I urged.

"Shit...Oli—"

"What?!"

"It's a goodbye text. 'Nybear something happened and I might have to leave soon. It's about my dad. You might not hear from me for a while, just know that I love you forever.'" She read the last part slowly, in a hush.

"Shit. Shit!" Xavi was calling me again. "I gotta take this, I'll call you back." I switched the calls. "Hello?"

"Tell me you're on your way."

"I'm on my way."

"You told me you weren't doing nothing shady," Xavi chided.

"I'm not. I didn't. I swear."

"Then what the hell is this, Oli?"

"I don't know, Xavi. I'll be there soon. I'll take care of it. You've got no part in this, don't worry—" But the call was ended.

The whole way there, my mind ping-ponged between being worried sick over Mina and the hell waiting for me at work. When I pulled up to the building where my storage unit was located and took in the sheer quantity of unmarked vehicles surrounding the building, I thought I might actually get sick. Xavi wasn't kidding, it had been a whole-ass unit and then some.

The question was, why were they here? Were they coming

for my source like Kiran warned they might? Had her husband pinned something on me?

I would give them my sources, TK and Mo. Those guys always promised me clean units, that was the deal. If they did something shady, then that was on them.

As soon as I stepped near the storage unit, an officer in full gear and carrying an assault rifle pointed the loaded weapon at me. I threw my hands up on instinct.

"Whoa!" I yelled out in surprise and a jolt of fear hit me. "I'm Oliver Mondell. Xavi called me, told me you guys were looking for me. This is my storage unit."

"I've got him!" the officer cried out to the others. The entire hallway and storage space were crawling with officers. They had black Kevlar vests on and all their SIGs were directed at me.

"Keep your hands where I can see them," the officer shouted.

"I am!" I emphasized my open hands by raising my palms as high as they went. The utter intensity of their distrust was terrifying. It was only when I took a closer look at my storage unit and observed multiple officers meticulously searching every corner that I truly understood the seriousness of the situation.

Past the two officers with their guns trained on me, I saw a glimpse of Xavi. He was cuffed and stood facing the wall of an adjacent unit.

"Xavi!" I called out. "He's got nothing to do with this. He doesn't—"

"Quiet! Hands behind your back." I did as instructed. "Turn around—"

"Just listen for a sec—"

"I said turn around! I won't repeat myself again." I did what he said. I felt my arms yank backward as he cuffed me, not wasting time trying to be gentle about it.

Panic shot through me as the metal bit into my skin. My mind flashed back without warning, straight to a memory I'd buried in Santa Clarita—a memory I worked hard to bury for good. I squeezed my eyes shut and clenched my fists, willing myself to stay present. *You're here. You're Oliver Mondell, your home is Los Angeles, California. You're not there. You're not him.* But the officer was pushing me toward a nearby wall, pressing me against it and I couldn't suppress the instinct to fight back. I pushed back against him. I fought against my restraints.

"Get off me!" I yelled. I was hyperventilating. "Get off!" I tried to pronounce the words clearly but my voice was unrecognizable. My pitch high, sounded like a shriek.

"Oli, brother, calm down. Yo, look at me...just do what they say!" Xavi urged. His eyes were round with panic. I focused on him. I didn't break eye contact with him.

"Listen to your friend. Stop fighting or I'll taze you," the officer warned. I stopped resisting and stood very still, muscles clenched but no longer pushing back against him. I let the officer frisk me without protest. I nodded to Xavi, grateful he was here. He nodded in response. The cuffs were tight but I could barely feel the pain through all the adrenaline coursing through me.

"I have a court order to search your property and seize your personal devices," the officer declared as he flattened out a document against the wall near my head. I squinted to skim through it quickly but the words swam on the page. "I'm going to take your phone—where is it?" he questioned.

"Front right pocket." I shifted my hip to give him better access.

"You can provide me with the code to unlock your device and cooperate with us or not...we'll get the information either way."

"I'll give you the code. I'll cooperate with you in every way." The officer took out a pad and wrote out my code. *563129.* "What's all this about?" I asked him.

The officer bagged my phone and the piece of paper with the code written on it in an evidence pouch and answered in a normal tone of voice this time. "Once we're done sweeping the unit, we'll ask you some questions."

Relieved that he was finally treating me more like a person, I caught my breath. "Okay," I said, sneaking a glance back at Xavi, who rested his forehead against the wall in front of him, hands cuffed behind his back, nervously jerking one of his knees. A rotten feeling of guilt gnawed in my gut at the sight of him in cuffs. This was all on me.

"Can he be released? He's got nothing to do with this," I argued.

"He stays until we're done here," the officer said, no room for negotiation in his tone.

I'd have to make this up to Xavi somehow. He must have completely freaked out. I couldn't imagine having this madness descend upon you, alone; not knowing what the hell was happening. He must have been scared out of his mind and pissed as hell at me. But this worry was postponed when a more frightening question slithered to the foreground. *What exactly are the cops here for?*

Ever since Kiran's warning, I'd made sure to triple-check my sources. I only dealt directly with brands now and only bought units from clients who had a track record with me and a history of making good on their word. Those guys always showed me their purchase receipts, and there was nothing more to it than that. As far as I knew, every unit I'd ever bought or sold was completely legit.

CJ was a powerful connect, a major exporter, but also an unpredictable maniac. Infamous for being bizarre and severing ties with his business relations without reason or warning, sending strange, threatening messages when he was dissatisfied with the way a client handled a deal or looked at him in a way he didn't like. Any minuscule thing could set that guy off and I didn't know him as well as I'd have liked.

Between CJ and his unhinged wife, Kiran, I had no clue what

rocky ground I was on. If she had thought it to be amusing to tell him about the time she took off her blouse in front of me after luring me into their penthouse and offering herself up to me out of boredom or God knows what, then I was a dead man walking.

CJ didn't feel like a dangerous man on his own, but it was damn clear to me that he was powerful. He had the intelligence, the money, and the connections to make anything happen. If I was on his shit list, I had an inkling that it wasn't a very cozy place to be. But I would do what Kiran advised the day she warned me I was being watched. I would cooperate with these guys. I'd answer all their questions. I'd give them everything they needed and I'd pray it was enough.

My heart hammered against my chest as I watched the men haul out unit upon unit of product. Xavi had everything organized and ready to ship out for this afternoon. If these units didn't go out, my customers wouldn't receive them on time and my account would immediately go under review. Online retail was no joke. People these days were ruthless when their packages didn't arrive on time.

I growled in frustration at the sound of box cutters ripping through packaging, as I thought of all the work that Xavi had done, gone to shit in a few minutes. Watching this scene unfold silently without saying a word in protest was the true demonstration of my developed control over my anger. I'd come a long way from the boy who arrived in Los Angeles just months ago, searching for a fresh start.

After the team was through cataloging the final boxes, they freed me from the handcuffs, hauled me inside the storage unit, and stood me against the far back wall. My eyes appraised the damage in horror. I'd never get these units out in time, but judging by the look on these guys' faces, that was likely the least of my worries.

"Mr. Mondell, have you ever seen these goods?" the officer

with short dark hair and a five o'clock shadow questioned me as he laid out laminated photos of pallets loaded into a truck and a closer image of a phone, likely the item that was stacked on those pallets.

"Yeah. I've seen thousands of those. I deal with SKUs like that all day...I'm in electronics."

"Did you acquire between thirty and two hundred units of these phones in the last week of September?"

"Possibly."

"Did you then sell those units to an exporter who goes by the name: CJ?" My heart thundered in my chest. *Just tell the truth. But what if this landed me in prison? It won't. You're still under-age. Not for long—your birthday's just around the corner and they could try you as an adult. You have the right to a speedy trial. Maybe you should ask for a lawyer? No, if you lawyer up, they'll come after you, hard.*

"Yes," I answered before I had the chance to change my mind.

"Are you aware that it is a federal crime to export stolen goods out of this country?" he asked.

"Stolen? No, I bought these units. I buy all my units and I have invoices."

"Where did you buy these units?"

"I bought my units from Tee. But he had receipts and everything," I explained.

"T?"

"T-e-e."

"You got an address on Tee?"

"No. I just have his number, it's in my phone. We usually meet at the parking lot of the grocery store nearby. Tee doesn't have a warehouse and I don't like to give out this storage unit to anyone, to prevent a robbery."

"You got the addresses on your most frequent meet sites?"

"Yeah, it's all in my texts with him. It's all there. You can look."

"We will. You said he had receipts? Where are those now? Those with you?"

"I don't have the original receipts, Tee has them…but I have photos of them. They're in my phone."

"Okay. Well…we're going to have to confiscate all these units until after the investigation is concluded and—"

"No! Please, man! These units have nothing to do with those photos. Those units are long gone through CJ. These are from Mo. I got them last week and all the units along the wall there in those boxes are direct from the dealer. Those aren't even phones, they're fitness watches!"

"You got invoices?"

"Yeah, of course. Let me pull them up. They're in my email… can I have my phone?"

"We can't let you access your phone until our investigation is concluded. You'll have to find another way to get us those invoices. Are there any other locations we should know about where you conduct business or keep merchandise?"

"No, I only keep product here, nowhere else."

"Keep in mind, if you are lying about having other storage units or omitting information about the other places you may be keeping product, you are interfering with an active investigation and we will prosecute you to the full extent of the law. These units…"—He pointed out the laminated photos again— "…were stolen from a freight truck in an armed robbery. Now, based on school records, you were in class at the time of the robbery, but…as I said, there is an ongoing investigation. So, we may come back with questions. Don't leave town."

My heart hammered in my chest, mind scrambling back to September, grateful that my ass had been behind a desk at school on that day. "I don't know anything about that. Tee always has receipts. Mo always has receipts. I don't buy hot units. I'll cooperate with you guys in any way you need."

"What is your relationship with Mina Arkova?"

The question hit me like a punch to the gut.

"What?" I must have misheard him.

"Have you ever, at any point in the past, accepted investment funds from Mina Arkova or anyone related to her?"

"No...what does Mina have anything to do with this?" I asked defensively. "How do you even know about her?"

"Have you ever conducted business on her behalf or on behalf of instructions she or any of her associates provided you?"

"Business on her behalf? Listen, I don't know where you're getting this information but it's completely off base. Mina's my...she—she's got absolutely nothing to do with my business at all. She's never even stepped foot in this storage unit. Why would you think that she'd be involved in any of this?"

"Because of who her father is, certain aspects have been brought into consideration," the officer explained vaguely, clearly assuming I already knew what he was talking about while leaving me completely in the dark.

"Who her father is? Who is he?" I asked. The officer's brows lifted as though realization kicked in and he shifted gears.

"So, you've never received packages from foreign countries?"

"You're not going to answer my question?" He looked at me with a blank, unwavering expression. "Received packages from foreign countries? Ever? I mean I've ordered a few things online..." I answered, thinking back. "Can you tell me what you meant about Mina's father?"

"Not retail purchases. I'm asking if you've received inventory from abroad in the past year."

"No. I don't import. I ship to customers domestically and only sell units that leave the country to an exporter. I don't export them myself. Is this about the attack on Mina and her mother? That's what you should be looking into...her attack. I've got nothing to do with this robbery and neither does Mina nor her father nor her mother nor anyone else I know—" I fumed.

"Her attack?" he asked and I couldn't tell if he meant it or pretended not to know.

"She and her mother were attacked in their home yesterday," I snapped.

"*Hmm.* I see. Well, while it's, of course, unfortunate what happened to Ms. Arkova, I deal with federal criminal investigations regarding theft and fraud. A home invasion is not my jurisdiction."

"Not your jurisdiction...right. That's convenient. Can you just ask around? A report's been made. Can you give us some advice about what Mina should do next?"

"No, I'm sorry. I don't believe I can. Like I said, it's not my jurisdiction," he declared, his expression unchanged.

"Fine. Can you please just, at least, let me show you the invoices for these units and let me keep them? If I don't ship these out to customers today, my marketplace accounts could be suspended. All of my money is tied up in these units and I need to pay rent this week," I pleaded, temporarily putting off my line of questioning about Mina or her father. The officer shook his head, no. I pulled at my hair, gritting my teeth in frustration. *Think, Oliver.*

"Xavi! Let me borrow your phone real quick to log into my email—"

"His phone's been taken in for evidence as well," the officer clarified.

"When will we be getting our phones back?" I asked.

"I can't say for sure, but it shouldn't be more than a couple of weeks."

"A couple of weeks? Are you serious?" I exclaimed.

"I'm afraid so—"

"What about all my units...where should I bring the invoices to get these back?"

"You can email the invoices to me at this email here." He handed me a white card with his name, Dalton P. Howard, a number and an email. "Once they're processed and cleared by our audit team, the units will be brought back here if everything appears to be in order."

"Right..." I muttered. *Wait, didn't I have a laptop here?* "Xavi, where's the laptop?"

"Yo, I think they took that shit, man, I'm sorry...I sorta blanked as soon as GI Joe over there busted through the door like he found Pablo Escobar's secret stash," he called back.

"*I'm* sorry, man. Trust me, I feel like shit that you had to go through that."

"What the hell happened, dog? I thought you said all this was kosher. What's all this shit about?" Xavi's voice drifted to me from just outside the unit.

He moved into my line of sight as a police officer who was aiding in the investigation uncuffed him. Xavi made his way toward me through the storage unit, rubbing his wrists and appraising all the work he'd done, now gone to shit.

"Daaaamn." He covered his mouth with his fist as officers continued moving around us to collect the boxes and bring them outside. "They're taking all your shit? Yo, what the hell, Oli? What went down?"

"Nothing. I mean, I have no idea. I bought them from my guy, Tee. The officer said there was a robbery. I told him that both of my sources always showed me receipts. I can't do much more at this point. They'll probably go talk to them."

"Listen, Xavi, man...I'm sorry this happened. I'm sorry you were alone and that I wasn't here—"

"Yo, Oli, I almost pissed myself, for real dog, I'm not gonna lie." He cackled loudly. I cracked a weak smile but I was torn inside. I wanted to ditch this place and go looking for Mina but I knew I couldn't leave the storage unit unsupervised while these guys were hauling away my entire livelihood. The feds might not be too keen on letting me out of here just yet anyway. "Yo, Oli, can I bounce now or..?" Xavi's question broke my trance.

"Of course, Xavi—"

"Wouldn't leave you like this, it's just, I got a shift at the dojo—"

"Trust me, I get it. I'm so grateful for your help. I'm sorry this happened. Nothing like this has ever happened before. And it won't happen again. I swear. It's why I'm trying to get off the streets and strictly into online retail. Here..."—I pulled out my wallet—"...let me pay you for yesterday and I'll give you extra for the trouble...but I hope you can come back later because I'm really gonna need your help with damage control emails."

I counted three hundred bucks and held it out to him. He hesitated a moment and glanced at the surrounding officers who were still going about the business of packing away, labeling, and hauling out inventory. Xavi took the money and shuffled through the cash, his eyes widening.

"Yeah, Oli. Yeah, I'll be back to help you, my man. I'll hit you up later. Oh, shit...wait, no, I won't...my phone, man. These guys have my phone."

"Yeah, I'll buy us some phones for the meantime." I was already making a mental to-do list that seemed impossible to complete. Find Mina, email invoices, find Mina, pray they bring back the units, find Mina, buy units at retail to ship to customers even if it means taking a major hit to the bank account, find Mina, keep my online retail account healthy at all costs, protect Mina, get Xavi to work with me full-time.

"Oliver?" Xavi brought me out of my head.

"Xavi, listen, man...I gotta keep the ball rolling. All I need is the invoices from distro for the watches, the drones, and the vacuums. I doubt they're ever gonna give back those phones, so I'll take a hit on those." I was pulling at my hair, racking my brain for a way out of this. "If you could somehow print those invoices, it'll say Gavin in the subject. Gavin's our distribution rep. Maybe I could stall them here in time for you to get back—"

"Eh—I got an idea...there's like an internet cafe on Hollywood Blvd, like two blocks down from here. You know the one on the corner? Why don't I run over there real quick?" he suggested, casual as a cucumber like it wasn't the most genius idea there ever was.

"Xavi! You're a frickin' genius. But what about the dojo?"

"It'll be all right. I'll only be ten minutes tops."

"You gorgeous, gorgeous man. You champ. Go! Thank you, thank you, thank you," he laughed as I shoved him toward the unit door.

"Mr. Howard!" I called after the lead officer. He was logging units, filling out a form on his black box clipboard. He hardly looked up as I approached.

"Mr. Mondell?"

"Please, Mr. Howard, what can you tell me about Mina's father? Do you know who those men are? The ones who are after her? Why did you think she was involved in my business?"

"I'm not able to disclose information about an ongoing investigation. And it's not that I personally think anything in particular, I merely ask based on the line of questioning that is agreed upon by the case supervisors. These questions are written down, here, on this form for me to ask. Not more to it than that, I'm afraid." He shrugged nonchalantly and returned his gaze to his clipboard before pausing and looking back up at me.

"But if you want some advice?" he offered and I stilled. I gave him a small nod in confirmation.

"Listen, kid, my advice to you is this: Stay far away from Mina Arkova and her father. While you're at it, stop buying electronics off the streets. Nothing good'll come of it. I've seen nice kids like you who are just trying to make a quick buck dragged into bad situation after bad situation. Beat up, robbed, and worse.

"Times are changing, people are getting desperate. It's not worth it. If you were my son, that's what I'd tell you," he noted with a shrug. He didn't sound too invested in his words, just laid it out like he was giving me directions to the nearest gas station.

About ten minutes later, as promised, Xavi was sprinting back toward the storage unit, printed invoices in hand. His eyes were searching for Dalton Howard, for the cars but they were all gone.

"Thanks anyway, man. Good try. The guy was a tool, in the end. He refused to wait a few more minutes." My mind floundered with worry. How was I going to pay rent, my storage fees, my van's monthly payment, the gas, my insurance?

I had just received my most recent disbursement from winning my foster care abuse case but had donated it to the Youth at Risk Foundation. The next installment from the state wouldn't be doled out until next quarter.

I didn't want to use any of that money. That money was going to help other kids escape, every damn penny of it. I had been so proud that I finally didn't need that blood money, didn't need it until now.

CHAPTER 10

MINA

The sound of the doorbell sent a jolt of panic through me, and I would've scalded myself with my brew of Ruth's Calming Meditation Tea out of sheer terror had it not been for the subsequent yell of a voice that steadied my hand. It was a voice I would have recognized in the middle of a raging mosh pit.

I cracked my front door open to find Nyah on my porch, eyes bugging out at me like I was a Martian on sabbatical.

"Wow, you're actually here...really, Mina? You think this is a good idea?" She gestured at my house then at me. My heart hammered from the implication that she knew more information about what was happening to me than what I'd told her myself, and that realization terrified me. *What did Oliver tell her?*

"Nyah, what are you doing here?" I asked stupidly.

"Nope. We're past all that." She bulldozed by me and I wobbled to keep the tea from spilling.

"Nyah—"

"I tried to come with my cousin, because Oli said it was too dangerous to go alone and that these low lives could come back any minute but my cousin wasn't picking up and Oli wasn't picking up, so I guess, here I am. Happy birthday, by the way…" —She pulled out a miniature gift bag from her pocket and handed it to me without missing a beat, the sound of a chain slinking around inside—"…and I was sure as hell not just gonna wait around while you figured this out on your own because, no offense, you don't make good choices when it comes to these situations."

"Oh, really? What's a good choice in this kind of situation, Nyah? Enlighten me…and thank you for the gift."

"Open it!"—She beamed, then frowned—"Well, let me tell you, first off, being back here in this house…alone…ain't it." I didn't fight her on that point because there was no way I could explain what I was really doing back here and without that context, she was absolutely right.

She rolled her eyes and grabbed the gift back from my grasp. She let the silver chain fall into her open palm: a necklace. There was a charm on it, a silver dancer mid-leap.

"Wow, Ny—" I gasped, pausing to get a grip on myself as another wave of emotion threatened to roll over me. It was painful, gut-wrenchingly painful, remembering that it was my birthday—that instead of celebrating together, Mama was unconscious, that I couldn't see her for more than half an hour, that before Nyah got here, I was sitting in my house, alone, coming to terms with having to not fight my own abduction.

The necklace was perfect—it gleamed as it caught and reflected light. I cleared my throat, avoided her eyes, and in a voice falsely bright I told her, "Thank you, it's beautiful, Nybear."

She nodded and unclasped it, encircling my head with her arms to try to secure it around my neck. I turned my back to her to make it easier.

"Why'd you run from Oli?"—Then, in a smaller voice she

asked the real question she wanted an answer to—"Why didn't you call me?" There was so much hurt in her voice, it made me feel ashamed.

"Nyah, it's dangerous," was all I could manage. I couldn't function an hour ago, so even this pathetic, oversimplified explanation was a vast improvement on the staggering mess I had become after the hospital this morning.

I'd been so empty and disoriented after seeing Mama in her broken state, somehow even more fragile and thin than she'd looked just the day before, that facing this house had proven almost too much for me to bear.

"There," Nyah pronounced, having fastened the clasp of the necklace. "Mina...were they the same men who left that mark on your face?" I turned back around to look at her, feigning confusion. She challenged me with a look that said, *Don't you dare try to evade me now.* "I know you said you didn't want to talk about how you got that scar but—"

"Nyah, you don't need any part in this damned mess, I swear to you. Just trust me." She shook her head in disbelief. "I'm begging you. I didn't call you *because* I love you. I didn't call you *because* keeping you the hell away from here is the best thing that I can do for you right now—"

"Please, Mina, let's get the hell out of here, come stay with me!"

"Are you insane? I'd rather die—I'd rather die than bring a death sentence into your house, to your family. Please, Nyah..." I willed steadiness into my voice and slowed my breath. "You need to go. I don't want to fight anymore. Not you, and not Oliver. I'm tired." My voice broke. Nyah stepped closer and pulled me up toward her as a sob broke through my throat at her touch. Her arms wrapped around me, the final crack in the dam. I heaved sobs into her shoulder and she took them in, hugging me tighter, pulling me against her as she walked us over to the couch in the center of the living room.

I stumbled to sit, still wrapped in her arms. Nyah sat beside me and pulled my head to her chest, stroking my hair while chanting rhythmic hushes against my forehead.

"It's going to be okay," Nyah said softly.

"It can never be okay, Nyah. I...I killed someone." Her hand stilled on my head for a beat then slowly continued its motion down then back up to the top of my head. I forced myself to meet her gaze. "I killed one of the men who attacked us here, yesterday," I finally managed.

"You must have been terrified." Nyah's eyes were round with horror.

I shook my head, slumping further down onto her lap. "I wasn't scared for myself. I was scared for my mom. She was all I was thinking about. I don't think I was even making conscious decisions. Something else took over and I just reacted..." I trailed off, recalling the blur of pulling a trigger one moment and then getting knocked to the floor the next.

"You did what you had to do, Mina—that's all that matters. I'm not saying I know what you went through. I don't. I can't even begin to imagine it. But if I handled it like you did, I'd have been proud of myself," she announced. Then, almost impercep- tibly, she asked, "How is she?"

I shrugged, feigning a level of detachment I did not have. "Only time will tell," I said, echoing the infuriating ambiguity all the nurses had been giving me.

I repositioned myself over her lap, draping one arm over her legs and the other under my chin, shifting until my body went slack around her thighs. I gave in to the exhaustion bearing down on me, drifting my heavy lids closed. *I'll lie like this just for a minute. Only one more minute.* It felt good here, warm, safe. Even though I knew it wasn't. A part of me was screaming for us to go. Get the hell away from here. But lying in Nyah's lap like this made me think of Mama. A sob tore through me, abrupt and forceful enough to fold me in two. I collapsed on myself, shoulders curling, stomach clenching in spasms as I heaved sob after sob against Nyah's legs.

When it passed, I was thoroughly spent and the soothing motion of her nails massaging my scalp made moving near impossible. I kept waiting for her to stop, to stand, to get tired but Nyah's hushes became melodic hums and the exhaustion made my head feel like a substantial hunk of granite, too heavy to lift.

I drifted off deeper. Despite how hard I fought against the lure of mental escape, my heavy lids ultimately fell completely shut and I began to dream of that morning, of the moment I realized with chilling certainty that there was someone in the house.

But the powerful hand yanking me upright and pulling me away from Nyah was no dream.

I knew they would come, I'd made up my mind. They would come and I'd go with them, I wouldn't fight it. It's why I was back in this house in the first place. But I didn't think they'd come this soon. I thought I'd be alone. Alone, they had no leverage...less leverage. How did they even get in? Did I leave the door unlocked?

Nyah was still on the couch, now cowering beneath a massive figure towering over her. It was him—the colossus who attacked me in the alley hovered over Nyah. Kiril. The one who had been sent by someone to scare me, to scare my father into doing something for them or paying them for something...I still had no idea what. My father simply told Mama everything had been taken care of and then disappeared again.

Kiril's blade left this scar on my cheek in the alley that day— a scar that was almost completely faded now, a glorified cat scratch, but the wound left deeper ramifications, I realized. Kiril's menacing glare, dark, deep-set eyes, bulging forehead, and ridiculous bowl cut had haunted my dreams almost every night since that day in the alley. My body was going into shock from the sight of him, my limbs uselessly limp.

I needed to do something. I panicked. I tried screaming. I fought with every millimeter of strength inside me to produce a sound, any sound, but my cry was muffled by the man holding me, whose hand still covered my mouth. His hand blocked me from releasing more than a stifled whimper. I clawed at his forearms with my nails.

There was a blur of sudden motion as Nyah momentarily broke free from Kiril, who grabbed her again and shook her violently like a rag doll.

"Stop, please! Leave her alone—you're hurting her! She doesn't know anything, she hasn't seen anything," I cried, ready to grovel...to beg when the bite of cold steel was thrust against my temple. There was a gun to my head. I went completely still for a sobering moment. I'd do whatever it took.

Quietly, through gritted teeth, I remembered my surrender and declared, "I'll go with you. I'm not fighting. Look, I'm going willingly, as long as you let her go—"

Kiril released Nyah, and her body slumped over the armrest of the couch; her head fell back at an awkward angle and my heart seized.

"Nyah!" I called but the man behind jerked me back, keeping my hands bound beneath his with ease. Kiril opened a gray, rectangular, plastic box with one hand and retrieved the contents, allowing the box to fall to the floor. He attached a needle to a cylindrical body containing a white fluid.

"Stop!" A scream tore through my vocal cords as the man behind me released my body to clamp his palm over my mouth.

"If you don't shut up"—he growled against my ear—"we'll kill her."

Kiril examined Nyah's arm before jabbing the syringe into her wrist and injecting her with something. Her eyes blinked open, then the life just seemed to drain out of her, and she slumped over again.

"Nyah?" I called, but she did not answer.

I turned toward the man who held my arms behind my back. "What the hell was that?" I jerked my head toward the empty syringe Kiril had thrown into an open duffle on the couch beside Nyah's body.

"She's not dead. Don't worry. She's just sleeping," the man who was restraining me husked against my ear.

Repulsion roiled in my belly from the smell of him too close to me, a strong tone of peppermint rolling off him toward me. I shoved him backward with one final, violent hip thrust then elbowed him in the gut. To my surprise, he released me and finally stepped away.

As soon as I couldn't feel his hold on me, I turned on him swiftly, ready to keep fighting but my jaw went slack from what I saw. He was a much older man than I had expected just based on the immense strength of his hold. But what did I know about older men and their capacity for strength? Not much.

I ignored my thrumming pulse. "Did you hear what I said? I'll cooperate...no resistance. Just leave my friend alone—"

"Anything else?" the man mocked, his voice gravelly and deep. He was of average size, his demeanor was calm, and his nearly serene expression was thoroughly unnerving, so relaxed it was as though this visit was entirely routine for him.

"Any other demands, princess? Although it doesn't look like you're in any place to dictate conditions to me," he taunted.

I didn't know him but I hated this man with a ferocity that sent a resolute tremor down my limbs and magma through my veins. My glare bored a hole in his forehead—a bullet-sized hole.

I swore to myself, then and there, that I would make him suffer. I would do to him what he did to my mother. I would make him pay for putting holes in her, for putting her in a coma, for the potential damage to her brain. I would end him.

These monsters that kept attacking us had no souls, no compassion, no mercy. There was no use wasting breath on pleas. The only currency these ghouls understood was power, so I was going to have to figure out how to accumulate it for myself. The question was how much power would it take? And how much of myself would I have to lose to get it? Where would I even start? I knew nothing about these people.

"How's Mama?" he asked, feigning genuine concern.

Rage—pure rage—took hold of me and I punched at his head, but he caught my wrist midair and rotated it until I was bending at my knees, crying out in pain. He released me and I landed on the floor.

The man bent down and gripped my chin roughly. He got sickeningly close to my face before his hot, minty, ashy breath invaded my space.

"You just promised cooperation mere seconds ago. Already going back on your word? *Tsk.* Shame. I despise liars."

I had never spat on anyone before in my life. But at that moment, I had an irresistibly potent urge to spit directly in the eye of this vile scum of a man. Once the thought manifested in my mind like the seed of a magic beanstalk, it sprouted beyond my control. I collected and released a thick, foamy glob of saliva into the too-short distance between us that—to his surprise and my gratification—landed square on his brow and immediately gave in to the force of gravity, oozing downward toward his left eye.

In one swift motion, the man released my chin, stood, whipped out a handkerchief, and wiped his face. I flinched as he lifted his leg to step over me on his way to our kitchen without saying a word. It unnerved me—his continued calm, his silence, the lack of a reaction.

Nyah was still slumped over the arm of the couch, out cold. I moved toward her. Before I could reach her, Kiril rounded the couch and grabbed a fistful of my hair, yanking back with a savage ferocity. As I winced, my mouth opened in surprise just as he raised his gun and shoved the long barrel into my mouth. The world froze.

All I could do was breathe slowly through my nose, fearful that any slight, sudden movement would send my brain flying out the back of my head. My eyes grew wider in horror as I realized this was it. I saw Mama in the corner of the room. She crossed toward me and knelt beside me. "Take a break, *lubimaya*," she said, smoothing the lumps in my ponytail and scratching my back in soothing strokes. I had been obsessively working on a summer packet for school that she was trying to get me to put off and have some fun instead. I did and we went for one of my favorite hikes, marveling at a double rainbow that appeared above the horizon after a refreshing drizzle of rain had cleared.

I was backstage at my first recital, upset with myself for forgetting a step in the dance routine. I was hiding in the corner of the changing area when Mama scooped me into her arms. "You were amazing, Minachka! Best artistry I ever have seen"— she cooed, then whispered in my ear—"and only a true professional know how to cover mistake so good that no one in audience even can notice. Not a one single person, except your Mama with her sharp eyes, of course."

I was eight and had wet myself at a sleepover after a bad dream. I snuck away to the back yard early that morning and called Mama on the flip phone she had given me in case of an emergency. It was cold out and the sun had not yet risen. She was there within fifteen minutes. She wrapped me in her cardigan, bringing me into the warmth of her embrace and wiping away the searing tears of humiliation streaming down my cheeks. "I'm here"—she whispered—"Mama's here."

Window shopping in December, nursing hot chocolates and

bundled under layers of clothes, convinced Southern California was having an East Coast winter. Painting rainbow hearts on our hard boiled eggs for Easter. Ugly crying after *The Notebook* then watching *Titanic* to soften the blow. Running with her into the freezing Pacific, side by side, shrieking with glee. Mama blowing my nose for me after I dislocated my finger and caught a cold at Disneyland. Matching green turtlenecks on St. Patrick's Day. Getting in a pinching war anyway. Iced coffees with soy milk. Sunday mornings. Homemade Halloween costumes. Her laugh. I shut my eyes to clear them of tears and kept them shut as another memory hit me, not as vivid as the others. More a feeling than a memory—a dreamlike, shapeless form of a feeling, nestled at my very core. Everything was dark. I was being held. I felt a rhythmic thumping against my body. The susurration of familiar melody filled the air. I was safe, surrounded by the smell of home. She was home. She was peace.

"*Hvatit*, Kiril! Enough." The man's voice cut through my reverie but it was too late. Nausea rolled up as Kiril's slight shift in the direction of the voice nudged the gun a smidge deeper into my mouth before he pulled it out, triggering my gag reflex. I covered my mouth with my hands but couldn't hold back the vomit. I jumped to my feet and pushed past the man in the doorway, heading to the kitchen sink.

"*Fu! Blyat.*" Kiril spat out, repulsion in his tone.

"Kiril, we don't have the time. Now she has to go wash upstairs. You must practice control over your impulses. You disappoint me," the man chided, clearly Kiril's superior. The man lowered his voice.

"Make sure you don't leave permanent scars on her this time," he hissed.

I kept my eyes on the men as I washed my hands and mouth with soap, heart still racing with fear. The man in the doorway turned from Kiril and walked back into the kitchen toward me.

I had nowhere left to move. I was trapped between him and the kitchen sink, staring at the floor, panting like a dog. He took another step toward me, reaching his hand out to tilt my chin up but not in the violent way Kiril had. He retrieved his phone and turned it toward me, holding it up in front of my face.

"*Posmotri.*" He wanted to show me something. I was paralyzed with horror when I saw her picture on his phone. My stomach twisted. The creepy paparazzi shot of my angelic little cousin on that scumbag's phone had sent a jolt through the fragments of my broken heart, slapping me back to the reality that there was a bigger picture at play here—bigger than my father and bigger than me. There was still so much more to lose.

"We have a far reach, *lapachka*. Even this sweet *kiska* is one phone call away from gone—your second cousin, yes? So precious. Your Mama's cousin Zoya is a looker for sure, makes beautiful babies—little Anya especially. You know what's interesting about a five-year-old...you can teach them almost anything at that age. They are so perfectly malleable, their brains absorb information like a sponge—so useful for training obedience.

"You should know, we have location access on them at all times. I don't have to say more. Do I? *Ty ponimayesh?*" I nodded without thought, that yes, I did understand his demented threat. He had pronounced the threat as casually as a waiter recites daily specials. I'd already known this, of course, that they'd use them, my family, use my little cousin to get to me. But still, hearing it out loud made the threat real in a way that sent sharp pressure into my lungs as I tried to breathe evenly.

"What do you want from me?"

"I want nothing from you. I don't like to do this. All of this..."—He motioned at Anya's photo—"...it's a nasty necessity. But...here we are. I need you to help me remind Papachka of some things he forgot. And this..."—He gestured back to Anya's photo—"...this is to keep you motivated."

The man's eyes were pools of tar, like a pair of precise ink blots made under intense pressure. He rubbed his tattooed knuckles in irritation. I could only make out the crosses on each finger—one shorter cross and a longer one with two horizontal lines passing through—as he smoothed back his groomed, salt and pepper hair. On his pinky finger was a half-shaded circle inside a square. The tattoos were old, faded and seemed out of place on the sharply dressed man somewhere in his late fifties.

Kiril crossed the kitchen and spoke quietly in the man's ear. "Gospodin Mikhailov, I should bring her in car?" *Mikhailov*. I repeated the surname in my mind until it was etched into my brain like a brand—a promise.

"No need," Mikhailov answered, coolly. "She'll do it herself. She'll go upstairs, clean herself, change, take her passport and a coat, and walk herself into the car. Now." His eyes bored into mine with a frightening intensity. Mikhailov's words were instructions, commands.

I trained my sights on the doorway to the stairs. Their lives were tied to mine now: Mama's, Nyah's, Anya's. If I made one wrong move, they'd get hurt. One look back at Nyah, and my decision was final. There wasn't any room for argument or hesitation. I had no doubt of that, of the fact that my life was no longer my own. I was owned by these people. I came back to this house to do this. I told myself I was ready for this, but the fear didn't pass; it intensified with each subsequent moment.

Love was powering every brain synapse that enabled my feet to move despite the terror I felt. I made my way past Mikhailov without so much as another glance in his direction.

I looked ahead, forged on, forcing myself to keep moving, through the doorway, up the blood-stained stairs, both hands gripping the rail along the wall.

Just keep going, one foot, now the other. You're climbing the same stairs you've climbed a million times. Nothing's different. It's almost over, I lied to myself.

This had only been the beginning of my trials—I understood that fact in the depths of my psyche.

In the bathroom, I stripped, showered, and dressed as a voice shouted through the door.

"Out," it barked. I jumped back so hard that I hit my elbow against the wall tile.

"Out," he repeated, a threat this time. I pulled my shoes on and flung the bathroom door open, hoping it would crash into him. He caught it with ease, raking his eyes over me as I passed him without acknowledgment. I was nervous to keep my back to him—unsure what he was capable of without the supervision of Mikhailov. I crossed the room to look for a coat.

"Kiril?" Mikhailov's voice carried from downstairs.

"Move!" Kiril shouted, crossing the room to grab me like a circus tamer attempting to wrangle a disobedient animal.

"Ow! Please, stop...wait! M-my coat—" I pleaded, resisting him as he grabbed hold of my arm.

"I say move!" His voice boomed so close to my ear, the reverberation felt like it nearly shattered my eardrum. I flinched and struggled to keep up with him.

Kiril dragged me out of my bedroom toward the top of the stairs. Mikhailov peered up at us from the foot of the staircase.

"Relax, Kiril. *Ana paslushnaya devochka*," he mused as though he was still undecided about it. So, he thought I was an obedient girl? Good—let him keep thinking it. Kiril loosened his grip on my arm and I took the opportunity to yank it away from him entirely.

"This whole place looks like it has already been turned upside-down," Kiril told Mikhailov in Russian and pinned me with an accusing glare.

"I've noticed a bit of that down here, as well," Mikhailov mused. He met my eye. "Has someone else been here after you killed Edgar?" I winced at the sound of the man's name. I didn't want it in my head.

"Just the cops," I said to them.

Mikhailov took a moment to mull that over before looking back up at me. "Take a coat and your documents, Miss Arkova. Quickly, please." With that, his gaze turned back down to his phone.

I ran into Mama's room, as Kiril loomed behind me, and I pulled on Mama's black wool coat with the burgundy buttons. Then I knelt by the safe in her closet where we kept our passports. I hesitated a moment, not wanting to open the safe in front of Kiril.

"*Bistreya*," he hissed. *How am I supposed to open a safe faster?*

I punched in the four-digit code, pulled the door open, and grabbed my passport. But before I could close the safe, Kiril shoved his ham hock of a hand into it. He shoved me aside like a useless piece of furniture and knelt beside me.

"Please—" I whispered, hating the desperation in my voice. I didn't want him to touch anything in there, not the money she saved up after all her years of hard work, not our family heirlooms and not the memories, none of it. "Let's go. He said to hurry," I said more firmly.

Kiril's mouth spread into a disturbing grin and he pulled out a ring, my mother's wedding ring. He got to his feet, examining it, then dropped it into his pocket.

"Put it back," I growled.

"Shut up," he commanded. "Downstairs, now. Let's go." He yanked me to my feet and shoved me forward.

You'll get it back, I promised myself and started for the stairs before he could grab me again. Another promise piled on top of the rest.

Entirely focused on survival, I moved as fast as I could. I followed Mikhailov outside as a dark SUV pulled up to the curb. My eyes scanned the neighborhood for a familiar face, any face, but there was no one. And there was no point.

"You keep moving. Keep your eyes down," Mikhailov

warned, as though he could hear my instincts screaming at me to run.

"Your mother could really use a break. Don't you think? Do what I say and maybe she gets one? Who knows...or we can send Kiril to get better acquainted with her? Up to you." Mikhailov squeezed my arm lightly and nodded toward the car, patting my back like he was glad I understood.

Courage helped me get into that SUV. Courage kept me there, motionless and silent in the back seat. Courage was all I had left—that and Mama's, Nyah's and Anya's lives, which were very much in my hands.

After being threatened at knifepoint in an alley on my way home from school, I used to stay up at night, crying, thinking: *What if those men come and kill us in our sleep?*

How are you supposed to live life with grace if you can sense the inevitable doom that awaits you—a haunting cloud shadowing a narrow path you are bound to take?

No, that won't happen, I convinced myself. *Father handled it. He wouldn't let something terrible happen to us. They just wanted to scare him, manipulate him into doing something they needed and it worked. It's over,* I would tell myself. But I was wrong. I did this. It was my fault. We never should have come back here.

I shut my eyes. In the darkness behind my eyelids was my mother's pale, motionless body cradled in my arms, surrounded by a pool of crimson. Her lips, blue—her face, white as a sheet, dark shadows looming beneath her soaked lashes.

Mama, the whisper escaped me like a prayer. *She's not dead. You saved her. You'll keep saving her. Whatever it takes. That's what you'll live for now. That's how you make it right.*

I looked out the window as the SUV exited the freeway, then turned right into a parking lot. There was a small sign indicating that a private airport was beyond the metal gates. *No. Oh, God, no.* I realized we would be flying somewhere—the passport, the coat, it made sense, but seeing an airport had the reality of everything coming crashing down over me.

The driver showed some documents to the security guard who stood in the doorway of a booth in front of the metal gate. After about a minute, he allowed us through.

My knees shook as we drove onward toward the tarmac, past rows of private jets until we pulled up to one of the largest jets in the lineup. The engine was on, and the staff was already waiting by the foot of the airstairs.

Mikhailov took hold of my arm and guided me out of the car, his minty breath too close to my ear as he whispered, "Behave. People are watching. If you disappoint me..." He gave me a knowing look that said *you know what will happen.*

"I know," I uttered.

"But that's not where we'll stop. We still have many to go: Babushka, Dedushka...big family in Sochi." My heart seized up when he said the word "Sochi."

"You're very lucky. Many options to keep you disciplined. Now, get on that plane and don't say one negative word, or they all disappear from this world...one by one. We'll save you for last. Is it clear?"

I nodded, swallowing back my disgust.

"If anyone asks you why you are traveling, tell them it's for pleasure."

CHAPTER 11

OLIVER

I was pacing back and forth from one corner of Mina's room to the other. Nyah was slumped on the floor against the side of Mina's bed, cocooned under a duvet as she rocked back and forth trying to soothe herself.

Everything in Mina's house had been turned inside-out. It was a disturbing sight. I had rushed here as soon as I could. After I had dropped the most urgent packages at the post office, I went to see if Nyah had found Mina at her house. If she wasn't there, I'd planned on heading to the store to buy Xavi and myself those replacement phones.

I expected to either find Mina's place empty or both of them there. I didn't expect to find a broken door handle and Nyah, semi-unconscious on the couch, disoriented, clutching her head, moaning in pain and crying to someone on the phone.

"We have to talk to the police, Nyah. I'm sorry, but—"

"They wrote a death threat on my damn arm, Oliver! They couldn't be any clearer—they spelled that shit out what they'd do if I talk." Nyah threw the duvet off her shoulders, jumped to her feet, and closed the distance between us as she rolled up her sleeve to expose the pen markings on the inside of her forearm. *MOUTH SHUT OR SUFFER.*

It was clear they meant business, but I had never been in any doubt as to that. The police were our best shot at finding her before it was too late.

"Nyah, you can't just pretend like it never happened. We need their help. They have access to information we can't reach."

"And if they don't? What then, Oli? These are the same people who shot one woman and abducted another right out of her own house!"

"I know, it's scary. I tried to get Mina to report the attack in the alley, but she was afraid it would escalate things, that they'd come after her family in Russia as punishment if she did that. But look, she did nothing and they still tried to kill her mother and kidnap her. Secrecy is helping no one but them. That's why they wrote that on your arm, to scare you into silence…it's a bluff—"

"I'm not gambling with my life on your hunch."

"We can't just—we can't do nothing."

"I know, Oliver. I know. You're right…I just…look…"—She raised her hands to me; they were trembling—"…you're right. But, I'm terrified. I don't want them to hurt me or my family."

"They won't. Listen to me. I'm gonna record a video of you on your phone, okay? Like a statement. You tell me what happened. You show your arm and explain why you're scared to come in and give a formal statement. I check on Lily, make sure they still have security by her door. You don't even have to come. I'll do it. How about that? Would that be okay?" I asked her, trying to muffle the desperation in my voice.

Nyah remained still for a while and just blinked at me, until finally, she said, "I need to call my mom. She'll know what to do."

A new nurse was manning the Critical Care desk when I got back to the hospital. I decided against pretending Lily was my mom this time in case they looked into it and didn't take me seriously if they found me untrustworthy.

"Hi, I'm worried about the safety of a patient, Lily Arkova. Her daughter is missing and—"

"Sir, Ms.—"

"I'm heading to the police station right now to file a missing persons report. Ms. Arkova is in a lot of danger. If anyone suspicious comes up here, you need to call the police immediat—"

"Sir. Ms. Arkova is no longer here. She was moved earlier today."

"What the hell are you talking about? Moved where?"

"I'm not authorized to disclose that. What is your relation to Ms. Arkova?"

"I'm—I'm a friend."

"In any case, I can't share any information except with her immediate family." I didn't know what my face must have done to prompt him to add, "All I can say is she's regained conscious-ness and is in stable condition," he assured.

"She—she's awake? Oh, shit—thank God! Is she talking?"

"I can't say more, I'm sorry." Then he added in a hushed voice, "I've never really seen them be so careful about anyone. We've had some pretty big celebs come through here, but this case...it's very intense. Lots of protocol from what the others are saying."

"Can you just tell me if she's still here in the hospital or if they've transferred her somewhere else completely?"

"I'm sorry." He pursed his lips tightly, probably sorry he'd said anything at all.

"Just tell me, is she safe?"

"Yes, of course. She's in good hands."

Clearly, I'd gotten everything I was going to get out of him. But I felt like Lily had to still be around here somewhere. I doubted they'd move her until her doctor signed off on it or until they finished tests to make sure she really was in stable condition. Maybe they knew about Mina? Maybe they knew Lily was in danger so they rushed it? But then, why didn't anyone come by the house yet?

"Sir?" I barely registered the nurse anymore, swimming through the sludge of my thoughts.

They might have been in a rush to move Lily out of here and had her testing prioritized, pushed through.

"Sir!" The nurse raised his voice to try to get my attention. He waved a hand in front of me as courteously as he could manage. At last, I returned my gaze to him. "I'm going to have to ask you to go back down to the waiting room. They've asked us to keep this area clear. I'm sorry."

I pulled Mina's cracked phone from my pocket, now secured in a Ziplock baggie. Nyah found it on the floor by the couch.

Nyah did what she said she would, allowing me to record her talking about what happened.

"I need to talk to your supervisor, now."

He looked surprised, then resigned.

"My supervisor is very busy at the moment. We've had several unexpected—"

"Tell your supervisor it's an emergency," I insisted.

"Umm...I-okay." He got on the phone, dialed a number, and said, "Hi... can you ask Shockley to come to CC-reception. It's about the patient who was moved, Arkova—no, I know. Just tell her there's someone here who needs to speak to her about it."— He smiled at me and nodded—"Great, thanks."

Shortly after, a ding resonated throughout the level, signifying the arrival of the elevator on this floor. A thin, preppy woman with a short gray hairdo rounded the corner. She wore thick black-rimmed glasses and smiled mechanically as she approached.

"Hi, how can I help you?" she asked generically, a hint of unease hid beneath the question.

"Who authorized Ms. Arkova's transfer?"

"And what's your relation to Ms. Arkova?"

"I'm a friend."

"I'm sorry. I'm afraid that's not enough. I can't—"

"Listen to me: Her daughter was abducted by very dangerous people just hours ago. We don't have time. Ms. Arkova's in danger. I'm going to the police about it now, but if they're here with her, let me speak to them. I have evidence they need to see."

She was staring at me, with her mouth agape, still deliberating whether to say more to me, so I went on, "Tell me it was cops who transferred her. Tell me they had documents and everything checked out. Tell me you took a careful look at those documents before releasing your patient to them."

Her brow furrowed and she tugged on the hem of her white scrubs. "Sir. I don't know what you are implying. Unfortunately, I'm unable to speak with you about Ms. Arkova because you are not a family member. I'm sorry, but unless you're a—"

"Tell me she's safe!" I thundered before I could stop myself.

The woman took several steps away from me and I couldn't blame her. I must have sounded deranged to her, with my tales of conspiracies and abduction. "Lower your voice, sir."

"I'm sorry. I'm sorry. Just forget it. This is a waste of time. I gotta go."

***

My hands shook on the handles of my bike throughout the ride over to the police station. I chastised myself for raising my voice in the hospital, and swore to myself I wouldn't lose composure in front of the cops. The police station was two miles away—a brick building with a bike rack out front. There was a small line to speak with a police officer who sat at a desk behind the glass.

I went around the line and spoke directly to the officer after apologizing to everyone in line and to the person speaking to him.

"I'm sorry, this is an emergency." I addressed the officer directly, "Officer, my friend, Mina Arkova, was just abducted from her house less than an hour ago by some Russian thugs who have been threatening her for the past few months."

"Wait in line, kid."

"Are you—we don't have time to spare—we have to move!"

He stared at me blankly.

"Hold on," he said to the person he was speaking with before me. "I'll get someone."

"Thank you," I said to him. "Sorry," I told the woman in line, who nodded and stared down at her phone, indifferent.

The officer returned. "Wait over there. Someone will come out and bring you in to take your statement."

"Thank you." I followed his instructions, yet the time passed, the line dissipated, and I was left waiting with no one coming to fetch me. The station was now practically empty. Had this guy played me? Or did he assume I was just another kid tripping my face off on drugs? At last, the officer waved me over.

I approached his booth but refused to lose my cool. "My friend—her name is Mina Arkova, she's been taken. She was first attacked in her home a few days ago. There should be a report on file because her mom was shot and taken to the hospital. They took Mina's statement there. The people responsible for that came again today and—"

"Hold on...slow down, kid. What's your friend's name? Meera?" The officer double-clicked his mouse a few times and began typing, slowly, with two fingers.

"Mina. M-I—"

"Can you spell that?"

"Yeah, M-I-N-A."

"Is that the last name?" He proceeded to ask me a series of questions as though we'd just gotten into a car accident and he was the insurance company. The only time I got any kind of real reaction out of him was when I told him that I had taken evidence from Mina's house.

"You don't do that, kid. You tainted the evidence. If the chain of custody is broken, evidence may be suppressed or deemed inadmissible in court. You may have jeopardized any chance of tracking these thugs down."

"I get that but I figured those guys could've come back and cleaned the place out. Here's the code for it. Oh, and I need to show you or I dunno who, the detective on the case a uh, a statement from a witness—"

"What witness?" His head flinched back slightly and he looked interested for the first time.

"Mina's friend, Nyah Wright."

"She was there for the alleged abduction?"

"Yes," I replied, ignoring the word "alleged."

"Where is this Nyah Wright now? Why isn't she here?"

"Because of this." I pulled out Nyah's phone from my pocket. It unlocked without a code. I pulled up the picture of Nyah's inner arm, the words MOUTH SHUT OR SUFFER glaringly legible in the photo. "I have a statement from her. A video," I pronounced in a hushed voice.

"Okay, kid, I'm gonna buzz you in. Come on in through that door and down the hallway into that open room there and uh, the uh officer assigned to this case will be in to take your evidence and such shortly." I nodded and turned for the door. "And kid?"—I turned back to him. The officer was struggling to maintain eye contact with me. He spoke in a quiet voice— "Sorry about your friend. You did the right thing coming here."

CHAPTER 12

MINA

There was a stabbing pain in my stomach as I trudged across the tarmac toward the jet. Flashes of Oliver's infectious, dimpled smile appeared so clearly in my mind. It was a smile he rarely revealed, but did the night he said he loved me and cracked the biggest smile I'd ever seen on him as we rode the Ferris wheel above a cluster of gleaming city lights.

But it was the photo of sweet little smiling Anya that Mikhailov showed me on his phone that drove my motivation—placing one foot in front of the other as I drew closer to the jet, contradicting my every instinct to run in the opposite direction.

Anya was an innocent little girl who didn't deserve to be tangled in my father's mess. I would make sure she was left the hell alone. I didn't care what had to happen to me in order to ensure that. I'd do whatever it took and I'd do it a hundred times over.

So, I looked ahead of me, past the horizon, past the pain in my right arm provided by the gorilla grip of the beast escorting me to God knew where. The part of me that had accepted my fate and that had understood what was to come was absolutely numb; the other part of me—the delusional bit, still clinging to desperate hopes and dreams of an old life with Oliver in it—was being smothered by its better half.

The first thing I noticed after climbing the airstairs and boarding the plane was that there were already other passengers there. There were about five or six of them spread out on both sides of the plane, and only one sat on the couch in the middle. She was the youngest and sat beside an older man in a suit who was scowling at his phone. She stared ahead blankly.

No one spared more than a brief glance in my direction as I made my way down the aisle. The presence of the others made me feel marginally more at ease but somehow unnerved me at the same time because of all the questions that immediately arose.

Two of the girls looked close to my age. One seemed tired and sick, with dark circles rimming her eyes. And the girl on the couch looked a lot younger than the rest of us, too young. Seeing that girl with her youthful features, her rosy cheeks, the fresh edge of fear in her wired expression, how thin she was—made my stomach turn.

They were dressed strangely: spaghetti straps and miniskirts, low-cut crop tops, and raggedy second-hand fur coats—an unfittingly cheap look for such innocent faces.

Were they here against their will like I was? Did they have families looking for them? They looked desperate and exhausted. *It's not looking too peachy for you either, sweetheart,* I told myself.

There were three more men wearing nice suits, similar in look and age to Mikhailov sitting near the back of the jet. Mikhailov pushed me to sit down in an empty seat in the front row.

"*Luchshe molchat,*" he suggested that it would be best for me to stay silent before he turned away and joined the others in the back.

After a few minutes, the flight attendant closed the door, and the jet taxied to the runway and took off.

My heart hammered as I looked out the window and watched my home, everything I knew, growing smaller and smaller. My heart tore. Whimpering, forehead against the glass, I said a silent goodbye.

Goodbye, Mama.

As soon as we reached altitude, the flight attendant, an elegant woman in an immaculately pressed red blouse, navy pencil skirt and sleek updo, delivered dark liquor in crystal glasses to the men chatting with Mikhailov.

They appraised her, giving her a blood-chilling twice-over before muttering something to each other and chuckling as she walked toward me. I smiled at her when she met my gaze, eyes still burning from tears.

"Can I get you anything?" she asked softly.

I started at the question, glancing back at Mikhailov, who seemed distracted. "Do you know where we're going?" I asked in a barely audible whisper.

She glanced back toward the men, eyebrows furrowing before looking back at me with something like pity in her expression. "There are many stops planned," she said quietly.

Mikhailov was beside us in a whoosh. "Excuse us," he said to her, all charm. She nodded and returned to her station.

He sat in the empty seat beside me unassumingly and wrapped his fingers around my wrist, squeezing firmly before leaning in to hiss in my ear, "What did I say to you? Make a scene, ask the wrong person the wrong question and see what happens. I make one phone call—" He raised his phone threateningly.

Panic entered my voice. "No, please. I'm sorry—"

"Keep that mouth shut," he cut me off and shut me up. I nodded quickly.

The flight attendant returned and asked Mikhailov, "Is everything all right, sir? Can I get anything to make you more comfortable?" She eyed me with a cautious smile. I forced one in return under the pressure of Mikhailov's glare.

"Yes," Mikhailov answered casually. "She's a nervous flier. Give her something for the nerves, will you, *kukla?*"

"Yes, of course, sir," she said and returned to her station in a hurry.

I looked back out the window without saying another word. I was an empty shell. I'd left my spirit in the hospital room with Mama. The possibility of not seeing her ever again sent me down a spiral toward the murky hell of hopeless thought. I didn't want to think about life without her, I couldn't imagine it. Then again, I couldn't even guess what the next twenty-four hours for me were going to look like, let alone the future itself.

I tried to focus on the things that were tangible in this very moment: my health, my mind, my memories, autonomy over my body. You're alive. Mama's alive. Nyah's alive. Anya is safe. Oliver's alive. Your grandparents are alive. Papa is alive, probably.

The flight attendant returned with a small packet of anti-nausea meds that usually just make me drowsy, but I guessed that was the point. She offered a small bottle of water with it. I nodded my thanks and looked away. She placed both items beside me and left.

I spent the rest of the flight with my eyes shut but too on edge to permit myself to sleep.

We landed sooner than I had expected. No one was talking

to me, but I could hear radio talk in the cockpit about preparing for landing in Las Vegas, of all places.

What were we doing here? Was my father here somewhere? The men from the back walked to the front of the jet and motioned for the girls to stand and follow them out. I stood, too.

"*Sadis*," Mikhailov commanded from the back of the plane, so I sat back down.

We waited another ten minutes. A black SUV pulled up near the jet. A new group of girls—similar in appearance to the ones who'd just left the plane—were brought aboard by two new men wearing dark suits. They all kept their eyes down as they passed me. The girls took their seats quietly, and soon the jet taxied back into line for takeoff.

I listened, waiting for information, news, anything that would indicate our destination. None of the other girls spoke a word, not to each other, not to the men, and not to me. They wouldn't even look my way. It was eerie how hopelessly uninterested they were in anything, their blank expressions unnerving me to my core. I finally looked back at Mikhailov, who was typing away on his phone.

I imagined running back there and shoving something sharp into the side of his throat. *What could I use?* Hypothetically speaking, of course.

I turned back to the front of the plane. The flight attendant must have something sharp enough with her up there: a wine opener or a metallic nail file. *Would a butter knife work?* Get real.

I looked back at Mikhailov fueled by rage and disgust when I spotted Kiril seated at the very back of the jet, by the restroom, scowling at me over everyone's head, which wasn't a challenge for him given his freakish size. His suspicious gaze bored into me and he gestured cutting my throat with his big, fat thumb. My heart thudded violently against my murderous little chest. I turned away and didn't look back again until the next time we landed.

Left with nothing to preoccupy my mind, grief rolled in, all-consuming and merciless, like dense sea fog. My chest throbbed as I chewed the inside of my mouth to keep from unraveling. The coppery tang of blood was on my tongue as I tried to refortify my emotional walls. I wouldn't give these cretins the satisfaction of seeing me break. I swore it to myself.

The minutes passed like hours and the hours felt like days. I tried not to think about Oliver, how he had no clue where I was, whether I was alive or dead, whether I would ever come back. I allowed myself to briefly fantasize that my father would mastermind a way out of this hell that he'd put us in, but I stopped because those useless fantasies were a delusional waste and they were feeding on what was left of my life energy.

One of the pilots finally announced that we were beginning our descent to Columbus, Ohio, the Bolton Field private airport to refuel. It seemed like a big jet with enough seats to hold close to nineteen people, but I'd never been on a private jet before. I had nothing to compare it to.

Refuel? That meant this wasn't our final stop. Where were they taking us?

When we landed in Columbus, the girls from Vegas were escorted off the jet by the men who brought them there. They filed out, no questions asked, just hollowed out, bruised, caked in makeup, solemn faces, eyes on the ground.

Watching them behave like terrified cattle made my stomach turn. I noticed that Mikhailov had made no move to exit the plane, so I didn't move either.

We waited as the crew refueled the jet. The remaining man in the back engaged in a hushed conversation with Mikhailov. I couldn't make out a word.

Just like last time—about twenty minutes in—a car arrived and new girls were escorted onto the jet accompanied by only one man this time. I was struck by how different they looked from the first group. The other girls certainly looked like they were having a tough go of it, but nothing some good food and sleep couldn't heal. These girls, on the other hand, were a different story. My heart sank with heaviness as I noted their strung-out gazes, blood-shot eyes, skin, sickly pale, marks and some of them had visible bruises. One of the girls was shaking—wrapped in a shawl—her forehead beaded with sweat as she shuffled past me. *Is this what they're going to turn me into?*

As the jet took off, I grabbed the Dramamine and shoved it deep into the folds of the seat behind me. I finished the water bottle and closed my eyes, pretending to sleep.

Whatever was to come, I wouldn't let them break me. I would fight, I promised myself. I would stay alert. I began to lose my sense of time as we flew. Still pretending to sleep, I focused my hearing on the hushed conversation between Mikhailov and an unnamed man who escorted the Columbus girls aboard.

"What's the rush?" the man asked. "Why was the timetable moved up? They never like transporting them like this; they usually give us time to detox."

"Don't question their timetable," I heard Mikhailov respond.

"I'm just curious. Unnecessary attention is frowned upon. This feels careless."

"There won't be another flight planned for several weeks, and they needed me to transport this one now. I don't ask questions. I propose solutions, I receive approvals and a timeline, and I follow through. For efficiency's sake—fuel costs, logistics, the flights had to be pushed up."

"See, was that so difficult? I just want to know why—"

"It's not your place to know why, Kartoshkov. Always assume the reason is sound and follow protocol. Everything else is a waste of everyone's time," Mikhailov snapped at the man.

At a certain point during the flight, Mikhailov came over to see how I was faring. My eyes were still shut, but I noticed the scent of peppermint that wafted through the air when his arm lightly brushed my shoulder, and he settled beside me.

"*Spish?*" He quietly inquired if I was asleep. I held my breath as he tucked a strand of hair behind my ear. After that, he didn't make any more contact. I must have drifted off to sleep at some point. The flight attendant's soft voice stirred me. "We will be landing in Amsterdam shortly. Can I get you anything else before we begin our descent?"

How long had I been out this time? I wondered. My head was still throbbing, and the kink in my neck was killing me from the awkward slumped-over position I woke up in. This had to be it, right? My neck continued to ache as I kneaded the sore spot.

I looked around cautiously, pretending to stretch. The girl across the aisle from me stared blankly out the window, her forehead banging against the glass in a dull thud each time the plane hit turbulence and took a dip.

I turned to see the flight attendant making her rounds, waking the sleeping girls up, and offering a sad-looking meal. I knew I needed to get some food into me, but I found it challenging to chew and swallow the salmon. I shuffled the spinach around before forcing myself to consume the plate's contents entirely. I kept glancing back at Mikhailov and the other men, but they didn't look up from their phones.

Each bite of food was a chore; each swallow uncomfortable and forced. But I pushed through it—I would make myself eat even when I had no desire to.

After we landed, no one moved. A man in a sky-blue uniform entered the plane, followed by a woman in similar garb.

From what I could overhear, they were special customs agents dedicated to inspecting private flight arrivals. Mikhailov approached them—cordial at first, then the handshake was quickly followed by a laugh and a pat on the back. They spoke like old friends. The woman smiled at him as well, like she'd somehow missed the fact that he was the scum of the earth.

Mikhailov handed the man a stack of passports. The man didn't open a single one. He counted us, then counted the passports. He pulled one out from the pile and lifted it.

"You've got a visa for this one?" the official asked Mikhailov. Mikhailov nodded in response and handed the man a document. The man barely glanced at it. "Good," was all the man said.

The woman filled out some documents on her clipboard, and Mikhailov signed them. As soon as they were gone, Mikhailov approached me. My heart hammered as he reached for my arm and pulled me to my feet. The blood rushed to my head and I swayed where I stood. Mikhailov steadied me. "Got up too quick?"

"Not like I had a choice."

"Why so gloomy? Poor girl—took a private flight, ate some wild salmon. The horror. You should be soaking this in. The rest may not be so...pleasant, I'm sorry to say." I swallowed down an insult that popped into my mind and I broke eye contact, staring ahead as though he weren't in front of me. Mikhailov turned and I followed him.

"Bye, thank you." I offered the flight attendant a polite smile, my lips barely twitching upward, but it was the most I could manage right now. She smiled back at me, a trace of worry in her eyes.

I stepped out into the bite of the crisp, morning winter air of Amsterdam in late October. I descended the stairs toward the first of the gray SUVs that were parked adjacent to the jet. I moved with Mikhailov as one. He opened the back door for me and I got in. As soon as Mikhailov was seated in the front passenger side, he turned and handed me a bottle of water. I thanked him but noticed the seal had already been broken.

"I could've opened it myself."

"My daughter always liked it when I loosened the top for her —old habit," Mikhailov said with a shrug.

"You have a daughter?" I asked in surprise that he was saying anything to me other than another command.

"Drink," he ordered and turned away.

I drank. When we drove out of the gates and into the public streets toward the highway, I tried to focus on where we were going.

After a few minutes, the signs grew blurry. My eyelids were drifting shut and I fought to keep them open, to keep myself upright. I noted how unremarkable the buildings by the airport were, almost like we were on a highway back home. That was the last thing I recalled thinking before everything went black.

CHAPTER 13

OLIVER

"S o, what's our next move?" I asked the police officer. He was done documenting the report.

"Our?" he asked, confusion entering his voice. He shuffled the papers around containing the copy of the original report filed on Lily's assault and her attempted abduction. He then shut the folder and folded his hands over it.

"*Your* next move...or the department's...you know what I—" I reasoned but he cut me off before I had a chance to clarify.

"You go back to your life. You do nothing. You stay the hell away from this case, from these people. You got that, kid? We keep our eyes and ears open. For now, that's about as much as either of us can do."

A hot flash of anger surged up my throat.

"Keep your eyes and ears open?" I exclaimed. "You've gotta be shittin' me! That's it?"

He sighed, exasperated. "Look...normally, we'd ask the neighbors to send us their surveillance footage. We'd drop by a few motels where associates of known Russian crime groups have congregated in the past. That's just on the small scope.

"On the large scope, we'd contact border patrol, give them a heads-up, make our rounds through all the private airports in the city, question the guards, check the manifests. All right? This department does some solid police work, but this case is different—our hands are tied, kid. So, save all that outrage for someplace else. I'm sorry to say, but there's red tape all over it and whoever's running it wants it hush-hush."

"Hush, hush—what the hell does that mean? They're just gonna pretend nothing happened? Is that a joke? She's a missing woman taken out of her own house in broad daylight in the middle of Hollywood!"

"I never said that. The case will be delegated to the most qualified department. This department deals with local crime. This case is out of our jurisdiction. That's all I can say. I'm sure you'll be hearing from someone about it soon. Just make yourself available for questions if someone comes around. And it sounds like you and"—he checked his notes—"Miss Nyah Wright are key witnesses, so be careful, kid. Avoid being alone for some time, all right?"

"What about the evidence? What's gonna happen to it?" I pressed.

"We've logged it and we'll send it where it needs to go," the officer said, clicking his pen.

"And Lily?"

"Lily?" he parroted.

I huffed out a short breath of frustration. "Ms. Arkova... Mina's mom? The staff at the hospital say she was moved—" I reminded him.

"Oh—yeah, again...can't really tell ya nothing about that, kid. Sorry."

I nodded and stood, holding out my hand to shake his.

"Thanks for being upfront with me. I know you didn't have

to tell me anything. I appreciate it." He nodded and got back to work.

My legs prickled from sitting on the hard metal chair for so long. When I stepped out of the station, the chill of the evening air took me by surprise. I pulled on my sweatshirt, the one that I had given Mina at the hospital. I'd found it in her room, tossed over her bed. The sleeve was stained with a coin-sized blot of dried blood but the sweatshirt also carried her sweet smell. I tucked my nose beneath the neckline and closed my eyes, surrendering to the pain of missing her. I couldn't remember the last time I cried. Actually, yes, I could. They were tears of joy after the jury in my trial against the state had stood up and ruled in my favor, sentencing the monster who abused me and others to life in prison, and granting me two million dollars for reparations.

The tears that threatened to spill at this moment were void of joy. I hadn't felt loss like this before because I'd never had anyone to lose. I had just begun learning to love Mina, the only unbroken piece of my heart belonged to her, and she had been ripped away from me right under my nose, that final piece gone with her.

I remembered the look on her face when she stood before me, dressed in this same sweatshirt, its warmth granting her a comfort that visibly soothed her. It felt so good that I was able to give her that. I wished it had been enough. I wished I could've done more—could've come up with a way to actually protect her and her mom.

It was fading faster than it had appeared, my happiness— vanishing right in front of my eyes. I squatted to relieve the burning in my chest, the ache from missing her and from not knowing what to do next. Every time I slowed down, like now, I felt like I was drowning. I needed to keep moving. I had to stay busy.

I jumped to my feet and rubbed the blur out of my eyes,

deciding that I was going to take the reins in this situation. These cops had their hands tied? That was fine. I didn't. I'd do it myself. Like the officer said, I'd start with the neighbors.

CHAPTER 14

MINA

I was lying on the floor of what seemed to be a dark moving container when I came to—my flaccid limbs rattled against a cold, hard surface like a loose pile of logs. I lifted my head and squinted through the dark. A bit of light streamed in through the linear cracks, revealing rows of potted plants all around me—something resembling tulips. It looked as though I was in the body of some kind of cargo truck.

We were moving fast. I sat up, disoriented, head splitting from a painful headache. Panic had set in quickly and jolted me to my feet. I almost fell when the truck made a turn, but I caught myself with my hands. I made my way farther into the truck, pounding my fists against the wall between me and the driver. It wasn't enough. *They wouldn't hear me, would they?* I yelled, "Hey! Hey!" as I pounded at the wall over and over again.

The truck finally slowed and came to a stop. I heard doors opening and slamming and deep, angry voices cursing. The back door opened, flooding the space with light, and someone climbed inside. I squinted and held my hand up to block the blinding daylight from my eyes. I could make out Kiril's silhouette at the entrance of the truck's body, and I backed into the wall, instinctively. Behind him was a highway along what appeared to be the edge of a forest.

He put a bottle of water down at his feet and pulled out some things wrapped in shiny plastic, and threw them next to the water.

"Where are you taking me?" I demanded.

I couldn't make out his expression clearly but his tone said it all. "No more noise. Not one peep from you. Eat. Drink the water."

"I-I need to pee." I glanced at the forest line as a suggestion.

"Uh-uh." He shook his head then gestured at the tulips. "Pee. Good for plant. They thirsty." With that, he swung the doors shut, locking me back into the darkness. My stomach growled and ached with a pang of hunger—I bent down to my knees and crawled over tulips and dirt and pots to reach the edge of the truck. I felt around for the bottle of water and the plastic-wrapped bars.

As my eyes adjusted to the darkness once more, the truck began to move again and my fingers found the food. I inhaled one snack bar after the other without hesitation. I found the water and gulped it down in a few swallows. I was so damn thirsty and my head was killing me.

How had I managed to be out of it enough to not remember being put in this truck? It felt like I was missing time and the more I fought to remember what happened and figure out my next move, the more my head went spinning. I fell to my elbows and then rested my forehead on my crossed hands. It wouldn't stop spinning. I was afraid I'd get sick when, pretty soon, everything went black again.

CHAPTER 15

OLIVER

The sky was turning from pink to gray, and it was growing late. I walked up a path lit by solar footlights leading to the decorative entrance of an impressive, two-story Mediterranean-style home at the end of a cul-de-sac in the hills of Sherman Oaks.

I rang the doorbell and waited after a faraway call—"One second!"—drifted through the solid wooden doors.

Moments later, the door swung open and Nyah was waving me in, scrunching up her hair that was still wet from a shower. "Hey, any news? Come on in."

I followed her into the overwhelming grand entrance of her home that boasted a double staircase, and I came face to face with an enormous vase on an enormous round table under an ornate chandelier. I craned my head up to take it all in.

"Wow. Nice house," I commented, closing my gaping mouth after processing the glamor of it all.

"Oh…"—She looked around like she'd forgotten this wasn't a norm for people—"Thanks." She shrugged and smiled politely.

"So, what happened? How's Lily?"

"She's gone."

"What do you mean 'she's gone'?"

"Nyah? Who are you talking to? Is someone here?" a woman's voice carried down from the second floor.

"Yeah! It's my friend, Oliver, Mom!" she called back. "What do you mean she's gone?" she asked me quietly, panicked.

"They're saying they moved her for her protection but they're not telling me where. But they did say that she woke up!" I told her, almost forgetting to mention the most important part.

"Holy shit! Does she know about Mina?" Nyah asked, eyes wide with worry.

"I don't kn—"

"You better not be leaving this house, young lady!" Nyah's mother called down again.

"I'm not! We'll be in the kitchen!" Nyah called to her before turning back to me. "She's taking a bath to de-stress after what happened and...left the doors all wide open to hear my every move, apparently," Nyah muttered. "Come on, you're probably starving."

I followed her through the living room, down a hallway filled to the ceiling with family photos, a majority of them professionally done, depicting a very happy family with impeccable genes and perfect teeth. We walked into a bright, spacious chef's kitchen. She pulled out a barstool at the marble island for me. The TV was on in the family room and a head of curly, dark hair was peeking out over the edge of the sofa.

"Is that your uh...sibling?"

"Oh...yeah, that's my brother, Chris. He's eight."

"Hey, Chris, what's up?" I said. When he failed to respond, I went on, "I'm Oliver." Crickets.

"Oh, there's no use, Oliver, he's in zombie mode. The world could end and he'd still whine, begging for five more minutes to play that stupid thing." She rolled her eyes. "Leftover pierogi and corn sound okay?"

"Yeah, sure…I'll eat anything. Can I help?" I offered.

"No, just sit and tell me what happened," she said and waved at me to stay seated. Nyah quickly got to work heating up the leftovers in a fancy-looking oven. "Is water okay or do you want something stronger?" She wiggled a juice box at me.

I cracked a small smirk. "Water's fine, thanks. Is it just your mom?"

"My dad, too. He drove over here like a bat out of hell when my mom called him and told him what happened. He'd been interrogating me pretty much the entire time that you'd been over there talking to the police. I had to give him every detail, down to the shoes those fools were wearing. I was like, sir, do you think I was checking out their footwear while they were forcing drugs into me?"

"Shit, you said that?"

She nodded. "What? It's true. And he started looking up how to install tracking devices on me after hearing that little detail. I swear, that man would install a GPS, a security system, and a camera on my ass if he could."

"Honestly? I don't blame him. So, where is he now?" I looked through the glass of the French doors to the back yard. Nothing out there but a playground, a tire swing, a trampoline, a pool, and a whole lot of yard.

"He took my car to a buddy's mechanic shop. Said he's gonna make sure there aren't any trackers on it or something. I wouldn't be surprised if he has them take it apart, put it back together again. And still probably end up selling it."

"Your dad sounds like a serious dude."

"That's one way to put it. Hopefully, he still lets me drive to school tomorrow."

"You're going to school?"

"Yeah...I have to, I have a midterm coming up. Why? Aren't you?"

I shake my head and take a swig of water. "I can't go."

"Yeah, I get that. It's hard. Just take a day or two. They'll understand."

"No, I mean I'm not going back until I find Mina."

"What do you mean? You can't just quit."

"I'm not quitting. I just can't go back, right now. I have to focus on tracking her down. It's not gonna be easy but—"

"You can't just give up on your life and go off playing private detective. Mina wouldn't want that," she argued.

"I'm not playing anything and I think Mina...would do the exact same thing," I argued. Nyah sighed in resignation.

"You're probably right. She would. But then again, she doesn't always make the smartest decisions," Nyah said with a quiet hesitation.

"Look, after we find her and figure a way out of this for her, for them, she and I will both figure out school and all the rest of it. Together." The word was a rubber band around the beating muscle in my chest.

She nodded, dropping the subject for now. "You think spreading the news about her disappearance on social media is a bad idea? I have a friend who knows the makeup artist of a hair guru who works on Traxi's gorgeous pink locks, and Traxi's really blowing up now in the music scene...soooo, she could really help us spread the word, maybe get a hashtag going?" Nyah suggested, eyebrows raised, a hopeful, questioning gaze lighting up her face.

"I dunno...it could be dangerous." I shrugged, not understanding half of what she said. She deflated. "I'm not saying no, Nyah, I'm just saying let's wait on that for now...give me a chance to look for her first. If we spook these guys with a public hunt, they'll hide her so well, we won't have a chance in hell of finding her and what if...what if it gives them a reason to..."—I had trouble verbalizing my worry—"...make her disappear?"

"Oh, shit, good point. I hadn't thought of that. So...what do we do? Like, these guys are no joke. My dad completely lost it when he realized we're dealing with organized crime here. He's all messed up now because part of him wants to go straight to the police, the press, the news, the whole nine yards but he's freaked out over the threat. Like he didn't even want me to shower because he thought I'd wash off 'evidence.' He called up his buddy who's in the Sherman Oaks PD—"

"Your dad knows someone in the police department?"

"Yeah, they served in the Navy together."

"Holy shit, what did he say?" This was good. Maybe this guy could give us something.

"Not much, just that he'd never seen the big mafia guys make this much of a disturbance around LA. He mostly deals with gangs affiliated with the cartels around here, like drugs and human trafficking cartels that they've seen a rise in. The Russian gangs around here, he says, deal with mostly financial crimes and stuff like that, but he said the threat could be very real and that we shouldn't mess around with these guys. They outsource jobs and hire thugs from all sorts of gangs to do their dirty work. Said I have to be very careful now...by the way, can I have my phone back?"

"Oh, shit, yeah...of course, here," I pulled her phone out of my pocket and slid it across the kitchen island toward her. In all the chaos, I forgot I still had it.

"So, what did the cops say when they saw it?" she asked. "My video...oh, and did you give them Mina's phone?"

"Yeah, yeah, I gave them all that. It was weird, I dunno...he said it wasn't their jurisdiction—that some other department's handling the case. He took everything, labeled it, documented it but that was it. He said they're being told to keep it quiet."

"What the hell?"

"Yeah...it's super weird. But I can't help but think it's somehow all tied together. Like...I get a visit from the Feds? Then that lady comes to the hospital—"

"What lady?"

"Some lady showed up at the hospital right when the police came to take Mina's statement. She walked right up and interrupted them, she like shows them some papers and demands to talk with Mina on her own and from the looks of it, she got Mina out of police questioning—"

"She did?"

"Yeah. After that, Mina was convinced she had to let these guys take her. That they were coming no matter what and that it was safer for everyone if we stayed away from her and she just went with them. And she wouldn't talk to me about what this lady said at all."

"That's crazy. That's what she was telling me too, before they came." Nyah was shaking her head in confusion. "She said something about her being a lawyer, but that doesn't ring true. That's so creepy. Look..."—She rubbed her forearms—"I've got goosebumps."

"Like, I just don't know...what the hell is going on? It's so damn frustrating. They just collected the evidence and said they'd forward it to the proper team or whatever. And the cop said not to be alone for a while, you or me."

Nyah gave an indignant sigh.

"Obvi! Shit, I'm not going anywhere alone anytime soon. I'm good and thoroughly freaked out, thank you very much."

I hesitated a moment but formulated my incoherent thoughts enough to finally ask, "Listen, Nyah...can—do you think you could talk to your dad? Convince him to ask his buddy for some information about getting a list of addresses, where these Russian gangs hang around most or do their business and stuff?"

Nyah's mouth dropped open.

"Oliver, there is no way in hell that—"

"Please," I interrupted, trying to soothe her with my voice. "Just ask. If he says no, he says no, if his buddy can't tell him, he can't tell him. But, please, I'm begging you, Nyah, just ask." Desperation laced my plea, as the look in her eyes told me it was the last thing she wanted to do.

"Time is running out," I pushed, "and you know what they say about missing people—the longer they're missing, the more likely we are never to find them again. We have to keep looking."

Nyah mulled it over as she pulled out the now-steaming dish of pierogi and the bowl of creamed corn from the warmer and placed them in the center of the island. I went on. "I asked Mina's neighbors if I could see their security footage." My face tensed at the memory. The tightness in my chest was returning, the same feeling I had when I first saw the footage with the SUV backing out into the street with Mina, likely, already inside. The camera footage didn't catch her getting in or the men getting out.

"They went north on her street and then turned left. I kept a list of timestamps in my notes for every time the SUV passed a certain house or a certain camera. For the next hour or so, I just knocked on the door of anyone who had cameras facing in a useful direction. Most of them didn't open the door or they slammed their doors in my face, but I was able to track the SUV all the way down to the 101 freeway—"

"Holy shit—"

"Then I went to the building that's right after the freeway. You know those offices? And I gave the security guard a twenty and the timestamp I needed, and I asked him to play back the footage from the camera facing the street corner and look for the SUV. He told me it didn't pass by there, so I know they got on the freeway—northbound."

"Wow, Oli, you did all that today?"

I nodded. "Before I got here. So, I don't think they took her south to the border. I don't know where she is, but there's a chance she's out here somewhere in the valley. I dunno, maybe I'm wrong. But we have to try. I'm trying. So, can you, please, just ask him?"

"Yeah, I will. Of course, I will." She still looked unsure but the determination in her eyes told me Nyah was a person of her word.

CHAPTER 16

MINA

The smell of wet cement overwhelmed my senses before the throbbing pain in my head came to the forefront. I curled into myself to resist the cold. I shook from the punishing chill, rubbing my legs and arms against themselves, desperate to ignite even the smallest bit of heat from the friction. My eyelids were heavy, working to shut out the discomfort, the pain, the cold. I needed to assess where the hell I was and evaluate this new threat.

It took time for my eyes to adjust before I could discern the source of the cold—an AC system was on at full blast. It was rigged into the adjacent wall of the small gray room—a euphemism for this ten-by-ten concrete prison.

This place likely hadn't seen the light of day in hundreds of years. I couldn't help but think the damp musk and bone-chilling frigidity spoke of the horrors endured here.

Something silver oscillated at the opposite end of the room. I turned my head downward, releasing the kink in my neck, but winced from the bite of rough concrete against the skin of my forehead. I strained to lift my head a few inches from the floor and squinted in the direction of the corner. A fan was rigged in my direction to blow the cold air around the room. This was deliberate. What did they want—for me to come down with pneumonia?

I squinted in concentration and trained my eyes on the room, looking around. The only source of light in the room besides the dull green glow on the AC screen and the reflection of light against the metal of the fan was a tiny white bulb across the room. My heart rate accelerated when I realized that this white light was attached to a camera, rigged on a tripod and trained on me.

I lurched forward, but my momentum was cut off by the pull of a chain tethering my bound hands. I followed the chain to a pipe attached to the wall beside my head. An uncomfortable pulsation rippled across my wrists, sending blood to my numb extremities.

My head was splitting from a sharp, growing pain, too severe to call a mere headache. I'd never experienced a migraine before. This must have been it—an inescapable, head-splitting burn like claws had cut the top of my scalp open, and kneaded my brain into dough for a brain pizza. I tried to curb the throbbing, rattling the chains as I gripped my head in my hands.

I folded in on myself, exhaling through my mouth to bring heat to my knees. My jeans were soaked. There was an odor of urine coming off me, I realized. *Ugh.*

"Hello?" I croaked out. There was no answer to my call. I shut my eyes and focused on bringing heat back into my body.

I drifted into a light, uneasy sleep until the sensation of a thousand needles hit me and pain erupted in my ear. I was drenched in what felt like a bucket of cold water. I huddled into a smaller ball but the water already made its way into my breathing passage. I was forced to roll forward, captured in a coughing fit, gasping as I tried to expel the water from my throat and nose.

My eyes burned as I forced them open. A blinding, bright light had turned on overhead. I averted my eyes downward and could see that my wrists were raw from the handcuffs that bound them together.

A dull ringing persisted in one of my ears more than the other. The throbbing ache on the side of my head lingered. I blinked against the sting of the cold water and the light but a sharp strike against my cheek had me jerking back, hitting my head against the wall behind me.

A pain whipped across my face—one, two, three weighty slaps. I fought to regain my balance, my blurred vision finally clearing and I focused on the piercing, blue foxlike eyes behind a disturbing, blank-faced mask that peered over me. A woman? I flinched away from her.

She wore a gray coat, white shirt, slacks, and boots. Her clothing, however plain, was ironed and immaculate. From the corner of my vision, I observed the camera was blinking red. There were wires connecting it to a laptop on a chair beside it. The masked figure moved deliberately, careful to keep her back to the camera.

"We've given you several warnings," boomed a low, distorted voice over an intercom. I shifted my gaze around, startled by the sudden sound that filled the room. The masked figure, tall and slender, stepped away, closer to the adjacent wall but with her back to the camera and her eyes on me. She remained there, unmoved.

"Lilia Arkova's death is on your hands." My heart hammered violently against my chest. My mind reeled, working to process what had just been said while I shook my head in strict denial of this lie. *No*, I told myself, fervently rejecting the information. *It isn't true; it couldn't be. She's safe.* Patricia had promised me Mama would be safe if I did this, if I went with them when they came for me. If I got her the location—this location. *I did it, I'm here...chained to a goddamn wall! Didn't she swear Mama would be safe if I did what they wanted?* I gave a sudden yell of anger and despair.

The distorted voice went on, "You have been unresponsive. That is unacceptable. If you are no longer cooperating, then you are a marked enemy. Every day you hide, your daughter will take punishment in your place. Her days will be spent tied to this wall like a dog." Were they addressing my father? Was the point of making this recording to motivate him to do their bidding?

A sound of footsteps echoed off the walls, growing closer through the corridor before at last, the metal door creaked open and the sound of wood on pavement entered the room. A second masked figure came into the space carrying another bucket and my stomach clenched at the sight of it. This person was tall and broad-shouldered with dark hair and taupe brown skin.

There was a feminine disposition in the posture of both masked figures, and their hair was pulled back each into a neat chignon. The second masked figure moved more hesitantly than the first. She stood next to the first, but unlike her, this one kept looking at me with worried eyes, dark and reflective. The concern in them contrasted against the blank expression of the mask over her face. She clasped her hands in front of her body and looked to the corner, waiting in silence. I noted a strange mark marring her slender hand, like a brand—a distorted circle with a long vertical and a shorter horizontal line crossing the middle. I shifted as far away from them as I could, splitting my focus across them, the door, my restraints, the fan, and the camera.

The distorted voice boomed across the room once more, "Each drop of her blood, each scream she surrenders is on your conscience." There was a long, uncomfortable silence and only the sound of our breaths. "We want our merchandise delivered in full, every last one of them. Prioritize the ones marked as specialized by their brands. Collect and deliver them alive, fully functioning."—*Alive?* My mind scrambled to put together a puzzle with far too many missing pieces. What merchandise did my father have to deliver to these people? Why would he have anything of theirs? Instead of answers, my mind filled with more questions.

I scoured the bare room for an escape but between these chains and the V for Vendetta twins, I stood no chance. I should never have come here, never have given in to them. I needed to get the hell out of here—run, hide, and never look back. *You can't. If you leave, they'll punish someone you care about.*

I named my reasons to stay: Nyah, Anya, my grandparents, my aunt Zoya, her boys. I imagined what I'd do if any of them were hurt because of my actions. Then I imagined what I would do if any of them were brought here. I'd find this place. I'd tear down these walls from the outside and fight anyone who stood in my way.

Mama's face came to my mind, and I remembered the sweet smell of her hair that enveloped me as I hugged her. I closed my eyes and buried my face in her dark curls. The pain of the mere possibility of never seeing her again was unbearable. The thought of never getting to do all the things we had promised we'd try cut me in half.

If she was really gone, would I find the will to keep pushing forward? I already felt myself falling into complacency, coming up with ways to feel less, to dull the senses, to exist merely for the sake of existing. But surely, I'd have felt it if Mama was really gone. Wouldn't I have? Wouldn't the massive hole at my core—where we had been tethered—have disintegrated from the inside out? Wouldn't there be an inescapable, hollow, nothingness to send me spiraling inward? Maybe there was.

The person against the wall with the piercing blue eyes

stepped forward to join her companion, who had been standing over me. They observed me in silence and I frayed at my seams until I was no more than a useless clump of thread.

One gave the other a nod. The figure nearer to me returned the nod but her dark eyes were racked with uncertainty. She shuffled toward me, her elegant fingers flexing under the long sleeves of her coat. She scuffed her boots along the floor, shaking her hands out as though to psych herself up for what was to come. I scrambled to protect myself, to brace, but nothing could have prepared me for the blow that came after she reeled her leg back.

"*Gaghhhh!*" I cried as she landed a sharp kick to my gut.

I couldn't catch my breath, not after a few seconds, not after a minute. Each half-breath I managed was agony.

"They said until she breaks," the one with the piercing blue eyes said in Russian to her counterpart, her voice cold but serene. She seemed eerily at ease in this place. The dark-eyed woman hesitated a minute longer. I winced up to find her shaking her head, her hands clenched into tight fists, knuckles pale with tension. Her knees were shaking.

"Please," I rasped, hooking into her hesitation, my voice barely a whisper. "Help me. I'm Mina Arkova, did they kill my mother? Is she really dead? Please. Help me. Tell me what to do. How do I make this stop?" I groveled.

"Be useful," a hushed, barely discernible mutter came from the dark-eyed one.

"Useful? How?" I croaked.

"Give them what they need. That's the only way to survive this place," she uttered, her eyes filled with pity and a kindness that didn't fit in a hell like this.

"What do they need—"

"Again," the blue-eyed woman commanded her counterpart. The dark-eyed one hesitated. The blue-eyed woman leaned in toward her. "Go. Again. Unless you wanna move back down here...I hear a room's gonna free up soon," she threatened.

With those words came my next blow. There was no more hesitation in the dark-eyed woman. She aimed to cut me down the middle like an ax to the trunk of an oak.

Was this a test to see how much pain I could withstand? To see how useful I could be to them? I'd show them what I was made of. I'd show them I was an asset, that it'd be a waste to dispose of me.

Absorb the pain, you are bigger than the pain, our dance teachers would say to drill endurance into us from childhood. Our toes would bleed, the soles of our feet would blister, our knees would turn black and blue, but they would say: *move through it, let the pain feed the story.* That's all I had to do now.

"Stop holding it in, damn you! Just break!" the dark-eyed woman hissed in frustration, all the while delivering blow after blow to my stomach, my legs, my side. I wouldn't, I wouldn't allow myself to break. I groaned through the throbbing, unable to choke the sound down any longer, rotating away and rolling in on myself. The stabbing sensation in my gut and ribs pulsed relentlessly. I had rolled onto my elbows to protect my organs from her strikes, but the movement sent such intense surges of pain through my body that a scream tore through me like lightning and the need to vomit overcame me. Nothing was coming out, though. I dry-heaved air and saliva on all fours, tears streaking my face as the sound of footsteps echoed off the walls once more.

Were the women gone? I didn't know. I collapsed onto my stomach. I heard the echoes of footsteps growing closer once more and gritted my teeth, prepared for the blow this time by flexing my abdomen instead of wasting breath begging. I was ready for the next hit, but instead of the blunt strike of a boot, the blue-eyed woman barreled over with a large bucket balanced on her shoulder and a wicked grin. A bucketful of bitterly cold water hit me like an onslaught of glass shards, the coldest yet.

A howl of anger ripped from my throat.

The sound of metal being dragged against concrete reverberated off the walls. They dragged the fan closer to me and cranked it up. The air was frigid and brutal against my drenched body.

They finally abandoned the room, leaving me quivering on the concrete under the torturous gust. The door shut behind them with a heavy thud but not before I managed a glimpse of the hallway just beyond the door. It was bare and concrete, just like the room. And although it revealed nothing, it reminded me that there was a world out there and that hallway was the way out. I just had to hold on.

I shut my eyes and focused all of my energy into healing my body.

The cold is good, I tricked myself. *It'll accelerate the healing. It'll help with the swelling.*

Father will do something. He'll get them what they need. He won't let them keep doing this to me.

I had to believe that, because if I lost that hope, I would die.

I forced movement into my limbs. If I didn't get heat into my body somehow, I would go into hypothermic shock. Moans of pain left me with every movement. Most movement was connected to the ribcage so I gritted my teeth through the anguish of push-ups. I did three before I collapsed. Later, I tried again. And again.

It was too soon when I heard the *whomp* of the door. The violent sound echoed through the room.

The clunking of footsteps grew louder. My heart pounded violently in my chest once more. *No. Not yet! I can't take another hit.* But the woman with blue eyes was back and this time, she was alone.

There was nothing I could do to stop her. She had one goal: pain. I could read it in her strides. I tried to crawl as far back as I could but I was a rat stuck in a cage. She knelt beside me and I flinched.

Suddenly, she punched me in the ribs but I covered my torso with my arm and took the blow there instead. I jerked back and threw my leg up, kicking her in the head, taking her by surprise by making use of my hyperextension. Her mask went askew as she hit the floor, catching herself and landing on her hands. She was back on her feet in a blur of motion, impossibly fast.

I kicked at her wildly, giving everything left inside me to fight her off. She absorbed the blows to her torso from my kicks like they were a mere nuisance and wrapped the chain around her hand until she held me at her mercy.

My breath caught and several more wheezes followed, each one causing unprecedented suffering.

"Ss-stahp...puh-please," I croaked. But she hit me again and again, breaking all my walls, cracking me open entirely. I was a boneless snail without its shell.

Every slight movement or breath sent jolts of pain shooting in a thousand different directions. I wanted death, I welcomed it with open arms. I was jealous of my mother. Couldn't they have killed me instead? *Don't let them make you cruel. You're stronger than this pain. Pain is nothing. Pain is temporary.*

I lay motionless, wheezing. There was nothing left of me. I was nothing. I felt nothing. I didn't know whether the woman was still there. I didn't care anymore.

I understood, now. This was what they needed. *Be useful,* the dark-eyed woman told me. I was a fool. They didn't want me doing push-ups. They needed me on the brink of death. They needed me broken on camera, so that my father could see me grovel and he'd do whatever was necessary to make it stop. Now that I understood the game, I would change my strategy.

I looked straight into the camera, red light still blinking, and let my mouth shape the words I never thought I'd speak.

"P-Papa"—I ground out, shaking from the pain pulsing through my abdomen—*"Papachka, pozhaluysta*...help me."

CHAPTER 17

OLIVER

"What did he say?" I was on the phone with Nyah, asking about her father for the fourth time that day. The first time, she told me that I was a lunatic to call up at six in the morning and that he wasn't even awake yet.

What I didn't tell her was that I had one of my worst nightmares since before the trial and I had not been able to sleep. Poor Xavi had run into my room at four in the morning worried I was being murdered by an intruder.

The second time I had called, she was in a much better mood and promised me she'd ask soon.

"Probably on the way to school since he insists on driving me," she said.

The third time I had called, she didn't pick up but texted back that she was in class and that she'd call as soon as she had an answer. It was hard to stay patient.

So, when I saw Nyah's name appear across the screen of my

new phone, I scrambled to answer, almost knocking it off the table in my haste.

"Hey, okay, so...he said his buddy told him something pretty similar to what that cop told you."

"He did?" So, there really was something bigger at play here.

"Yeah. Sounds like this case is sealed up real tight. His buddy said the case notes are heavily redacted. Still, from what he told my dad, he managed to put a list together of a few places that match what we're looking for. You know...like places with a history of those gang associations. But he says the list is pretty outdated and it's unlikely that they're still using those."

"That's okay. I'll take them. Gotta start somewhere. Thank you, Nyah—"

"Listen, my dad flat out refused to help. He doesn't want me looking into this at all or telling you anything about it. He was pissed I even told you about his friend. He was like, commanding me to drop it. Period. But I told him he was dead wrong if he thought I could ever do that. Then, I reminded him who we were talking about here, and legit brought out our old family albums where there were pictures of Mina's baby-faced, eleven-year-old, irresistible, chunky-monkey self as she stayed over at our house every Saturday that summer and made a certain grumpy someone a friendship bracelet that melted his old, grouchy heart. He told me he still had that bracelet in his drawer and I asked him: Is that the girl you want us to 'just forget' to 'just drop it' and move on from? Then he actually cried. My grown-ass daddy bawled like a baby. So, yeah, he got the list but he won't just give it to you and he doesn't want me anywhere near this list or these places. He says if you wanted to check these places out and ask around, he'd have to go with you."

"Oh, shit," I let out an exasperated sigh. "All right. Tell him yes. I can come by now. Does that work?"

"Hold up, he's still at work," she said.

"Can I call him?" I asked. We had no time to spare. If he insisted on coming with me, we'd have to go sooner rather than later.

"Uhhhh…yeah, I guess?" Nyah seemed hesitant.

"Don't worry. I'll make sure he's safe. Text me his number. Thank you, Nyah."

"Uhh…yeah, of course."

I was still cleaning the mess the police had left in my storage unit. There were open boxes and packing slips scattered everywhere. Packing material and office supplies covered the floors, from air packets to packing paper to rolls of tape—the place looked like a bomb had gone off.

I replaced our phones and bought replacement units for the items that needed to be shipped out to customers as soon as possible. I picked Xavi up from the dojo after leaving Nyah's place. We managed to fulfill most of the online orders by midnight.

I felt indebted to Xavi, big time. I had invited him to stay with me at my place last night after work instead of letting him sleep at the storage unit like he had before. When he raised a feeble protest, I told him it was the least I could do. I'd been excited to finally make use of the pullout couch in the living room.

I gave him both my pillows and the duvet: he resisted but I explained that they ended up on the floor of my room anyway. I told him I slept better without them, and he responded with a strange expression of disbelief. He didn't pry, however, and accepted them with a word of thanks. I hadn't gone into detail with him about my past yet but he knew I had grown up in foster care, so he probably filled in some of the gaps on his own.

He was a bit stiff when he first arrived at my place, like he didn't know what to do with himself. After he woke me from my nightmare, I figured he'd grow more distant and bounce. Contrary to what I thought, by the morning, everything was back to normal—he was cracking his usual jokes and burping his way through breakfast.

It was actually kind of nice having someone stay with me. I hadn't realized how lonely I'd been until he was there. Something about hearing the sounds of another person in the next room put me at ease in a way I didn't know I needed.

He seemed more motivated than ever. After breakfast, he was already making plans for growing the business and building our website. By lunch, he suggested we buy a whiteboard for ideas.

"Let's spitball some domain names! But we need a board... see, I told you it'd come in handy!" he said, full of enthusiasm.

I wasn't feeling as motivated for an expansion as he was at the moment. "I have to work on getting the units back from those fools and I gotta call Mr. Wright about looking for Mina."

I'd filled Xavi in about everything that happened to Mina when we got home the night before. At first, he didn't believe me. He thought I was messing with him but after he saw my face and realized I'd never joke about something like that, he apologized and offered to help in any way he could.

"Did you email the uhh...that officer dude last night with the—"

"The invoices...yeah and I got Tee and Mo to text me images of the receipts for the units they took. I gave them a heads-up about what's coming. They're spooked, but tried to play it off like it's no big deal. We probably won't hear from them again."

"Any response from the officer or whatever?"

"Nah...not yet. But with the wholesale stuff slowing down now and the amount I spent on replacement units last night, my rent's due this week and my accounts almost tapped out. I might have to make a trip later this week. Maybe tomorrow."

"Oh, all right...yeah, I can clear out, just let me know when—"

"No. I want you to stay, Xavi. We're gonna get a disbursement from the units we just sold and you can talk to our reps to place the next order if I'm...I dunno what's gonna happen when I go looking for her, so you might need to take over. I'll pay you for your time, of course."

"You sure?"

"Yeah. One hundred percent," I promised.

"Oli, man, I really appreciate this. I got good friends who never even...I'm just grateful for you. God bless you, man."

"I'm grateful for you, Xavi."

"Dude, should we hug? I feel like we should hug."

"That's okay. I'm not a—" But he already was walking over with his arms stretched out. "Okay," I said, letting him hug me, patting his back a few times. "Xavi, I. Can't. Breathe." He let me go and I shoved him off, playfully.

"Ahhh, that was nice, man," he beamed. I chuckled stiffly. "So, you're going out of town?"

"Santa Clarita."

"What's in Santa Clarita?" he asked, but Nyah's text notification rang for a second time and I excused myself to make the call to her dad.

He picked up on the second ring. "Hello?"

"Mr. Wright, thank you for agreeing to help—"

"Who is this?"

"I'm sorry. This is Oliver. Nyah told me you'd...umm...help us look for Mina."

"Oh, right..."

"She...umm, said you were at work but she gave me your number and I was hoping we could go today. Could I come by right now?"

"Right now? I'm at work, son, I can't just—"

"We're running out of time. The longer we wait, the more likely she'll be moved."

There was a pause, and then I heard him sigh. Maybe he was starting to waver.

"I'll be wrapped up here around six—"

"Six?"—I interjected—"I can't wait that long. Anything could happen. Sir, listen, can I drop by and grab that list from you? Look, I promise I won't do anything stupid. I'll just drive by a few of these places and if I see anything suspicious, I'll call the cops—"

"I don't think that's a good idea," Mr. Wright retorted.

"I won't tell the cops a thing about the list. I won't mention you or your buddy or Nyah, I swear," I promised. I held my breath as the line went quiet. After several seconds, Mr. Wright released a tense sigh.

"If you see something, you call me. Right away. Is that clear? If I let you pick up this list...you make me a promise my Nyah is nowhere near these places. Is that a deal?"

"Yes, sir. I swear," I assured in my most authoritative voice.

"You got a car?"

"Yes, sir," I confirmed.

"You stay in your car. If you see anything suspicious, you report it and then, you call me."

"Yes, sir," I lied.

"All right then. Call me when you're here."

CHAPTER 18

 MINA

Something moved in my hair. A tickle stirred me back to consciousness. My hand shot to my head to swat away whatever it was but the chains stopped it. I flinched and looked up to find the dark-eyed woman kneeling beside me on the floor. Her mask was gone. She looked young, about my age.

"It's okay. I'm not gonna hurt you," she said in Russian with a slight Middle Eastern accent. She had a smooth clay complexion, rich and taupe. Her obsidian hair, high cheekbones, full lips, and dark eyes with flecks of carnelian came together in a beautiful outer image. Too bad she was a torturous bitch.

I scurried away from her touch but didn't make it far when pain erupted in my abdomen.

"Try not to move," she urged and pulled the gray cloth blanket—she must have covered me while I was unconscious— up a bit higher.

"What do you want?" I croaked in Russian.

"Nothing. I'm just checking on you," she said softly, not

meeting my eyes. I appraised her with suspicion. She seemed to be unarmed. I thought of something and turned to check the camera. The red light was off and the laptop was gone. Could that have been the end of it? Was it possible that I wouldn't have to suffer anymore?

"My name's Starling," she announced.

"Congratulations," I snapped gruffly.

"I've been here, where you are. I have to say...you're strong. I pissed myself after the first blow. You held on longer than I ever could."

Her words surprised me. I didn't know what to make of them. The idea of her being in my shoes raised so many questions.

"If you understand this suffering, then why are you inflicting it on me?" I accused, anger seeping out with every syllable.

She couldn't hold my gaze. "I don't get to choose," she answered simply. "But I'm glad you understood what you needed to do. How to play their game. You're smart. I'll tell you this..."—She finally looked me in the eye, seemingly determined to offer a kernel of something—"It's not always about showing endurance or strength down here. It's about figuring out the game they're playing and giving them exactly what they need so that you suffer less. That's your goal, Mina. Do anything to suffer less."

"Perfect, thanks," I groaned, rolling off my aching arm.

Starling moved to help me but I shrugged off her touch and gritted my teeth through the pain.

"Here, drink some water," she said, lifting a cup to my mouth. I gulped the water down eagerly. "Slow down, you're probably dehydrated," she warned as I fell into a coughing fit.

"I can help you tilt your head up so I can feed you some of this." She revealed a bowl of mush that looked like a cross between oatmeal and mashed potatoes. I shook my head, certain I was unable to stomach anything right now.

"You have to try to eat something. They might not offer food again for some time. You never know when they'll feed you when you're down here, so just force some of it down if you can," she said, her voice impossibly soft for someone who had delivered such devastating strikes.

"Where are we?" I ignored the spoon of mush as she tried to feed it to me, and I shook my head.

"I can't say and I don't know. No one does. The location of this place is kept so heavily guarded that even the staff don't know where it is."

"How is that possible?" I asked.

"I'm...I can't say."

"What staff? You mean like the guards?"

"Sort of..." She hesitated.

"Are we in the Netherlands?"

"No." With this confirmation, I realized they must have driven us out of the Netherlands on that cargo truck.

"Russia?"

"Not exactly." Her voice was so soft, it was difficult to discern what she was saying; even soft one-worded answers were muffled. Maybe my hearing was damaged. "We're in Belarus," she whispered.

"Minsk?" I offered. She didn't answer. "Is this place a prison?" I asked her.

"Down here, it is...yes, you could call it that, I guess. Although I'd say this is worse than a prison," she said.

"Down here?" I questioned her choice of distinction. She nodded and looked away, clearly nervous to say the wrong thing. "If this is the prison...what's up there?"

She parted her mouth but she shook her head. "Eat something...please," she pleaded. I shut my eyes from the nausea rising in my throat. She tried to prop me up to lean against her and forced the spoon against my bottom lip. I growled and turned my head away.

"Please. Eat...trust me."

I was determined to try to keep up my strength but the thought of her feeding me right now made my stomach turn. I stilled, attempting to reason with myself. Starling tried again.

"They kept me down here for two months. It's the longest anyone's endured."

"Well done." I refused to look at her for too long. The sight of her enraged me, and I kindled that fire. My rage might just be the thing that was keeping me alive.

"I'm not trying to brag. I'm trying to say...I've done everything you are doing. I've refused the food, the water. I starved myself. I tried to drown myself in one of those buckets. I choked myself out with those chains when they thought I was asleep. I cut my wrists against the edge of a can. Eventually, they send someone down with sutures and antibiotics." My eyes fell to her wrists looking for the scars. They were so faint, they were hardly noticeable.

"Weak attempt," I commented, refusing to let compassion muddy my anger.

"No, trust me, I messed myself up pretty bad. The infection that set in gave me a fever. Thing is, as good as they are at hurting, they know how to cover it up just as well. Take it from someone who's been where you are—they don't give a rat's ass about you. You're a commodity now, a property. Don't make it worse on yourself. Take all the comfort they give you with no questions. All that rebellion is only hurting one person—you. They don't care. They got what they needed out of you already. They wouldn't have sent me to feed you otherwise."

Anger still boiled through me but her advice was starting to add up. I sensed she was telling the truth. I was surprised at the softness that remained in her, even after all that.

"How long ago was that?" I asked, still not looking at her. "When you were down here, I mean."

"Two years ago," she answered.

"You've been here for two years?" I repeated in horror. "Here in this place?"

She didn't answer. I realized that she couldn't elaborate. She kept looking up at the video camera in the corner of the room. Someone was watching. A wave of pity rolled through me and I couldn't help but sit up a bit. I opened my mouth for the spoonful of porridge she held, and I finally met her gaze.

She blew on the spoon before delivering it to my mouth with a small smile of triumph.

"What's with the other one? That other girl who was in here with you?"

"Swan?"

"Starling? Swan? I'm guessing these are not your real names?"

Starling shook her head, no.

"Did you choose it?"

She shook her head no, again.

"Right. Well, Swan? She's…" My lips turned down from the memory of her.

"Yeah…she's—"

"A psychopath. She obviously liked it, hurting me," I accused.

"She's intense. I don't think she *likes* it. But she's obsessed with doing well, with pleasing them. This is all she knows. She was raised here," Starling answered in a hushed voice, using the action of feeding me by hand to lean close and whisper her response.

"In Belarus?"

"She was raised *here*." Starling gestured to the ceiling.

My eyes widened. Only knowing the walls of this place and nothing else? How could someone have lived their entire life like this? "What is this place? What's up there? Is the rest of it like this room?"

Starling shrugged, her conflicted expression unreadable. Then, she removed emotion from her face entirely, like a drawbridge that she'd retracted. An eerie blankness was all that remained of the sad, conflicted girl. "When's the last time you spoke with your father?" she asked.

I furrowed my brow at her sudden transition. "I don't know," I answered, slowly. "Why? Do you know him? What did he do to these people?"

"He's stopped cooperating, he's sabotaged the transfer of important merchandise, and now, he's off the grid. That's all I've been told. Has he ever mentioned anything to you about his business? What he was doing in Russia? His plans?" Starling went on. Observing her increasingly tense tone, it was clear that her true objective was to extract information from me..

My suspicions grew but I kept my reaction even and answered simply. "He's an architect."

"Really?" she asked, raising her brows in disbelief.

"Yeah. We never talked about work. He usually just asked me about me and what was happening in my life. I'd ask him how he was doing...like emotionally, how he was feeling, his state of mind, things like that," I answered truthfully, but even if I had known more, I wouldn't have told her a damn thing.

"What about your mother?" she asked. I tensed at the mention of Mama.

"What about my mother?"

"Did your mother ever talk to you about your father's ties in Russia? People he particularly trusted? Any mention of close family friends or even—"

"Why are you asking me this?" I snapped at her, fed up with the bullshit. "Do these people really think I know something about my father that they don't already know? Is that why I'm being tortured in this prison cell? I don't know anything about him. I haven't heard from him in years!"

Starling closed her lips into a tight line and appeared to

deliberate on a new approach. "If you had to guess where he could have gone...for instance, does he have old ties in Stavra—"

"What the hell is this? Are you hard of hearing? I just told you, I don't know anything!" Unable to contain my anger this time, I pushed the next spoon of porridge away and it clattered on the floor. "If they don't know where my father is, then who's the footage for? Why did they need me sobbing and begging for my life?" I nodded to the camera on the wall.

"They may not know where your father is currently hiding, but that doesn't mean they can't send him footage through the dark web. They need footage that'll encourage him to come out of hiding and cooperate sooner rather than later," Starling replied dryly.

I shook my head at Starling incredulously. Just as I had suspected, they hadn't sent her in here to feed me. They sent her in here to butter me up and extract information. And I almost fell for that good cop-bad cop bit they played. "Get the hell away from me. Tell them I don't know shit, they're wasting their time. They need to let me the hell out of here—"

"Mina—"

I was consciously redirecting months of pent-up rage at this girl who wasn't responsible for any of it, and I knew that but I couldn't help myself. "You heard me. I don't know anything" —I turned to look her dead in the eyes and she flinched from the intensity of my glare—"You can tell them that you suck balls at this and that they should let you stick to kicking innocent people chained to a wall. That's all you're good for. Because you're about as subtle as a blunt ax," I bit out in a low tone.

Starling's eyes glossed over to mirror my own. Good. I turned away, curling into a ball against the cold, hard floor. I shut my eyes as Starling moved to go. Her footsteps halted when she reached the far side of the room. "You can use the bucket to do your business," she advised before rolling it closer to me and shutting the door behind her.

The lights went out and everything was swallowed by darkness. There was nothing but mind-numbing silence, the whir of a metallic fan, and the occasional quiet whimper coming from a beast that was once a girl.

CHAPTER 19

OLIVER

"This doesn't feel right, either," I noted.

"Well, what's it supposed to feel like? Oli, you don't look so good. You been sleeping?" Xavi asked, concern furrowing his brow. He had insisted on coming with me to scope out the places on this list of past mob hotspots.

I shook my head, then nodded. "I'm fine. I feel good."

Xavi and I had just finished looking around the first floor of the third motel we'd visited on his list. The truth was, I was fighting a raging headache with nothing but water and air, and last night, I'd only managed about an hour and a half of sleep, tops. But we'd had no success so far. I couldn't stop now. It's not like I could sleep anyway.

The first location was nothing but a construction zone. The motel once standing there had been leveled. We found nothing but tweakers and low-level dealers at the second one—no one recognized Mina or admitted knowing anything about the Russians.

We started with the locations closest to Mr. Wright's work

address, and this was the third we'd seen so far. Based on the camera footage, I decided we should focus on the valley.

I stared at the pages Mr. Wright had handed over to me in the parking lot of his office.

"All right, let's go to the next one," Xavi suggested.

"No, wait…let me talk to that guy up there," I replied.

"That guy? Come on, Oliver, that guy looks like trouble."

"Doesn't matter. Gotta try," I insisted, moving around Xavi.

Xavi blocked my path but I maneuvered past him and climbed the stairs to the second floor, making my way toward a filthy man in a torn pink beanie who was mumbling aloud to himself while gripping the balcony rail. As I drew nearer, I noticed he was fiddling with a broken skeleton doll tied around his neck and hissing curses at it.

"Oli…" Xavi called after me but I continued my approach toward the tweaked-out scarecrow of a man. His clothes were soiled and torn. He had a wild look in his eye and couldn't seem to focus on a single point. A pang of sympathy for this poor soul rang through me. He was pacing a triangle between two rooms and the balcony rail. The shades on the rooms were drawn but muffled sounds came from inside.

"Excuse me, can I ask you—" I began as the man whipped around to face me, fixing me with an unblinking glare. He whipped around again to check if anyone stood behind him before turning back to me. He performed this paranoid little dance over and over, mumbling something incoherent under his breath.

"Have you seen this girl anywhere?" I pulled out Mina's photo on my phone and turned it toward him.

"Try me! Try me!" he screamed and yanked a makeshift shank out of his back pocket just as Xavi reached me.

"Oli…" Xavi cautioned. "This guy's not in his right mind. Let's just leave him alone."

"This girl is missing. Have you seen her? Please…" I pleaded.

He lowered his duct-taped, wood and glass shank and took a step toward my phone. My heart sang hopefully when his frantic gaze finally focused on her photo. I zoomed in closer so he could get a better look at her features.

"*Mmmhhh*," he moaned. His gaze dropped to the floor then the wall then the upper corner of the roof then back to the floor. "Yeah...yeah, I seen her. Yum-yum. I can tell you. You got a bump? I'll tell you if you got a bump."

"Oli...he's a junkie," Xavi said in my ear, pulling me back toward him. "He'll say anything for a hit."

"You seen her or not?" I bit out in desperate frustration.

"Yeah, yeah. Yeah. You got a bump?"

"Oli..." Xavi warned.

"Maybe he's seen her?" I reasoned. "It's not impossible."

"Oli, bro, look at him...this guy wouldn't recognize his own mother. And even if he did, he'd sell her for a hit," Xavi muttered beneath his breath.

The sound of clattering shutters drew my attention to the window of the room marked 2B. Someone was watching us behind them. After a few moments, the gap in the shutters closed again. I turned my attention back to the junkie. He was pacing side to side, pulling coins from his pocket and counting them. I took out a twenty and held it up.

"Hey," I called out. He jerked his head in my direction. "I'll give you this..."—I said, waving the twenty—"...after you tell me where you saw this girl. Tell me everything you know and you can have this. "I pocketed the twenty and waited for his response. His eyes went wide, tracing my head movement to my right pocket.

His eyes didn't leave my pocket as he said,

"I saw yum-yum. I saw yum-yum." His eyes were still wide and trained on my pocket.

"You saw Mina? Where did you see her?"

"Down..."

"Down where?" I tried to get him to look at me. I shifted my hips away from his eyesight and tilted my neck to the side to catch his gaze. "Down where?" I repeated, fury starting to bubble in my gut.

"By the river," he muttered, nodding in the direction behind me.

I turned to Xavi. "You know if there's a river around here?"

"Oli…"

"Is there a river or not?"

"It's not a river, I think there's an underpass but—"

I turned back to the man. "When did you see her?"

"By the river—"

"When did you see her? Today?"

"Ughh…maybe two days. Not yesterday but ya…yahhhh, by the river. Three days ago. No. Yeah, yum-yum. Saw her two days ago." He nodded up and down frantically and my stomach sank. Xavi had been right, this tweaker would say anything to get his fix. My eyes grew cold, flinty. I took a step toward the junkie, who jumped back and whipped his shank up toward my face.

"Oli…what are you—"

"Give it to me!" the junkie yelled, frantically swiping through the air with his blade. "You said-you said!" he accused.

I pulled out the twenty and threw it at him. "Take it!" I bellowed. I turned and led Xavi back down the stairs to the first floor as the junkie banged on the door to one of the rooms in a frenzy, releasing a cackle of glee.

Heat flushed through my body as I marched down the final steps toward the street level. I peered into every window of every room on the first floor of the motel. *What a dump.* The open windows were vacant, and the rooms carried a potent odor of mold and something putrid. The occupied rooms had their shutters closed.

"Mina!" I cried out in a desperate attempt to get answers.

"I'm no narc! I earned this. I earned it!" The junkie's incessant knocks turned into shouts, the racket drifting down from the second floor.

"What the hell?" Xavi looked up at the balcony over our heads and I followed his gaze. "Didn't I tell you not to bother with him?" The junkie's back hit the balcony rail and he scrambled to the end of the hall. From the sounds of it, he was trying to score and they weren't selling. The sound of heavy footsteps making their way across the hall and down the stairs set my nerves on edge.

"We should get out of here," Xavi urged. I knew he was right but I wasn't ready to give up just yet.

"You go. I'll keep looking," I insisted. He didn't argue. I turned and started checking the windows again. I was looking around for an office or someone to talk to when I noticed Xavi unlocking the van and getting in. It was parked by a meter on the street.

Click-click. I froze at the sound of a round being chambered. As I headed toward the stairs, two men made their way down to meet me. One was bald and pot-bellied, while the other was short and bearded. The short one was looking around for who I was with and the bald one aimed his Glock at my head. I threw my hands up, palms open.

"Whoa, hold on," I stammered. "Hold on!

"Where's the other one?" the bearded man questioned. I didn't dare look toward Xavi out by the van on the street.

"What do you want?" I asked, urging calm into my voice.

"Why you up in here asking questions, giving out twenties?" said the bald one, waving the Glock around in my direction. The two men were adorned with tattoos, but the most prominent ones were skull and blade designs.

"What in the hell? Put that shit down!" I urged, growing more wired by the second at having a gun trained on me.

"I asked you a question!" the thug repeated.

"I'm looking for my friend. That's it. I was asking around if anyone had seen her."

"You with the police?"

"No. Now, can you please just lower the gun?"

"Who was that—who was with you? Was he a narc?" asked the bearded man.

"Easy...easy," came a voice from behind the bald one with the Glock, startling him. In less than a few seconds, Xavi disarmed him and had him in a chokehold. Xavi held the man's own gun to his temple. I felt my heart racing at the thought of how badly things could have turned out.

"Yo-what the—" The bearded one pulled out a switchblade from his pocket and held it out, making a move toward me. I jumped back. He used me to shield himself from the Glock that was now under Xavi's control.

"Stop...hold up, you got this all mixed up. We don't want trouble," Xavi assured with firm authority. His grip on the gun and the guy was unwavering. The bearded man slowed his frantic movement, blade still at the ready, unsure what to do next.

"We're just looking for a girl, that's all. Have you seen her?" I held up my phone toward the men with Mina's picture pulled up.

The bearded one with the blade glanced at my phone a few times before returning his focus to Xavi, who still held a gun to the bald one's head. The bald one spat out, "Naw, we haven't seen no one like that round here."

"You sure? Take a better look," I insisted and moved toward him.

"Yo, I'm about to slice you to pieces if you come at me, narc," the bearded one threatened.

"I'm not a narc. We need to find my friend. That's all," I insisted, hands still raised in submission.

"I said: we ain't seen her. Now, get!" the bald one repeated.

"Come on, Oliver," Xavi urged. He shoved the bald one with enough force to make him stumble to the ground. Xavi grabbed onto my shirt sleeve and tugged. The bearded one still aimed his blade in our direction as we backed away toward the van.

"We're gone," Xavi ensured them, gun still raised. A middle-aged woman passing by with a young boy shrieked at the sight of the standoff and ran in the opposite direction. We were drawing attention, now. We were almost at the van when Xavi lowered the gun entirely. He and I jumped in.

"Hold up," Xavi exclaimed as he wiped down the Glock with the bottom of his shirt, lowered his window, and dumped the gun.

"Don't come back around here!" the bald one called out to us in warning, rediscovering his voice. "Next time I see either of you, you're clipped." With that, Xavi and I sped away. Trembling, he rested his hands on his legs while I gripped the wheel with shaky hands.

"All right, what's next?" I asked, after several moments of silence, as if neither of us had just been confronted at gunpoint.

"Oli, I think it's important that we keep a low profile while we do this."

"I get what you're saying," I told him, pocketing the list. "But when I show up at these places, my heart starts jackhammering and I just picture her out there somewhere in one of these rooms, scared. And it brings out this rage in me. I just don't want to miss my shot at finding her by being quiet or scared."

"I really hope we find your girl, but we can't go getting ourselves killed by being reckless. We gotta be smart."

"It's hard to be smart when you're desperate," I noted. Xavi's frown deepened. "I'll try," I amended, tightening my grip on the wheel.

CHAPTER 20

 **MINA**

As hard as I had tried, I had found no way of tracking time. It could have been days since Starling had been in to feed me. A week, even. It felt like it. My screams for water, for food, for light had been unanswered at first—met with radio silence. Only when I was too weak to lift my head did they scrape cold soup and stale bread across the floor toward me on a metallic tray.

I was filthy, and my skin itched. The bucket that I had managed to drag over with my foot carried a putrid stench, and I kept it as far from me as I could while still within the chain's reach.

One October, you could be scooping out pumpkin seeds, planting a rubber spider in your best friend's shoe, staying up all night for a horror movie marathon while stuffing your face with popcorn dressed up as your favorite Tim Burton character —and the next October, you could be chained to a wall in a bitterly cold concrete cell, terrified out of your mind, writhing in agony, going through every mental riddle, rhyme, and mathematical equation you can recall, just to stay sane. You could be so far gone that it seemed reasonable to leave scratches over your arms in a weak attempt at keeping time.

You could be so desperate to move that even through the nearly unbearable pain in your destroyed ribs, you push through sit-ups, push-ups, and leg lifts—just to stay sane, to stay warm, to keep feeling like a person. And despite your resolve, you could slowly be losing grip on the very slippery sliver of hope sliding down a grate in the slimy subway that's now your soul.

Time sneered at me like it was playing a cruel little joke. In here, time seemed to stand still, only each passing meal, each additional repetitive motion, the clanking of chains to mark it here, then gone.

Out there, it was speeding by, forgetting me. Life was rushing past, moving on and I couldn't hold it, not for one second. I couldn't breathe. I was suffocating—crushed under the panic of the fact that my life as I had known it might well be over.

How much time had passed? I thought instinctually it was October, but it could just have easily been December. It probably was. The new year could have come and gone and I wouldn't have known—couldn't have felt it.

The lights came on without warning, blinding me for several moments. I shut my eyes, then blinked rapidly to adjust to the glare as the clanking of the door and the echo of shoes against the cement drew nearer. A dark figure trained something on me, a weapon in the shape of a firearm.

Facing the barrel of a gun—even through hazy vision after eons of darkness...was a gift. I was overcome by grief over things that hadn't happened, experiences I hadn't felt, places unseen, foods and sounds unknown, dreams unrealized. I saw my future unborn children, my grandchildren, the crooked smile of a stranger on the subway, the smell of fresh lavash baked in clay ovens in the ground as I strolled through a village market. I could hear the songs of the sparrows that were perched in cherry blossoms by a pond. I couldn't face the unending dark, the fear of what came after. The fear of the nothingness.

This wasn't the first time my life had hung in the balance of a trigger squeeze, and it very likely wouldn't be the last. Melancholy washed over me like a draft in the winter and then, a flash flood of anger took everything in its path.

Lilia Arkova's death is on your hands. The words had been replaying in my mind since they first sliced through my eardrums—a curse, wearing away at my sanity like water at stone. Rage burned through me, unrestrained. I unleashed it, thoughtlessly, on the only person I could, despite the weapon trained on me.

"If you don't show me..."—My unused voice cracked through the patched Russian syllables—"...my mother right the hell now, and if she isn't on the road to a full recovery, I swear..."—I growled—"...I will kill every last one of you sons of bitches." My voice was hoarse and broken. My vision swam. The figure crossed the room fuzzed at the edges.

"Zapisivai!" he barked, instructing someone to start recording. After several moments, a guard rushed into the room and opened the laptop on the stool. The red light on the camera began blinking, sending my heart to thrash wildly against my chest. Too soon, it was too soon. I wasn't ready—I hadn't healed from the last beating. Something inside me was already broken. Time—I needed more time.

I remembered the pain in my mother's eyes on the stairs of our home after the attack she had endured—the pain she was trying to hide from me, to protect me from. I drew on that strength. "Please, just tell me. Tell me something. Tell me she's alive. Tell me she's—"

"*Zatknis*," the voice hissed at me to shut my mouth. A sharp, crackling pain shot through me. Before I understood what had happened, I hit the floor, convulsing in spasms, one after another. The shocks had me clutching my stomach, curling in on myself.

The shocks passed and I lay, motionless, but the residual spasms rocked through me soundlessly. Moisture pooled at the bridge of my nose before overflowing to the floor. I sensed a warmer kind of dampness flowing between my legs, urine.

I didn't utter a sound. The room was filled with a strange echo. The voice spoke again.

"Mina Nikolaevna Arkova," a male voice pronounced. A distinct chuckle filled the room and triggered a dormant misophonia that I hadn't sensed in years. The sound grated against my eardrums, my spine. It got beneath my fingernails. The passive, repetitive tone was unnerving but a silent promise of violence thrummed in my veins.

Whoever he was, he was amused—bastard. I squinted to make out the face. "I've come to congratulate you on your last performance," the voice cooed in Russian. "Very effective. We go further, just in case."

"I-in c-case?" I stuttered through the sounds, my tongue clumsy, swollen.

"In case he loses his way again. You'll likely be upstairs by then and we don't want to waste time rehabilitating you twice, do we? Easier to pre-record some fresh material. More efficient this way, we learned from past mistakes."

My vision was clearing. I could now make out the man. A sneer twisted his lips. His black and silver hair was slicked back, greasy and flaked at the roots. His piercing eyes were colorless. "I was worried you had some kind of congenital insensitivity to pain. I didn't want to have to start removing body parts so soon.

They don't like when I send cripples upstairs, too distinguish-able. We have to pace these things out. You're a very tough nut to crack."

He was tall, slender. He wore a sharp suit. His cheekbones and jaw were pronounced. Everything about him—his hair, his shoes, his forehead—looked wet, slick. Slick's nostrils gave him a reptilian air.

My voice was barely audible but I pushed the sounds through, "Do you have a daughter? What if someone was doing this to her?" I rasped but my words were slurred. My mouth felt as though it were filled with cotton, like my tongue had been inflated to three times its normal size. I waited for him to say something. He gave nothing—just cold ambivalence. This filth was incapable of empathy.

I tried again.

"I c-could getta loan...I'm supposed to go to u-university...if it's about m-money, I c-can figure something out...I c-can s-send m-money." His mouth grew wider into an eerie grin. Slick pulled a mask over his face and drew closer, kneeling beside me. I tried to move as far away as I could but only managed the slow scuffle of an emaciated prey. A faint whimper fell from me as I shrank away.

He cocked his head to the side. "*Shh. Shh-shh-shh.* You're clever. I'll make sure they know just how clever you are. Strong, too. That kick to Swan's face...*whoo*—she did not see that coming. Too bad, really, that I had to edit it out of the movie—clearly untrained but so much potential..."

He trailed his gloved hand up my leg. I shuddered, jerking away. He went on. "I'll pass it along, your potential. I'll send word to the top of the chain, if you cooperate. But about your demands...you should know, this..."—he gestured to the cell and continued in Russian—"...is not my call. I just film the scenes and cut them together. I'm not the movie producer. I'm a minuscule component in an unstoppable machine. If I don't function properly, they replace me, like a broken cog. They instruct, I obey. So, save your demands and threats for the top of the chain. If you want my advice, though, accept your new reality. It'll be so much easier for you that way," he purred in Russian. He was slimy. I wouldn't trust a word from this snake.

He continued toying with my shin through his glove and I had run out of space to recoil. "Why me?" I bit out, words slurring but clearer than before. I was desperate to distract him from touching me. "He doesn't even c-care about me. C-can't you tell? My father and I haven't seen each other in years. He cares only about himself, so, if they want 'cooperation,' they should just take *him*."

It came out as harsh as a swear.

"Bet you they'd get everything they wanted out of him, real quick," I gritted. Shame washed over me at the sound of the words that dripped from my mouth with venom for my father that had started brewing somewhere deep within the instant I first saw Mama in the hospital bed. I didn't realize how potent that venom had become.

"Such a lovely little dove with a beak sharp as a blade. It's understandable, your hate." His eyes lit up with the word. "Young person, I have a lifetime of experience extracting the precise emotion that I need from different kinds of people. Every case is unique, of course. Each human experiences and expresses pain in their own beautiful way." He caressed my cheek like he was recalling a treasured memory. I jerked my face away. "One thing always remained the same after decades of observation—threatening the person's life never works quite as effectively as a threat to the lives of their loved ones, especially lives of innocents," he said, his cold eyes reflecting the clinical lights overhead.

"Besides, they need your Papa to perform a task. He can't very well do that while being chained down here. Can he? Trust me..."—He patted the back of my knee and I flinched—"...Papa's

properly motivated and I'm confident he'll continue to cooperate without hesitation." His lips spread thinly into a grotesque
grin. "Especially if he ever has to see the tape we're about to
make." My pulse quickened at the threat. I was going to be sick.

"This time..."—he hissed—"...let's get you there faster. And
don't hold anything back. Give me everything—really show us
what it feels like. I know you're a strong girl and that's good.
Useful, up there, but not in here. In here, give me all the drama.
Yes?" His mouth widened into that same disturbing grin that
didn't reach his eyes.

I wished I could claw his glowing eyes out with my fingernails. He moved to grab me and panic shot through me, my
hands restrained, unable to stop him. Before I could stop myself
and think it through, I did what I had done to Mikhailov—all I
could do—I filled my mouth with the loathing I'd been carrying
trapped down here like a rat. I unleashed a stream of spit onto
his face.

Regret shot through me like adrenaline. But I had acted on
instinct and nothing could have stopped it. I winced, preparing
for the blow in response, awaiting it, preferring it to electrocution. I'd been conditioned, I realized. Somehow, I was already
convinced that I deserved the punishment. I welcomed it, but
nothing came.

Slick's eyes narrowed into slits and in a blur, he shot
forward, leaning in so close that I could see the bubbles in my
own spit as the blob slid down the side of his face.

"Bad. Very bad," he barked out. He glared at me with a
haunting grimace. His chest was heaving with audible exhales. I
couldn't begin to guess what he'd do to me for this. Slick
produced a handkerchief from his jacket pocket and wiped the
spit from his face. Without pause, he forced my jaw open by my
bottom teeth and shoved the handkerchief into my mouth. I
gagged as soon as the fabric touched the back of my throat. I

lurched forward but he held me up against the wall by my shoulders.

I tried to push the handkerchief out of my mouth with my tongue, but he placed his palm over my mouth, sending tears to my eyes. He leaned in to whisper in my ear as I choked on the fabric—convulsing in waves—his body flush against mine as we knelt.

The mind-splitting pain in my ribs was fighting for attention against my need to clear my airway. I didn't know which was more urgent.

He let go of me and yanked the handkerchief out. I gasped, starved for air.

"I am a mere cog, yes. But—" Slick enunciated each Russian word with sharp exaggeration as he stroked his fingers down my ribs. "I'm not a cog that you want to disappoint. After all, I am in charge of your torture, little dove," he hissed against my ear as his hand rubbed roughly against my ribs.

I tensed and pushed back against him. His nails dug deeper into my skin. My whimpers turned into screams and screams turned into gurgles. My heart sank deeper into my already broken core.

CHAPTER 21

OLIVER

"Yo, Oli...you look like shit, bro," Xavi commented at me from the open bathroom.

"Thanks, Xav," I called back from my place on the couch.

"Yo...I'm starting to look like shit, too. If you keep screaming every night like these past few weeks, we're both gonna be walking around like the undead." Xavi was wiping steam off the bathroom mirror and leaning in to look at his face.

"You're pretty enough," I joked.

"How long have these nightmares of yours been going on?" Xavi leaned against the frame of the bathroom door and crossed his arms.

"It used to happen a lot when I was younger but hasn't happened in a while," I managed. Xavi nodded. He understood why. He turned and knelt to collect something up off the floor. It was the list of addresses from Nyah's dad. Xavi shuffled through the pages with his eyebrows raised. The list must have fallen out of my jeans when I was in the shower.

"I've been trying to come up with a way to narrow this list down."

"Most of these are crossed off. You haven't been going without me...have you?" Xavi asked, frustration lacing his tone.

"I haven't been able to narrow the list down enough," I deflected. "The surveillance footage all suggests they went north and that's all I've got for now. That and some BS online forums where people run their mouths about places you can get drugs and pick up working girls. But none of those places were on this list so far."

"Yeah, I've been meaning to ask, where did you get this list? You never said." He studied me, folding the list back up.

I chewed on the inside of my cheek. "Not really supposed to say, but the source is legit," I replied as I typed out a text to CJ, my exporter.

> yo, sri i've been MIA...when can we meet?

"How have you really been holding up, man?" Xavi asked me, cautiously, watching me watch my phone for a response from CJ. "No bullshit. Just be straight with me."

"Yeah...no, I know I've been..." I trailed off, ruffling my hair, which was wilder than usual. "I'm sorry my nightmares have been keeping you up, too."

"Naw, don't get me wrong...don't be sorry, I'm not complaining. Me? I'm fine. I've slept on the streets, Oli. A little screaming is nothing, brother. I'm grateful for you, trust me. I'm just worried about you. It's not just the dreams. I don't think I've seen you eat much of anything lately. You gotta keep your energy up somehow if you're gonna keep going like this. Here, let me make something for you right now—"

Xavi moved toward the kitchen.

"Don't worry about me. I'm fine."

"I dunno...you don't look fine." Xavi opened random doors

of our cupboard. "Yo...where's the pasta?" he asked, rummaging through a snack drawer.

"It's fine, just toss me one of those cheddar cheese things," I deflected again.

"You can't just keep eating chips all day. Do you have any pasta or noodles or like, I dunno, rice or anything?" he asked.

"I usually order food, not cook it," I confessed, scratching my neck.

"Yeah...nope, nothing here but protein bars. Listen, we should do a quick shopping trip. It'll save us so much money on food if we stop eating out twice a day. You know I used to work in a kitchen—"

"All right, calm down, Wolfgang Puck," I joked, leaving out the part about how pots can trigger memories of Jack Burns' foster home, and that's why I avoid it when I can—cooking anything I used to make there.

I had been the oldest in the Burns' home, so he had me cook for the younger ones. If I didn't cook, they didn't eat. He allowed me out to shop for food, but it was so seldom that I had to ration the produce. It could be a month until I'd manage to convince him to let me go buy something. He ate fast food for breakfast, lunch and dinner and he licked every plate clean. Only thing left was the bag and the paper napkins.

In the bad months, I'd go around the restaurants and beg for leftovers or the expired stuff. When things were really desperate, I'd steal some potatoes or rice from a store. Once I stole a chicken and my balls nearly froze off from the chill when I hid the frozen bird in my pants. I learned to get creative and turn rotten rations into soup. The soups would last longer than anything else I could think of making, and it fed all the mouths.

These days, I couldn't look at soup the same way again and would avoid anything that reminded me of it...including pots.

"I'm good," I pressed, putting an end to the discussion. But Xavi was right. I was far from good. My head was killing me and my body was operating on diminished reserves. I needed answers that I couldn't get on my own. I needed help and all my hopes were currently pinned on CJ. He was the only connection still talking to me after the raid on my storage unit. As I had anticipated, Tee and Mo were lying low and had shut me out. Word must have gone round about the raid because all my old connects were icing me out and business was slow, too slow.

My phone buzzed with a message from CJ. I read it in a hurry.

CJ

> I can meet up later tonight, come by warehouse...how many units u got for me?

My stomach sank. I had nothing for him but he wouldn't meet me for less than thirty units of product. I'd have to figure something out. I replied.

> 30

CJ

> y so few?

> I've been dealing with some fallout.

CJ

> fine wanna talk to u anyway...come through @ 9

I looked up from my phone at Xavi, who was playing music off a laptop on the couch. I walked over to find him listing product online and cataloging costs.

"Where'd you get this laptop?"

"School," he answered without looking up.

"School? What school?"

"I rented it from college."

"You go to college?" I asked, surprised by the new information.

"Yeah...I enrolled thanks to you, actually," he said with a smirk. "Figured since I'm always on the computer now anyway, and I cut most of my shifts at the dojo to work with you...I dunno, might as well get a degree. Right? You said that I should? Remember? Almost all of my classes are online—"

"I'm glad. I just—I didn't know. What's this playlist?"

"You like it?" he asked, his eyes lighting up in excitement.

"Yeah, I do," I answered. "What is this?"

"It's my mix! It's R.E.M.'s 'Losing My Religion' mixed EDM style with Gregorian chant vocals. You really dig it?"

"Hell yes. It's insanely good."

"I used to DJ. You want me to send you some tracks?"

"Of course. Wait, you were a cook, you DJ'ed? What *didn't* you do?"

"Yeah, oh man, I had so many unfinished mixes on my old laptop, but it got jacked last year. I'm trying to remember some of my ideas. I wish I just uploaded them somewhere."

"What are you studying in school?" I asked him.

"Programming, but I'm in it for the perks. Get to borrow this baby," he chuckled, shaking the laptop, making it do a little shimmy.

"That's great..." I trailed off, my thoughts running away from me.

"So...what's the plan, boss?" Xavi asked. "Oliver?"

"Hmm?" I responded, still thinking about college and how derailed all my plans had become.

"What are we doing after this? I'm almost done listing these. I'm gonna enter the costs next, and cross reference with our general workbook numbers, but I can already tell just by looking at this that we're not cutting it this month...the rent and car payment alone—Oli, my man, you don't wanna get evicted from the storage unit and the guesthouse and lose the car…something's gotta give—"

"Yeah…no, I know. I'm on it. I've been distracted but I just need to get my hands on thirty units for CJ by tonight…then, I'll focus on covering rent and the van," I assured him.

"Thirty units? Oli…where're you gonna get thirty units by tonight? There's no way. We don't have the funds."

"Didn't we just get a disbursement?" I argued.

"Well…yeah, but that's going out again to the distro tomorrow for our allocation on the s9s, m6s and the 255Ss."

"Oh…well, we have terms, just push it—email Gavin—"

"I don't think that's a good idea, Oli. We fought for the allocation. If we push terms, they won't give us the units next time…they'll just allocate to someone else."

"No one moves these units like we do, and CJ will wire me tonight," I reasoned, growing tired of explaining myself.

"It'll still be a loss—no one has those units for the prices he's buying at right now," Xavi argued.

"How do you know?" I asked.

"I checked for you yesterday…remember?" Xavi said, confusion over my question furrowing his brows.

"That's right," I feigned recalling. "Either way…it's gotta happen." I wasn't budging on this. I needed to talk to CJ.

"All right…but you're just digging a bigger hole. Why do you need to mess with CJ right now? Just wait on it—" Xavi argued.

"Don't tell me how to run my business, Xavi. I have to make that sale, okay? I just do. Either put two and two together or leave it alone," I snapped, exasperated at being backed into this corner.

"Damn, tell me how you really feel," Xavi joked, but the smile didn't reach his eyes. Xavi averted his gaze from me, clearly dejected by my outburst.

"Sorry," I muttered. "Where's the list?" I checked the bathroom for it but it wasn't there. I checked the kitchen next; it wasn't there either. I checked the cupboard, the counter. I even checked the fridge in my panic.

"I dunno...it's around here somewhere. Maybe on the counter?"

"It's not here, Xavi—you were just looking at it! Where the hell did it go?" I couldn't breathe. My throat was closing up.

"Relax, dude. It's here," he assured, looking around the floor, on the couch, and under the pillows. "Oh, shit, see...here! I was sitting on it...my bad."

"Give it to me," I snapped. "Is that all of it? All the pages?"

"Yeah, I think so," he muttered.

"You sure?"

"Jesus, yeah...I'm pretty sure. Calm down. If it matters so much to you, make a copy," he suggested while shaking his head at my outburst. I wasn't proud of it and he was absolutely on point. How had I been so stupid not to take photos of the pages?

I admonished myself and immediately laid the pages out on the floor to take snapshots of them with my phone.

"All right, I'm gonna head out," I told him, my mind still running through possible gaps that I might have missed in my search for Mina. I was beginning to question my ability to reason and think clearly. Maybe I was biting myself in the ass by not sleeping, and that was hurting the search more than it was helping. Maybe I needed to start seeing a therapist. Again.

"I'm going with you," he insisted.

"No...stay. Finish listing those units. It's important."

"I'm finished listing," he insisted before shutting the laptop and impressing me into silence. "I'm going with you." It wasn't a question. I nodded my response, not realizing how much I needed to hear those words until the weight on my chest lifted a fraction. Four simple words and suddenly, I wasn't suffocating in isolation anymore.

CHAPTER 22

MINA

I couldn't remember what light had felt like but I had come to accept the lack of it. I preferred the darkness, where my mind wandered freely without the constraint of sight. I'd been living in darkness so long that I could make out the shape of my legs without truly seeing them. I never stopped moving—sit-ups, crunches, pushups, whatever I could manage—even on the worst days, through the worst pain. If I could manage two and collapse, I would. Lately, I'd been having a hard time breathing. I did do half a crunch before I collapsed, and I finished the exercise in my mind. Those, I would never stop—the mental crunches.

Oliver's train leaves the station one hour after Mina's train but Oliver's train travels 20 mph faster than Mina's train. Oliver is on an express train. If Oliver's train catches up to Mina's train in 2 hours, what is the speed of each train? Let x be the speed of Mina's train and y be the speed of Oliver's train. Speed is distance over time. The distance traveled is equal when Oliver's train catches up with Mina's train.

$$y=x+20$$
$$s=d/t$$
$$d=s(t)$$
$$x(3)=y(2)$$
$$3x=2y$$
$$3x=2(x+20)$$

Mina was traveling 40 mph and Oliver was traveling 60 mph. Mina would see Oliver through the window of the train for a fleeting moment and then he'd be gone. Mina's train would get derailed. The moment, however brief, would change the trajectory of Mina's path in a way she wouldn't understand until eighty-seven thousand, six hundred hours had passed.

Euler's identity said that the base of natural logarithms to the power of the imaginary unit multiplied by pi plus one was equal to zero. It was deemed the most beautiful equation ever written. It wasn't. The most beautiful equation ever written would be the one that optimized a path from negative infinity to infinity where P, pain, approached zero. It was being written in my mind—my mind, the one that was nearly lost.

I kept track of time with meals. First, the lights went on, then I'd shut my eyes to let them adjust, and finally, a masked person would come in carrying a metal tray with the lukewarm mush of the day and a piece of stale bread. I had been brought fifteen trays since Slick had been here. Sixteen days could have passed or it could have been a week. It could also have been less, but less would have meant three meals a day, and my vacant stomach told me that figure was unlikely.

When a mask (because I'd started thinking of them as masks, not people) walked in with my seventeenth meal, something came over me. A whisper that turned into a thought that turned into an idea that turned into an urge—an urge that turned violent. I grabbed the old tray that lay at my feet and I jammed its edge with all my might into a lateral hit to the knee. There was an ugly crunch and the mask crashed to the floor. The voice behind the mask cried out in pain. I didn't think I had the strength to really hurt anyone.

"I'm sorry," I whispered as the mask scrambled to their feet and roared from the agony of their injured leg. The mask whipped around toward the cameras in a panic before quickly turning back to yank the old tray out of my weakened grip. Mask now askew, they limped away, fell, clambered back to their feet, and continued limping.

My breaths grew short and quick. Soon, two more masks filed into the room. One of them pulled a breathing apparatus over my head and fastened it around my neck while the other held my arms still and barked orders at me.

"Stand! Hands on the wall. Don't move."

"How long?" I asked, yanking my body from their grip.

"Don't move," snarled the one holding me. I prepared to fight, but seconds later, my hands were bound by the chain I wore and the air holes on the gas mask they'd sealed me in were covered. I was suffocating. My chest tightened until it burned so badly that I collapsed to the floor. The rag covering the air supply to my mask was removed.

Time was slipping—I was trying to hold on but I had fallen into a vacuum. The walls of my mind were closing in on all sides and I was bolted down as water poured in all around me. I knew I'd drown in my own mind.

The gas mask was pulled off my head. The back of my head hit concrete. Two masks looked down at me. I tucked into myself, covered my head, and shut my eyes. Instead of beating me, the two masks worked on freeing me of my chains.

A sliver of hope tinged with skepticism glinted in my mind, deluding me into believing that this could be the moment of my release. Something heavy scraped against the concrete floor down the hall. I watched in horror as a third and fourth mask approached, dragging a bulky wooden plank behind them.

They are going to beat me with this plank of wood until there is nothing left of me but a pile of flesh and guts, I thought. A hard shock of fear ran through my system. I winced and dug my heels into the floor as hands dragged me forward after my hobbled attempts to resist had failed. I kicked and fought and screamed as they dragged me closer to the camera, closer to the plank of wood.

They dropped me to my knees and I caught myself from hitting my face against the floor. I felt a boot on my back and the plank shortly after. Hands groped my elbows and wrists, forcing my arms over the plank and the plank under my armpits. My wrists were knotted together, as were my ankles. They tied my hands to my feet behind my back over the plank of wood.

A cry tore through me, all breath and bile. The bite of the ropes was punishing but compared to the ache in my muscles, it was a tickle.

I lifted my head, rotated my body to look into their eyes to find something distinct under those masks, to say: *I see you, I'm watching you, I'm witnessing you be this beast.*

I locked eyes with one in particular. There were two small moles under her lash line. Evidently, she didn't like being seen, because she rotated her face away until I couldn't look into the eyeholes of her mask.

I wanted to lunge at them, to claw their eyes out.

I wanted to know if the blue-eyed girl from before—Swan— was in the room right now, enjoying herself, but a gnawing pang ate into the muscles of my legs and again, I was gone, there was only pain. Pain moving toward infinity.

I'd been wrong. I began wishing for blows to the stomach instead of this. *Hit me. Break me.* At least that was something concrete—something definite, something with a beginning, a climax, and an end. This was unbearable. I'd be reduced to a useless pile of gelatin.

In a room that had been barbarically cold, I was soaked in

sweat and tears within minutes. I wanted it to end. I wanted life to finish.

"P-please..." I shook, pushing to get the words out like two-ton boulders off a cliff. "J-just k-kill me."

Ropes were cut and my limbs unraveled to the floor like an unbound stack of toothpicks. There was a blessed relief as the worst of the pain ebbed. Was this what they'd wanted all along? For me to ask for death?

The last thing I felt before drifting away completely were my chains suddenly returned. The room fell away as I slipped into darkness with eager anticipation—my beloved darkness, where I knew I'd see him. I summoned him toward me. Where the chains had wrapped around my wrists, Oliver's fingers were now.

You're here, I spoke in my mind but I knew he heard me because he answered aloud.

"Of course, I'm here. This was my idea. You are so deceiving, by the way," he said, smiling his crooked smile. His luminous eyes lit up as he spoke. "You pretend that you're this dainty little thing. 'I'm terrible at climbing...my arms are weak.' But here you are, moving like a mountain lion," he chuckled lightly.

Oliver was breathing heavily, sweat glistened off his chest, and the sun was at its peak overhead. We were surrounded by trees and wilderness, climbing up the side of a daunting cliff.

Oliver jumped from one boulder to the next and I followed. Soon, he began to ascend a steeper cliff side. I looked across the expanse and realized it was the left abutment of a dam. I followed him closely, growing less confident in my ability to keep up. I grabbed the rocky boulders for support but they were scorching hot from the sun.

My foot slipped. My kneecap smashed into a jagged boulder. I dug my fingernails into the rock, struggling to hold on.

"Wait!" I cried.

"There's water at the top, we can cool off." He smiled down at me, not worried in the slightest. "You good?"

"Yeah." And I was. As long as we kept going, I was confident I could get through. The tips of my fingers were burning from the heat of the boulders but I pushed on, not looking back, not looking up. Not until I sensed Oliver slow down ahead. We'd reached the top of the dam.

Oliver climbed up onto the ledge of the dam and offered his hand to pull me up alongside him. I shook my head, not taking his hand and risking throwing his balance off. I climbed onto the ledge on my own.

I slowly straightened from a crouch to standing and turned to survey the lagoon awaiting us on the other side of the dam wall. An expansive 100-foot spillway divided the lagoon from the rocky creek, 100 feet below, and we were balanced on the ledge of that divide. One misstep meant certain death. Oliver shuffled farther down along the ledge.

"It's beautiful," Oliver remarked, his eyes scanning the wild expanse.

"And terrifying," I added, eyeing the drop. Oliver reached his fingers out to me. I considered crouching back and lowering myself into the lagoon, the water so secure and tempting, glistening under the light of the sun, gem-like and luminous. I changed my mind and shuffled close enough to reach Oliver's outstretched fingers with my own, closing the distance between us with one gentle touch.

Gone were the fear of the 100-foot death drop inches away and all the rest of my reservations. Oliver was in focus and everything else was fading away. He parted his lips to say something, but hesitated, and as my eyes drifted down to his mouth, he seemed to swallow the words.

Oliver laced the length of his fingers through mine, locking them into a tight embrace and using the leverage of his hold to pull the rest of me against him. I inched forward, deliberately slow, resistant but permissive until the only way further was to merge.

But before I could press my open mouth against his soft, slackened lips and melt into Oliver fully, like oozing, molten lava, before I could even tilt my head forward, I felt it—him— speaking in my mind. The reverberation was like a caress of sound.

"I need you." The rough timbre of his voice echoed in my mind. An energy that traveled down through me, into the concrete of the ledge, into the dirt, up the roots of the nearest trees, through the leaves that shook like a cacophony of cymbals. A tight, coiled tension rotated and compressed in my stomach with each syllable that rang through my thoughts as the surrounding wilderness rumbled.

"We are more than the sum of our parts. We are our intangible souls. We are the springs of a stretched cord suspended in time and space, drifting through the ethos." I felt both loose and tight as his voice echoed within me. Those strange words—his and not. They belonged to an Oliver I hadn't known yet.

Every syllable vibrated within my heartstrings—creating a melody that gave rise to goosebumps covering my skin. I wanted him to need me, have me, consume me. I wanted him to absorb me until we were one entity, overfilled, welded together —so messy in our union that no one could even begin to identify the seam.

He squeezed my fingers urgently and it was as though fingers squeezed my mind. I let out a gasp, eyes widening. I reveled in the sensitivity it elicited in my every nerve ending.

"Oliver..." I breathed as he brushed my cheek with his other hand, the light touch somehow sending waves of pleasure rolling through me. "I don't understand what you're saying," I whispered the admission.

"Yes, you do," the voice echoed in my mind while his perfect lips remained closed, a corner turned up into a slanted smile that faltered.

"You're gonna have to jump," he whispered. His eyes had grown dark and his words heavy. The fear in them was palpable.

I chuckled at his dramatic tone—recalling the sheen, tempting water in the creek beside us. I peeled my eyes away from him, ready to tease him about being a baby and make a point of how tempting the water looked when I spotted it—the dry basin, once a lush lagoon.

"The water"—I sputtered, baffled—"it was just there...how's that possible?" I pulled my hand from his and crouched to feel the emptiness, just to be sure. It was a far drop to the dirt at the bottom.

"Looks like we're out of luck," he remarked.

I followed his line of sight. He was peering down over the other side, and there it was—the water that had been up here moments ago was now at the base of the treacherous 100-foot drop, so far down that it made my head spin.

"You'll have to jump," his gravelly voice echoed in my mind and shook the leaves all around us. His arms were open to me, awaiting my embrace. I stepped back from his offer to thoroughly examine the drop.

"There wasn't any water down there, Oliver. Where did that come from?" He shrugged, eyes down. I followed his line of sight again, fighting not to get dizzy from the height. A fear that he could jump, gripped me. "It's too far down. We could die. We don't know how shallow that water is. We saw rocks down there earlier, remember?" I urged. There was an eerie silence.

"Oliver?" I whispered, but I knew even before I looked up from the drop that he was gone. I looked behind us, where the dried basin remained empty. I turned to stare down the dam wall but he couldn't have fallen. I would have heard something. No. He had simply disappeared, like the water. Here one moment, gone the next.

I turned around clumsily and desperate to find him, eyes combing the surrounding tree line. As I rotated my foot, it slipped off the edge. I threw my arms out to grab for something but I only managed to grasp air, plummeting like a stone, arms flailing.

My throat seized up. I couldn't take a breath; the speed of the drop was choking me. I had the sudden remarkable realization: *I'm asleep. I'm dreaming.*

But something *was* choking me. My eyes burst open. There was a man on top of me—a guard. Cruelty marred the lines of his scowl. He wasn't wearing a mask, and I didn't recognize him.

He covered my mouth with his hand. My hand moved to my face, desperate to pull the obstruction away but he was too strong and my energy was drained.

I pulled on my chain, wrapping the slack around my hand and securing the makeshift knuckle-ring in my palm. I had one clean shot. I needed him closer, in case the chain didn't reach. I grabbed the back of his neck, rolled back, using the inertia to bring his head closer, then released him before rotating my chain-wrapped hand back to punch him square in the eye.

He hollered a curse and before he could recover, I followed up with two swift jabs to his throat. A heady grunt escaped him. His chin dropped and his body toppled back as he released me to grab at his throat.

I thrust my hips up forcefully to buck him off me and kicked with all my might, but he was so heavy, it barely budged him. Enraged by my fighting, he restricted my legs with the weight of his own, my arms with only one hand. He fumbled with my pants. I bared my teeth in search of a vulnerable piece of flesh to bite, rotating my head, jerking around wildly. Fast footsteps approached from beyond the door into the cell. The unfamiliar man was quickly shoved aside, replaced by Slick.

Slick was fuming. For a brief moment, I felt relief. Slick's expression was livid as he turned his rage on the unfamiliar man. Slick pulled out a pocketknife, directing it at the guard.

"You weasel! You thought you could sneak in here and I wouldn't notice...again? I won't screw them after you, you filth!" Slick screamed in Russian, throwing a tantrum. My heart turned to stone.

"What does it matter?" the guard argued, rubbing at his eye socket. I reveled at the sight of the broken skin, the blood oozing out of the wound. "You'll get your turn, you always do" —the guard spat—"But you're sloppy, you stretch them out, tear them apart and leave behind a mess so slimy, it's like a crime scene! Who can enjoy that? Not to mention, you take too damn long! There's no time today. There's an inspection scheduled, so, screw off," the man hissed, his hair disheveled from jerking his head around as he spoke.

Slick mimicked collecting falling tears into his palm before his humor faded and his expression fell. "Respect the hierarchy," he commanded. The other man shrugged and grunted, dabbing at his bloody eye with one hand and rubbing his throat with the other.

My mind—groggy only moments ago—was now highly alert. I was wide awake. I clenched my fists, body rigid with tension. Slick turned to me and moved forward.

"Stay away from me! Stay the hell back!" I cried, crawling as close to the wall as I could. I kicked out at him, threateningly. My body was shaking, overcome with terror. "Please," I cried, uselessly. "Please. Please! No!" My vision blurred. A deeper, more frantic panic set in as Slick lowered over me, still holding his knife. I locked my legs, pressing them tightly together.

"Kill me. Please, just kill me," I pleaded.

"*Dura,*" he hissed. "I can't kill you. You're not mine to kill."

He squeezed my chest through my shirt. He tried to yank my jeans down without unbuttoning them. I kicked him away, but each subsequent kick was weakened by the excruciating pain coursing through my ribs. I was chained to a wall, after all, trapped like an animal with nowhere to run. "I love it when they fight. This one has so much fight," he chuckled. I looked at the guard, stupidly, as if to seek his help. He rolled his eyes at Slick and turned away from us with disgust on his face.

Slick's enthusiasm didn't distract me; it made me fight harder, with every ounce of strength that remained. Growing frustrated, Slick flipped me over in one sickening motion. The chain still wrapped around my hand twisted and rattled. A scream tore from my lungs as pain ripped through my hand and a second one followed as Slick's weight pressed my ribs against the concrete.

I heard the sound of fabric tearing as Slick sliced through my jeans with his blade. He let out a groan.

"She reeks," he complained to the guard.

"Hose her down, for God's sake," the other cried.

"No. You were right, there isn't any time." The metallic clank of his blade hitting the ground echoed through the room as he yanked my jeans down with a few rough jerks of the fabric, exposing my bottom to the frosted air.

Good. I hoped I was filthy. I hoped he choked on the stench, gagged on the putrid odor of the filth he and his kind were responsible for. I hoped the reek would haunt him until the day I could slice his ball sack open.

"Sometimes you gotta even out the playing field to have a chance. Only a weapon—a gun, a knife, a bat, a pencil, whatever is lying around—can help you do that." Oli's words came to me, now. A knife. A knife. There was a knife in this room with me. It was here and I had just heard the sounds of it clattering on the floor. I turned my head to the side, and there it was.

Slick pinned both my hips down with his knee. My free hand could reach the knife—it had been lying just a few feet away, just right of my head. I had one shot at this. I probably couldn't kill him with it unless I was able to get close enough and maneuver it into the throat or slice through an important artery. I practiced the grab in my mind, over and over. I'd time it perfectly. I'd wait. I'd be patient. I'd be precise. I heard the sound of his zipper. One. Two. I reached across under my chin, ignoring the stabbing pain through my entire ribcage, I twisted and rotated until my fingertips connected with the pocketknife, my pinky wrapping around the part closest to the blade. I quickly closed my fingers around the handle. I kicked up with my leg to hit him in the backside as a distraction. Meanwhile, in one swift swing, I wound my arm back around and jabbed, jabbed, jabbed, jabbed. His screams echoed off the wall as he fell away from me. The other man, still rubbing his bloody eye with his palm, ran forward.

"What is it? What happened?"

"*Suka! Suka! Shto ti natvarila!*" Slick's screams filled my ears with a ringing. I turned back over, sat up, and scrambled against the wall holding the bloody knife out, ready to slice, kick, claw, and tear this scum to pieces until my very last breath. Slick was clutching his bloody groin, weeping.

"What the hell is going on here? Have you lost your damn minds?" The husky voice cut the cold air like a blade and I almost dropped the pocketknife I held in my shaking fingers.

Mikhailov was accompanied by two men who trained their guns on us, one on me and the other between Slick and the bleeding guard.

Slick jumped to his feet, still clutching his sliced-up gut. Once more, I was flooded with the insensible reaction of momentary relief to see Mikhailov, as though he were not the one who had put me here.

"G-Gospodin Mikhaila-lov, please forgive me...I-I didn't expect you so soon. I was just...we were, just celebrating the

completion of Miss Arkova's time with us but then sh-she—"
Slick stuttered to Mikhailov in Russian.

"Celebrating?" Mikhailov was tamping down his reaction
beneath a steely expression. His mouth twitched with irritation,
anger even. Never in my most deranged nightmares did I
consider I might ever be happy to see Mikhailov's repulsive
face.

"Gospodin—"

"What are you hired to do?" Mikhailov asked Slick in
Russian.

"Gospodin Mikh—"

"I asked you a question. What are you hired to do?" he
repeated.

"To encourage cooperation in insubordinate agents and
document motivational material for persons of interest, sir."

"And when you've completed your task?" Mikhailov continued, blank-faced.

"Sir, I came in here and found Ghalupkin forcing himself on
her. She fought him, look at his eye!" Slick pointed to the man
in the corner of the cell.

"Nyet—" the man argued but Mikhailov cut him off.

"Arkova, you did this to him?"

I hesitated then croaked out, "Yes."

"He attacked you?"

"Yes," I repeated in a small voice.

The man opened his mouth to argue but his arguments were
cut off instantly by the deafening sound of Mikhailov's gun as
he fired a burst of shots into the man's chest without warning.
The man's blood splattered against the wall. I winced and
turned my head. Mikhailov fired two final shots. I jumped with
each one. Finally, it was quiet.

I looked up to find the man's motionless body bleeding out a
few feet away from me. I could see holes in his chest and head,

unable to look away as blood pooled around his torso and skull. The gunshots still rippled through the room; they reverberated off the walls, the floor, the ceiling, and echoed in my mind. Somewhere in the chaos, I had lost my grip on the pocketknife. I scrambled to pick it up. Mikhailov trained his sights back on Slick.

"What is the protocol after you've completed your task?" Slick looked horror-stricken as he turned to Mikhailov to beg for his life. He raised one trembling hand in the air as though attempting to slow Mikhailov's decision with it.

"P-Prepare p-property for transfer and awa-await your arrival," Slick answered fearfully. I scooted as close to the wall as I could, slowly pulling what was left of my jeans back into place, gritting through the pain of every laborious movement.

"You failed to prepare our property for transfer. You decided to risk our property with an STD and then got yourself stabbed," Mikhailov ground out in Russian. His face was tinged with a reddish shade. His voice was eerily calm. Even from across the cell, I could see the bulging vein of his temple.

Slick laughed nervously. "I don't have an ST—"

"You're stealing from the company. You're using company property for your own pleasure. What do we do with thieves?" Mikhailov raised his gun and I flinched.

"Please, sir. Never again. Please!" No part of me took pleasure in hearing the man beg. The instinctual pity I felt for him made me sick. That small sliver of the old Mina that was still somewhere deep inside me was afraid to witness more death. Mikhailov pointed the gun at Slick's head. Slick took a few steps back, eyes widening as Mikhailov continued his scolding but did not lower the gun.

"You know better. We've never let a thief walk. Have we? What kind of message would that send?"

"Please, sir, I understand. I—I'm sorry…never again."

"Ms. Arkova's father stole from us. So, we stole from him."

Mikhailov pointed a finger at me, but avoided direct eye contact. I hugged my knees and rocked, my teeth chattering from nerves and cold.

"The question is, what to take from you? How long has this been going on?" Mikhailov asked Slick, waving his finger in the direction of the dead man on the other end of the room.

"Sir, this has never—"

"Don't lie to me. I'll find out and double the punishment," Mikhailov threatened, taking a step forward. Slick cowered and lowered his gaze to the ground before answering in a quiet voice I couldn't imagine belonging to him.

"From the beginning, sir—"

Mikhailov's eyes widened. "All this time?" I stared back and forth between Mikhailov and Slick. I remembered the knife. I used this distraction to wipe it against my jeans, close it, and slip it into my pocket. Then, I curled up against the wall like a dog by its bone. Mikhailov turned to look me dead in the eyes, fully acknowledging me for the first time. He kept his gun on Slick. My heart accelerated.

"Did he violate you?" Mikhailov asked me, face solemn. The question pulled a manic cackle from me. I glared into his cold, dark eyes.

"Did he violate me?" I shot back, my voice a croak. "He's been violating me under your command for-for...well, I don't know, actually. How long has it been now? How many weeks?" I genuinely craved to know. To know how long I'd been torn away from the life I loved. From Mama, from Nyah, from Oliver, from my dreams, my art, my future. Their absence was like a cavern in my stomach with a bone-chilling draft wafting through.

"Did he violate your womanhood?" Mikhailov clarified, irritably. "Should we call a nurse to inspect you?"

My "womanhood"...the nerve—a low chuckle rumbled through my vocal cords, triggering a violent cough. My throat felt like it was seizing up, it hurt to swallow, and my body felt so cold. I was shaking more than usual. "I think my ribs are broken," I rasped. Mikhailov's lips thinned into a hard line.

"No, he didn't manage to force himself on me but I, I wasn't a virgin, if that's what you were worried ab..." But the cough returned and I was unable to vocalize my disgust with him. The memory of the violence I carried out against this man—regardless of how vile he had been—settled on my shoulders, an excruciating weight to carry on top of the load already slung there.

Mikhailov released a short exhalation of near imperceptible relief, but at which part of the information, I wasn't sure. "We need to get her to the infirmary and have the nurse look at her," Mikhailov mentioned to his men. He turned back to Slick, reset his sights lower, and shot him in the hand. I flinched from the sound.

A gurgled scream escaped Slick as he nursed his maimed hand. He fell forward, convulsing with violent sobs.

"Thank you for your honesty. I'll only take one hand," Mikhailov assured, generously. Only a few feet from him, the unfamiliar man whose name I'd already forgotten lay still, blood draining from his body and surrounding him in a reflective pool of darkness. I shut my eyes to escape the hellish sights and sounds of this damned place.

"Clean her up. Carefully. If her ribs are broken, she must be handled with caution. Put a chair in the shower then carry her to the infirmary," Mikhailov instructed his men. They approached and I flinched from them although I had just heard his instruction. It was pure instinct, now.

"They won't hurt you," Mikhailov assured, as though his word could mean anything to me. "You've done well. The worst is over. Your father has reaffirmed his cooperation." *What?* He spoke with the flippancy of someone who had managed to tame a difficult child. "I'll ask the kitchen to send something to the infirmary for you, shortly," he said, the warmth in his voice throwing me off-kilter entirely. "Oh, and Miss Arkova? Please, don't stab any more of my men with that pocketknife you've so cleverly tucked away." My hand reached for the lump in my pocket automatically, but Mikhailov turned and left.

CHAPTER 23

OLIVER

"And who's this?" CJ inquired. He hadn't said a word of greeting since Xavi and I pulled into his warehouse. Instead, he ordered his security men, who I had nicknamed Titus #1 and Titus #2, to accept and process the units we brought. I nicknamed them that because they refused to tell me what they preferred to be called, and hardly ever spoke or looked me in the eye if they could help it. CJ never addressed them by name in front of me.

"CJ, this is Xavi," I answered.

"Is he the new Mina?" CJ chuckled, his dark eyes gleaming with amusement as he took another bite of red rice.

My brow rose in response to his joke, or perhaps he was genuine.

"Ey, naw, man—" Xavi began, but I signaled him not to with a shake of my head. We had more important things to discuss.

"He's my partner." I ignored CJ's little joke as though he had not made it, and I silently felt proud of the new level of control I had mastered. "CJ, I wanted to ask you about something—"

"Please...sit. Join me. The chicken tikka poutine is quite good." He gestured to the food before him.

"Thank you," I said, pulling up two chairs for Xavi and myself as the warehouse employees began processing and logging our units. "CJ, I wanted to ask you about something," I tried again.

"So, did they confiscate everything or just the one SKU?" CJ asked, inquisitively but with concern underlining his inquiry.

"They?" I asked, feigning naïveté.

"Oh, come on, Oliver, just be straight with me, will you?"

"About what?" I asked.

"That you got raided by the police. Come off it, don't be tedious."

"How'd you know?" I asked, genuinely curious.

"I had you followed," CJ answered as though he'd been telling me about his rock collection.

"For how long?" I asked, outraged, all the while, unable to recall a single time I suspected that I was being followed.

"After I saw footage of you entering my home with my wife..." he answered, cool as a cucumber, though all the while my heart was palpitating like a jackrabbit.

He'd known. I couldn't believe it. He'd known all this time. I opened my mouth to speak but words failed me. Xavi looked from CJ to me and back to CJ, his shoulders tensing, sensing my growing panic.

Finally, I managed, "Nothing happened."

"I know nothing happened. I wouldn't be breaking bread with you if anything had," CJ scoffed. Xavi released his clenched fists and took a step back, easing up a bit. I nodded at him.

"I just came up because she said she needed help with a tech issue..." I went on although he hadn't asked me to.

"I know," he stated simply. How many times had I met up with him since that day? Jesus...it must have been a handful of times, at least, and this whole time, he knew. I wanted to ask

him about his wife, Kiran. Were they still together? Had he...
gotten upset with her? I didn't dare ask.

"So...?" He awaited a response but to what, I didn't know. I
noticed my thumb tapping the table repeatedly and stopped the
movement.

"I'm sorry, I don't follow...'so'?" I questioned.

CJ stood and went to the counter at the back corner of the
warehouse, his back toward us. Xavi nudged my arm and whispered, "This fool is so weird. Let's get the hell out of here?" I
hushed him and shook my head as CJ brought over two mugs
from the sink. "Water?" he offered, bringing back a jug of ice
water with lemon slices and placing it in the center of the table.
He went back to grab a mug for himself as he said, "So...did
they take all your inventory or only one SKU? My PI said it was
a big haul."

"Yeah...they took all of it," I muttered.

"They're not supposed to do that. They're only supposed to
take the units they are investigating," he noted.

I shrugged. "They seemed adamant about taking all of it.
They turned the place inside-out."

"Really? Interesting," CJ commented. "All right, here's what
we'll do. I'll give you my lawyer's contact info. He's good." CJ
was on his phone and my phone pinged with a notification
within seconds. "Send him the leading officer's information and
give him a copy of everything you gave them. Sign the paper-
work he sends you so he can act on your behalf and he'll take
care of everything. I bet he'll get the rest of the units back
within the week. Did you cooperate?"

I hesitated, then answered, "Yeah, I gave them names."

"Good."

"But my guys had receipts so they should be all good..." I
reasoned. CJ chuckled at that as though I were missing something obvious. "Not to sound ungrateful, but why are you

helping me, CJ? Kiran said..."—CJ's expression stilled—"Kiran said you didn't like me."

He gave a short, sour laugh.

"I like you just fine. But now, I *trust* you."

"CJ, tell me it wasn't a test...tell me Kiran coming on to me wasn't another one of your insane trust tests," I breathed. My blood was boiling at the mere thought of that idea.

"No. It wasn't a test. Kiran was acting out as Kiran acts out from time to time. She was upset with me and was trying to get even— get a rise out of me by sleeping with you," CJ said in such a calm tone that it was difficult to discern his true emotions. He poured the water into my mug as he went on. "She knows I have cameras hidden all around our place. She wanted me to watch, the little devil. She was so frustrated when it didn't pan out with you and I... well, I was grateful," CJ expressed, his shoulders relaxing slightly.

"Jesus," I muttered, rubbing my forehead. I went for my mug of water and almost knocked it over.

"It's rare...to come by someone you can fully trust. Isn't that right...Xavi, was it?" CJ turned to Xavi, who choked on his water. Xavi coughed, trying to play it off.

"Yeah, *ahem*...'scuse me. Trust—trust is...rare. Oli's a real one." Xavi nodded, keeping his gaze anywhere but on CJ.

"Indeed. I think we have that trust now. Don't you, Oliver?" CJ questioned.

"Yes," I lied, every facet of my intuition telling me that underneath his careful facade, CJ was every bit as unhinged as his wife.

"Good. That's why I'm helping you," he said.

"So, why did you have me followed if you knew I wasn't sleeping with her?" I asked, exchanging a look of discomfort with Xavi, whose eyes were wide in amusement and disbelief.

CJ smiled as he filled his own mug with water and deliberated over a response.

"Curiosity," he offered. "Something else is happening, isn't it?" CJ observed me under his scrutinizing gaze. "Something that has nothing to do with the police raid on your units." I met his eyes.

"Yes," I told him.

"You've been by the hospital an awful lot lately, visiting some questionable places...driving around all hours of the night. My guy was complaining, I had to pay him double for his efforts," CJ remarked. *This is unbelievable: he has me followed and has the gall to be irritated about it.*

"Yeah, something happened to Mina," I confirmed, unnerved by the idea that I'd been followed all this time without knowing it. If I'd missed CJ's guy, couldn't others—far more dangerous, more threatening—be following me, too?

"That's a pity. I hope she's all right. You wanna talk about it?" CJ offered, coyly.

Xavi leaned over, cupped his hand over his mouth, and said in a low voice, "Yo, you sure you wanna tell this fool anything, Oli? He's giving off shady-ass vibes bro—I think his barber did him real dirty and he's been out for vengeance ever since."

"No choice, Xavi," I muttered, stepping up to speak into his ear. "What I'm doing hasn't been working out so great."

"Her full name is Mina Arkova. Her father is somehow connected to the Russian mob, but exactly how, I'm unsure. She was threatened by some Russian thugs in an alley on the way home after school a few months ago, around the time you first met her. They said something about her father owing them money or that he took something from them, it was unclear... the only thing that was clear was that hurting her was a message intended for him."

"Oh, how awful," CJ commented, his voice entirely devoid of emotion. Xavi looked at me with concern in his eyes; he'd only known she was taken—I hadn't given him the details as to why.

"Her father ensured that his dealings were settled...that

there'd be no more problems with these men in the future. So, Mina and her mother came out of hiding and returned to their lives here. But the men came after them again. Her father must have done something to really piss them off because they hired some local guys to go to Mina's house this time. They shot her mom, Mina fought back, and one of the guys got away and the other one...Mina killed the other."

Badass girl," Xavi breathed.

"Indeed," CJ agreed.

"But the original guys came back for Mina, anyway. They took her from her house the next day. I was able to trace their route with surveillance footage all the way to the 101 North. I have this list of places she might possibly be. I can't say where I got it but—"

"Does it have something to do with the motels you've been visiting lately? The man you met with, a Mr. Jerome Wright? I believe you were spending some time with his daughter, Miss Nyah Wright, last month," CJ remarked. Xavi turned to me, his brows lifted. This was news to him, of course. The knowledge that CJ had sent men around to follow me was troubling, and frankly, it pissed me the hell off. But CJ might be the kind of guy who could actually help me with this.

"Yes," I said through my teeth. CJ smiled at my look of distaste. I ignored him and went on. "I need help narrowing the list down or asking about some of the places that may not be on it. It's a list of locations where some of the Russian underground organizations have operated in the past. I was gonna see if you knew about any of these places or knew who to ask. I've been to all of them, shown her picture around, and I've found nothing. I've gotta be missing something. A home invasion, murder, and abduction in a quiet family neighborhood—there's got to be word on the street about it, to someone who's connected. Working solo, I've come up bust every time. I'm running out of time to find her. I'm worried they'll move her—if they haven't already. If they do, I may never find her again," I said to CJ to express the gravity of the situation, even though I wasn't ready to unpack that possibility myself, yet. Xavi leaned forward in his chair, shifting his foot closer to mine, concern filling his gaze after hearing me confess my fears.

"You said they hired local guys to hit the house first? How do you know these guys aren't locals themselves?" asked CJ.

"I don't know. They could be, I'm just taking a guess. They have heavy accents and the big guy in the alley—he was massive —weird clothes, all leathery and black, European fashion. Oh, and he had this creepy haircut, like an upside-down bowl. Have you ever seen a Russian dude like that around? He had this big, lumpy-ass forehead. I think his name was Kiril."

"No, I'm sorry. I have not," CJ answered. He seemed genuinely upset that he couldn't be of more help, which was an odd change of attitude from CJ. "Why not come to her house themselves? Why send some hired locals first, do you think?"

"I have a feeling something happened with her father. He must have done something rash and maybe they needed to move quickly before her father had a chance to reach out to Lily and Mina and warn them?"

"Mmmm...that's possible," he mused. "I wonder what his involvement actually is. What did you say her surname was? Ark—"

"Arkova," I told him.

"Arkova. So, he would be Arkov, then. That's how they do it, I believe. The Russians, the ending is an 'a' for the females and the 'a' is dropped for the males. Arkov...Arkov." CJ played with the name.

"So...you think you know who you can ask about it?" I inquired. CJ chewed on the piece of meat he held between his fingers, looking up at the ceiling thoughtfully.

"No, it's unlikely that he does, sweetness," a woman's voice came from behind a stack of boxes piled on a packing table nearby. I recognized that voice. "But I may know just the person to ask," she said in a sing-song inflection. The sound of a stool scratching against concrete filled the warehouse as Xavi and I exchanged a look.

The clanking of heels grew louder and Kiran Kaur rounded the corner of the packing table, revealing herself in all her curvaceous glory. She was in a purple, body-binding suit that complemented the dark tones of her skin and brought out the warmth in her honey eyes. Her hair swayed with her hips as she walked.

"You been playing hide and go seek back there?" Xavi asked. "Or were you in time out?"

"I picked out the precise location of my desk strategically," she purred in that smooth British accent of hers.

"Dammmmn," Xavi muttered under his breath. "You said no to all that?" He stood and ran to peek around the packing table, clearly checking the veracity of her story. "Nice yoga ball. You sit on it in...uh, in that?" He gestured to her outfit.

"Yes, why not?" she asked in amusement of Xavi's interest.

"It's just..."

"It's what...?" she teased, flirtation and playfulness entering her tone.

CJ rolled his eyes. "Kitty, are we completely shameless today? I'm right here, you know?"

"Oh." She shrugged, innocently. "Must have slipped my mind. I'll make sure to have more discretion next time. You know, like you're so good at doing."

"Kitty—"

"Looking good, Oli," Kiran cut CJ off. She took me in with her gaze. "A bit...knackered, clearly. But in a delicious, grunge-rockstar-melancholy kind of way."

CJ grunted his disapproval with her. I stood from my chair, awkwardly. My headache was earsplitting, but I needed their help. I just had to be careful not to land in the middle of one of their twisted little games. I walked over to join Xavi by the packing table.

"You said you know someone you can ask?" I addressed Kiran, veering away from her comments and back on track.

"I know of someone who's very, very knowledgeable about local Russian dealings—" Kiran replied with a lilt in her voice.

"You'd better not be speaking about who I think you're speaking about—" CJ uttered, looking seriously displeased by where she was going with this.

"Some may even say he's at the heart of the Russian underground in New York. He happens to be in town for the holidays, visiting family," Kiran continued, ignoring CJ entirely.

"How do you know that?" CJ interjected.

"I could give him a ring...set up a rendezvous. If it means so much to you that you would arrange an entire meet just to ask this favor of CJ." Kiran's gaze intensified on me before she turned to CJ with a pointed expression. He understood the upper hand she was offering him. I'd owe him big, thanks to her.

"Oli..." Xavi warned me, probably feeling just about as sick in the stomach from this conversation as I was. Xavi, from the brief time I'd known him, despised dishonesty. Kiran, however, seemed to enjoy playing games.

"Yes, Kiran...I'd owe CJ," I confirmed in a hard voice.

"You'd owe *me*, sweetness," Kiran corrected in a voice that was almost wistful, leaning against the table and crossing her legs slowly. "I may use it or...if CJ behaves, I may gift it to him on an anniversary, maybe Christmas...or I may just forget about it and remember years and years from now, after you've grown a bit," she said drolly.

"Business only"—I stated my terms—"nothing weird. Are we clear on that?"

"Boo!" she pouted. "You were such a fun grump when we first met. Now, you're just...a grump. What happened?"

"Someone I love was terrorized and kidnapped. Tends to suck the fun out of things. Don't you think?" I responded in a low, hollow voice.

"It happens," she said, meeting my eyes. Xavi mouthed *it happens?* like it was the craziest thing he'd ever heard someone say. He should've seen what she'd done to me on the balcony of her penthouse.

"So, who is he? The guy you're gonna call?" I asked her, trying to get back to the reason I was here but still reining in my desperation.

"His name is Anton Zaharov." The name danced off her tongue. "He's based on the East Coast. Dabbles in all sorts of business. He's from England; we grew up together, actually. But he has Russian roots, so he might know some things."

"What kind of things?" I asked, my curiosity and hope growing.

"Oh, well, you know...all sorts of things. We haven't been in touch in years but from what I hear, he deals in oil, diamonds, antiques, caviar, exotic animals. Like I said, all sorts of things. He's likely acquainted with a variety of people."

"He's Russian?" I asked.

"I told you—I believe he's of Russian descent."

"You think he knows people in the Russian crime organizations? The groups in New York? Or the ones in Russia?" I asked, seeking clarification. My mind reeled with questions.

Kiran let out a slight laugh. "I'm not familiar with the contents of his Rolodex. I met him as a child. He attended Harrow School, an all-boys boarding school in my hometown. We were about the same age, around fourteen years old at the time, I believe. My group of friends would hang out with his group when they snuck out into town.

"He was quite friendly and fairly popular, a bit wild. All I knew was that his parents and his younger brother lived in Russia because he'd often mention missing them. But a few

222 • EMILIA ARES

years later, I believe both his mother and his brother moved to London permanently. He'd told me that his father had died, and we bonded over that. Mine had just died in a car wreck around the same time. Freakish coincidence.

"His younger brother, Alexei, started at Harrow School as well. Serious fellow, that one was. A bit strange, always seemed angry, and a bit of a loner. Not Anton, though. Anton Zaharov was a lover of booze, intrigue and friendship—"

"Darling, is this walk down memory lane quite necessary or are you just enjoying yourself?" CJ interjected, seemingly unnerved by her recollection of Anton.

"Always enjoying myself, sweetness. I thought it might be useful for our Oliver to understand Zaharov's background before meeting him." I nearly flinched at 'our Oliver.' CJ's mouth was a hard line. "So, he knows how best to proceed. Right, well, as I was saying, last I saw him was a couple of years back in New York. We all had a bit of a reunion, our group of friends, and he seemed like the same old Anton. Just a bit more unhinged and much more connected. He walked through the city as though he owned it and he might as well have, because everywhere we went, ropes were opened, carpets were unrolled. Nothing was off-limits and when my bonkers friends would ask for this drug or that one, or some rare wine, or dinner at an impossibly exclusive place, Anton had the connection. Always. It left an impression," she reminisced.

"Would you say he's...unreasonably unhinged?" I asked.

Kiran chuckled and sighed. "There were rumors about the supply of cocaine and heroin on the East Coast—they say he's involved to some degree. But one night, we were both thoroughly smashed and he vehemently denied it when I brought it up. He actually called drug dealers scum. Sounds reasonable to me. So, he can't be that bad, right?" she remarked casually.

"Right," I pronounced, unsure of what to make of all that.

"Well, maybe we don't show him the list, then? Just in case he is…dangerous?"

"Oh, don't get your knickers in a twist, Oliver. We don't have to show him your little list. I don't care one way or the other. You're the one who needs answers. You can ask him whatever you want. I can't guarantee he'll give you the answer you're looking for, though. He's temperamental and quite unpredictable." Kiran shrugged. "Just know, men like him don't do favors. So, if you want to be foolish and waste a perfectly good bargaining chip…fine. But be ready to give him something else. Better you offer something up than allow him to come up with what he wants to take in return."

I thought on that. CJ ate his rice in silence, and Xavi sat down to eat with him. I walked back to the table, as well, and finished my glass of water.

Later, I joined CJ's men to help them log the units I had brought. Soon, CJ approached. Xavi was busy devouring the rest of CJ's take-out. I chuckled at his attempt to check Kiran out discreetly as she sauntered over to the electric kettle and brewed a pot of tea.

"If you find yourself in a position of weakness with Anton"— CJ muttered to me under his breath—"if you end up in need of something to barter for the information you're seeking and you're serious about not wanting to hand over that list—which, by the way, I respect—then, you can tell him you have a connect at the West Coast ports. A man like Anton may value a connect at the ports from the sound of it."

"But—I don't have a connect at the ports, CJ," I said slowly, in disbelief of what he was offering.

"But *I* do," CJ offered on a platter with a small smile. At that moment, I both admired and distrusted him. I wasn't sure which feeling was more potent.

"Why would you do that for me?" I questioned.

"I like you, Oliver. I like working with you. You are in a

predicament. I can appreciate that this predicament was not of your own making and I can help, in a small way. So, I'm helping. Nothing more to it," he ensured but I didn't buy it. I decided to let it go for now. CJ continued stacking the units along the wall and nodded to one of his men, who left and returned with a handheld scanner.

"What should I say when he asks me about this connect at the port?" I asked CJ, who was scanning the units into his system.

"You can tell him you'll arrange the meet...after he gives you actionable information," CJ instructed. "There," he remarked, finishing up the cataloging task and directing his full attention to me. "How much are you losing on these, Oliver?"

I blinked at him in surprise at the change of subject. "*Ahem*, about twenty bucks a pop," I answered with a small chuckle, at how well he understood both my situation and why I was really here.

He answered my chuckle and patted me on the back, his dark eyes glinting in the fluorescent light of the warehouse. "I like that about you, Oliver. You don't care about the money, you have principles. It's truly so rare a quality. Good thing to know I wasn't wrong about you. I'll wire you the difference."

"You don't have to do that, CJ," I insisted.

"I know I don't." He nodded in agreement. The crinkles at the corners of his eyes nearly camouflaged the cold calculation hidden behind them.

CHAPTER 24

MINA

Mikhailov's two men carried me on a stretcher through a large old manor. This place was not what I had thought it to be. I somehow imagined the rest of it much like my cell, an extension of concrete and musty darkness. But like a bright, well-preserved relic from long ago, it bore the elegant curves of the late eighteen hundreds. It had surely belonged to a prestigious family, at some point.

The men held the cloth stretcher as still as they could. I distracted myself from the pain by focusing on the floral carvings along the columns and on the ceiling as we reached the bend of another staircase.

Like an old estate that had been left to grow increasingly worn over the years but later was restored in a hurry, this place carried signs of a rushed restoration. The walnut panels were covered in a fresh stain that preserved the dark markings of past leaks. The plaster had been touched up here and there, a few shades off from the original. The walls were adorned with wallpaper, something that looked vaguely like a mural of the French countryside.

The romanticism belied the solemn energy of this place, highlighted by the stern face of a woman in a dark gray suit whom we passed in the hall. The woman's gaze rolled over me impassively before moving her attention to the stack of papers she carried. She appeared entirely unmoved, as though a girl being carried by two guards through the hall on a stretcher was routine around here.

Past her, inside the room through the open door, stood a line of girls. My heart pounded as I recognized one of them. It was Starling, standing in the line—not a form, not a group nor a circle of girls, but a perfect line. Equal distance between each of them and the next. Expressions blank.

Subtle curiosity conquered their faces as they moved into the hall and discreetly watched me pass. They were all dressed in the same uniform, white collared shirts and long gray dresses, their hair braided back. Some of the women were younger than me, some were older, but each had a severity about her. They seemed stoic—no softness in sight. They stood and watched as I was carried by.

It was like being in the twilight zone. They were moving through the halls like this was a normal place to be—like a school. No, not a school. Something even more familiar than a school. Something more intimate, a home—their home. Hadn't Starling said that the other girl, Swan, had grown up here? This must have been what she meant—where she meant.

The enormity of the rooms and the height of the ceilings made my head spin. I squeezed my eyes shut and imagined I was back in the cell. I clawed at the cotton cloth that covered the rails of the stretcher. The phlegm in my throat was thick, my lungs felt heavy, and they hurt when I inhaled.

The darkness, I needed darkness. I covered my eyes with the palms of my hands to close out the light entirely. I rotated as much as my body would allow. Better. My breath eased, the tightness in my chest loosened.

The men placed the stretcher down on the tile once we were inside the spacious communal bathroom, the wooden door swinging shut behind us with a resounding clank. My heart would not, could not stop hammering wildly in my chest.

Rows of showers lined the wall. This room had clearly been recently remodeled, as it was much more modern in design and hardware than the rest of the manor. One of the men left the room while the other approached me to remove what remained of my pants. I jerked back from his fingers on me.

"I'll do it," I rasped in Russian.

He shrugged then nodded. He turned his palm up and held it out to me. "*Nozh?*"

I exhaled irritably, reluctant to part with the one weapon I'd managed to defend myself with, the only thing that had granted me a sliver of security. I shook my head, retrieving the pocketknife, only to grip it in my hand tightly.

"Don't hurt me and I won't hurt you," I warned the man. He scoffed. The other one returned carrying a plastic chair. He placed it under the showerhead and brought over a bar of soap in a dish. He placed the dish by the foot of the chair.

I tried to stand from my place on the stretcher on the floor and maneuvered myself toward the chair, on which I sat down heavily.

"*Pamagiti*," I called to the men. As one of the men reached for the lever, I clutched the pocketknife, keeping it hidden and folded in my palm.

"It'll be cold at first," he warned in Russian. I shifted my body to the left, but the cold water hit my torso and legs. This was nothing. I didn't even flinch. The water warmed and it was bliss until minutes later and the warmth quickly began to wane.

I tucked the blade under my thigh as I scrubbed my skin, my face, under my nails, my hair. I dropped the bar of soap and the guard who turned the water on walked over, picked it up, and handed it to me without a word. He didn't stare at my naked-ness. He looked only in my eyes and then away. This was kind-ness to me, now. That's how low the qualification had sunk.

Still, I clung to the pocketknife, even when I had to dry myself and put my arms through the armholes of a crisp linen hospital gown. I held onto Slick's carver all the way up to the infirmary room, where a turned-down bed awaited me.

There was a chill in the air of the infirmary, but it was nowhere near as cold and dank as my basement cell had been. But even in the warmer air, it was becoming increasingly painful to breathe. My cough was taking over and I felt like I was dying.

The nurse observed me with a *tsk* of disapproval on her tongue. She had a hard mouth and hard eyes but a kind touch. The first thing she did was offer pain medication in a small bean-shaped dish. For that, I vowed to myself that if I ever got out of here, she'd be remembered as my favorite person in this cursed place. Her fingers were delicate as they moved across my limbs, nudging and rotating lightly to examine the bruises and cuts up and down my body.

Depleted of energy, I rested my eyes and cradled my ribs, wincing—tears running down my freshly scrubbed face.

Eventually, the nurse covered my trembling body with a wool blanket, and the sound of an electrical device buzzed nearby. I peeked through a slit in one eye to discover a heater pointed toward me a few feet away, connected to a long exten-sion cord. The label suggested it was an infrared heater.

There was a glass of water on the cart table beside me and a cup of white pudding next to it. I took a long drink of water, then reached for the pudding. I hadn't tasted anything this good in what seemed like forever.

Not an hour ago, I had been assaulted. Now, I was under a blanket with my very own therapeutic heater and a cup of pudding. My, how I had moved up in the world. A low, rumbling laugh took hold of me but quickly turned into a cough.

The painkillers must have taken effect because my sight had grown soft, and the lines of the monitoring machines and the bedrails had gone fuzzy. I smiled, despite my circumstances. Through my grief, I smiled—stupidly. I felt relieved to be spared from the agony that had become my life.

At first, I thought I was losing my mind, feeling happy, grateful, even, to be up here instead of down there, because I knew that up here, I wasn't any freer than I'd been before. But I decided that I wasn't losing my mind. No, I was being exactly who I was raised to be, a survivor.

Mama wouldn't have wanted me to give up. She would've wanted me to fight by any means possible—to find the hope. It wasn't my time to die. I had fight in me. They hadn't broken me, or maybe they had but I didn't know it yet, like a dismembered insect that keeps moving and twitching as though it could still run away. Maybe hope itself was just an instinct.

I needed to speak with Mikhailov. I needed to come up with a plan of some sort or I was as good as dead.

So, what did I know? I knew diddly squat. All I knew was that my father had done something to upset the wrong people. And Mama said it was a financial institution with ties to the mafia. I needed to figure out which mafia. I needed names.

The medication was sublime. I dozed into a delicious dream, barely aware of the portable x-ray machine that was wheeled in and angled over my chest. At some point, I fell into a deep, dreamless sleep.

Cold, rough hands shook me awake. There was movement— my blanket being pulled off of me. I started, opening my eyes to find a guard over my infirmary bed. I recognized him as the one who had given me a heads-up about the cold water in the shower. He kept his dark hair buzzed short, and it blended in with his black clothes and dark brows so that his bright, arctic eyes seemed to gleam in contrast. A tattoo of a black serpent in a fine-line ink style crept up along the olive skin of his neck from beneath the collar of his black shirt.

I sat up and yanked the blanket out of his grip and back up to my neck. For the first time, I noticed an IV drip connected to my wrist. The pole to which it was connected rattled with my movements. I looked around the room, wondering if there were cameras here, too. If there were, I couldn't see them.

"The doctor's here for an examination," the guard explained, and he released his grip on the blanket and stepped away. As he moved aside, a second guard escorted in a frail, gray-haired man.

The doctor pulled a pair of spectacles from his pocket and put them on. He wore an oversized tweed suit and carried a large, dark-brown leather satchel into the infirmary.

Mikhailov followed them closely, emerging from the hall, casually sipping coffee as if all this was nothing more than a mundane routine.

The pale-faced doctor approached and nodded at me. The nurse rushed in after Mikhailov and swiftly handed the doctor a marked file.

The doctor placed his satchel at the foot of my bed and walked over to examine X-rays against the light of the window. The plastic paper vibrated in his trembling grip. He handed the nurse the documents without a word and approached my bed.

"Can I use the restroom first, please?" I whispered to the doctor. His gray eyes were unreadable and when they met mine, I recognized pity in them. He shrugged, glancing back to Mikhailov nervously before bowing his head and busying himself with his satchel. Hands still shaking slightly, he fumbled through his medical bag.

"Speak up," Mikhailov demanded. He must have heard me.

I cleared my throat and asked him, "Can I use the restroom?"

"Restroom? Of course. Artyom, *pamagi*—" Mikhailov instructed but the guard with the snake tattoo was already by my side to help me up without Mikhailov's command.

"No need," the nurse chimed in from the far corner of the room. "I inserted a catheter last night to avoid unnecessary movement. It's normal to feel an urge to urinate—the catheter can trigger that sensation," she explained to me. "I'd like to get a handle on her pain before removing it. Walking, even being lifted, will place additional strain on the recovering tissue and bone," the nurse justified to the men, speaking in Russian.

The guard named Artyom nodded and moved away quickly. I shifted my legs under the blanket uncomfortably, trying to feel for the catheter tube, disturbed by the thought of this nurse putting something in my body without my consent, regardless of the reasoning.

"Vladimir Rostislavovich, *prodolzhayte*," Mikhailov encouraged the doctor to continue.

"I'm going to examine the damage," the doctor said softly to me in Russian. I gave a small nod. He reached forward to pull the wool blanket out of my iron grip.

"May I please have privacy for this?" I asked, looking directly at Mikhailov.

"No," Mikhailov answered, leaving no room for negotiation.

The guard, Artyom, redirected his gaze from me toward the window after my request. The second guard did not. Mikhailov sipped his coffee and watched with a bored expression.

Tears streamed down my face as the doctor tucked the blanket down at the foot of the bed and lifted my linen gown to my collarbone. I stared at the ceiling as the doctor, or Vladimir Rostislavovich, as Mikhailov had called him, audibly inhaled from the sight of my naked body covered in large, ugly bruises.

I shivered from nerves, hunger, and the cold touch of his soft, wrinkled fingers. He placed them lightly on a particular spot where pain shot through like a knife—I cried out. He moved his fingers gently to the lower side of my ribs and added pressure—I groaned and nausea rolled through me.

"I'm sorry," he whispered to me in Russian, so quietly that I could barely make out what he had said.

The doctor turned to Mikhailov after evaluating a series of breathing and coughing tests that he had me do. "I'm afraid there's a hairline fracture. You can see it there on the X-ray and significant, deep contusions as you can see.

"There's something else that concerns me, though. She's just on the brink of developing pneumonia. It's good the nurse here had the sense to start her on an antibiotics and pain management regimen already. I noticed the notes on her chart." I had a suspicion that something was very wrong with my ribs, but somehow, hearing pneumonia inspires a different kind of panic.

"Treatment?" Mikhailov asked.

"The pneumonia was forming because she couldn't take deep enough breaths due to the pain in her ribs. With her pain managed, this issue will be addressed. It needs to be monitored, naturally. The infrared heat lamp is a good idea and I suggest pairing it with salt therapy.

"As for the fracture, it will heal on its own, with time. There looks to be no organ damage or serious lung impairment." The doctor turned to the nurse, who was standing at attention across the room, her posture rigid. "I recommend pain management, acetaminophen for the following weeks, as needed. Ice. Breathing exercises to help with the cough and avoid future lung infection.

"The bruising should disappear within two weeks but the deeper hematomas can take up to a month. You can offer the usual supplements to speed up the process." He turned to Mikhailov. "She should avoid physical strain and risk. Naturally, I would recommend holding off on combat training for at least a period of four to six weeks." *Combat training?*

I stretched my legs down and shut my eyes, losing the fight against the spreading numbness throughout my body.

Think only about your breath—nothing else. I was drowning again. My chest was rising and falling trying to catch up with the short breaths, but failing.

"Well? Anything else?" Mikhailov finally insisted. His voice sounded like it was coming from underwater.

The doctor's response of "no" sounded like a muffled echo from far away.

"Good." Mikhailov's response came from somewhere even farther away. Four-four-four. Oliver. Four-four-four. *Breathe with me, Mina*, his voice echoed inside me.

"Gospodin Mikhailov, if that is all, I'll send my schedule over, in case you require me to conduct further examination on this patient in the future," the doctor echoed. There was shuffling of feet and the sound of footsteps. Some growing quieter, others approaching. I kept my eyes shut until a scraping sound grew closer and Mikhailov's voice echoed from somewhere nearer than before.

"Miss Arkova. Do you hear me?"

I nodded but kept my eyes closed.

"You won't be tied down or restricted in any way unless you disobey. You will follow the necessary steps to recovery, and you will fulfill each and every task required of you," ordered Mikhailov. He sat in a chair, a few feet away from my bed. Between us was an empty rollaway table cart covered by a linen dining cloth. Mikhailov placed his coffee down and rested his elbows on it as he spoke.

"If you do anything foolish—harm yourself, or impede your recovery in any way, I will have you drugged and kept sedated while you heal, which I'd rather not do, as it's not recommended for extended periods of time. Your brain can melt into a puddle, like ice cream in the California sun, understand?"

The nurse approached with a pack of ice and an elastic wrap.

I winced, inhaling sharply as she lifted my hospital gown and began massaging a cold, clear substance on the bruises. She placed the large ice pack against my ribs over my thin gown and started the wrapping process around my ribs as she maneuvered my body to the side. I faced Mikhailov head-on. He now held out a screen in front of my face, and on that screen was the moving, living, breathing image of Mama in a room just like this one.

"Mama..." The sound left my open mouth like a prayer. The relief that coursed through my body was like a hundred-pound weight removed from my sternum after months and months of pressure. My chest shook with sobs.

"S-she's...M-Mama—Thank you. Thank you. Thank you, God."

"She's recovering—" he commented and quickly put the screen away.

"Wait! Please, let me see! Please!"

"That can be arranged," he explained in a tone so calm, so controlled that I wanted to gouge his eyeballs out with the pocketknife beneath my mattress. "It all depends on you, really."

"What do you mean?"

"If you can show me that you can cooperate, I will show you I can cooperate."

"I can. Of course, I can. I will. Gospodin Mikhailov. I will do anything. Sir, listen to me. I'm smart, I can be useful to you. Is this a school?" The thoughts and ideas kept coming and coming. I'd do anything to see Mama. I'd say anything. "It looked like a school when I was carried here. I saw a few classes and—and there were teachers, weren't there? Tell me what you need. I can work. I speak perfect English. I can teach English," I urged. Mikhailov raised his palm up to silence me. I stopped.

"I've reviewed the notes on your time with us, Mina Nikolaevna. I must admit, there is tremendous potential, despite your lack of control and those nasty sporadic outbursts. The endurance you've displayed, the natural predisposition required for skilled combat—you possess the agility and strength required. Not to mention the ease with which you psychologically manipulated one of our agents. You are Lavidian material."

"Lavidian?" I asked.

"And, now, I can see that your mother will serve as an ideal tool to help you stay in…control of your impulses," he finished carefully.

My limbs shook in anger at his implication as the nurse finished the wrapping and helped to roll me to my back. Artyom entered the room with the second guard carrying trays of food. They placed both trays on the table and after Mikhailov waved them away, both turned to wait by the doors of the infirmary as Mikhailov unwrapped his utensils.

He had a plate filled with barbecued meat and fish, rice, and salad. He had a warm loaf of bread and pickled vegetables. I had a bowl of warm broth before me and a spoon, but there was a salt shaker beside it and for that, I was grateful. Still, I didn't touch the spoon. How could I, after what he had just said—just threatened me with?

Mikhailov bit into his food. He looked at me, my hands clenched under the blanket.

"Eat," he commanded, a threat in his tone. This was it, the test. Would I be cooperative?

I could flip the soup over. I could throw it in his nauseating face. But it wouldn't help—wouldn't change things. It would only make matters worse.

Mama's alive. My heart soared. I would do anything—everything they asked of me—I realized. I took my hands out from under the covers of the wool blanket and gripped the spoon tightly, then I placed it back down on the table. I brought the bowl of soup to my chest and lowered my eyes to sip from it.

"Good," Mikhailov purred, evidently pleased. "We have your mother in one of our secure facilities, rehabilitating, much like you. But her condition can easily worsen, if, for example, you make moves the organization deems uncooperative. Similarly, they can get her the best care available if you prove to be valuable."

"I'll be valuable. What do you need me to do?" I urged.

Mikhailov chuckled as though my sudden enthusiasm amused him. I didn't let it bother me. "You need to heal first. You will begin attending classes as soon as you're able to sit through a lesson."

"What kind of lesson?" I asked.

"Our approach with you will be more specific than the other girls. There will be a curriculum. You will follow it. This is a very special program. Studying here is a privilege, an honor." He widened his eyes to emphasize his point.

"Yes, sir," I obliged.

"We do not train outsiders. This is a rare exception. I made your case to my superiors and they agreed to allow you to train among our agents on a trial basis. Absolute loyalty and obedience are expected of you. When you begin this program, you will no longer be called Mina Arkova. You will relinquish your name and your identity to become a pupil of this program. Do you understand?"

"You can call me whatever you'd like. My name doesn't matter to me, sir. I will do anything to help my mother."

"Good. Rest now. In two days, your work begins."

CHAPTER 25

OLIVER

"Yo, Oli, that shit was crazy...I can't believe they brought it all back! Boss level," Xavi remarked and jumped back into cataloging the units into our system, box by box. He'd hardly believed me when I had called him to say the merchandise had all been returned, and that he needed to get to the storage unit asap.

Everything CJ promised that his lawyer would accomplish for us, he accomplished. This man must have been a magician because our merchandise, phones, and the laptop were all returned within a few days of me reaching out to him. All I provided the lawyer with was the same information that I'd already emailed the police myself. But time and time again, I learned the lesson that a lawyer meant power and the right lawyer meant results.

A lawyer had gotten me out of an abusive home, put a sadistic monster away, and now, saved my ass yet again. Fitting that becoming a lawyer was one of Mina's greatest ambitions.

I smiled at that thought and another came to mind: remembering the dimple in her brow and cheek that formed when she twisted her mouth in concentration over a challenging prompt in Gerald's AP Gov class. Lately, I'd been lost in more and more memories of her. I was forgetting the details I'd come to learn so well, like the exact curve of her cheekbone and the sound of her hum when she was reading and got to her favorite part in a book. I missed her.

Over the past few days, Xavi and I had staked out almost all the locations in the valley that were on the list.

I'd learned that I was more likely to spot her or one of the men who had her at night. In the daytime, only the most desperate junkies and low-level drug dealers showed face.

At night, these spots saw far more traffic. Motorcycle crews did meet-ups, musicians threw ragers, and pimps were openly conducting business from most of the rooms.

Some of the spots on the list were regular motels with no suspicious activity or illegal stuff going down at all. Still, I'd peer into as many rooms as I could, site after site. Even after asking the wrong people the wrong questions and being met with angry looks, or on several occasions, getting shoved to the ground, kicked around, told to get lost, I persisted on my fool's errand. They must have thought I was a lunatic or maybe a pathetic stalker who was desperate to find a working girl I'd become obsessed with.

Sometimes, I'd just sit on my bike and eavesdrop on conversations, keeping an ear open for Russian language, and even that pissed people off, especially the pimps. They kept coming by and threatening me. They were probably concerned that I might have been scaring off their customers. And maybe I was. I didn't care. Xavi cared; he didn't approve of my less-than-subtle methods of questioning.

Xavi bumped my shoulder to get my attention as a curvy woman jogged past our van. We were sitting in my van, parked outside one of the final valley locations on the list. The days were growing shorter and darkness came earlier every day, but that was to be expected with winter fast approaching. The holidays were just around the corner. I shook my head at Xavi as he escorted the curvy woman down the street with his gaze.

"Oli, are you going to answer me?" Nyah's voice came through the speakerphone.

"What?" I asked, not recalling her exact question.

"I asked if you wanted to grab a bite at my place. My dad was asking about you."

"I...uh can't come by today. I've gotta—wait, hold on...I have another call." I looked at the display. "It's CJ. It might be about Kiran's guy. Let me take this...I'll hit you back. Sorry, Ny." I answered my second line. "Hello?"

"Oliver. Kiran will text you shortly with a time and a place for tonight. He doesn't know you're coming," CJ said.

"You think that'll be a problem?" I asked.

"I'm not sure, to be completely honest with you. Only God knows which way the wind will blow with that one."

"Hey..." Xavi leaned in to tell me something in my ear. "Ask if I can come with you. I don't want you going alone."

I shook my head to show it wasn't necessary but he nodded, insisting. "Can Xavi come?"

"Who? Oh, yeah, your associate. It might be better you go on your own with Kiran. He'd be more likely to give you something with fewer ears around. I've given her my blessing to accompany you. Plus, I'm sending both my men, so you should be fine. Just don't piss her off—she can be...vicious, my little Kiran," CJ chuckled. Now that I'd seen their dynamic for myself, I highly doubted that Kiran needed CJ's blessing for anything.

"Thank you, CJ. It means a lot to me," I stroked his ego but also meant it.

"I do hope you find the answers you're looking for, Oliver. But let me also say...prepare yourself for some difficult news. These organizations are not known for treating vulnerable women very hospitably. It's likely your friend may never come back from wherever she is and if she does, she'll hardly be the same. You should prepare for—"

"Mina's strong," I snapped. "Okay, thanks, CJ. We'll talk later."

Moments later, Kiran's text indeed came through. But there was no address or time, just: *see you tonight Mr grump* accompanied by a kissy face emoji.

I wrote back, *where? What time?*

Kiran didn't respond right away, and Xavi and I were still checking out the last address on the list. We spent about half an hour inspecting every open window. I called Mina's name. We knocked on every door and showed her picture to anyone who would take a look. No one recognized her.

Dejected, I returned to my van and Xavi followed. I rolled down my windows and listened. The chill had a bite and Xavi cupped his hands around his mouth for warmth.

"Screw what he says—I can still come. I don't gotta be right next to you. I'll just be nearby. In case—"

"It's cool, Xavi. I'll be fine."

"All right, but hit me up if anything feels shady," he insisted.

"Yeah, I—"

My phone vibrated with a message.

KIRAN

> sorry love, getting my bikini waxed atm let's talk details later?

Then, she sent a smirking emoji.

> we meeting at a pool party?

I joked.

Xavi read the texts over my shoulder. "Man, she's something," he chuckled under his breath.

KIRAN

there's my fun grump! Make sure you bring HIM
out tonight

Her response made me regret my retort but I knew damn
well that I couldn't help it sometimes.

I can't bring fun grump anywhere if I don't know
when or where we're going

I texted.

KIRAN

Anton's not gonna get there till it's thoroughly
going. headliner on at midnight so we'll collect
you at your place 11ish?

headliner? tell me it's not a rave

I texted back, frustrated with the lack of information.

KIRAN

not rave its at Spaces

what's spaces?

KIRAN

sweetness, does it matter? it's a venue...u
need these answers or not?

I'll be there. dress code?

I asked.

KIRAN

> you could come in disco gear and I get the feeling they'd still open the ropes for you. But if you're asking what I'd have you in...I certainly wouldn't mind you in a dark dress shirt, sleeves rolled up, a few buttons undone, perhaps?

She sent a winking emoji.

"Daaaaamn, dog...you in trouble. This lady gonna eat you alive, I swear," Xavi joked. I shot her a quick text back.

> just lmk when u figure out the exact time.

"You think I gotta dress differently than this?" I asked Xavi, gesturing to my hoodie and jeans.

"I don't get it...is it a club?"

"I don't know. She said, 'venue' and 'headliner.' But if it is a club...I've never been to one," I admitted. Xavi shrugged.

"I mean, I'm not a club rat or nothing but I've rolled through a few spots when a homie was spinnin' and hit me up to come through. I wore a dress shirt like she said, and looked fine as aged wine, believe me."

"I believe you."

"Ey, it's gonna be loud as hell, though. How you supposed to have a conversation with this fool in a place like that?"

I shrugged. "Guess I'll figure that part out after I'm there. You got anything I can borrow? A dress shirt or whatever?"

"You wanna borrow something from me? I mean...shit, sure. I've got like...one. But it could use an iron and some Febreze." We both laughed at that.

"All right, I'll just stop by somewhere and pick up a few of those for us both. We'll probably need them eventually anyway," I offered.

"All right. Yo, so what's up with that girl you were on the phone with?" Xavi asked, trying to sound casual about it.

"Nyah? She's my girl's best friend. She's been helping me find Mina. Her dad's the reason I have the list—"

"No, yeah, I know that," he said.

"Then, what do you mean what's up with her?" I asked.

"She was asking you to come by her place for dinner."

"Yeah…so?"

"So, let's roll through…"

"Why?"

"Why? She's got an awfully sexy speaking voice and I wanna see if it matches the rest of her, that's why."

"Xavi, you think everything about every woman you ever meet is sexy," I joked, but not really.

"Not untrue," he confirmed. "But like, is she as cute as she sounds?" He waggled his brows at me, grinning from ear to ear. "Just blink twice for 'yes.'"

"Not answering that," I said, shaking my head at him but smiling for the first time in a long while.

"Gotta eat, Oli. Gotta eat."

CHAPTER 26

MINA

oday would be the day. I woke up before the first light of the sun touched the window pane of the infirmary. I awaited the arrival of the nurse and listened for the birdsong I had grown fond of hearing, a sound that had never penetrated the brick and concrete walls of my old prison downstairs. One of the many perks of my new, gilded confinement.

The nurse had at last entered the infirmary and I wondered where she slept.

"Good morning, Katya," I told her brightly.

"Do not call me Katya, girl. It's forbidden. I asked you once already," the nurse scolded but managed to still sound gentle. She had let her name slip late last night, after a long day on her feet. I asked and she answered. Then, she covered her mouth in horror and asked me never to repeat it. Yekaterina Borisovna. I thought she'd meant not to repeat the full name, but it appeared the nickname wouldn't do, either.

"Yes, of course, nurse," I agreed.

I'd been eager to leave this room, even if just for a few hours, and today was meant to be the day that I would be allowed out. The nurse hadn't let me get out of bed so far. The most movement she'd allowed was the tilt of my hips for the insertion and removal of a bedpan—a mortifying process.

"Please, I can walk to the restroom. Let me try," I would beg her, but she wouldn't hear it.

The past twenty-four hours were all anticipation and routine. Ice packs along my ribs every forty minutes during every waking hour, medication every four hours, examination—the nurse's hands all over my body to apply salve every six hours on the bruises that covered me from neck to ankle.

I would tell her, "Allow me to apply the cream myself, I can do it." But she insisted she could do a more thorough job. There were five meals a day—three big ones and two snacks. I could hardly stomach them because firstly, the pain in my ribs was still too keen. Secondly, I was no longer used to this much food. Thirdly, I hadn't been as active. The only exercises that Katya allowed me to practice were breathing exercises.

The nurse had her hands full with more than just me as her patient. Three other girls had come into the infirmary yesterday, which was quite eventful, although no one addressed me or so much as glanced my way. I listened to their exchanges while pretending to sleep. One girl had dislocated her ankle. The nurse was able to pop it back into place and send her off with an ice pack.

"How's that?" I heard Katya ask her.

The girl answered, "Good," and walked off without another word.

The second girl sounded very young, I'd say around twelve years old, and had gotten a splinter under her nail. I opened my eyes and watched as Katya managed to remove it in less than a minute. The girl looked at me for a few moments, as though to appraise me in her own way, then like the first, she turned and left.

The third girl was brought into the infirmary on a stretcher, carried by two guards like I had been, except she appeared to be unconscious. The guards told Katya that the girl had been hit on the head in combat training. The nurse nodded like this wasn't a rare occurrence, then brusquely asked the guards to transfer her onto the bed carefully.

After the guards had carried the stretcher away, Katya opened a small bottle of something and waved it under the girl's nose, causing her to wake with a start. Katya opened a file cabinet that was kept under lock and key and retrieved a file. She performed a series of tests on the girl to look for signs of a concussion, I supposed, and took detailed notes before asking her to stay for a few hours of monitoring.

The girl was visibly uneasy and her gaze jumped to the door every time there was a noise, as though she was afraid of who might come through it. I had tried to smile at her on many occasions as she lay there, but she pointedly ignored me.

"How did you get injured?" I whispered to the girl and she finally looked my way.

She had opened her mouth to answer when Katya's voice quickly interjected from across the infirmary, "This is a space for quiet and rest. No talking."

"I'm sorry," I offered. Something told me I could trust Katya despite how strict she seemed.

Today, nothing could keep my inquisitive mind at bay. As soon as Katya arrived this morning, questions filled my head. Where were they keeping Mama? Was she also somewhere in Belarus? Was she near? How could I find her? Was it possible she was in this same building? It certainly seemed big enough to hide many secrets.

"What is this city?" I asked Katya.

"We don't speak about locations here. It's forbidden," Katya responded sternly.

"Did you grow up somewhere nearby?"

"It's considered forbidden to speak about your personal life to one another in any way," Katya warned, but I wasn't discouraged.

"Where does the staff sleep? On cots in a communal room? Or on beds? And the girls? Are there bedrooms? How many?"

"This is for you." Katya placed an envelope on the empty cart beside my bed and went to her supply closet to begin her daily inventory count on schedule, ignoring my questions. I was too distracted by the envelope to insist on answers from her.

"Zhavoronok" it read. For a moment I wondered who this Lark was, then realized it was my new name. I recalled Mikhailov's words. *When you begin this program, you will no longer be called Mina Arkova. You will relinquish your name and your identity.* I was ready to relinquish everything about myself, even my likeness if I had to, if it meant protecting Mama and Nyah and my little cousin, Anya.

I opened the envelope. Inside were two pieces of paper with today's date, the word 'Lark,' and my schedule typed neatly. But the date was what I was staring at. It read November 27th, which meant it had been over a month and a half since I'd been taken from home. *I've been here more than six weeks?* That amount of time made my head spin. I forced myself to focus on the rest of the schedule.

It looked like my first class, named 'Society 1A', would be right after breakfast, in precisely one hour. Afterwards, I'd have to check back in with the nurse for an evaluation, treatment, and medication. There would be a nutrition break shortly after and the next class was 'Psychological Strategy 1B', in the afternoon. Lunch was scheduled shortly after, but again, it appeared that I was expected to return to the infirmary and check in with the nurse for treatment. The last class scheduled was 'Diversion 1Y', followed by dinner and bedtime.

I ate my breakfast quickly and had been studying my schedule when a girl burst into the infirmary.

"Nurse!" she cried. It was Starling. Her hand looked like it had been badly injured, and the blood trailed down her elbow and dripped into a tidy, dark crimson puddle on the tile. The nurse rushed to her at once.

"What's happened?"

"I was…it was an accident." Tears fell down her cheeks.

"Did someone do this to you?" the nurse asked.

Starling shook her head, no, and her eyes darted to meet mine. Now, with our gazes locked on each other this way, it was clear she was lying. Someone *had* done this to her, I was suddenly certain. It hadn't been an accident.

"Come." The nurse pulled her along toward the sink in the back of the infirmary. She washed the cut, which from my vantage point didn't seem to stop the bleeding. Katya worked quickly, retrieving herbs from her cabinet of medicines. She looped a silk thread through a needle and began stitching the laceration with confident, steady movements of her hand. All the while, Starling watched me. I went on eating my breakfast, mixing the berries into the oatmeal and chewing as I watched Katya work. I felt nothing for Starling, maybe a twinge of pity, but I suffocated it as soon as the feeling arose. Finally, Katya covered the wound with a green paste and wrapped the hand in gauze.

"Come back for a fresh dressing at lunch," Katya told Starling, whose eyes still bored into mine. Katya looked between us in disapproval. "Starling! Off you go. And keep out of trouble. You must be more careful with your dominant hand." Starling nodded and disappeared in a few swift strides.

"Kat-I mean Nurse, what can I wear today?"

"I have a few spare things I picked up for you this morning."

Katya went to retrieve a folded pile of clothes that she had left on a bed when she had come in this morning. I motioned to sit up, eager to get out of this bed.

"Wait!" Katya urged and ran over to help me stand, throwing the clothes down onto my bed.

"I'm fine. I can stand, you don't have to worry." I turned to examine the clothes, which were quite plain. Three dark cotton pants, three collared white button-up shirts, a long gray dress, a dark wool coat, several pairs of clean white underwear, and gray, wool socks.

"Are there any shoes?"

"Right, what's your size?"

"Seven."

"Seven? Is that a US size?"

"Yes."

"I'll find you a pair of boots that fit. They keep hand-me-downs in a room downstairs. You can wear your slippers meanwhile. Go on, start getting changed."

The nurse had brought over my toothbrush and toothpaste. I took them and nodded gratefully. I had redness and swelling at my gum line that were slowly healing with treatment. I joined Katya near the sink to brush my teeth. She eyed me warily like she was worried I'd collapse.

"I'm fine," I insisted. "Would it be possible for me to get my hands on a hairbrush?" My hair was quickly becoming a tragedy. I'd been working through the tangles with my fingers all this time, but a brush would have gone a long way toward making me feel human again.

"I don't have a brush up here for you. I'll put in a request for one. They'll have to forgive your appearance for now. I'll run down right now and look through the storage room for some boots for you to wear. You can't go barefoot. A US seven, maybe that's around a size thirty-eight?" She appraised my feet.

"Thirty-seven probably." I remembered Mama letting me

borrow a fancy pair of European shoes for a school dance, the first time I wore heels. The sole read 37. They were a bit loose then, but I'd probably grown into them by now. The memory ached and I pushed it away.

"I'll lock you in here. Please, change in the meantime. If you feel faint, lie down."

"Yes," I promised. As soon as the door clicked shut, I finished brushing my teeth as fast as I could, flossed, applied the white paste treatment to my gums, changed out of my hospital gown, and tried to braid my hair out of my face, but the pain of lifting my arms was overwhelming and I gave up. Instead, I took the unprecedented opportunity to snoop around.

I had to be quick. I went to the file cabinet first, but it was locked. I looked around for the key. It was nowhere near the sink or the countertop. It must have been with Katya.

That's when I saw it, Starling's file, above another file on the far counter. I ran to it, checked the door, and opened the folder quickly.

STARLING
Azra Kader
Ethnicity: Arab
Religion: Sunni Islam
Status: Refugee
Notes: Subject volatile and displays signs of aggression and rebellion.
Subject refused nourishment for several days.
Unresponsive to punishment and cold shock therapy.
Unresponsive to light deprivation.
Highly invested in wellbeing of younger sister, strong motivating factor and behavioral shift into more

amenable disposition upon mention of younger sister's involvement with the organization in place of the subject.

Subject has become highly cooperative after the threat of younger sister replacing her was more explicitly discussed.

Subject no longer rejecting food or water.

Deep lacerations to upper forearms, torso, and legs.

Amoxicillin needed for infection spread in wound.

Treatment necessary for severe rash formed around ropes.

Full compliance and cooperation achieved.

Subject has abandoned all religious affiliation and devotion.

Released to infirmary for therapy.

Treated for lacerations, rash and malnourishment in infirmary under Nurse A.

Notes:

Fluent in Arabic, Russian and English.

Mentioned exceptional proficiency in swimming, skiing and chess.

Training revealed a notable aptitude for hand-to-hand combat and long-distance shooting.

She said she's been here for two whole years. They must have taken her when she was about fifteen and threatened to replace her with her even younger sister. It was their strategy, I realized. And it worked every damn time.

I wondered for a horrible moment if they would take her

sister anyway, if they would take my little cousin, Anya, anyway. Time was running out. I checked the door to see if someone was coming, then I went back to my snooping. The file beneath Starling's was blank—no name. *Maybe it's mine.* I wanted to read it, needed to read it. I checked the door once again and grabbed for the file. It was as I thought.

Mina Nikolaevna Arkova
Ethnicity: Russian
Religion: Unknown
Status: US Citizen
Notes: Subject unresponsive to strikes and displays unusual resilience to punishment.
Subject highly invested in wellbeing of mother. Subject expressed bouts of rage and denial.
Subject continued conditioning exercises after severe strikes to torso.
During second beating, subject demonstrated advanced potential for combat proficiency and strong defense instincts. Subject quickly understood new objective and proceeded to produce necessary emotional distress for suitable torture footage to motivate subject's father into compliance.
Subject displays highly acute understanding and control of emotional manipulation and was able to extract information and emotional distress from trained Lavidian pupil.
Recommendation to consider subject for Lavidian Program submitted.

Subject took a trained Lavidian agent down in an attack with a food tray, dislocating agent's kneecap.

Subject withstood oxygen deprivation in gas mask without losing consciousness.

Subject requested termination of life after a trial of plank binding.

Subject attacked senior Lavidian guard in self-defense utilizing chains.

Subject attacked senior supervisor in self-defense with the supervisor's pocketknife, leaving multiple, non-lethal lacerations to the groin.

Released to infirmary for rehabilitation.

Treatment for early onset pneumonia, hairline fracture in rib 9.

Notes:

Fluent in English and Russian.

I knew all of this. I needed something else—a location, information on where they could be keeping Mama, but before I could flip the page, there was a clicking sound at the door. I shut the folder hastily and threw it on top of Starling's file. I refilled my mouth with baking soda water and gargled as the nurse reentered the infirmary carrying a pair of boots.

Her eyes went straight to the files, which were clearly misplaced from where she had left them. Katya dropped the boots at my feet and went to the files at once. My heart froze. What if she reported me? What if they hurt Mama over this? Why had I been so careless? She picked up the files, stacked them neatly, and placed them across the room.

"You should go. You'll be late," she said coldly. She said nothing more. I wouldn't give her the opportunity to grow angry. I nodded appreciatively and bent down gingerly to pick up the boots, not with little effort on my part.

Katya tsked. "Sit, I'll help you put them on."

"I can manage—"

"Sit." She brought my medication over on an oval tray along with a glass of water. "This should help with the nausea and the pain for a few hours."

"Thank you." I took the pills as Katya worked on my boots. They were a bit loose on my foot but a far better alternative than if they'd been too small. I thanked her again before leaving the infirmary.

It had all been so easy in my mind, theoretically, leaving the infirmary, stepping out into the hallway. But as I faced the prospect now, the unknown out there made my fingers grow cold and shaky. I squared my shoulders and forced myself to step into the hallway.

One step. Two. Three.

I had faced so much already. I wasn't going to be defeated by a hallway and my own fractured mind. I clenched my hands into fists until I could feel my nails sinking into the skin. Four. Five. Six. My breathing grew ragged. I grew closer and closer to the wall, dragging my shoulder along it to stay on my feet.

The eastward facing windows of the hallway brought in so much light from the winter sun that it burned my unconditioned eyes, which were now grown accustomed to the drawn shades of the infirmary.

In a daze from the onset of stimuli, I put all of my weight against the wall in an effort not to slide down to the floor. Girls brushed past me so swiftly, like ghosts, in those perfect lines. A teacher rushed through the hall to unlock a door in front of a line of girls who were already waiting.

I noted the guards at the ends of the hall, marching down the center of the corridor, checking that everything was in order.

My head spun and my breath caught. I tilted my head up to

the ceiling and opened my mouth to catch the air that was so quickly escaping my lungs. Where was I going? I realized then that I had no idea which of these doors would hold the Society class that was written on my schedule.

I froze and stared down at one of my hands; fingernail marks marred the inside of my palm in ugly c shapes. Where is that schedule? I patted my pockets. Did I leave it at my bedside? I hadn't gone far from the infirmary. I could just turn and go back. All I had to do was move my feet.

My mind understood what I had to do, but my body was frozen. I rotated toward the wall until my palms were flush on the wallpaper and my forehead rested against it. It smelled like chalk and wet paper.

"What are you doing?" The low, rough voice cut through the ringing in my ears. Then, there was a strong grip around my arm, a guard pulling me off-kilter. I lost my balance, knees buckling as I nearly fell to the floor. If he hadn't been holding me up, I would've hit the floor hard. The guard pulled me back up to my feet in a rough motion, keeping a painful hold on my upper arm.

"I'm...it's...release me—" I stuttered.

"You belong in the infirmary. What are you doing in the hall?"

"I'll take her—" said a voice behind me. A gentler touch accompanied the voice. The guard with the vise grip on my arm eased up his hold at last and I leaned into the more open-palmed support of the masculine voice behind me. I knew before seeing him that it was Mikhailov's guard, Artyom. I'd learned the sound of his voice by now. It brought an unexpected ease to the tension coiled in my gut.

"Thank you—" I breathed and righted myself, taking a small step away from him. Artyom nodded and looked at my open palm, shaking his head.

"I was held up. I would've come sooner," he excused himself.

"I'll escort you downstairs, now—show you to the room on your schedule. Try to pay attention so you can find your own way back," he advised. I nodded and followed. He turned and went in the opposite direction than I was originally heading. "All the 1A classes are on the first floor, the 2s are on the second, and the 3s are here on the level of the infirmary. Combat, Arms Training, Weapons Training, and Diversion Training are all outdoors. Be very aware of your surroundings in those areas. Getting distracted when someone is knife throwing, ax throwing or shooting can be life and death."

I was shaking as I held onto Artyom's forearm, keeping distance between our bodies but as we approached the stairs, I slowed. Feeling drained, I took my four steadying breaths and began the descent, leaning heavily into him. I poured my pain into my exhales. Artyom watched me carefully as I descended each step. I turned to meet his eyes for a moment—the color, a clear and brilliant azure—then looked away quickly. I missed the next step and almost stumbled down the stairs. He compensated for my misstep and wrapped his wide arm around my waist to steady me.

"Arkova, focus," he scolded, then quickly closed his mouth into a tight line. "*Zhavoronok*," 'Lark,' he corrected.

"Why are we birds? Why do you get a name, Artyom?"

He stopped in his tracks and looked at me, a flash of anger or frustration in his eyes. "Know your rank. You don't address me by my name."

"What do I call you, then?"

"You don't call me," he said. His tone wasn't unkind but he meant what he had said with a finality.

"If I'm Lark, you're Serpent," I tested, my eyes flashing to him for a second. He ignored me and moved us along. We reached the bottom of the stairs. Artyom stopped in front of the third door on the right.

"Here," he said. "Go in." And he left me without a word or a glance back.

The door was closed. A small oval brass tag with the engraved letter *A* hung around a nail in the door. "Society 1A," the schedule had read. Next on schedule was "Psychological Strategy 1B." I took note of the door with a *B* tag farther along the hallway. I returned my attention to door *A*.

Was I supposed to knock or just enter? I didn't know. I knocked. The muffled voice coming from inside grew quiet before the clicking of heels approached. The woman who opened the door stared at me blankly. I peered inside, my heart thumping loudly in my chest.

The class was filled with children, all girls, none of whom looked over twelve. They were clearly children on the cusp of puberty.

"I'm sorry. I was brought here. This must be the wrong place. I'm looking for Soc—"

"Silence, or I'll tape your mouth shut for the rest of class. Is there a reason you have arrived late and disturbed the pace of my lesson today?" the woman snapped.

I closed my mouth and looked at the floor, shaking my head.

"Lark, sit. Do not speak unless spoken to." I nodded, more than happy to oblige, my head spinning from the excursion of walking down so many steps.

There was exactly one empty chair in the very back of the small room. I moved to it without hesitation. There were nine chairs total, three rows of three. The girls in the chairs were silent, focused solely on the teacher and the image projected on the white screen in the front of the room. The girls were dressed in the same uniform as I was, but each of them wore her hair in a neat chignon whereas mine was braided in a tangled mess with strands already falling forward into my face.

Society was less of a class and more a dictation of facts. The teacher—I did not know her name nor did I dare interrupt to ask as she droned on—listed names of noteworthy families in current positions of power and influence. She projected images of their faces and the logos of the companies they owned.

We were expected to memorize this information, by the looks of the lesson. We weren't given any paper or writing utensils to take notes. The other girls simply stared at the images and listened in silence for two hours as the teacher droned on and on. The pain in my ribs grew louder with each passing minute. A bead of sweat had formed above my brow and began to slide down the side of my face. My breaths became heavy and audible.

"Zharabovsky, Igor. Owner of Yakut Oil Company," the teacher said and changed the image projected to a bald man wearing glasses. The faces were all starting to look the same. "Born September 23, 1966 in the town of Avdiivka, Ukraine. Graduated from the Moscow State University of Technology-Stankin with a degree in Computer-Aided Design in 1989. Married, with three sons." She went on to describe the shopping habits of the wife, the drug habits of the mistress, and the weaknesses of all three sons. It went on this way for all the heads of the major energy companies in the country. Where they lived, how many houses they owned, where they traveled, and how well they were favored at the moment. The girls listened in silence, as did I, and then it was over.

They stood so abruptly, I almost fell out of my chair from the uniformity of their movement. The two before me marched to the front of the room and blended into a line. I fought to follow in step but was too slow. By the time I managed to file in, the pain in my ribs had grown to be nearly unbearable. I needed my medication desperately. I thought of the six flights of stairs ahead of me and groaned.

"Shut up, you cow, or we'll all be punished!" sniped the girl before me and stepped back onto my boot with her heel.

"What's wrong with you?" I hissed at her in Russian, biting my tongue to keep from crying out.

"Silence! There is no talking during class, Lark!" The teacher barked. I grew quiet, knowing better than to draw more attention to myself, especially in my weakened state. I'd bide my time. I needed my strength.

I followed the line outside but kept a healthy distance between myself and the brat. I let them leave quickly and stayed behind to speak with the teacher.

"Ma'am?" I observed as she pinched the bridge of her wide nose. Her washed-out features became even paler.

"Yes?"

"Are we supposed to learn the names and details of these people you have been describing during the lesson?"

"Are you an imbecile?"

"No."

"What else are you supposed to do with the information I give you but learn it, of course?" She let out an exasperated breath and rested her hand on her hip.

"Will we be tested? And what if I can't remember certain details?" I asked her.

"There are no tests. These facts you must know like the alphabet. When an agent is given an assignment out in the real world, you will prepare in a similar fashion. You will be expected to learn your subject, their world as well as your new identity."

"Do we call you by a name or just ma'am, or teacher—?"

"You don't…call me," she snapped, echoing Artyom's words. "You are called upon. Otherwise, you are silent. Clear?" She shoved me out the door, swung it shut with a hard click, and locked it with her keys. She turned and left me in the hall, blinking after her.

I was in a cold sweat by the time I crawled back into my bed in the infirmary. The nurse rushed over to me, shaking her head.

"I knew it was too soon. I'll have you know, I insisted on more time for recovery but I was denied. Two weeks has been the standard for almost all post-basement level rehabilitation, especially considering the severity of your injuries. I'd up your dosage but I don't want to risk you becoming dependent on the painkillers. These can become a problem," Katya rambled.

"I'll be fine," I panted. "I just need to rest for a minute." Kicking my boots off, I burrowed beneath the sheets that carried the sterile, medicinal scent of detergent. "It's those stairs that get me and my foot...this little witch stepped on me, on purpose. She looked like she was aiming to break my foot—why are they like that?"

"Who was it?" the nurse asked, not at all surprised.

"I don't know, the one in front of me in line. Nasty little thing, no remorse, no human softness in her eyes like some of them have, just cold, hollow eyes," I explained as I glanced toward the similarly cold eyes of the nurse. But Katya's eyes were different than those of the girl. I could see that Katya had a warmth inside her that she fought to camouflage with cold indifference. Her purpose was to heal, to revive, to recover, and that purpose easily shone through her every action. She deliberated, glanced at the door before returning her gaze to me and the hardness in her expression softened just the slightest.

"The ones who have been here longest, especially the ones who were raised here since infancy tend to be...different than the rest." She leaned in closer and lowered her voice, fingers busy tidying the top of my sheets into a neat fold. "They are exceptionally bright, efficient, impressive in more ways than one, but they look at life like a game. Even in everyday life, when they aren't on assignment, they are tallying points in their heads. They don't like to lose. The easiest way to win sometimes is to make your opponent endure a tougher time than necessary. Be wary of the career girls. Stay out of their way," the nurse warned, her gaze darting back and forth between my eyes and the door.

I nodded in admiration of her bravery to speak frankly with me despite her apparent fear of being overheard. It felt like I could trust her. She seemed to be one of the only remotely decent people I'd come across in this horrid place.

"Where are the dormitories? Am I to sleep somewhere else tonight?" I asked her, worried.

"I'll bring it up to my superiors that you should stay here for as long as the beds are available. Of course, when there's an injury, you'll be expected to forfeit the bed. As I understand, they are eager for you to assimilate to life at Lavidian. The dormitories are all on different levels and dispersed based on division along the east side of the manor," Katya explained as she rushed around the cabinets, sorting my medication. "Here, take these quickly and eat some pudding. We don't want to upset your stomach. These are herbal-based; they shouldn't conflict with the pain medication I gave you a few hours ago. They won't be as strong but it should hold you over for the next few hours. Be careful on those stairs, Lark."

I took the capsules from the dish that she held out to me, along with the glass of water, and I nodded.

"Good. Now, do the breathing exercises while I bring over your ice pack."

When I first read "Psychological Strategy 1," I'd imagined a lecture on old psychological philosophies and terminology with, maybe, some pointers on how to withstand torture sprinkled in. As I sat in the lecture and attempted to focus on the words coming from the teacher's mouth, my body remained in a state of fight or flight. My exhaustion and the tension in my neck from the inexplicable fear of an attack from behind were weighing heavily on me. Inexplicable because I was sitting in the last row—there was no one behind me. There would be no attack.

Tears would spring to my eyes sporadically throughout the class. I'd wipe them away quickly before anyone could notice and when I looked around, I masked my expression to make sure no one had seen.

It was surprising how composed the other girls always seemed. I remembered myself at that age. I was full of hyper energy and found it difficult to sit still for very long. I was always giggling at something, shifting around in my seat, asking questions, obsessing over how much the world had to offer. These girls looked to be the same group who had been in Society 1 with me. There was a heart-wrenching deadness behind their eyes, like someone had drilled a hole in the top of their heads and vacuumed out all their hopes and dreams. Then I remembered that if I got the chance to observe my own reflection, I would bet the look behind my eyes would not be very dissimilar to theirs. We were kindred spirits, now—the girls in these halls and I—kindred ghouls.

My gaze raked over the class, observing them carefully, looking for a crack in their composed expressions. They'd all been taken from their homes, I guessed. Maybe not all, but probably most. I couldn't see the evidence of it. If I had been taken at twelve years old from my friends and family, I'd be a wreck. I wouldn't be sitting quietly in a lesson. They all probably had people they were protecting, people they were here for. Maybe their old lives were worse than what they had to endure here. Maybe they were content here. Maybe they even felt fortunate, chosen. Maybe they didn't know about the cells in the basement, yet.

"If you are facing a shortage of time or resources, however, your aim is to change the appearance of your most distinct feature," the teacher explained as she switched the image on the projector to a slide of a woman with untamed, red hair.

"If you have bright curly hair and you are seeking cover, your best bet is to put on a wide hat or cover with an umbrella, as this will protect your image from most aerial surveillance. It's important to note that stealing a disguise isn't always worth the trouble of attracting attention as a thief—discretion must take precedence. Take from those who don't value their possessions. This is determined by body language. How tightly is the possession being held? Are the knuckles white with tension? How financially secure does the victim appear? This can be evaluated by noting jewelry, watches, quality of fabric, shoes.

"When seeking a direction for your disguise, if the hair is curly and dark, you make it light and straight. If you're short, you wear heels, if you're young, add some gray into the hair. When using contouring makeup, here are areas of the face where shadowing can alter the width of the nose, the size of the forehead, and the shape of the jaw. Take note where the dark areas are drawn on here." The teacher switched the slide to the face of a woman with dark brown marks on her temple, the sides of her nose, the hollows of her cheeks, and along her jawline.

"This is how you narrow your features and then blend, and here is the result. And this is how you blend and shape your face to round out sharp features. Again, this will only serve its purpose if done dramatically to avoid some wide-angle surveillance detection. Facial hair and prosthetics are much more successful in achieving full disguise," the teacher explained. "And when it comes to a personal assignment—some of you have already had the privilege of experiencing a true field assignment—"

A girl with wavy dark hair sitting in the chair diagonal to

mine turned to give a meaningful look at the girl with short blonde hair and bangs sitting beside her—the little witch from earlier. It was that twisted little look in her cold, dead eyes that gave it away. The blonde rubbed a place on her inner wrist and pulled up her sleeve to reveal a tattoo of a raven. She must have felt my eyes on her because she glanced at me suddenly and yanked the sleeve back down over her wrist.

The girl in front of me turned back to look at me as well. I avoided eye contact. When both girls returned their full attention to the front of the class, I began scanning the other girls for signs of markings or tattoos. Most wore long sleeves so it was difficult to tell if anyone else was marked that way.

"—you will curate a style and a look based on your profile background. Your appearance must be informed by your profile history. If your profile indicates that you are poor, your hairstyles and clothing must reflect mass trends of the general public of the region.

"Take into account if the profile specifies social media consumption, specific region origins. Ethnic backgrounds must be taken into consideration. Above all else, appearance is the emotional connection that will tether you to your subject. You must find the thing missing in their life and become the thing that brings them fulfillment. This goes back to the basic attachment principles we've been discussing from the first days of our lessons. Without the emotional attachment of your subject, you have nothing and all your work will be worthless.

"What does your subject crave more than anything? To be understood? To be heard? To feel powerful? Important? To be touched? If yes, then touched how? With reverence? Passionately? With fear and respect? You must find the nuance in their persona. Their profile will inform some of that but a lot of it will be discovered in moments of communication and must be delicately extracted.

"Have they lost a child? Have they lost their self-worth?

These are vital kernels that, once weaponized, will prove a vital tool in your arsenal."

Weaponizing the death of a child against a subject? I shuddered at the thought. My skin crawled from the depravity of what this woman was programming into the minds of these girls.

They were so young, certainly too young to be told any of this. They were still children in my eyes. I looked around at their faces, so eager to learn, to absorb information, to prove themselves. Ambition and obedience rolled off them in waves.

At lunch, Starling returned to the infirmary. I was pushing boiled vegetables around my plate when she hurried in, then stopped dead in her tracks upon seeing me.

"Can I help you?" I asked her. I noticed purple tinges of a new bruise beneath her left eye. *That wasn't there this morning. Could she have gotten in trouble for some small kindness shown to me down in the cells?* "Ouch, what happened? Did you try to snuggle with the wrong bear?" I joked, but my heart involuntarily ached for her. She seemed so fragile, and after reading her file, I knew now that she was doing all this to protect her little sister. I understood her in a deeper way that I couldn't ignore.

Still, I was angry with her and thought it was cheap and cruel, how she tried to slither her way into my head when I was so vulnerable. At least now, I knew she hadn't done it purely for sport, unlike the others had seemed to—unlike Swan and the young girl with short hair and bangs who tried to shatter my foot—the ones who were raised inside these walls, who only knew this place and the survival mentality they bred around here.

Starling's gaze fell to the floor before lifting toward Katya.

"I think the dressing from this morning is still okay," Starling said quietly.

"Still, we'll refresh it," the nurse insisted and went to work without pause. Katya went to retrieve an ice pack for Starling's eye.

"What's wrong? You can't fight?" I asked her, placing an overcooked piece of broccoli in my mouth.

Starling looked at Katya—who was still rummaging in the freezer—and then looked back at me, hesitating before speaking. "I can fight. But with Swan, sometimes, fighting back and winning is not worth the cost. She thinks she's better than all of us—they teach them that from birth. I'll let her keep believing it. What's it matter to me?"

"Starling!" Katya scolded, returning with the wrapped ice pack. "You know better. Don't take advantage of my tolerance. I'm already on my second warning from the organization." Katya looked between us, face red with frustration.

"I'm sorry," Starling voiced at the same time as I asked, "Why?"

"You are not to discuss career agents or openly criticize or even identify ideals that are reinforced by Lavidian. Is that clear? If a guard were to walk by and overhear you and make note that I didn't report it, I would be the one punished," the nurse explained. And though she turned away quickly, I saw the terror in her eyes and felt it twinned in my own.

As I reached the bottom of the stairs to the first floor after lunch, my lungs seemed to burn from the amount of breath it took to get here. *Now what?* I moved through the hallway, staying as close to the wall as I could manage. I scraped past door *A*, door *B*, a lavatory, a window, an office of some sort, on and on until I reached the end of the hall, where a door led to the outside. I halted before it, a nervous energy gripping me. Why did I feel like I was doing something wrong? Diversion training was held outside. I needed to leave the manor in order to find the class. My heart thundered in my chest. I realized then that this was the first time in over a month and a half that I was going outside.

I suppressed the feeling of dread and pushed through the door. I took a step out, then another, but as I did, a veiled sense of terror crept back in, quietly enveloping me. I looked out and absorbed the sight of the open, sage sky.

There was a sound ahead, a scuffle of a shoe against dirt, near a bald birch tree. Slick. His eyes met mine, as I noticed him nursing his bandaged hand. A second later, he simply disappeared. *Am I hallucinating? Or have these bastards actually driven me insane?*

I must have conjured him up. He wasn't here, and I had no reason to believe they'd kept him around. He hadn't been to the infirmary; he hadn't been treated by Katya. What were the odds that there was a second infirmary on the manor grounds? I doubted it. Still, I'd been dreading—fearing—running into him in the halls. I was certain my mind would snap from it.

The wind hit me first and my heart seemed to stall abruptly. All the air and noise that surrounded me earlier had been suddenly muffled and there was merely a vacuum of wide endlessness ahead of me.

There was a thin layer of snow on the ground as far as I could see. I could feel the wind on my exposed skin but my lungs felt like there was no air to breathe. I felt like I was being smothered beneath a pillow. I could hear my heart—it pounded, beating faster and faster. I saw the ground before me, vast, muddy and covered in patches of white. I could see the gravel, the bald trees beyond, the vast grounds, and the forest surrounding the perimeter of the property. But it felt like it had been fog, an illusion just like Slick. Maybe I was an illusion too. Maybe I wasn't really here at all? Maybe I was dead on the floor of my house in Los Angeles, shot in the head by that intruder.

I tried to move but I just shook and shook. My nails bit into the flesh of my palms. I attempted to force a step forward. It was like the cosmos and all the multiverse within it stopped at the toe edge of my boots and if I took one step forward, I'd fall into the void. It was so open. I shut my eyes. *I'm no agoraphobic. This is all in my head, that's all.*

I didn't recall the outside world feeling so wide before. The day I'd stepped off the plane was the last time I had seen the sky without a pane of glass separating us. The sky was so expansive —had it looked so endless at home? I felt like I was going to be sick. I wanted to go back to the infirmary. It was the only place that felt safe, solid. I wanted to press myself into the infirmary bed and feel the mattress beneath me, the ceiling above me, Katya beside me.

Staring down at my boots, which were now wet with melted snow, I sensed the loss of feeling in my toes. I felt tears irritating the corners of my eyes. The panic had been rising inside me like a storm. A lark had been caged inside my chest, beating itself to death against the metal bars, desperate to escape. I covered my mouth with my hands to keep from hyperventilating. I sat down hard on the ground. Through the muffled drone in my ears, a voice grew clearer, cutting through the fog.

"Lark, you need to stand," Artyom's deep timbre vibrated through the crisp, dry air. He hovered over me, a familiar scowl decorating his face. He lifted me to my feet and directed me back inside the manor through the open door. The hallway was empty except for a few agents who walked past briskly. Artyom supported my weight and led me back to door *B* on the first floor, unlocked it with a set of keys—he had an entire ring of them—and led me into the empty room, locking the door behind us.

He offered a chair and I took it, gratefully. "I am making my rounds and imagine my surprise when I find you lying on the ground in the freezing cold doing…doing what exactly?"

"Sorry…I'm sorry—" I gasped. "I'm—I don't know what

happened. I don't know what's wrong with me..." I took a shuddered breath as I stumbled over the words.

My lungs felt flat, like all the air had been vacuumed out of them. The world was sliding away under my feet and I was stuck on an escalator moving in the wrong direction. I couldn't stop trembling. I was all alone here in this void. If I tried to scream, I wasn't sure I could even make a sound. No one knew where I was. No one was coming. I was lost.

"Stop," growled Artyom. His pale eyes flashed as he stared at me. "You are not permitted to sit around playing in the snow or contemplating the meaning of life or whatever was going on out there when you should have been in a required lesson. They will assign punishment for that, and you are in no condition to endure the cells again anytime soon. Do not give them a reason to find you dispensable. I won't report it this time. I'll say you got lost."

"I—I...I can't—I don't know why...but—I saw him and I couldn't breathe suddenly," I stammered.

"Calm down," he commanded in an icy tone. "Saw who?"

"That-that monster—the one who was in charge down there...orchestrated my torture." I pointed to the floor.

"Impossible," Artyom stated factually, with a shake of his head. "If that's what prompted all of this, then know that he can't harm you here. You're safe."

A sharp sneer left me and I twisted my mouth in distaste.

"Safe?" I huffed, exasperated at the ridiculous claim. "This place is a goddamn landmine," I retorted. I focused on the solid feeling of the chair beneath me and stared down at my still-wet boots as I worked to regain control over my breathing.

The anxiety attack ushered in by the disorienting vast sky and grounds began to ebb now that I had four walls around me. I was in a room. I was with a guard who seemed like he had no particular interest in harming me. I was in a chair. I was safe. Slick was gone. He wouldn't hurt me anymore.

I took in a measured breath and counted to four. I released the breath gradually. My heart slowly stopped pounding, but my body was tired. Now that the numbness washed away, my side hurt.

"Let's get you to your lesson. Come." Artyom stood and held out his hand, almost a plea.

"You'll be punished," I said to him suddenly. His gaze returned to my eyes, brows knitted. "If you don't report my panic attack or whatever, they'll punish you if they find out."

"Then, let's make sure they don't find out," he said. I blinked at him, not expecting that response. I took his hand and allowed him to lead me back out into the hallway, and back into the bitter cold.

Artyom led me around the perimeter of the manor toward the back, and we moved across the grounds until we reached the tree line. I paused, looking out across the expanse of the forest. This was real wilderness, I could feel it in my bones. This wasn't some tame park or a few preserved acres in the hills of Los Angeles. I turned back to take in the facade of the manor for the first time. It was even bigger than I'd imagined. The gray, three-story mansion stood out against the dense forest of trees that surrounded it.

As though he could read my mind, Artyom said, "We are surrounded by one of the oldest and largest forests in Europe. Don't come out here at night."

"Are there...wolves?" I asked in a constricted voice.

"There are plenty of carnivores that live in this forest, and winter makes them lean and hungry. Don't wander into these woods, because if you get lost—and you *will* get lost—it's likely that the freezing temperatures at night and lack of food will kill you faster than the wolves."

"Then, where are we going?" I asked, unable to peel my eyes away from the places in between the snow-dusted trees.

"Not much farther. Come." He tugged on my arm. About 100

meters into the tree line, an expansive low-rise concrete structure came into view. I hadn't noticed it before, not through any of the windows of the manor. It was very well-hidden, likely from an aerial view as well. I spotted the foliage hanging over the side of the roof, the colors helping to camouflage the building within the wilderness surrounding it.

There was a small, locked side door, barely visible. That's where Artyom and I entered. My eyes lingered a moment on his fat key ring. He probably had key access to every room on this estate. I filed the observation away for later use.

Inside the flat concrete structure was a staircase that led down into an impressive training facility. The walls reverberated with the sounds of practice and training. Shots rat-tat-tatted from a firing range, though they had been totally inaudible from the outside of the structure.

Outside, it had been eerily quiet. In here, my ears were ringing from the rounds of bullets, the panting and grunting of physical exertion, the sounds of impact, and even screams. The ceiling must have been at least thirty feet tall while the outside structure appeared only ten feet tall, so they likely had excavated down pretty far. That took large machinery and funds. With this level of equipment, Lavidian and the people behind it were clearly much more powerful than I had realized.

It was becoming apparent how powerless I was to escape this imprisonment that had become my life. The hardest pill to swallow was that nothing I had dedicated my life to before this —not books nor grammar nor calculus nor AP Government— offered any kind of solution for the situation in which I now found myself. I didn't know how to get through it and for all I knew, my sentence here was for life.

Maybe I should walk into those woods at night and let the wolves end my suffering? But even that felt like an impossibility, a luxury, a selfish choice that only a brat would make and it would lead me straight to hell. I shelved the thought to the back of my mind and zoned in on my surroundings.

The training space was sectioned into several separate training divisions. One in particular was equipped with rows and rows of wooden painted targets. Training mats were in a nearby section. A rock wall and rope obstacle courses were in another section of the warehouse.

"You look pale," he remarked.

"I'm...I'm still recovering." I placed a light hand against my ribs. He nodded.

Before he led me to my lesson, Artyom made a detour into a multi-level, tactical training area near the back of the warehouse. Once inside, he gestured to a crate. I paused a moment to make sure I understood him correctly before squatting to sit on the crate. His eyes lit up as he boasted about the design of the tactical training bunker, the hallways, the stairs, the breaching doors, and a catwalk recreated for nearly every combat scenario. It seemed that Artyom was giving me time to pull myself together.

By the time Artyom brought me back down to join Diversion Training, I was feeling much better but the powerful ache in my side resulting from my meltdown hadn't subsided. After I just barely missed an elbow to the head from an agent who had been preparing to throw knives in some sort of target practice training, we approached the Level 1 Diversion Training group.

I recognized the other young girls in the group, and took my place behind them. The instructor exchanged quiet words with Artyom and nodded toward me before he walked over.

The instructor, a tall, slender man with a gray beard and thinning hair, handed me a book without explanation and walked back to the front of our group, where he was leading a seminar on the significance of practicing misdirection in front of a mirror as often as possible to become intimately familiar with what the mark was seeing.

"It's the fluidity of motion that is necessary when it comes to maneuvering the eye-line of your mark." I turned the book in my hand right side up to read the title, Bill Tarr's *Now You See It, Now You Don't*. I furrowed my brows at it. *He's given me a book on magic?* I looked up to find our instructor handing out fluffy red balls the size of a walnut.

"Using these balls and a partner, you will take turns creating the illusion that one ball in your partner's cup has become two without detection. Once you have mastered this illusion no less than three times, we will increase difficulty and introduce an item in your partner's coat pocket that you must retrieve, undetected."

We worked until our fingers were numb from the cold and our noses were red as cranberries. My partner was a quiet girl like all of them, but I was grateful that she didn't seem like a heartless hag. She even cracked a small smile when I successfully managed to replicate the illusion and swipe the rock from her pocket on my fourth attempt. Sounds of intense combat training filled the air with nearby grunts, screams, thuds, and thwacks. I would sometimes flinch from the sounds and my partner giggled at me; she thought I was amusing.

"What's your name?" I whispered to her.

She froze and looked around. Then, to my surprise, she turned back to me and whispered, "Dove."

"I'm Lark." I smiled at her. She smiled back, her freckled cheeks glowing red from frost.

We ran a series of exercises where we passed by each other as though on the street or in a store, and practiced swiping a rock that was in one of our coat pockets from one another, using the distraction of bumping into our mark to divert attention from the sleight of hand maneuver.

Dove was tall for a twelve-year-old, almost exactly my height. The simulation of this particular scenario was the hardest for me to complete because each collision against

Dove's shoulder or torso caused me tremendous pain. Dove noticed and made sure to collide more gently. The gesture, both subtle and unexpected, almost brought tears to my eyes.

"Hey, Dove?" I whispered as I leaned in. "You seem to have a kind heart. Keep that close... if you can." She nodded subtly, showing only a hint of curiosity that I could perceive. "Don't let them make you insufferable, all right?" Dove responded with a faint smile, yet her eyes reflected a sense of warmth.

Maybe, just maybe, I finally had a friend.

CHAPTER 27

OLIVER

"What in The Real Housewives of the Valley is this?" Xavi pronounced under his breath as we walked through a display of twinkling robotic reindeer toward Nyah's impressive front porch. Her house had been miraculously transformed into a winter wonderland since the last time I had been here. Giant nutcracker soldiers stood guard on either side of the massive doors. Oversized red ornaments rested at their feet. Rich garlands lined every window of the house. The roof and columns were outlined with sparkling lights, while hundreds of shimmering snowflakes danced in the evening wind.

"Yeah, it's nuts. Isn't it? Wait till you see inside," I muttered and rang the doorbell.

"Coming!" Nyah called to us from somewhere within the house. Moments later, the door swung open and Nyah's cheery face greeted us, her cheeks flushed and her hair pulled up. She was wearing an apron. Nyah waved us in but she didn't linger. Xavi's smile faded and his eyes rounded slightly before he pulled his phone out of his pocket in haste, suddenly scrolling through his feed.

"My dumplings are in high heat, gotta get back to them," Nyah called over her shoulder. "Come in! Oliver, show your friend to the kitchen, will you?"

I quickly checked my phone for a message from Kiran but after seeing that nothing had come through, I pocketed it. I stepped inside and took in the holiday décor in the foyer. The rails of the double staircase were strung in rich, green garlands, and the large round entrance table now held a miniature Christmas village. A nearby high-top featured a display of seven candles. I turned to clock Xavi's reaction.

"Nice, right?" I commented, but Xavi was still staring down the hallway that Nyah had disappeared into.

"Yo..." I said, waving my hand in front of his unblinking eyes.

"My maaaaaaan," Xavi whispered. "The voice."

"The voice?" I questioned.

"The voice...it doesn't do her justice. She's..." He trailed off, head over heels already in typical Xavi fashion.

I chuckled at my lovesick new friend who always fell for every pretty girl he met. "Come on, man," I said and tugged him along to the kitchen.

"How do you know her, again?" he asked.

"My girl's best friend," I explained to him for probably the third time.

"Right. She dance, too?" he asked in a hushed voice as we walked through the hallway filled with family photos. Xavi lingered by one of Nyah with her leg extended in a pose worthy of a dance magazine. "Yes. Yes, she does," he confirmed to himself and hooted like a squeaky little owl.

"Don't be creepy. Come on," I urged him.

In the kitchen, Nyah was cooking up a storm. There were meatballs and spaghetti in a large bowl already on the table.

Beside it was an even bigger salad bowl. Nyah was plating dumplings and I got the feeling it was going to be more than just the three of us for dinner tonight.

"What were y'all whispering about in the hallway?" Nyah prodded in a tone of amusement. She was wearing an apron that read *That Ain't Burnt, That's Flavor.* I checked back with Xavi, who was suddenly very interested in the cabinetry.

"Nyah, this is Xavi. Xavi, Nyah," I introduced the two to each other and joined her behind the counter. "Let me help with something," I offered.

"Nice to meet you, Xavi." Nyah gave him a glance before pointing at a cabinet and saying, "Plates are in there if you wanna set the table." I got to it.

"Smells good in here," Xavi finally said as he leaned against the kitchen island, scrolling through his phone again. I'd never seen him on his phone so much. Nyah turned to him, smiling at the compliment, but her smile faded a bit when she found him buried in his phone.

"Xavi and I work together," I explained, not recalling how much I'd told her about him before. I'd mentioned him here and there and I was sure she'd heard him in the background a lot on our phone calls. Nyah was becoming more and more vital to my sanity. She was so grounding and calm as she bustled about the kitchen. She made me almost forget for a moment that my world was completely falling apart all around me.

"Work together, live together. We're practically married, dog," Xavi joked. We shared a laugh at that but when Xavi's eyes met Nyah's, he quickly looked back down at his phone.

"Xavi, help me set the table," I asked him, trying to distract him from his phone and placing a stack of plates in front of him. "Are your parents and brother joining us?" I asked Nyah.

"My mama's changing for dinner. She'll be down soon. Chris! Dinner!" she called after her brother, who shouted something indiscernible back at her from upstairs.

"Dad should be home soon. He's stopping by the store for Mama's favorite wine. So, yeah...let's set it for six," Nyah clarified.

I added two more plates to the stack, and looked through drawers for the silverware. Xavi circled aimlessly around the kitchen island, still holding the stack of plates and looking lost.

Nyah watched Xavi's pacing with a hint of amusement and pointed toward the door at the other end of the kitchen. "Sorry, I should've mentioned that the dining room's through there."

"Yeah, I know," Xavi told her.

"You know where my dining room is?" Nyah asked in confusion.

"Yeah, like...I figured it would be there," Xavi retorted, his cheeks suddenly flushing.

"Okay," Nyah pronounced slowly and went to check on the boiling pot. I sent Xavi a bewildered look and mouthed *what's up?* But he just shrugged and stalked off to the dining room.

"Everything looks delicious," I told Nyah. "Thanks for having us over."

"Is your friend okay?" Nyah asked.

"Xavi? Yeah, he's cool, he's amped, actually..."

"Amped? That's amped?"

"Yeah, he was just telling me the other day how much he was craving a home-cooked meal and how he hates that we always order in."

"Hmm..." Nyah mused, unconvinced.

"Be right back," I told her as I found the silverware drawer and counted out six forks and knives before following Xavi into the dining room. The wallpaper was tropical and filled the room with vibrant color. Xavi was still holding the stack of plates and standing by the French doors, looking out over the vast back yard.

"Yo, what the hell is up with you?" I asked in a hushed voice.

He wheeled toward me, knocking the stack of plates into a dining chair but managing to hold onto them.

"Shit," he said. "Ummm...I think we need those like...things to put under the plates so we don't mess up the table," he remarked. "You know—like coasters, but big-sized."

"Oh, yeah...you're probably right," I agreed. "Hold on, I'll ask her." I turned to go back but Xavi continued.

"Ey, Oliver, man, I think I'm gonna head out—"

"Xavi, what? No—"

Xavi was worked up. "Yeah, naw, dog...I forgot that I promised my buddy—"

"No, you didn't forget shit. Tell me what's really up."

He didn't answer, but just stared at the stack of gold-rimmed plates in his hands instead.

"Come on, man...it's not that bad. I mean, trust me, I get it. This place is a lot, I know. But Nyah's not like some random rich girl or anything like that. She's cool," I promised.

"Yeah, she is. But the thing is, I thought 'dinner' meant we'd grab some tacos or eat some pizza on the couch or some shit. I didn't know her whole family was gonna eat with us like in a fancy feast style—and her dad's gonna be sitting here like who the hell is this fool in his house, I don't—" His eyes were wide with a new anxiety now.

I laughed almost imperceptibly. Damn, Xavi was fully smitten!

"Xavi, he won't, okay? He's cool. He trusted me with the list. He seemed decent when I met him. Plus, I don't think they're like that, her parents...you know? Uptight or judgmental or anything, not from what I've heard. Listen, Xavi. It's chill, it's no big deal. We're already here. Eat. Relax," I insisted.

"Okay," he said, nodding like he suddenly had this under control. I turned to go back and ask Nyah what to do about the tablecloth or the place mats but turned back to Xavi first.

"And stop staring at your phone every time she looks at you —it comes off...rude," I suggested, carefully.

"Word."

Xavi hardly uttered a syllable at dinner. Mostly, Nyah and her father kept the conversation flowing. Her mom, a bubbly and hospitable woman, who thoroughly relished drinking her favorite wine by producing thunderous sounds of appreciation with each sip, had a great laugh and enjoyed quietly observing both Xavi and me with mild curiosity throughout dinner.

Meanwhile, Nyah's younger brother, Chris, lost no time consuming his fill as fast as he could possibly manage and insisting that school was "good" and "nothing new happened" before asking to be excused to "work on a project." Her brother surprised me by mumbling "nice to meet you" as he brushed past. I smiled and returned his pleasantry.

As soon as Chris left the room, Mr. Wright cleared his throat before asking, "So, Oliver, how's the search coming along? Any leads?" Nyah's mom gave him a disapproving look and quickly refilled her wine glass to the brim in response to the introduction of the subject.

"Umm...well, no. Not really. I did, umm, ask a colleague about it and his wife actually knows someone who might have some background knowledge on the—well, you know, on the Russian groups with ties to whoever might have Mina. I'm hoping to meet him soon and get a chance to ask him some questions." I struggled through the explanation, not quite sure how much I wanted to divulge here.

"That's good. But anyone who knows about that kind of information, knows very dangerous people. Approach him with caution," Mr. Wright suggested.

"Yes, sir. Of course, you're completely right," I agreed. "I will be careful."

"Keep me in the loop if you need any help," Mr. Wright insisted.

I agreed, "I will."

Xavi was chewing loudly beside me, working on his fourth helping of spaghetti and meatballs, nodding in appreciation. The conversation grew quiet and we all turned our attention to him. Nyah's mom watched Xavi with curiosity while sipping her wine. "You seem to really be enjoying the Bolognese, Xavi. Is it a favorite dish of yours?"

Xavi froze, mid-chew. He looked up, surprised to find all of our eyes on him—everyone smiling but Nyah, who appeared to have made up her mind about him from an earlier impression.

"Mhmm." He nodded, his mouth still full. "Not bad," he mumbled, sounding like a reticent critic on a food show. I shot him an incredulous look and hit his knee under the table. Why was he being such a dick? Nyah's mom smiled politely while Nyah rolled her eyes and stood to begin clearing some of the dishes. I shot to my feet and helped clear the table as Xavi kept eating.

"You cooked. Let me help. You take a load off," I told Nyah. "Thanks for having us over."

"Dinner was delicious, sweetheart. Thank you," Mrs. Wright complimented her daughter.

"Thank you, Nybear," Mr. Wright agreed. He wiped his mouth with his napkin, leaned over, and kissed her forehead. Then, he stood to help me clear the table.

"We all needed a night off from Mama's gluten-free recipe book," Nyah teased.

Mrs. Wright chuckled reflexively. I started toward the kitchen and Mr. Wright followed closely. As I cleared the plates, he rinsed them.

After rinsing the second plate, he spoke. "When will you be meeting this person? The one who may know some information about the people responsible?" Mr. Wright asked, his tone grave.

"Umm...really soon. Tonight, actually, but I'm still waiting on a confirmation," I answered honestly, and checked my phone again. There had been no news from Kiran.

"Listen, Oliver, I meant what I said. If anything feels off, get out of there. If something happens and you need help, you can call me," Mr. Wright insisted.

"I really appreciate you saying that, sir," I told him, meaning it. It felt pleasantly strange to know I could lean on him. I wouldn't. But it felt damn good to know I could. "Thank you."

There was a resounding crash in the dining room, and a small yelp of distress.

"Oh, shit! My bad." Xavi's voice carried from the other room. I groaned inwardly. A few moments later, Xavi stalked into the kitchen balancing the leftover Bolognese in between the cracked pieces of a serving bowl.

"You good?" I asked him, moving forward to help.

"Yeah, yeah, yeah...no I'm—I'm one hundred—wasn't me, slip-slippery bowl." Xavi nodded toward the cabinet under the sink. I opened it for him. He tossed the pieces into the trash. He straightened, holding his sauced fingers in the air awkwardly and meeting Mr. Wright's gaze. Xavi gulped audibly.

"My bad, sir. Let me...ugh, let me pay for that?"

"Nonsense, son. Life does not consist of an abundance of possessions. Those porcelain bowls are pretty damn slippery." The sound of muffled giggles drifted from the dining room. Xavi dropped his head a fraction as a flush crept into his cheeks. I patted his back in reassurance as Nyah floated into the kitchen, biting back a grin.

"Dessert anyone?" She smirked, eyes dancing around the room and landing on Xavi.

CHAPTER 28

 **MINA**

I began to settle into my schedule and the parade of a routine: breakfast, stairs, rich business prick profiles, stairs, lunch, stairs, mental manipulation strategies, stairs, meds, stairs, magic tricks, stairs, dinner, staring out a window into silent darkness, sleep, repeat. This had become my life. Dreary and Sisyphean, yes, but anything was better than where I'd been two weeks ago.

But when Nurse Katya passed along my new schedule a couple of days ago, that uncontrollable falling sensation resurfaced. I would be moving onto the second floor this week. Society 2A, Psychological Strategy 2B, and Weapons Training. My heart pounded its maniacal, familiar war drum against my weary chest.

I hid the new schedule under my sheets as though that would make the changes disappear.

Why was I being moved so early? What was the rush? I was still vastly lacking in knowledge and skills compared to the other girls, especially when it came to European politics, facts about prominent families, and who was or wasn't in good standing with the current administration.

I still didn't understand most of the psychological manipulation strategies expressed using advanced Russian terminology. My Russian was good but many of these words I had never heard before, and questions to the teacher were clearly unwelcome. I learned the hard way when I asked what a word meant and the teacher forced the entire class to stand for the remainder of the lecture as punishment. The dirty looks I received from those angry Level 1s had me promising myself never to interrupt with a question again.

Artyom, much to my relief, had showed up at the infirmary to walk me to and from my lessons. The escort had come in handy especially that day, as the Level 1s appeared to have it out for me after the punishment.

On the days Artyom wasn't there, another guard replaced him. But the ones who took his place were always rough with me, holding my arm like I was a prisoner. I preferred being alone. I would shake them off, insisting that I could manage on my own, and they kept a few paces behind me.

I heard the girls whispering about me to one another. *Why are the guards escorting the American around Lavidian? Who is she? Who does she think she is? Americans all think they're celebrities, don't they? Look how pleased she is with herself.*

Despite all this, the presence of a guard, especially when it was Artyom, had kept my panic attacks at bay.

Classes on the second floor were not much different than the first but the Level 2 girls were older, somewhere between fourteen to fifteen, I'd say. The profiling methods being taught were much more intricate. The teacher brought in case files of past assignments, discussing successful choices that agents had made on assignment and highlighting fatal mistakes that had cost agents their lives. I found this type of lesson far more interesting than straight dictation because of how elaborate many of the cases were, and how meticulous the plans against each target needed to be to achieve success.

From securing unique friendships with lonely older women in power to entrapping kinky oligarchs in compromising positions after weeks of preparation, the details of each case varied greatly, but the absolute trust each agent managed to secure from their targets was impressive.

I found myself shifting from a perspective of utter disgust to subtle intrigue and later to admiration over the detail in the work displayed, the realization of which was deeply disturbing.

I wasn't sure how I was going to hold on to the Mina who was repulsed by these psychotic people. I was losing her inch by inch the deeper I was submerged in my all-encompassing brainwash of a schedule.

All meals will be consumed in the dining hall. Report to the Division 2 monitor.

The time I dreaded had finally come. Now that the nurse had properly weaned me off my pain meds, I took my medical cocktail once a day in the morning and was expected to eat my meals with the rest of the girls in the dining hall. This plagued me deeply. I'd become accustomed to eating alone, being alone in the infirmary with only an occasional injured agent or pupil coming through every so often. It was peaceful and more importantly, controlled. No one could hurt me here. I felt truly safe.

But I'd known all along it was only a matter of time before they'd move me into a bed in the dormitories with the rest of the girls. I dreaded that time more than anything.

The dining hall was simple and sparse. A faded beige, floral wallpaper covered the top of the surrounding walls, while a deep wood paneling covered the bottom half. There were six large windows around the left side of the room that looked out over the grounds, which were now covered in a thin layer of snow. Several oil paintings depicting forests, mountains, and streams warmed the hall along with four large but minimalistic chandeliers—curved metal accented by incandescent bulbs.

A fire was roaring near the table, where seats were filling up with teachers and administration. Mikhailov was among them. He eyed me warily as I passed but my attention was diverted by a freckled redhead with striking fox eyes that made her look fairylike. She stood in my path with a wide but genuine smile on her lips. Smiles were rare around here. There wasn't much to smile about. I scrunched up my face in response, baffled by her demeanor.

"Lark, I'm Magpie, vice-monitor of your table. Follow me. I hear it's your first time in the dining hall?" she asked.

I nodded.

"Welcome. Newcomers sit at the far end of the table. Every table has a monitor and a vice-monitor. I'm the vice-monitor for Division 2, and Cardinal—she's the one wearing the dark rimmed glasses over there—Cardinal is the monitor," the girl announced with a tone of pride. I nodded but kept my eyes on the others as we made our way past the girls. I casually scanned their faces, looking for ones I recognized, like Swan and Starling.

I spotted Swan at a table near the very front of the room.

"That's where the agents sit," Magpie remarked. I didn't comment. "That includes anyone who's been on assignment," Magpie clarified.

As I passed, I could practically feel Swan's manic gaze bore into me, searing a hole in the back of my head. I scratched my neck uneasily, remembering the look of satisfaction in Swan's eyes as she kicked me, with the intention of breaking me. I didn't want to be anywhere near her.

I noticed Starling next. She sat alone at the end of the second table from the front with the other Level 3s. She met my eyes and her gaze flickered with shame before morphing into blatant irritation. Either her shiner was healing nicely or she had gotten her hands on a good concealer, but her palm remained bandaged. The cut must have been deep.

"Monitors come in early to set the tables. We enforce the rule that only proper topics are to be discussed at meals..."— She rolled her eyes at that, which almost made me chuckle—"... ensure that etiquette is upheld, and clean up at the end," Magpie said without pause.

I nodded and followed her down the dining hall as she led us to our table, not at the very end where Level 1s were seated but somewhere in the middle of the hall.

"Don't talk more than you have to and mind your table manners," she advised.

There were six tables of about nine or ten girls, two tables of guards, and one large table for the teachers and directors or administration or torturers or bastards or whatever they called themselves.

Shortly after a bell was rung and we were all seated, the cooking staff carried out serving dishes and salads to the tables. I took the spot at the very edge of the table beside Magpie, and across from a quiet girl with dark messy bangs who didn't even look up from her empty plate when I sat down.

The food was placed at the far edge of the tables, and the table monitors and vice-monitors served it to the rest of us. Cardinal, the monitor of the table, did not pass out an equal amount to everyone. She favored certain girls, I noticed. So, the monitors held some power.

A jug of water, salt and pepper, and a small vase with a plastic yellow flower sat in the middle of the table. White empty plates, polished but simple silverware, a starched white napkin, and an empty glass stood at every place setting. Breakfast was scrambled eggs and fruit salad.

"What are the teachers in Level 2 like?" I asked Magpie, taking a bite out of the omelet. It needed salt.

"Division 2 teachers? They're good, they're very knowledgeable," she answered after first looking around herself and then at Cardinal.

"They don't beat us, then?" I asked in a hushed voice.

"No, the pupils and the agents keep the order. They believe in group punishment—the teachers call it group spirit. So, if one fails, everyone fails and everyone suffers. Therefore, we tend to keep each other in line," Magpie explained, expression animated. She had a rare energy I hadn't noticed in any other girl around here. It was magnetic. I found myself leaning closer to her as though the energy would somehow wash over onto me.

"Can you please pass the salt?" I asked Magpie.

"I wouldn't," she said in a hushed voice.

"Wouldn't what? Use the salt?"

"It's considered rude."

"It needs salt. It's bland."

"You'll get used to it," Magpie assured.

I reached across her to grab the shaker, checked it, and added it over the eggs. "Life's short. I want salt."

A clatter sounded from across the table. I looked up to find Cardinal glaring at the salt in my hand. Her intense gaze, filled with scrutiny, flickered up to me through her thick-rimmed glasses. "Next time, ask someone to please pass the salt. No need to behave like a neanderthal, newbie."

"Promise," the reply flew out of my mouth. I winked at her. What was I doing? I wasn't sure, but it felt as good as coming up for air after holding my breath for far too long. Like I was standing in front of a funhouse mirror and finally, my vision had focused and I recognized the girl in the reflection. Magpie snorted.

"You're fun," she commented in a quiet voice after Cardinal turned her glare away.

"Are there hidden cameras anywhere?" I found myself brave enough to ask.

"No, I don't think there are. I've never heard of any. I mean they wouldn't risk it, would they? Cameras can easily get hacked. It seems like a liability that a place that isn't supposed to exist can't afford," she reasoned.

"Right."

"Besides, that's your surveillance system right there." She eyed the table of agents, teachers and guards. "They've got eagle eyes, sharp ears. They take note of what's going on, of who's doing what, saying what," she whispered, her gaze lingering on the table of men closest to the windows. I looked at each of them until my eyes locked with Artyom's. He nodded slightly. I looked back down to my omelet quickly.

"Mikhailov's in charge?" I asked, trying to sort out his place in the hierarchy.

"Who?"

"That man with the emerald kerchief in his suit pocket."

"I don't know who that man is. I've seen him come and go a few times. I thought he must be a regulator or a director of the agent program perhaps. He seems important. But, no, the headmaster is the old man there in the middle of the table."

"What do you call him?"

"We don't really ever have a chance to address him. Headmaster or sir, I suppose if you had to speak to him, but he rarely speaks to pupils. He's more of a figurehead. He's been here as long as some of the oldest career agents from what they say," Magpie explained.

"And how long have you been here?" I asked her before I could stop myself.

"Let's eat. There's not much time left. I still have to clean up before lessons," Magpie cut me off. She wiped her mouth and stood, starting to collect empty plates from the rest of the table. Almost everyone was finished with breakfast. I worried that I had overstepped with Magpie with my questions, but she didn't seem visibly upset.

At lunch, I sought Magpie out once more and sat beside her. She offered a cheery smile, confirming that she didn't mind all my questions this morning. I decided to test my luck and see how much more I could learn from her, so far, the only person willing to speak to me.

"Why are some called agents and some called pupils?" I asked, eyeing Cardinal before salting the bland roasted potatoes, wishing the onions were caramelized instead of raw. Cardinal was busy barking orders at a squirming girl who sat across from her.

"The ones who've been out in the field, even on just one assignment, those are agents. If you are chosen, you're marked, and if you survive the assignment, you are an agent. You sit separately from the pupils."

"Because they talk about assignments?"

"You never discuss assignments—it's forbidden. It's one of the gravest offenses there are, and would result in immediate isolation and punishment. No, I think they do it to preserve rank. There are clear ranks among them, as well. The more experienced agents are ranked higher. There are ranks in everything around here. Even ranks amongst the guards," Magpie explained. I looked at the guards' table. Artyom hadn't escorted me down today and now he was gone entirely, a vacant chair among the guards. I turned to search for Mikhailov. He seemed to be missing as well. Artyom must have been Mihailov's personal guard.

"What about the guards with the snake tattoos on their necks? What does that mean?" I asked her.

Magpie looked around before speaking. "He's a senior guard. Regular guards usually stay here at Lavidian. Senior guards outrank them because they have extensive combat and weapons experience and they come and go. They oversee the agent assignments. But I heard about a gang in Omsk that has snake tattoos as symbols. He might have been one of them before, gotten arrested for something, and then was recruited from prison. Many of these guards were once prisoners who were offered work in exchange for a semblance of freedom," Magpie said in a voice so low I could barely hear her.

"So, the guards are prisoners, too," I muttered.

"I guess you're right, if you look at it that way," she mused.

"The prisoners guard the prison. What keeps *them* from running?"

"They're tagged. Anyone who gets to leave this place gets tagged," she says, serving a second helping of the chicken dumplings to herself and me.

"Tagged?"

"It's a GPS technology that gets implanted under the skin. I heard the agent in our year, Duck, talk about it. She told her bunkmate about the process in confidence at night when she thought everyone else was asleep, but I was awake and I overheard. They perform a surgery on the wrist to install it, but that's not all. Later, they mark you, permanently—"

"Mark you?" I asked.

"With a tattoo," Magpie clarified, and a thought came to mind at the mention of a tattoo.

"There was a girl in Level 1—"

"Division 1," Magpie corrected.

"Right. She had a raven tattooed on her arm. It's her code name. So, she must be an agent, right?" Magpie nodded as she poured herself a glass of water and did a visual scan of the table. "And that means she's been out on assignment before?"

"Yes," Magpie confirmed.

"But she's so young...aren't Division 1s like twelve?"

"Raven is a career. They send careers out on assignment young because they've been trained since birth and their combat and weapons training is unparalleled. We will never catch up to them. That's why I think the organization uses us only when they need a very specific skill set that one of us fits. When they are looking to profile someone with a particular physical attribute or a talent that an assignment calls for, that's when they put one of us to the test. That's what I'm guessing, anyway." Magpie shrugged and reminded the girl across from her to please chew with her mouth closed.

"Duck isn't a career. She wasn't raised here," Magpie added. "She's been sent on assignment twice, I think. I can't know for sure, of course. But the reasoning has to be either because of her horseback skills or her fluency in French. She boasts about them often. Ugh, I'm so envious. Hopefully, they require a gymnast someday soon," Magpie pouted.

"You want to risk your life? For them?"

"I want to prove myself. I want merit. Life around here changes after you've proven your worth. The others..."—She nodded to the older girls—"...they don't touch you. They leave you alone because the agents, they all have each other's backs. Every girl in here wants that," Magpie insisted, nodding toward the table of agent girls. I looked over my shoulder at the table perpendicularly arranged to mirror the guards and the administration. Everything was symbolic. They weren't one of us anymore. Swan, Duck, Raven—the tiniest of the group—and seven others sat in silence eating their soups in eerie synchrony.

I turned my attention back to Magpie, shaking off the unnatural image. "Are you saying you're treated badly now?" I asked, unable to imagine anyone treating Magpie poorly. She was so amiable.

"I used to be," she answered, glancing at Cardinal, who was busy scolding the squirming girl for not keeping her hair tidy.

"We always have to watch our backs. Just the other week, a Division 3 girl went to grab her toothbrush and someone had taped a razor blade to the handle. She cut open her hand—"

"Starling..." I realized.

"Yes. And it could've been worse. Things like that happen all the time. The longer it takes to prove your worth, the longer you're subjected to the degradation," Magpie whispered in between bites. "That's why I became vice-monitor. A little bit of authority never hurts." She winked.

"How do you become a monitor or vice-monitor?"

"You challenge the standing monitors in hand-to-hand," she answered, unblinking. My expression must have been doubtful, because she added, "Listen, I was a gymnast. People underestimate how strong we are."

Privately, I had no trouble envisioning Magpie as a total badass.

———————

At dinner, Mikhailov and Artyom were back. Artyom stared at me with an expression that was both intense and impossible to read. He scratched his beard and finally averted his gaze. The unease that crept over me was hard to shake.

"What happens when you, I dunno, age out of Lavidian?" I asked Magpie after she passed me the dinner rolls during the table rotation. "Where are all the older girls?"

"Well, I assume after you've gone on enough assignments and proven yourself in the field, they continue to use you as an agent but you live elsewhere...but I don't know. The teachers, for example."

"The teachers were agents?" I asked.

"Yes, of course. Can't you tell?" Magpie looked over her shoulder at the administration table. I looked, too. They did carry themselves with a certain strength. Their posture, their attitude—how had I not seen it before?

"Yes, now that I look, I suppose it's obvious. But there are only like twelve of them. Where are the rest?" I asked.

"You think this is the only program of its kind? Some probably get transferred. But, Lark, many die in the field. As I'm sure you've understood by now." Magpie's smile faded but returned quickly before she stood to pass out the string beans with a set of silver tongs. The beans were piping hot. I warmed my frigid fingers over the steam.

"Manners, Lark!" Cardinal ground out at me from across the table, eyes searing. I pulled my hands back and sat on them instead.

"Earlier, you said 'career girls.' Are those—"

"Yeah, that's what we call the ones who were raised in a program since they were five years old or younger," Magpie explained.

"I haven't seen any of the little ones around," I noted.

"Yes, they keep them in the other building until they're ready for Division 1. A good thing, too, or we would never get any sleep with all that crying. Do you know when you'll be moved into our dormitory yet?" Magpie asked.

"No, I don't know," I confessed, then, remarked, "They turn out strange, don't they, the career girls?"

She shrugged.

"It used to be worse when they segregated them from us entirely. Our Psychological Strategy 2 teacher explained once that when the program first started, Lavidian kept the career girls separate from the ones who were brought in, like us, so that Lavidian could control what they knew about the outside world, but what ended up happening was that they behaved so differently, like you said, 'strangely,' that when they were sent out on assignment, their marks would notice the behavioral differences and comment on them. So, Lavidian started integrating them with us in Division," Magpie explained.

"The career girls learned to mimic our mannerisms and way of speaking. I've always figured that's why they let us talk at meals, so that they can learn to blend in with us and with society, but there are restrictions, of course. Things we can't talk about. Things that make girls disappear," Magpie whispered, eyeing Cardinal, who was engaged in her own conversation with the girl beside her. Magpie lowered her voice to a barely audible whisper.

"You can't trust any of them—they'll sell you out on a dime. You can't even trust me. We all have a motive to be here and one way to get ahead is to report others for infractions. But I can tell that you're no silly goose. You're a serious player. I can feel it," Magpie remarked, scratching an itch on her freckled cheek.

"What do you mean?"

"There's an air about you. I'm good at sensing these things—reading people. It's kind of my gift. And with you, my warning senses are tingling. I know better than to mess with you. No, you and I will be allies. If I'm lucky, you'll end up teaching me a thing or two."

"Agreed," I said and nodded at her, still confused about exactly what she meant but deciding to drop it. I'd rather have been friends but allies would work. After all, in a place so inhumanly cruel as this, an ally would be handy. "But I gotta say, Magpie, the way things work around here is pretty goddamn disturbing," I remarked lightly.

"What did I just hear?" Cardinal snapped at me from across the table. "You there, what sort of language was that?" The table grew silent. All the girls turned their heads in my direction.

"What language?" I asked, heart pounding in my ears.

"Don't give me that. Stand up," Cardinal barked as she stood.

After a hesitant moment, I stood up, my eyes never leaving hers.

"Come here." I walked around the table toward her. The entire dining hall went quiet. Chairs screeched as most of the girls and some of the teachers turned in their seat.

"Close your mouth," Cardinal commanded, picking up a fork from the table. I took a step back, eyeing the fork in her hand with suspicion. "Don't move." She lunged, flicking the fork toward my mouth. Was I expected to stand there and take the punishment in submissive silence? My instincts kicked in and I blocked the blow with my right hand. There was a sharp *thwack* and the fork clattered to the floor. Audible gasps filled the dining room. Cardinal huffed, enraged by my insubordination.

"You little—"

But as she curled her arm back to strike me and my body tensed for a fight, a large hand wound around her wrist. Artyom, who moments ago had been seated at the guards' table, shot over in an instant to stop Cardinal from striking me. My chest heaved from my ragged breaths.

"Lark has been granted special protection under the authority of the senior guards. I am under strict instruction that until further notice, she is not to be harmed, by anyone, for any reason," Artyom instructed, his voice steady and low. Cardinal seethed but nodded her understanding. My shoulders were tense with unused energy from the fight for which I had been prepared. I didn't understand. Since when was I under any kind of protection? Electrocution was fine if it served their purpose, but this was where they drew the line?

Cardinal took a step around Artyom to look me in the eye when she bit out, "Mind your language at the table, newbie. Sit down."

Besides plenty of arctic glares from Cardinal and a few of her allies over the next few weeks, lessons were going fine. I dedicated my full focus on excelling, figuring that the more I appeared to be invested in the program, the more they'd buy that I had given up hope of escaping and would not pose a threat to them.

I figured if I managed to convince them of my value, they'd give me more freedom, and maybe I'd even find a way to make Mama's life more comfortable. Maybe they'd even let me see her someday?

It felt a lot better being in lessons with girls closer to my age. There was a smaller height gap between us, as well, so, I didn't feel like such a beanpole.

I was doing fine for whatever that was worth—I was at least managing to get through the motions of my new schedule. But it wasn't just a new schedule; it was a new life. Somewhere in my brain, there was a disconnect with that reality. I refused to fully accept that this would be it.

This is just for now. Not forever, I promised myself to tame the enraged animal inside me. It was easier when I was absorbed in the lessons because despite the depravity of some of their strategies, the subject matter and skills being taught were intriguing.

Everything changed the morning I woke up with the same headache that I had the day I found myself in the basement of this cursed manor—a situation I suppressed so entirely that I had managed to cope daily without falling apart.

Panic rushed through me like a tidal wave as a sharp pain—a searing burn—came from a focused place along my inner arm. I sat up in one breath. I was still in the infirmary but it felt like someone had put out a cigarette on my bare arm.

I lifted my arm for a closer look. It was bandaged. I peeled the medical tape and removed the gauze. There was a gel-like substance along the small incision on the inside of my lower arm. The aggravated skin around the site was lightly red.

"What the...? *Ohhh...*Christ," I hissed at the pain. "What the hell? What is this?" I mumbled. Something was very wrong and almost immediately, I guessed what it was. *Have they put that GPS tracker in me?*

"You're awake?" Nurse Katya's voice grew closer as she rushed to my bedside.

"It's all right! Don't touch it!"

"What the hell is this? Who did this? What ha—*ah*, Jesus…did you do this to me?" I seethed.

"It was instructed. You have been enlisted in the agent program. The memo was sent last night. Normally, pupils are made aware and spend a night in the infirmary, but I was given instruction not to discuss it with you in detail."

"What the hell is it? Is it a location tracker or surveillance equipment—"

"I am not authorized or qualified to discuss the details of the program beyond giving you instructions regarding the minor surgery that you underwent." I squeezed my eyes. Flashes of my memory were returning. The anesthesiologist had come in and I had tried to resist, but they restrained me and there was a sharp pinch and then, nothing.

"An antibiotic was administered. I made a small incision to install the tech—"

"You're insane…you people are psychopaths!"

"There's no need to be alarmed. I used a laser and a medical glue to close the wound after a diagnostic was run on the device to ensure it was functioning properly. The incision will be almost imperceptible with time. The entire process did not take longer than twenty minutes."

"Oh, so it was quick. Fantastic," I mocked.

"It has a full charge upon installation but you will need to wear this bracelet to charge it." She gestured to a thick gold cuff, about the diameter of my lower arm, that was plugged into a cord that ran to an outlet. Her expression was stern, unreadable, but her eyes gave away the hopeless resignation that plagued her.

I wanted to scream. *Get it out of me!* But throwing a fit wasn't going to help me. I swallowed the outburst as thick tears fell down my cheek.

Katya shook her head. "Breathe, Lark. I told them this wasn't the way," she muttered under her breath. I threw my head back against the pillow and shut my eyes, my mind reeling, analyzing what this would mean. I was trapped now; there'd be no escaping. Nothing would help me now, not Artyom's kindness, not his ring of keys, not Magpie's information. Why did they do this? Did they suspect my desperation to run? Or would I be leaving the manor soon on a mission?

I reached down to scratch the skin around the incision. The nurse grabbed my hand to stop me. She released me after a few moments and brought her hands up to squeeze my shoulders.

"Be careful. Try not to tamper with it," she warned. "The bracelet is a power bank—it will keep your device charged. This detail is vital. If the device in your arm loses charge, it..." There was a slight hitch in her tone, almost imperceptible, but I saw the disapproval on her face. "If it loses charge, it can be very dangerous for you. You need to notify an authority figure right away. If you ever feel heat or burning in the incision area, notify someone. Do you understand?"

"Fine." I refused to look at her. I couldn't believe they'd done this to me while I was unconscious. Tagged like the newest cow in the herd. I felt violated, powerless. I wanted to curl up into a ball and harden until I was stone. I had thought this room was safe. I was a goddamn idiot.

"It's life or death with that device, Lark. Do you understand?"

Go to hell, Katya, I wanted to say. "I understand." My voice was hardly more than a whisper.

I heard her exhale heavily and walk away, but she soon returned with the gold cuff in hand.

"You'll need to put it on at night to charge the device and

keep the cuff on the charger during the day. It's waterproof but try not to wet or damage this arm for a few days. The magnet will keep it in place at night. If it gets dislodged by friction or force, it will continue to charge, just at a slower rate. Best to try to keep it in place."

I shook my head in disbelief of her attempt to normalize this cruelty. I looked away from her as she covered the incision with a thin rectangular bandage and clipped the gold cuff back to charge. I didn't want to think about the repercussions this device would have on my health.

Katya walked back to her station and scribbled additional notes into a file, likely mine. Now that I'd snuck a look at my file, I could imagine what her most recent notes read:

GPS installed successfully.
Subject displays signs of insubordination and rage.
Instructions on cuff: provided.
Comprehension of potential lethal damage from misuse: unknown.

Despite my foul and slightly defeated mood, I took my meds and went through the motions of the day. The long sleeves of my uniform hid the incision. At some point a few hours in, I even managed to forget about it until the meds wore off and the incision started throbbing and itching again. It was the middle of weapons training when Magpie—who partnered with me for training—spoke up.

"What's with you today? You seem...different," she asked after pulling knives out of the chest of our wooden target and replacing them on the table for me.

I shrugged and checked the distance to the target like the teacher instructed. I estimated one and a half rotations would be sufficient, so I held the knife by the blade instead of the handle. Grateful that the incision was made on my non-dominant hand, I positioned a blade between the fingers of my left hand, bent my elbow the way Magpie taught me, and stepped into the throw. I repeated the motion until all of the knives were in the chest of the target and one was in the head.

"At least your knife work is better than your appalling archery," Magpie teased. She walked to the target with me to collect the knives.

"I heard Starling got pulled away at lunch—did you notice?" Magpie remarked under her breath. I shrugged and shook my head. I hadn't lifted my eyes from my plate at lunch. "God, when will it be my turn? I'm itching to get back into the world," she moaned. "Jesus, would you look at Crane?"

I looked over my shoulder at a petite girl with silky hair tied in a thick, low knot. At first glance, she was unremarkable. If I passed her on the street, I wouldn't think to look her way except to admire her dark hair, perhaps. But observing her once she was in motion was like watching a panther hunt at full speed.

"A career girl, right?" I asked quietly.

"Now you're catching on!" Magpie snorted.

We mere mortals aimed and threw, pointed and shot. Meanwhile, Crane was performing an entire ballet of violence. She trained in a corner with another girl, likely another career girl, who blocked Crane's target with her body. Crane performed a rotating turn to swipe her opponent out of the way, kicked up a bow from the floor with her foot, and caught it in one hand as she aimed an arrow at the target with the other.

After successfully striking her target, Crane blocked a leg kick attack with her forearm and responded with a combination of strikes before ducking and throwing her leg in the air for a powerful round kick that knocked the wind out of the other girl. While Crane was ducking, she picked up a discarded gun, released the empty magazine, pulled a new magazine from her holster in one smooth motion, and slid it into the gun midair.

302 • EMILIA ARES

She rapid-fired a round into the center of the head of the target before retreating behind the table, diving for cover.

I found myself staring, mouth agape.

"Wow, she's incredible," I admitted.

"Don't pour salt on my wound," Magpie retorted, not without humor.

"It's all consistency and training. We'll get there."

"Yeah, in ten years, if we don't die first," Magpie commented, and I wasn't sure if she was joking.

At dinner, Artyom was missing from the table of guards again. Mikhailov was not seated with administration for dinner either. Magpie had been quieter than usual when she suddenly leaned in and spoke in a hushed voice.

"You asked how long I've been here. It's been almost two years."

"Wow, same as Starling! That's a long time," I commented.

"Yes. Starling and I started around the same time. She was a year older, I believe. She had a really hard time here, in the beginning," Magpie remarked, looking over her shoulder.

I turned and looked for Starling as well. She wasn't in her usual spot. I looked around the rest of the Division 3 table. Starling wasn't there at all. Where the hell was she?

An unsettling distress fell over me and I realized that I'd been concerned for Starling, and I didn't like the feeling one bit. I looked back at Magpie, who somehow managed to remain consistently cheery despite everything going on around us. "How do you do it?"

"Do what?" Magpie asked.

"How are you okay here? You're always in such a normal, I'd dare say happy mood."

"I don't know. What else should I do? My mother—she died

when I was eight and sadly, I don't even remember her face that well anymore. One thing that I do remember about her pretty clearly is how she'd touch my cheek and say, 'Smile, little one.' I'd ask her why and she'd say, 'It makes my pain go away.' I believed her, so I got used to smiling." Magpie's dark eyes glinted with a memory.

"I'm sorry about your mom. Sounds like she was wonderful," I said, dropping my gaze to the roast on my plate.

"My father always told me I reminded him of her. I like to think that we're exactly alike."

I offered Magpie a small smile, pushing away painful memories of Mama and poking my fork into the small piece of roast on my otherwise empty plate. Cardinal had just finished serving roast to the last few girls. She'd made a show of giving me the smallest piece of meat. Magpie compensated by giving me an extra helping of mashed potatoes.

"Does he know where you are?" I asked Magpie quietly after she had finished serving our table, looking around to ensure no one was listening.

"He's the reason I'm here. My father was diagnosed with cancer three years ago, and a man came around to speak with him, which, in hindsight I realize was really strange. My father didn't trust him at first. When the man offered advanced medical care in exchange for allowing him to bring me here, my father grew very suspicious. Send me to some boarding school abroad, to be trained, fed, and educated, in exchange for them taking on my father's medical bills?

"My father told the man no. He also forbade me to leave the house, afraid I'd get kidnapped or something. But they bided their time. They didn't return until my father couldn't walk, until there was nothing to eat," Magpie recalled.

"Then, they came back. This time, I took the offer myself, I spoke for myself. A shame, really, as I had top marks in my classes and I was trained in rhythmic gymnastics since I was three—I was good enough to get the attention of Olympics recruiters at nationals the year before and everything. Then, one day, no more gymnastics, no more school. This place or he dies." Tears filled her eyes at the memory.

"Isn't talking about our lives outside of this place...our lives before we came here...isn't it forbidden? That's what the nurse told me," I whispered.

"Really? That's strange. I've never heard that spoken as an actual rule. For us, it's always been a no-brainer. It's rarely spoken of, that's true. But, in whispers with someone you trust? What's the harm?" she said, taking me entirely by surprise. *She trusts me!* Hearing her say it so directly softened a small part of my heart that I thought had entirely hardened.

"Was your father...angry with you for coming here?" I asked, eager to get back to our conversation, and mentally kicking myself for interrupting her. I hoped I hadn't scared her off from sharing more with me. We had been whispering quietly enough that it was unlikely anyone else could hear.

"No. He couldn't be. We were very poor," she went on. "The kind of poor you don't often see in America." I exhaled internally, glad she was still willing to talk.

"He had trouble getting food on the table. The factory he worked at paid him meager wages and probably exposed him to the chemicals that caused his cancer in the first place. So, there wasn't much of a choice. He was just glad I'd be fed and have a roof over my head. They told me upon orientation at Lavidian that if I ever overheard quality information and reported it, they'd find a place for my father in a competitive experimental cancer trial. I'm sure I wasn't the only one who was given some kind of incentive," Magpie alleged, eyeing the other girls.

"That's how they achieve total surveillance without risking a leak from an actual surveillance system." She shrugged.

"And did you...report quality information?"

"Yes," Magpie answered without hesitation or remorse.

"And did they keep their word about your father's treatment?" I asked.

"Yes," she confirmed. I tilted my head back in surprise. "But the trial didn't work. He's still in the fight."

"I'm sorry," I said. Silence fell between us. I took a moment to evaluate the conversations of the other girls at the table. The four girls nearest us were engaged in a debate about the dominant misdirection strategy. The others were listening to Cardinal boasting about the accuracy of her aim.

"And if he goes into remission...can you leave?" I asked.

"Come on, Lark. I think you know the answer to that by now," Magpie exhaled, resigned.

"So, we're all stuck here, owned by them, forever?"

"We know too much. They'd never allow it to be any other way."

"Why are you telling me all of this? Wouldn't it be wiser for you to keep it to yourself and try to get information out of me?"

"It would probably be wiser. But like I said before. I want to be allies," Magpie admitted, almost coyly. "Here's the thing: I heard about what you did to Starling in the middle of your torture session. You manipulated information out of her, and then, you made her cry. You broke her. You were untrained and under duress. Swan told the other agents and Duck gossiped about it at—"

"At night when everyone was sleeping?" I guessed in a whisper.

"Now you're getting the picture." Magpie smirked.

A finger tapped my shoulder. "Let's go."

I turned my head quickly to find a large, square-faced guard with dark wavy hair and a full beard, standing beside me.

"Why?" I asked.

"No questions. Stand," he commanded in a low voice.

"Do as you're instructed," barked Cardinal from her place across the table. I turned to her slowly and offered a sarcastic smile, dabbed my mouth with a napkin, and stood slowly. Magpie furrowed her brow but offered a small nod of encouragement as the guard escorted me out of the dining hall.

Once we cleared the hallway, I yanked my arm out of the guard's punishing hold, grateful it wasn't the incision arm.

"You're hurting me. I can walk on my own," I insisted, emboldened by the knowledge Artyom shared with Cardinal a few weeks ago, that for whatever reason, I was not to be harmed by anyone. I had long since lain awake at night pondering the possible reasons that was so, but came up short on any ideas that made sense.

Why would they care if anyone hurt me? They obviously didn't care about pupils getting their hands sliced open, concussions, sprains, dislocated joints, and on and on. Why was I any different?

We reached the end of the hallway passage and I followed the guard outside. The sun had set and the sky had already grown dark—gray clouds loomed over an indigo sky. The new layer of snow crunched and spread beneath our boots. I hid my fingers in my coat pocket as I followed the guard across the grounds, careful to avoid possible patches of ice.

We entered a second manor, not far from the main building —not as large as the first but much taller and it had a tower. I had often observed it at a distance. This was where the careers grew up in Lavidian as infants, toddlers, and children. Why was I being brought here?

I followed the guard through the main entrance, past a series of doors until we reached a narrow, winding staircase that we climbed to the second floor. The guard led me down another carpeted hallway, and sounds of crying babies and the eerie resonance of melodic shushing echoed off the walls in the distance. I peered into rooms as we passed them, hope blooming in my chest that Mama could be here somewhere. But most of the rooms were dark and seemingly empty offices.

The guard escorting me stopped at an unlabeled wooden door. He knocked three times.

"Enter," declared a voice from beyond the door.

Mikhailov was seated behind a desk while Artyom stood by a window, looking out of the spacious office. He turned and watched my approach as the other guard joined him by the wall.

"Is Kiril a guard?" I asked Mikhailov, wondering why I hadn't seen the giant oaf around here.

Mikhailov quirked an eyebrow in surprise at my question. "No. Kiril is an associate."

"Does that mean Kiril is an agent or—"

"Please, Lark, have a seat," Mikhailov insisted, cutting my question short.

I approached his desk and sat down slowly. The same tension from this morning returned to my shoulders.

"Where are you keeping my mother?"

"Has the nurse explained the function of the device that's been activated in your—"

"Has she told me about the thing that was shoved in my arm against my will after I was drugged? The thing that could kill me at any moment if it's tampered with or loses charge? Yeah, she has—"

"Watch your tone," the guard who escorted me here warned. I didn't take my eyes off Mikhailov, whose mouth curled to reflect amusement.

"No, that's quite all right. It's perfect, in fact. It's exactly what we need. We need a spoiled, outspoken, overconfident, little brat for this assignment. It's the assignment after that where we'll have to extract some of that hidden elegance to the surface." The way that Mikhailov emphasized 'extract' made my stomach turn. I didn't speak.

Mikhailov turned and nodded at Artyom. He and the other guard left the room. After the door clicked shut, Mikhailov retrieved a folder and placed it on the top of his desk. He pushed it forward toward me. I picked it up. He nodded and I opened it.

Inside was a profile similar to the files they kept on us, but this one was slightly different. It reminded me of the oligarch profiles we studied in our society lessons.

"Maria Yuriyevna Berezova," I read aloud. "Who is she?"

"*Ber-yo-zova*"—he corrected, irritably—"The accent is on the second *e*. Who is she? She is you. You are her. This file contains preliminary data on your identity. The file also contains information on your targets. Only access the file when in solitude in a designated assignment study room. Never allow the file to be seen by anyone other than you. Never discuss details of an assignment with unauthorized personnel. Notify me at once when you have learned the information contained in the file to its completion so it can be destroyed," Mikhailov instructed.

"You are Maria Berezova, daughter of the reclusive media magnate, Yuriy Berezov. You have excellent English, grew up in the States, and attend Columbia University. Your targets for this assignment are the Mohorenski twins, Pavel and Margrette, heirs to the gas and oil enterprise owned by their father, Levon Mohorenski. The family is taking a ski trip to Artybash in the Altai Republic. The organization will scout the ideal location for you and Starling to run into the twins on the slopes."

"Starling will be there with me?"

"She will take on the identity of a close girlfriend," Mikhailov explained and I accidentally let out a snort. He scowled, unamused. "She, the daughter of a wealthy sheik, a colleague of your father's. They would be guarded if you were there alone. They've been taught certain strategies, growing up as children of a billionaire, to avoid being targeted and played. Starling is perfect for the profile—she has impeccable English and the regal look appropriate for a Saudi princess with a generous allowance."

"I don't know how to ski. I snowboard—"

"It won't be necessary in this case. You will wear skis, of course, but you will feign an injury and Starling, who is an excellent skier, will act as any good friend would and find help. Our team will coordinate the incident to ensure the help she finds is none other than the Mohorenski twins. Starling will ask to borrow a cell phone from the twins to complete her part of the assignment. Your skiing accident will legitimatize the need for her to borrow the phone in the first place. You are the diversion. Afterward, your new objective is to befriend them, gain their trust, and create a circumstance where they feel comfortable around you. You must be one of them. Do you understand?"

I didn't understand. I felt more and more frozen in place as Mikhailov elaborated on the strategy. Still, I nodded.

"We are looking for information linking their father to international money laundering through offshore accounts. Discreetly observe how they spend their money—what does the payment method look like? If it's digital, you need to sneak a glance at the type of payment. If it's a card, is it a bank card or credit? Find the name. Find out their most frequent travel destination, specifically where they travel as a family the most. Encourage them to indulge in large purchases. Test their spending limits, when dining together, order the most expensive caviar on the menu and ask for their rarest wine, and when the bill comes, make no move to pay. They won't think twice about taking care of the bill; it's simply the swipe of a card for them. Their resources are supposed to be virtually limitless," Mikhailov explained, standing up and walking over to his bar cart to pour himself a drink.

"We are also establishing a history in their community of a Maria Berezova, so that, when you are on assignment with your next mark, your true mark—"

"Who is my 'true' mark?"

"One thing at a time. As I was saying, the Mohorenski twins—"

"What does this have anything to do with me? What do you want from me? What is happening with my father? Where is my father? And where are you keeping my mother? Answer me!" I interjected, my frustration brewing into an aggravated boil.

"Enough! That will be the last time you interrupt me. Speak one more word out of turn, go on...I'm waiting...one more word and we will arrange for you to see precisely how fast your mother's condition can devolve. Your father? Your father is busy with his own assignment. So, I suggest you focus on yours—"

"My father is an *agent?*" I was so overtaken with incredulity, I had forgotten not to speak. Mikhailov's eyes widened in annoyance and I scrambled to apologize, "I'm sorry...I'm sorry, I'll shut up I swear, please don't..."

"Go on, speak over me again..." Mikhailov's nostrils flared. I didn't dare speak. I held my breath, eyes wide at the very real threat in his words. He downed the rest of his drink in one gulp and placed the glass on the table with a loud clank. "Good. No, your father is not an agent, but he's back on task with renewed focus, thanks to you. Now, follow his example and give me your undivided attention. I will not repeat myself again."—Mikhailov did not wait for a confirmation—"The Mohorenski twins will establish your identity in their world. This is more vital than anything else. We need you, Maria, to have a physical encounter with the Mohorenskis because they are a powerful family and they love to gossip. Word about you and Princess Adel will quickly spread. It will establish your place in their world, that you didn't come out of thin air. Is that clear?" he asked, expression hard as steel.

"Yes." My voice quavered. I didn't know if I could actually do this. It felt too soon. Just the thought of leaving, of being out in the open, petrified me. But I could look for an opportunity to get word to Oliver, or even Nyah when I was on the outside.

I remembered losing control on the ground outside, staring out at the expanse, unable to move, frozen like a wood frog in the dead of winter.

"You have six days to study the file. In this first case, a plan will be formulated on your behalf. As you progress through the program, you will begin to draft your own detailed plans, clearly citing sources from previous cases as to why your method is optimal. After you have committed the details of the plan to memory, you will make note of possible challenges you may face when attempting to enact the plan. For example, as you said, you cannot ski. That is something you would write in your notes. After your notes have been submitted, reviewed, and logged by the senior superior agent, expect to spend the following days working in private lessons with Starling and various specialists. Is everything that I have detailed to you thus far clear?"

"Yes...except, I really don't think Starling can pull off pretending to be a close girlfriend of mine," I argued. "Maybe if you consider someone like Magpie for—"

"Starling will pull it off. As will you. There is no discussion. Starling will continue to work with you into the next assignment. The work you will do in Artybash will only lay the foundation for the next phase, the far more important assignment. Understand this, Lark: You don't belong here. Being here, being part of this program, becoming an agent is an honor, a blessing, really. The sheer fortune that fell upon you when you happened to fit the profile we required for the next assignment is incalculable, and it is the only reason I have worked tirelessly to keep you out of a whorehouse despite the wishes of my superiors.

"Don't prove them right or you'll quickly learn that the cells beneath Lavidian are a luxury resort compared to what awaits you in Amsterdam." My knees trembled at the threat in his words like ice had been injected into my veins. I thought Lavidian was hell and that Mikhailov was the devil, but I was beginning to realize that I had no concept of how deep the depths of hell truly went and how many devils ruled it.

"Do you understand the consequences of failing to maintain absolute discretion regarding the nature of your assignment?" Mikhailov questioned, pressing his lips in a hard line.

I opened my mouth but couldn't push the sounds through.

"Answer me," Mikhailov demanded.

"Yes," I breathed through clenched teeth.

"Do you understand the consequences of failure?"

I shook my head. "I will t-try my best, but what if—"

"Failure is unacceptable. Your mother will suffer for your failure. Equally, she will reap the benefits of your success." After several seconds of silence, Mikhailov stood, walked to the door of his office, and held it open for me. "Go."

When I returned to the infirmary, Starling was lying in one of the beds, a bandage covering the inside of her arm. She was asleep.

"Get some rest. How is the healing of your incision progressing?" Katya's voice carried from the back corner of the infirmary.

"It's fine. It's itching like hell, though."

"That's good. That means it's healing. Let me take a look at it." Katya approached me as I undressed and changed back into the hospital gown. I met her at the sink. Katya carried over a fresh bandage. "Drink this—it will accelerate your healing." She held out a vial of a clear liquid. I took it and downed it without question, knowing it was fruitless to pretend I had any choice in the matter.

"Does she know?" I gestured toward the sleeping Starling, her exhaling breaths now producing a soft snore. "Or did you drug her, too?"

"She knows. She was conscious during the procedure. I don't know why the instruction was that you be sedated. Perhaps they thought it would be too traumatic if you were aware. I was briefed that you had been experiencing trouble with managing anxiety after the cell. They worried your vitals would be problematic had you been conscious for the procedure. They wanted to minimize complications. Regardless, I am sorry for how it happened," said Katya. I could see she meant it but I was distracted by the bitter pang of disappointment that hit my gut when I realized that Artyom reported me.

Artyom might have played down the severity of the issue because had he conveyed the full truth, I doubt they'd risk sending me out on assignment. Still, Artyom wasn't to be trusted, no matter how decent he appeared, and I would never forget it.

CHAPTER 29

OLIVER

"So, what exactly is this place?" I questioned Kiran. We were on our way to whatever the hell 'Spaces' was supposed to be.

"It's like a superclub, nothing to be worried about. You need to relax. Oliver...don't look so stiff. Here..." Kiran handed me her gold flask. It passed as a cologne bottle, as did the taste of the liquid it contained.

"Thanks." I sipped half a mouthful under Kiran's intent watch. I returned it and wiped my mouth with the back of my hand, wincing from the taste. "You'll have to excuse me for being nervous about meeting someone who may or may not be 'dangerous,'" I pronounced.

"Oh, Lord, don't say anything like that in front of Anton. All right? He's self-righteous...he actually believes he's a good person," Kiran warned, a look of genuine trepidation overcoming her features.

"Obviously not. I'm not stupid. There's too much at risk," I assured.

"He doesn't know I'm bringing you, and he doesn't know you want anything from him. If he did, he'd tell us both to bugger off. So, here's the plan—you accompany me like you're my fun, new boy toy and he'll think I'm flaunting you to make him envious. He might play nice or he might entertain himself by having a laugh. It depends on his mood."

"Envious? Doesn't he know you're married?" I asked.

"Keep up, sweetness. If CJ gets to play with all the toys in the sandbox, he certainly shouldn't expect me to sit there twiddling my thumbs and waiting. I run the sandbox now, sweets," she explained. I nodded like I was following, but she lost me.

"And Anton was another...toy you played with in the sand-box?" I asked, seeking clarification.

Kiran smirked gingerly. "Anton was a grenade that my fingers happened upon while I was digging a hole in the sand to bury CJ in."

Her expression grew dark. "It's important that you don't insult him in any way, Oliver. Not with your words nor your gestures nor your body language. He doesn't seem it, but he's sensitive so he'll close right up. If he's pissed, he won't share a damn thing."

"Right, well, I'm not looking to intentionally piss him off."

"That's the idea. Keep him happy. Be friendly, but not too friendly or he'll distrust you. He's sharp—got a good nose for bullshit," she clarified. I nodded in understanding. "Most importantly, Oliver, don't bring Mina up. Not until I've given you a signal that it's okay to do so. It's a delicate subject. It's got to be brought up naturally or his guard will go straight up. He'll boot you and blame me. Don't make me look bad."

"How do I bring something like that up naturally?" I wondered aloud.

Kiran touched up her lipstick in a compact mirror. "I'm confident that you'll...figure. It. Out." She winked at me and focused back on her own reflection. She was devastating in the

316 • EMILIA ARES

sheer red dress through which a burgundy corset was visible. *She's definitely making a statement tonight.* The statement was: Look at me. And if my eyeballs were any judge of things, she was making damn sure that it would be hard for Anton not to.

"Are they both coming in with us?" I gestured toward CJ's security team. One of CJ's men was driving, Zavier, I think his name was. I called him Titus 2 because he was shorter than Titus 1, sitting in the passenger seat. I'd tried warming these guys up to me with no success. I'd asked where they go for coffee, what their workout secret was, but they refused to answer like human beings. I guess that's what made them great at their jobs.

"Zavier'll stay in the car nearby, but yes, Jason will accompany us inside. Just in case."

"Just in case of what? And won't Anton think it's weird to have CJ's guy there?" I asked her in confusion. Kiran shook her head with a naughty smirk in response. Interesting couple.

We were pulling up behind a long line of black SUVs, slowly getting closer and closer to the entrance of the club, where a substantial crowd had gathered. When we were adjacent to the central entrance point, near the red carpet and main ropes, Zavier put the car in park and Kiran squeezed my arm.

"Showtime, sweets," she purred and gave me an encouraging wink. Jason got out and opened the door for us. I climbed out first and held my hand out for Kiran. She took it, delighted at the gesture. "What a gentleman," she cooed.

We walked to the place of entry, where a long line extended as far as the eye could see, wrapping around the street corner. I was hoping the line moved quickly and I motioned forward, ready to walk toward the back of it but Jason blocked me off, redirecting us through the crowd. Jason escorted Kiran and me to the velvet ropes where a woman with a clipboard stood guard. She wore a white suit and festive fedora.

She met my eyes briefly before she appraised Kiran up and

down. She seemed satisfied by her overall appearance and didn't seem to mind mine. "Joining a table?" the woman presumed.

Kiran's assessing gaze made me uncomfortable and I stepped a bit farther from her, putting some breathing room between us. Kiran held onto my arm tighter still and rested her hip against mine with a subtle sway. "Yes, darling. We're with Anton tonight," Kiran told her, all the while not taking her eyes off of me. The woman in the fedora lost her grip on her pen at the mention of the name. She chuckled nervously and bent down to retrieve it before rushing to open the ropes for us, which seemed uncharacteristically clumsy for the generally aloof and resigned persona she was initially presenting. The woman nodded us forward.

"Right this way," she pronounced in an anxious, breathy tone, keeping her eyes off Kiran and me entirely. Jason followed us closely.

The building was dark and simple on the outside, almost inconspicuously plain. But inside, it was lavish. The decor made for an ambiance of tropics and luxury. There were hundreds of potted palm trees throughout the dimly lit warehouse. Bottle service tables were scattered around the space. Elegant rugs, velvet couches, and low brass tables elevated the otherwise sparse warehouse.

The music was smooth and rhythmic. The DJ was spinning on a stage against the far wall on the opposing side of the room.

The cocktail and bottle servers were tall and attractive, unusually so, like they all had just stepped off a runway. Appetizers and drinks in fine glassware were being ushered around on gold trays.

"This is not what I was expecting," I mentioned to Kiran as we followed the woman in the fedora along the path toward the private booths. Kiran looked back at me over her shoulder and smirked in satisfaction.

The woman led us through a division that separated the

general space from this more private section, isolated by additional ropes and tighter security. The woman in the fedora stamped the inside of our wrists with invisible ink of some kind and gestured toward a corner table that was even more inaccessible to the crowd than the rest.

Broad men in dark suits with unsmiling expressions guarded the table. As they clocked Kiran's approach, they turned to check with one of the men sitting on the couches. After a clear nod from the one who lazily stood to greet us, the guard stepped aside and allowed Kiran and me to pass. Jason remained by the perimeter of the table.

Kiran shimmied her shoulders playfully and offered me a charming smile before turning her full attention to the man greeting her with open arms. This had to have been Anton.

There was an intensity in his presence, even at a distance. His gaze locked on Kiran, searing her to the spot. It was both alarming and adrenaline-inducing and I wasn't even the recipient of the gaze. My body buzzed with a nervous, electric energy.

He was tall, but still a bit shorter than me and appeared quite broad-chested under his dress shirt. I wasn't sure what I was expecting, exactly, but this wasn't it. In fact, if I hadn't been warned by Kiran about his temperament and dealings, I'd have mistaken him for just a regular guy. Apart from the tattoos peeking out above his neckline and under the cuffs of his sleeves and his wide-eyed, somewhat wild expression, he looked fairly normal.

The men surrounding him were much the same. They all wore toned-down clothing, bland and functional—dark pants, crisp, white dress shirts, and each of them wore a nice wristwatch. They looked like businessmen, colleagues, financiers— just regular guys out for a night of debauchery. The only thing that gave them away were the tattoos on their arms and the intensity behind their eyes.

Upon closer examination, he had the coldness of a predator. It was like looking into the eyes of a wolf. Kiran offered her hand to him. He looked down at it and quirked a brow, expression unreadable. He left her like that for several moments, her hand out in the air toward him, while his arms were open wide for her awaiting an embrace. He seemed to enjoy playing with her as much as she did with him.

I wondered what her next move would be if he did not take it.

She had said that he was not expecting me. She had not warned him that she was bringing anyone along. Was this a test of wills? Was this their game? He was remarkably unreadable.

Finally, he took her hand and brought her closer to him with a yank. She lost her footing but regained balance by leaning against his chest for support.

"You fallin' for me, Kiran?"

"You wish," she breathed.

I didn't know what I was meant to do. Kiran had said Anton would assume I was her "new toy," but what did that mean? Was he marking his claim? Was I supposed to pretend not to be okay with this? We were only friends, weren't we? Wasn't that the story? I kept my expression composed beneath a solid deadpan. I thought it would be best to keep Anton guessing about our dynamic.

I turned back to the men at the table before me. The three men sitting to the right of Kiran were still evaluating me while murmuring remarks to each other. My ears pricked up at the sound of a Slavic language.

"You presenting your hand to me like you're the queen of England is my favorite moment of the week, and so thoroughly, Kiran," Anton chuckled and brought Kiran's fingers up to his mouth, pressing them against his lips before biting the pads of her fingers playfully. "As if this hand had never been..."—He leaned in and said something against Kiran's ear. I couldn't catch it but she hit his chest and chuckled, throwing her head back. She seemed younger around him. I could see a glimpse of the girl she must have been back in London.

"You animal!" she teased.

As he glanced at me over her shoulder, a questioning expression appeared in his eyes. His charm disappeared and his guard went firmly up. He did not offer me a smile or a greeting of any kind.

"And what's this?" he asked Kiran with a forced levity in his voice.

"This is my friend, Oliver," Kiran announced with a shyness in her smile that made her nearly unrecognizable. Anton's gaze raked over me in appraisal and darted to Kiran. He threw his head back, laughing like she'd just said the funniest thing he'd ever heard—revealing all his teeth like the wolf that he was. He recovered, offered Kiran a seat on the couch and plopped down beside her, wrapping his arm around her shoulders and leaning in to speak into her ear.

I remained standing, unsure what to do with myself. I looked at Jason, our bodyguard, who like the members of Anton's security team, had his back to us. Seemingly not paying attention.

The man on Anton's left regarded Kiran with an indiscernible expression, laced with a hint of annoyance or distrust. Whoever he was, he didn't like her and didn't want her here. This man appeared to be around the same age as Anton, who was likely in his mid-thirties. The man was dressed sharply, his suit immaculately pressed. He had two pens and a folded handkerchief lined up along the front pocket of his suit jacket. From the way he was glaring at Anton's hand around Kiran, you'd think this man was in love with her, except he glared at Kiran just as angrily and his eyes even shot darts at me.

"Hello, Alexei," Kiran addressed the man. She must have felt his searing gaze on her. *Didn't Kiran mention a younger brother of Anton's with that same name? Is this him?*

Alexei's disapproving glare eased slightly as he nodded and replied, "Hello, Mrs. Kaur," emphasizing her married status.

Kiran chuckled almost seductively, pulling my attention back to her. She was whispering something into Anton's ear. Whatever it was, he raised an eyebrow at her and said, "You're full of surprises, Kiran."

"Always," she promised. She turned to me and summoned me with her curled finger. She scooted closer to Anton—practically sitting on his lap—to make room for me on the couch. I sat.

"I'm Oliver." I held my hand out to Anton. He simply looked at my outstretched hand for a few moments, making no move to shake it.

He narrowed his eyes at Kiran slightly and tsk tsked at her in a scolding tone. "Let me guess"—he went on—"waiter slash runway model?" He shrugged dismissively as though the combination was the lowest form of occupation someone could have. "Tell me...were you working this event when my Kiran dragged you over here? Did she have you hide your tray in a planter box somewhere?" He looked me directly in the eye for the first time. I wasn't sure whether he was asking as a joke. I decided not to respond until I had a better understanding of his humor.

"Still punishing CJ, I see. He *is* pretty," Anton conceded, loudly, discussing me as though I weren't there. "Does he speak? It seems like I've left him speechless. Or maybe you prefer your playthings to be seen and not heard?"

Kiran rolled her eyes. "He's a colleague. Envy doesn't suit you, so be civil. He's brilliant. Actually, I think you'll quite like him."

"Is that so?" Anton mused with intrigue and perhaps mild irritation that he had misjudged me.

The bottle server appeared with a tray of empty glassware and a plate of sliced citrus fruit. "Pour us a round, will you, darling. Thank you," Anton requested, gesturing at the bottle in the bucket of ice and making a circular motion with his finger. The server nodded and obliged. She served Kiran first before pouring a glass for each of the rest of us. Anton downed his glass in a fast swig, gesturing for another one before he was even finished swallowing the first. She bent to pour his next drink, when Anton remarked, "Bottoms up. A very, very nice bottom is up. Careful, sugar, or one might mistake all that swaying for an invitation." The server froze. She forced a smile but shifted her backside away from him. Just as I opened my mouth to put the bastard in his place, Kiran and Alexei chimed in simultaneously, "Anton!"

"Yesss?" Anton bobbed his head to the sharp beat of the bass. "What? I can't say something nice?"

"Anton," Alexei warned and gave a sharp shake of his head.

"Oh, lighten up, it was a joke." Anton winked at the bottle server, making her cheeks flush red. I refocused my gaze on a stain on the glass tabletop, trying to release the tension that had my jaw locked into a painful clench.

Anton downed his second glass, poured a third, and tipped it against Kiran's mouth. She welcomed the drink, parting her lips for him, swallowing. She even let him place a lime wedge between her teeth. They had a strange chemistry, Kiran and Anton. She seemed to enjoy his unhinged nature. And he seemed to enjoy eliciting an oscillating cycle of irritation and amusement from her.

I was growing uncertain if I'd be able to coax answers of any kind from someone like Anton. For starters, who was I if not a potential thief of Kiran's attention?

He gazed past Kiran, lasering in on me once more as though hearing my thoughts. Before I could say anything, he jumped up and grabbed my hand.

"We drink!" he exclaimed. Anton yanked me to my feet forcefully and poured two glasses of tequila. *Not vodka? Interesting. Maybe he's grown tired of it.* I already had a drink in hand from earlier and now he handed me a second one. I looked at him in confusion.

"Catch up. Then, we drink together," he insisted. I hesitated only a moment. I considered telling him I didn't drink or that I wanted to take it slow but I needed to loosen him up, warm him up to me so I could get a feel for what he knew. This was the first chance he'd given me, and I would take it.

I finished my first glass, then worked on the second. The second one didn't go down as easily. I winced. The liquor was smooth and almost sweet on my tongue but it left a peppery feeling in my throat.

Anton let out a whoop of elation and nodded enthusiastically. I was slightly disarmed by the sudden shift and the seemingly genuine nature of his smile.

He poured our next drinks into shot glasses, not bothering to wait for the bottle server. He poured to the rim but managed not to spill a drop. He seemed pleased at having found his new drinking partner for the night. He held his glass up to me and I mimicked his gesture.

"Bottoms up." He smirked.

"Cheers," I pronounced and he beamed at me before we took back our third shot in synchrony.

"*Ahhh.*" Satisfied, he smacked his lips and patted my back in praise.

"Tell me, Oliver. What do you do to stay in shape?" He grabbed my biceps, squeezing hard to test the muscle. I tensed, instinctively. My jaw worked as my body went rigid with unease under his hold. My heart rate immediately shot up. I worked on my breath.

"I was about to ask you the same thing" I deflected, patting his chest slightly harder than casual and plastering a grin on my face. He jumped at the question.

"I train with the boxing champion of the world," he

announced enthusiastically, leaving me at a momentary loss for words.

"So...not just for show, then? These have function?"—I gestured to his biceps—"Too bad your world champ can't show you what to do if you get tackled down to the floor," I teased, holding my breath for his response. His grin grew wider and he pounced on this information.

"Ah! You do MMA, yes?" he guessed, squeezing my shoulders. I nodded and smiled, stiffly.

"Yes," I confirmed.

"Brazilian jiu-jitsu?" he asked.

"Yes."

"What belt?"

"Blue," I said.

"I'm blue abadi-abuda," he sang. "We sparring tonight?" His face grew serious and I felt pressured to nod in agreement.

"Why not? Let's do it," I promised.

I pushed my hesitation back, reminding myself of the necessity to get this man to warm to me. I'd do anything to make that happen. I'd take any quantity of shots, let him win against me in any game, let him tease me, poke fun at my expense, whatever it took to get what I needed out of him. But I had to confirm that he held the answers that would make doing all of this worthwhile.

"So, you live out here?" I asked, fighting to sound only casually interested.

"New York." He provided a clipped response and eyed his brother, Alexei, who was clearly having a silent conversation with him.

Anton said something to him in another language and there was my in. The man's scowl deepened and he answered Anton in a harsh tone and my eyes lit up. *That definitely sounds like Russian.* I wasn't an expert but I was fairly sure. Anton rolled his eyes to the ceiling in response and feigned getting shot in the chest. Anton began to laugh at himself but the other man remained cold, his eyes unblinking.

"My brother's such a killjoy. Always 'no'...*blyat.* I helped change your diaper! How are you so serious with me?" Anton turned back to me. "Okay, only one diaper. And I put it on his head. Heh. But, still...where's the respect? You know?" he asked, but didn't wait for a response. He poured the next round of shots into fresh glasses, once again to the rim, once again not a drop spilled. He handed the shot to his brother, who refused with a curt shake of his head.

"Alexei!" Anton exclaimed something indiscernible to his brother, who answered with another glare before resuming his conversation with the man beside him. Anton shrugged and handed Alexei's shot to me.

"*Davai,*" he shouted. I wished I could refuse him, not accustomed to drinking this much or at all, really. But I had to play the game the way he wanted to play it. So, we sent another one back. Our fourth? I was losing count.

"You have a British accent but you speak another language and you live in...New York?" I clarified. He eyed me, incredulously.

"Yeah...so?" he asked, like it was entirely common.

I smiled but shrugged. "It's cool. You seem like you've seen a lot of the world. Where were you born?"

"I was born in a faraway land, my *rodina,*" he announced, half-jokingly.

I furrowed my brow in confusion.

"The motherland," Anton clarified.

"Russia?" I asked.

"No, the North Pole...ho-ho-ho," he said in a voice devoid of humor. "Why? Where were you born? No, don't tell me," he said, squinting at me. "North Hollywood."

"Pretty much," I answered with a shrug. His eyes grew a bit cold and he looked away, watching the crowd that had doubled in size since we'd first arrived. The music was louder now, bass thumping into my spine through the vibrations of the floor. I could sense Anton's irritation and unease at being questioned, but I had to know if I was wasting my time. I couldn't afford to waste any more time.

"So, you in LA just to party?"

"We're visiting family for the holidays."

"Oh, nice. I thought you guys were doing business for some reason. Must be the suits."

"The suits?"

"Yeah," I said with what I hoped was a casual chuckle. "California's a pretty laid-back place. Suits mean business in LA."

"These aren't suits. This is a sports jacket and slacks. It's casual," he commented.

"Oh," I said, stupidly. "So, what do you do?"

"What do *you* do?" he threw back.

"Me? I'm in resale," I explained, vaguely, but he must have known. Kiran did say we worked together. He must know that she and CJ are exporters and that I must be a supplier.

"We do the same thing," he said.

"Resale?" I asked and he nodded. "Well, I deal with electronics mostly. What about you?"

"I deal with more eclectic goods."

"Oh, nice, like what?"

"Rarities," he answered vaguely. I didn't like the sound of that.

"How's business?" I asked.

"Booming. Another recession's coming." He smiled.

"And that's...good?" I clarified.

"Recession fuels escapism," he explained.

"What sort of rare escapes do you provide?"

"The kind that Oliver of North Hollywood wouldn't understand and couldn't afford," he said, flatly, not as an insult, just a statement of fact.

"You'd be surprised," I challenged.

"Would I?" He raised a brow. "All right, I help my people by finding out precisely what thrills them, and then connecting them with my other people who can provide them that particular thrill. I am the thread."

"Do you know a lot of people?" I asked, hope blooming in my sternum.

"An opulent quantity of quality." He smirked.

I chuckled, "Who talks like that?"

He patted my back and laughed. "You see, Oliver, that is precisely why I love Los Angeles. The bar is set on the floor. You do the bare minimum, you put on a casual sports jacket, you wash your arse after a shit, you use some basic vocabulary like 'opulent' and just like that, people will fall over themselves to know you."

"Well, I'm not falling," I insisted. "Just talking."

"I can see."

"Well, maybe you can help me?" I was gonna do it; I was gonna shoot my shot.

"Help? I only help my own people."

"Maybe I can be one of 'your people?'" I blurted without thinking. It must have been the shot of tequila kicking in. I wasn't used to it and the barrier between my thoughts and my words had thinned.

"Not quite so fast." He smirked at my ardor. "What is it?"

"A friend of mine was-is…in some trouble with…well, first, actually, let me just start by asking: Do you happen to know anything about underground Russian organizations with uhh… reach here in LA?" I asked, stumbling through the words and regretting them as soon as they left my lips. Anton's expression grew rigid. *Too soon, Oli, you idiot. Too late to back out now, though. Fix it.*

"Sorry—let me give you the backstory. There was this man… Kiril. He threatened a friend of mine on behalf of a Russian group, I think they were from over there; they had thick accents. This guy, he was—" But I didn't get to describe him. Anton grabbed my arm and dragged me toward his guards. He shouted an order at them over the music. The two guards grabbed me on either side, and began to drag me away from the table.

"Hey! Don't! Hey, get your damn hands off me!" My mind was spinning from the tequila and the sudden eruption of activity. Kiran jumped to her feet and shouted after us, "Anton, what are you doing? Have you lost the plot!" Kiran tried to stalk after us but her guard, Jason, restrained her. Alexei and another man followed closely.

The guards dragged me through a hallway. I kicked and jerked against their hold but their grip was too powerful to fight. I let my body go slack the way we were taught in defense training, as this was supposed to enable me to slide out of their grip with my body weight, but they simply dragged me along. They were impossibly strong.

The cold night air was on my face as we busted through a back door and into the dark alley behind the venue. There was no one and nothing around aside from a tent and a few large trash-bins. The men pushed me up against the far side fence and Anton approached. He raised a hand and they released me. I fought to catch my breath. "What the hell, man?"

"Why are you asking me about some guy named Kiril? Hmm?" He turned to his brother and the other man, saying something in their language before they all turned to study me.

"I—I was just...I didn't mean to piss you off or I dunno, why are you so angry? I was just—"

"Who sent you?"

"*Sent* me?" I looked at Anton, Alexei, and the other man, all dead serious. "No one sent me!"

"I could just have them beat it out of you." Anton shrugged.

"Anton..." Alexei chided in warning.

"I'm only joking." Anton threw his hands up in exasperation.

"It isn't funny," Alexei scolded. "Just leave him. Let's go." Alexei turned to go back in just as Kiran, escorted by Jason, blasted through the back doors into the alley. Relief flooded through me at the sight of her.

"What's going on, Anton?" Kiran was fighting Jason's hold on her. "Let me go or you're fired," she warned a frustrated Jason and returned her gaze to Anton. "I was just trying to tease you with him. Don't beat my friend up over me. Oliver's an absolute sweetheart. You'll love him. No need to be jealous... he's a nice boy. He knows how to share," she insisted, gingerly.

"It's not about you, Kir. Why is he asking me about some oaf named Kiril? Is he a narc or ain't he?"

"'Ain't he?'" Kiran teased but Anton wasn't having it. *Shit, that damned tequila.* My vision grew hazy but cleared a bit as I squinted. *I messed up. I had too much to drink and went in too soon.* Way too soon.

"You brought him to my circle. Can you vouch for him? I'm dead serious, Kir. I'm not playing with you."

"A narc? Are you out of your mind? What in the bloody hell would I be doing hanging out with a bloody narc, Anton? The real question is, what have you been up to of late that's got you all worked up about potential narcs, hmm? Enlighten me..." Kiran's voice took on a new intensity. Her outrage was sobering to Anton, who looked like the blood had drained from his face. He ran his fingers through his dark hair. Kiran stepped forward, placing herself between Anton and me.

"Oh, my, Oliver," Kiran chided. "Anton, you're clueless. Oliver here is the sharpest little hustler I know. CJ trusts him completely—and that's saying something." This seemed to mean something to Anton. He raised his brows at her.

"He just got a tad overenthusiastic. Forgive him. He was probably trying to relate to you, to get to know you...make you think he knows your world, do a little name-dropping, bless him. He was excited to meet you. Can't you see he looks up to you? Give him a break. Remember you at this age? You were a wild card! It was impossible trying to shut you up or calm you down. Who are we kidding? It still is." Kiran stepped toward Anton and stroked his cheek. Anton raised his chin out of her reach. "Oliver—apologize for being a nosey little know-it-all."

I took her cue. "She's right. Kiran told me a bit about you on the drive over and I was stoked to meet you. I figured you had some Slavic roots when I heard you speaking to Alexei in your language, so I asked about pretty much the only Russian I knew. I thought it would impress you. I'm sorry. It was rude. I'm sorry for upsetting you."

"Good," Kiran purred and patted my back, moving me toward the doors, not giving Anton a chance to deliberate.

Alexei crossed in front of us toward Anton and said, "Slow down on the tequila, brother." He patted Anton's chest and headed inside followed by the other man, Kiran and me. Kiran didn't so much as glance back at Anton before leading me past the roped area, straight toward the center of the club space in front of the stage. The bass was pounding more aggressively and the rhythm was quickening.

Kiran guided my hands to her hips as she sauntered toward the dance area. I leaned in and said against her ear, "Thank you."

"Thank me by dancing with me."

"This is just to keep him guessing, okay?" I moved my hand to a more neutral place on her back.

She turned her body to face me, her nose inches from mine.

"You want to keep him guessing, darling?"—she purred. "Be convincing."

Kiran placed my hand back up toward her waist, then closer to her breast. But before I could pull away, she warned, "He's coming." I squeezed her ribs in a nervous response. "And don't be foolish. Don't randomly ask him about those guys. Don't ask him anything. You must uphold the illusion that you have all the answers—that you are a well of information. Powerful people don't share intel with the weak or the clueless," she whispered in my ear in one breath.

"But then, how will I—"

She cut my sentence off with a hard kiss. "*Shhh*," she muttered against my mouth. I nodded and pulled away.

Through my peripheral vision, I clocked Anton's approach. He circled us like a shark and closed in behind her, caging her in between himself and me. His hand slid up the side of her body as he drew his face to her neck. I stiffened and stopped my movement entirely—unsure how to play this. I looked at Kiran for guidance, questions filling my eyes. She pushed me to continue swaying with her. I tried to.

Anton wrapped his arm completely around her stomach and pulled her against him. There was nothing subtle about the grind of his hips against her backside. I could feel the brush of his knuckles on my stomach throughout the movement. It was too much.

I pulled away, stumbling back a step and stopping only when I reached the bar. I leaned against the bar top and turned to watch the two of them continue their display along the dance floor. They merged completely, like liquid on liquid.

My vision was already a blur, but I followed their movements. They took turns glancing back at me, surely receiving satisfaction of some kind from me watching them. This I could do, as long as they didn't lay a damn hand on me. If they wanted me to watch, I'd watch.

CHAPTER 30

MINA

I spent the next two days poring over the contents of the target file obsessively, not unlike the way I would cram for an AP exam or finals week. I understood this kind of pressure. I thrived under this kind of pressure. I memorized the contents of the file from beginning to end.

I learned everything there was to know about Pavel, who went to Eton and was now at Yale, and Margrette, who was also at Yale. There were screenshots of their social media pages, blog posts, achievements, and a record of any acts of rebellion that were carefully brushed under an expensive rug.

I was now Maria Yuriyevna Berezova, daughter of a media magnate, Yuriy Berezov. I had also been raised abroad, attended a private school on the East Coast, and was now a poli sci and international relations major at Columbia, but my real passion was art.

Starling would pose as Adel—Adel bint Sultan bin Abdulaziz Al Saud of Saudi Arabia. Adel and I happened to be on winter holiday at the same ski resort as the Mohorenski twins.

Ultimately, Starling and I had different assignments. From what I understood, her objective was to install a bug of some sort into Pavel's phone.

Upon a second, more detailed debriefing, Mikhailov promised that Mama would receive physical therapy from the best in the field if I managed to extract financial information about where the twins' funds were being held. Nothing was going to stop me from getting that information. Mikhailov made another thing clear, an unexpected detail that it was imperative I mention to the twins: I was looking to purchase a unique, exotic gift as a surprise for Adel on her approaching birthday. Margrette and Pavel would know just the people for such an ask. This would also establish a need to exchange contact information and stay in touch.

Over the next week, Starling and I were instructed to spend every moment of the day together. The goal was to seem close, to be believably friendly, effortlessly casual with one another.

At first, she called me Maria and I called her Adel. It was like being a method actor, studying for a part, and never leaving character. Even during meals, we would sit at a small table near the agents, but separately from everyone else and we would chat as though we really were these girls.

It felt wacky, at first, but when I saw how seriously Starling was taking the task, I rose to the challenge as well, remembering what was at stake.

Throughout the week, our measurements were taken and clothes were shipped in for both of us. From what I understood, we were meant to look like a million bucks, or at least as though a million bucks was the valuation of the contents of our walk-in closets.

On the fifth day, there were clothes laid out for each of us in the classroom. It was everything from ski clothes to après ski to dresses to loungewear to lingerie. The fabrics were luxurious, and the quality of the clothing was extremely fine. Whoever had selected these had exquisite taste. The clothing was labeled by name and everything fit perfectly—no alterations were needed.

"Adel, our ski suits were made in Portugal," I commented.

"This design is very flattering," Starling raved.

"The material is very thin. Won't we be cold in the snow?" I commented.

"We will be absolutely fine in the cold, Maria. I've heard of this company. This fabric is revolutionary, a patented design, specially crafted for this sport," Starling/Adel assured.

"Our conversations still sound a bit stiff," I observed. *They need to sound more laid back*, I thought. "Maybe when we get there, we can have a drink and it'll help us loosen up, get out of our heads," I suggested.

"I don't drink," Starling/Adel replied quickly.

"Why?" I asked, but I already knew the answer from her file. She was religious and drinking was against her religion. The file stated they forced her to give up her faith. I smiled inside, realizing they hadn't managed to do so.

"Adel is Saudi; it's against the law in her country and against her religion," Starling explained. I nodded.

"You're right. Our banter has come a long way from where we began, a significant improvement either way. It'll do." I smiled. She returned my smile and surprisingly, it felt genuine.

The following day, additional packages awaited us. There were skis, ski boots, helmets, and goggles. Everything we would need for a ski trip—the gear appeared to be top-of-the-line— not that I knew much about it.

I knew close to nothing about ski clothes besides the fact that they were very flattering on feminine curves compared to the saggy snow pants I was used to wearing for snowboarding.

Our private instructor, a dark-haired woman with a sleek bob, demonstrated how to get in and out of the ski gear. She also demonstrated exactly how I should limp after the injury I would be feigning.

"Don't overdo it. Just remember to stay consistently limping on the same injured foot," she reminded.

Starling and I spent day and night together intensifying our profile work and immersing ourselves deeply into the lives of our fictional Maria and Adel. I was beginning to feel more comfortable as Maria, especially given how committed Starling had been to becoming Adel. She had stayed in the infirmary with me every night since the tech had been implanted. I supposed they continued to monitor our recovery from the implant to minimize the chance of any mishaps.

It was surprising to witness Starling behaving like an entirely different person than she'd been in my first weeks at Lavidian. She had been lifeless and cold before, isolating herself from the other girls and by all appearances behaving like an unfeeling robot. At meals, I once remarked that the careers had more life in them than Starling did.

Now, she had morphed into an entirely different person, literally unrecognizable. I'd attempt a joke as Maria and she'd giggle, actually giggle. Starling had clearly shoved her prior discomfort with me and with her circumstances somewhere deep inside herself. I wondered idly how they'd incentivized her to succeed in the mission and if it had anything to do with her changed attitude.

"Mar, do you remember when our fathers tried to cannonball off the yacht in Greece and your dad lost his trunks?" Starling had started calling me Mar. I liked it. It was casual.

"Mar. That's perfect. I'll call you Addie," I told her.

"I like it," she said, smiling into her fruit salad.

"Yeah! And when your dad freaked out and screamed at you to get inside the cabin while my father dived for his trunks," I played along. Addie burst into laughter and I joined her. I could feel the other girls' eyes searing a hole into the back of my head as Starling and I talked.

I turned over my shoulder to find Magpie locking eyes with

me. I smiled at her. "I miss you," I mouthed. Magpie looked around nervously, gave me a small sad smile, and looked down at her plate. *I do miss her.* Things hadn't been the same without Magpie these past few days. I'd been so preoccupied with the assignment that the time had flown by, but what I had with Magpie was real. This thing with Starling, it was fabricated. I had to remember that. Lavidian was taking from me, again, and I hadn't even noticed it.

Every time I had tried to speak with Starling about our real situation or anything that truly meant something to her or me, she would change the subject. I vaguely implied that I was doing this for my mother and my young cousin, hoping to inspire Starling to trust a similar confidence with me. But she brushed it off like I hadn't said anything of consequence and carried on pretending to be Adel. She drew so heavily on her profile, on Addie, to the point that I was unsure whether she was becoming delusional or simply brilliant at agenting.

Starling continued our thread of thought, fabricating more stories for our past together. She crafted a memory of a prank we played on her cousins that involved chocolate and bedsheets when I stayed over at her Saudi penthouse.

I crafted a more detailed history of the summer we met and the games we played aboard the megayacht our fathers chartered to Greece.

We discussed each other's favorite snacks—mine: chocolate meringue cookies, hers: blueberry angel food cake. When you have private chefs in your kitchen, why not?

Starling's Addie was into Bach, *Downton Abbey*, and *House of the Dragon* while my Maria was into MGMT, *Loki*, and *Bosch*.

Starling and I were both nervous about never having attended university, but we were both fairly certain that we could pull it off with enough study. We consumed hours of footage of the Columbia campus. We were given supervised access to social media to research the latest posts from students on campus. The whole time I sat in front of the computer, my fingers were itching to type Nyah's social media handle into the search bar, just to see her, just for a brief glimpse of happiness; but I knew better than to put a target on her back considering the pair of eyes behind me, watching my every move.

On the sixth day, Mikhailov called us into his office and let us know that Starling and I—or Addie and Maria, more accurately—would be making a stop in Minsk. The purpose of the stop was to establish our friendship in public and conduct further recon on several wealthy heirs who were spending time in Tsentralny, Minsk.

"You will study how they speak and behave—the artistry is in the detail," Mikhailov noted passionately.

Starling and I were to spend some time in a popular café where the offspring of the rich and famous, commonly known as nepo babies, tended to congregate. We were also instructed to take plenty of selfies together, on the jet and in the city, to fill our phones with adequate recent photos to supplement the doctored and implanted ones—thorough identity work, as our private instructor had labeled it.

A few days prior, an extensive photoshoot was arranged for Starling and me, set in front of a greenscreen backdrop. Those images were fed to an AI, modified, and posted to various media outlets, added to the private social media pages of the girls. The posts would be backdated by Lavidian hackers.

When the time finally came, Starling and I were loaded onto a jet to be flown to Minsk before we set off for our final destination, Artybash. We were escorted by two agents masquerading as our private security team. I approached the jet on the tarmac slowly as a nauseating sense of deja vu washed over me.

Has the sky always appeared to be so endless? I felt like I was going to be sick. The last time I was on a plane, I had been forced onboard. *The circumstances really haven't changed. I know nothing.* The overwhelming pull to return to the infirmary took me off guard. I yearned to feel the hard mattress of my bed beneath me, to see the beige, arched, stone ceiling above me, to hear Nurse Katya sorting through glass vials or flipping through her files.

My heart seemed to stall abruptly as all the sound and air around me was sucked away. Panic gripped me by the throat. I took a ragged breath. *Not again, not now.* I fought to force the breath into my lungs. *One. Two. Three. Four.* My eyes widened as the sky expanded farther out then rushed back in all at once and suddenly, it felt as though the universe ended at my toes. One step closer and I'd fall right in. A hand squeezed mine. I looked to find Starling by my side, squeezing her palm against mine. An onslaught of jet noise attacked my eardrums. Sound returned.

"Don't be nervous, think of it like a yacht...with wings," she assured and gave my hand another squeeze. I snorted a laugh and it was just the distraction I needed, an unexpected jolt out of a toxic trance. The tightness in my gut released and my feet somehow shuffled toward the jet.

I didn't meet Artyom's gaze as he studied me. I refused to allow my disappointment in him to distract me from the task that lay ahead. I walked resolutely past him without a word, climbing the stairs to board the jet, only releasing Starling's hand once inside.

Our luggage had already been packed for us. The only things that we added to our carry-ons that morning were our cuffs and their corresponding chargers. I snuck my pocketknife into my carry-on, as well. I likely wouldn't need it but it granted me inexplicable comfort.

A stern-faced Mikhailov distributed our new phones and coordinating documents just before we departed Lavidian. He handed Starling an additional device, miniature gadget, which had something to do with allowing Lavidian hackers remote access to Pavel Mohorenski's phone—extracting the data they needed and making a copy.

I clicked my seatbelt and looked out the window as the jet began to move.

I reviewed the plan in my head once more and checked my carry-on bag for the ear coms, which would allow us to communicate if necessary. They were safely tucked into the small zipper compartment in a compact magnetic case. On our final day of training, we were instructed on how to operate the coms and when to hide them or dispose of them.

Starling and I knew the plan inside out. We had the layout of the mountain memorized. We learned the ski slopes the way you would learn a map for a geography test, but I was still worried about navigating the trails. What if the ski runs weren't as straightforward in real life as they appeared on paper?

Luckily, we wouldn't be alone—our babysitters would be there to hold our hands through this one. I was confident that they'd get us exactly where we needed to be for my "injury." The rest would be up to us.

I posed for a selfie as Starling/Addie maneuvered her phone to find a flattering angle.

"That's cute. Let's do one smiling," I suggested. We both flashed our grins, showing off bright, toothy smiles.

It felt strange, almost unnatural, to be out in the world again, pretending to be normal, to be free. It felt like breathing fresh air for the first time after being stuck in an echo-chamber but then learning that the air was fabricated—a simulation, a reverie.

Through the small window, I carefully observed the terrain we had departed. The region around Lavidian was surrounded by seemingly endless acres of forest. We landed in Minsk in less than an hour, which meant Lavidian was about a four-hour drive away.

Artyom and the second guard, a short, round-faced, clean-shaven man in his late forties, were our acting security team. They waited for us to change into our high-heeled boots and accessorize with scarves and jewelry before escorting us into a black Mercedes sedan in the parking lot of the airport.

Artyom and the second guard drove us into Tsentralny, Minsk, which was about a half-hour drive. By the time we pulled up to the Café de Paris on Karl Marx Street in the Lenin District, I was thoroughly Maria Berezova. I walked hand in hand with Addie, having left both Mina and Lark behind.

Café de Paris was covered in twinkling lights even in the daytime, and felt as though a piece of the European city it was named after had been plucked up and brought into Minsk. The atmosphere was luxurious. The guests and the staff were sophisticated and well-dressed. Addie and I chose a corner booth overlooking the cozy dining room near a roaring fireplace. The walls featured large, gold-framed renaissance paintings and tall bookshelves filled with the classics. Sculptures were scattered throughout the space and potted plants hung from the ceiling, draping over the decor.

We ordered lunch and snapped a few more photos together. Artyom and the other guard, Fox, sat at a table nearest to the entrance with their backs to the wall, eyes discreetly scoping out the lounge.

When a young, trendy group of five occupied the booth near us, Addie and I put our conversation on pause to observe and eavesdrop.

They were dressed in monochromatic matching sweatshirt-sweatpants combos with designer shoes, handbags, fanny-packs and pricey-looking wrist pieces. They were garrulous but spoke with a sort of elongated, drawn-out intonation.

"Did she say her stepmom keeps grabbing things from her?" I checked with Adel in a hushed whisper.

"No, she said, *S'menya khvatit*, not *khvatat*—it's an expression. It means, 'I've had enough'—she's fed up with her stepmom for competing with her over some feature on a magazine cover. They're both models who used to be friends," Adel whispered back.

Wow. I'd been completely off. I strained my ears to listen more carefully. If the Mohorenski twins spoke in the same fashion, it might be a problem. I'd have to keep them speaking English to level out the playing field.

I continued listening in, mentally drilling myself with the colloquial expressions this group spouted throughout their chat. I guessed at the meaning and tried to commit them to memory. Unsure if I was allowed to, I risked jotting a few phrases down in the notes of my new phone. I resisted the potent urge to connect with the cafe's Wi-Fi and send Nyah a message.

I noted that most of the clients in this place who ordered lunch rarely uttered the words "Thank you." "Please" was thrown in from time to time but very seldomly. The staff was equally unceremonious with the clients.

The group of friends Addie and I were observing laughed loudly as they ate with their hands. Their manners weren't perfect, but then again, it wasn't clear who they were, exactly, or how they had been raised. They could very well have been new money.

Would Adel and I be expected to behave this way in each other's company? Perhaps, when we were children, manners had been drilled into us with etiquette lessons and the like. But maybe some of those trust fund kids had rebelled from that level of performative propriety after a few years of living independently. I mean, why not?

A change on my phone screen caught my eye. I looked down and noticed a line of text that appeared beneath the phrases I jotted down in my notes earlier.

In a few minutes, visit the bar, order a drink.

The phone was being monitored. Of course, it was. I quickly typed, *Ok*, under the message as my heart thudded loudly in my chest from the unexpected intrusion. I looked up, glancing at Artyom and the other guard. They continued scoping out the lounge, not paying any particular attention to Adel and me. Neither of them had a phone in his hand.

I looked back down to the text in my notes. The lines were gone; the screen was blank.

The group of friends didn't ask for a check. One of them handed a card to the waiter without even looking at the bill. The waiter returned with the sales slip and the group got up and left without a word of thanks. Neither did the waiter thank the group. The dining room soon grew quiet and empty.

"Addie, I'm gonna go sit at the bar for a bit. Be back soon," I told Adel. She gave me a short nod and continued scrolling through our photos on her phone.

I gathered my handbag, which was a gorgeous, brown leather piece that I was growing fond of, and I snaked a path through the vacant tables and chairs toward the bar. The only other patrons near our targeted demographic were seated there.

An empty barstool stood between a man in a navy suit and two women gossiping animatedly over drinks. I wasn't sure what I was meant to do here besides order a drink, so I figured I should take a seat and await further instruction. The women were caught up in conversation, so I asked the man in the suit if the empty seat was occupied. The man was drinking a cappuccino and watching the muted television showing the news. He had a handsome profile, a stately nose and an angular clean-shaven jaw that sloped down toward a pronounced chin. His broad, dark eyebrows drew together, making him look deeply concerned by what was being reported on the news.

"Is this seat occupied?" I repeated.

He glanced my way and shook his head. At first, I thought he was telling me I couldn't sit there. I motioned for the unoccupied barstool in the corner but stopped when the man turned his face toward me, inhaled a deep breath, and after a few moments of appraisal, nodded at the empty seat.

"Thank you," I said. When he did a double-take, I realized I may have done the wrong thing. Was thanking someone really so rare? Or was this not an appropriate occasion upon which to thank someone? I'd have to investigate further.

At least Maria—my current persona—had been raised in the States. That would be my excuse. I took a seat beside the man and held back an automatic smile as I turned to the bartender who approached.

"What would you like?" he asked.

"I'll have a chardonnay," I answered quickly. It was the first thing I could think of. I'd never ordered a drink at a bar before. I was supposed to be a college student in Europe, after all. Maria would've ordered a chardonnay, I felt sure.

The man in the suit was still looking at me; I could sense it through my peripheral vision. I turned toward him, noticing the dimple in his chin. He immediately turned his attention back to the news.

I sipped my chardonnay and listened to the woman beside me complain to her friend about what an inadequate lover her husband was, and how she feared she'd never achieve an orgasm with him. Her friend, instead of encouraging her to be open with her husband, offered the contact information of an ex-lover who was excellent in bed but had been alarmingly neurotic from time to time. The woman beside me replied with an eager "Yes." I checked my phone for further instructions but the notes remained blank. *What exactly was I supposed to be doing here?* I took another sip of my chardonnay.

I glanced over my shoulder to check on Addie, who was still scrolling through her phone. She looked up at me and I lifted my glass to her. Addie furrowed her brows in confusion. I considered standing up and rejoining her when a loud exhale from beside me pulled my attention. I turned and quirked a brow as the man sitting next to me huffed, releasing a quiet growl that rumbled out at the end of his breath.

"Bad news?" I asked the man, looking between him and the television screen. It was mounted to the wall of the bar display, set in a gold frame to match the paintings. I was curious to speak to him, to anyone outside Lavidian. I wasn't exactly sure if I was allowed to do so or if I was supposed to be doing something completely different while I was over here. I checked back with Artyom and the other guard, Fox. They both watched me intently from where they were perched, but made no move to stand or interrupt the conversation.

The man with the dimpled chin slowly turned his gaze back toward me, but his body remained facing forward as if to broadcast a clear message of disinterest.

"I'm not looking for a professional, thank you."

"A professional?" I frowned.

He turned and nodded toward Artyom and the other guard, then at me. I followed his gaze and it hit me what he meant. This guy thought I was an escort.

"Oh, no...I wasn't..."—I sputtered before recovering from my very Mina-like fumble and reclaiming the emotional neutrality that someone of Maria's stature would possess—"I wasn't coming on to you. I was just trying to have a conversation," I remarked and started to get up, planning to return to Addie.

"Forgive me," the man apologized. "It's the bullshit they spew on this programming that has me infuriated. I may have projected my displeasure onto you." I nodded but remained aloof. "To think people actually believe this garbage. It's endless threats and ultimatums with this regime and people blindly support it," he continued mostly to himself. I looked up at the screen and read the apocalyptic rhetoric scrolling at the bottom.

It reminded me of a quote I memorized for my poli sci background work.

"'We must continue the process of humanizing mankind until men can learn to live in peace, and cooperate in constructive activities instead of competing in a mindless contest of mutual destruction,'" I quoted, ecstatic to put the words of William Fulbright to use like the insufferable know-it-all that I was. For a brief moment, I felt like myself, like Mina, the girl who once had a bright future ahead of her. I released a mournful sigh, fighting to hold onto levity.

"What are you studying? No. Let me guess…International relations?"—the man in the navy suit perked up—"Clearly, you're from the States with a quote like that," he added, amused with himself.

"You're not wrong." I smirked, impressed. "I'm guessing you studied international relations, as well?"

"That and—"

"Political science," we both said simultaneously and chuckled. I let out a bemused snort and covered my mouth.

"Of course," the man muttered with a smirk. "'Those who tell the stories rule the society.'"

"Is that a quote?" I asked.

"Oh, come on…they teach Fulbright but not the ideals of the world's first political scientist?" the man exclaimed, rubbing his dimpled chin in bewilderment.

"Is it Plato?" I postulated.

"It seems all hope is not lost," he remarked, half-jokingly. I rolled my eyes at that. "What brings you to Minsk?" the man asked after another sip of his cappuccino.

"I'm meeting my friend." I nodded toward Addie.

"Then, why aren't you with your friend?" he asked, inspecting Addie from across the dining lounge. She glanced up at us from her phone with a question in her expression.

"I was craving a chardonnay and my friend doesn't drink. So,

I came over here, just in case it made her uncomfortable. Plus, I enjoy conversing with strangers. Although they're usually less crabby," I jabbed. He quirked a brow to that. "But, it's always a surprise—who you meet, what you learn—Plato." I finally released my smile, unable to help it. He was slightly taken aback by it. I looked away quickly and checked my phone for a note, and after a moment, a short message appeared.

> That's enough. Return to your table.

I looked back at Artyom and Fox. They were still watching me but neither seemed to have a phone in his hand. Artyom nodded toward the table, gesturing for me to return.

I finished my glass and stood.

"Can I buy you another?" the man in the navy suit offered, rushing through the words.

I considered it. I smiled down at him. "Not today, Plato, but thanks," I said with a wink and returned to Addie without another word.

Artyom and Fox had already checked us into the resort when we arrived in Artybash. All we had to do was present our passports to reception, sign a document, and the keys for our deluxe suite were handed to us. I started to smile, to say, "Thank you," to the team behind the reception desk but hesitated and nodded my thanks instead.

It was imperative that we establish our presence as guests of the resort to the twins, familiar faces—before they encountered us on the slopes. Our private psychological strategy pedagogue insisted that it would expedite the trust between us and ultimately, make our work easier.

According to internal recon, the twins should pass us in the hall on their way out of their suite as they headed to dinner. They had a 17:00 dinner reservation.

Right on time, I heard the sound of a door opening and conversation filled the hall. I saw Margrette first, a tall brunette in simple jeans and a gray sweater. She wore her hair down and had little to no makeup on. The yellow lights of hallway sconces reflected against her round glasses.

Pavel followed her closely, muttering something indiscernible as he scrolled through his phone. He had curly, dark chestnut hair in the same shade as Margrette's, wore boxy spectacles, and like his sister, was dressed rather plainly. Addie and I stood out in our patterned leggings, faux fur puffers, and platform boots.

I smiled at Margrette as we passed. She did not return the smile. That was all right. Smiling at strangers for no reason was considered strange in their culture, but since I was technically a university student who spent most of her time in the States, despite who my father was, I figured it would be consistent if I expressed a similar disposition to the way Americans normally behaved.

Pavel did not look up from his phone as he passed us, so Addie veered ever so slightly to the left to create a collision. He slammed into her shoulder with his phone. Addie clutched her shoulder and turned to Pavel.

"Be careful! Try looking where you're going," Addie warned, in a soft but firm tone before leaning into me, linking her arm with mine, and sharing a quiet giggle as we hurried to find our suite. Based on his surprised expression, Pavel wouldn't forget Addie anytime soon.

"Come on. She's right, you know," we heard Margrette chide.

As soon as Artyom and the other guard swept the suite and gave us the go-ahead, Addie and I appraised our accommodations. Lavidian had booked us one of the finest suites in the hotel. There were two large beds in the bedroom, a walk-in closet, a clawfoot tub, a rain shower, a living room, and a kitchen—luxury at its finest.

I jumped onto one of the massive beds and spread my legs and arms like I was making a snow angel. It felt like heaven. I savored the luxurious feel of the high-thread-count sheets against my skin as I closed my eyes. It reminded me of the hotel opposite the hospital. Memories of Oliver flooded my mind. I remembered how he clung to me in his sleep, his arms wrapped around me possessively, as if he never wanted to let me go. I heard someone clearing his throat. Artyom crossed his arms and quirked his brow in amusement, leaning against the doorway between the bedroom and living room. Addie giggled and followed my lead on her own bed. It was unusual to see her behave so freely but I wondered if this was who she would have been had she not been taken by these people. Sudden anger at that thought of a young life cut short and a fierce protective instinct for her washed over me.

"Can we have some privacy?" I asked Artyom, a demand in my voice. His amusement fell away. His eyes fell to the floor at the clear judgment and distrust in my eyes.

"Be ready for dinner in twenty minutes," he advised us, but before he turned to go, I wanted to clarify what had happened in Minsk.

"What was I supposed to do at the bar in Minsk?"

He considered my question and looked at Addie before answering me, "You did everything you were supposed to do." Before I could question him further, he quickly turned and left the suite.

Sprawled out over the soft, luxurious mattress, with my head turned to face the window that looked out over the winter wonderland beyond, I finally understood what Magpie meant when she said she was desperate to go on assignment and be in the field. *This is... thrilling!* I felt alive in a way I hadn't thought I'd ever feel again.

I had been concerned I might have another panic attack when I boarded the jet to Artybash, but as soon as I saw Artyom by the airstairs, without his coat, in a tight, black turtleneck that was way too small for him, I almost laughed out loud. It was a welcome but short-lived distraction. My heart began to pound almost on cue, the closer I walked toward the jet. Then, I felt Starling's fingers interlace through mine and the knot in my throat loosened as it had before. I looked at her now, sprawled on the other bed, and smiled at her. She returned it.

"I'm glad you're here," I said to her, softly, too softly. Her smile faltered. She could sense I was speaking as Lark, as Mina, not Maria Berezova. She turned her face to the wall. Stung, I jumped to my feet and went for my suitcase, blinking away the moisture puddled in my eyes.

We had precisely a half hour to eat breakfast, and forty-five minutes to get changed, and get out on the slopes. The twins would likely have completed their first run by the time we made it up the ski lift. The other guard, Fox, had been running surveillance on the twins, who had breakfasted earlier than we anticipated. Pavel recognized Addie and even mumbled a perfunctory, "Good morning" as he passed.

Addie and I ate breakfast quickly and billed everything to the suite before heading back to change into our ski gear.

Our ski run would have to be timed perfectly before their third run down. Adel would seek out the help of the twins. Artyom and Fox would act as our personal security. One would remain on the twins and telecom with us, while the other would remain in the lodge to fulfill his own assignment in keeping Mr. and Mrs. Mohorenski occupied while we dealt with their kids.

This assignment in and of itself was a test, I realized. I had learned from my research that this family—this mark—was a low-level priority and their operations had historically been aboveboard. The financial information Lavidian was fishing for might not even exist. This was my test run, dipping my toe in the water and demonstrating how I would fare. How useful could I be? It was imperative for me to do well because now that I'd had a taste of freedom, I couldn't go back to being locked up at Lavidian. I just couldn't.

"In two minutes, get on the ski lift," Artyom's deep timbre came in through my earpiece. I looked around to make sure no one was watching and with the guidance of Addie, practiced walking forward and backward in the skis. She gave me a crash course on how to brake, just in case.

"Skis in snow plough position to go slow—the kids call it 'pizza,' and to stop suddenly, just drive the backs of both skis downhill, like you're trying to spray snow on someone. When we get to the top, we'll make sure no one of importance can see us and I will support your weight all the way down to the site of your accident. It's a bit steep around there, so snow plough your legs to slow yourself down. Just make sure your skis don't cross. Keep your legs wide and your skis parallel to each other. Okay?"

"Sounds easy enough," I muttered and shrugged. It wasn't. As soon as my skis hit the snow at the top of the lift, I ate it. To my credit, I got back to my feet quickly enough that no one familiar had taken much notice, but most of the skiers getting off the lift were clearly skilled veterans.

"How unlikely would it be that the daughter of an oligarch didn't grow up skiing?" I asked Starling.

Her eyes went wide and she looked around frantically. "Oh, Maria, your humor is so...unique. You're just a bit out of practice is all. Don't worry, it's like riding a bike," she insisted in her best, lighthearted Addie voice.

"Uh-huh," I muttered as Artyom gave us the go-ahead through our coms to start the descent to our target location.

"Take the expert trail designated with a black circle. That's the one Pavel and Margrette have been taking today. Take a spill at the right side of the run, a few meters after the first left sloping turn," Artyom reminded.

"Piece of cake," I grumbled, looking at the much less daunting blue circle and green circle trails longingly. "Why can't they have been skiing those trails?" I whined, eyes widening at the steep slopes of the trail marked with a black circle.

"We're just lucky they aren't off-trailing. That reminds me, be careful of the trees," Starling advised. Be careful of the trees? What were they going to do? With no one watching, she turned in her skis so that she was skiing down the slope backward and rested her hands on my shoulders to start me on our way down but control the speed.

"Maria, I'm going to need you to help me and brake the whole way down. Do Pizza! Brake! You're gaining too much speed! I can't keep holding you up at this speed. Maria, slow down!" she screamed and we plummeted down the steep slope. I pizza'd my legs as much as I could but the drop was too steep.

"Brake! Snow plough! Just fall! Fall with your body uphill!"

I rotated my right foot inward slightly more aggressively. Just as I feared, my ski-edge ate snow and I went down like a rock. Starling moved out of the way in time so I didn't swipe her off her feet.

I was shooting down the mountain full-speed. I lost one ski, then both sticks. I was plummeting straight for the tree line. *Shit, shit, shit!* I used the last of my strength to propel myself around and dug the heels of my ski boots into the snow, making enough friction to slow my descent just as I plowed into a massive pine tree, smashing my knee into the trunk. I tried to right myself but I careened into empty space, my body plummeting into a tree well of unconsolidated snow powder, which closed around me like quicksand.

"*Aagghhhh!*" I screamed, trying not to move and cause more snow to fall over my head. I held onto the trunk of the tree and a branch I grabbed on the way down. I nuzzled my face around to create a breathing hole in the powdered snow. "Help! Addie! There's a tree well! Be careful!"

"What the hell was that?" Artyom's voice boomed into my ear. Relief filled me that someone knew where I was. I'd never been so happy to hear his voice. Thankfully, my helmet had kept the com in my ear.

"Ar-Artyom! I'm stuck! I n-need help...I fell-I fell in a hole. I'm in a hole by a tree! I can't-I can't move, I c-can't breathe—"

"Lark! Don't panic. Whatever you do, stay calm, take slow controlled breaths with me. Are you near the planned accident site?"

"We overshot it by a few hundred yards, I'd say," I estimated, trying not to shift my weight and holding onto the branch for dear life. "Addie!"

"Maria!" I heard Starling's voice faintly in the distance. "Artyom, tell her I can hear her. She's close. Addie!" I yelled.

"Maria!" she called out. "Maria, hold on! I'm coming!"

"Breathe with me, Lark," came in Artyom's voice, even and grounding in my ear like the pulse of a steady heartbeat. "How did this happen?"

I breathed in slowly. "The brakes on these things suck."

I heard the rumble of his low chuckle. "Good, that's good, stay calm just like that, Lark. What is your position? Are you inverted or head up?"

"Head up."

"Good, that'll be a much easier rescue. Try not to move. How far down do you think you fell?" Artyom asked. My wrist was scraping against the trunk of the tree.

"I don't know, uhh...I can't see." I squinted up but all I could see was snow.

"Call out to Adel right now, right now, as Maria. I've got a lock on your location; she's right on top of you."

"Addie!" I screamed, trying to hold onto the branch. "Addie!"

"Maria! I've got you! Help! Someone, help us!" she cried, her voice sending a soothing wave of calm through me. I felt something reach down from above.

Fingers wrapped around my wrist and pulled with fierce effort. In between pulls, Starling's voice cried out, "Help! Help us! Please, help!"

"Hey! You need some help?" I heard someone call to her from a distance.

"Yes!" Addie and I cried together.

"My friend is stuck in a tree well! Help me pull her out! Please!"

"Okay, hold on!" the voice boomed back.

"Lark. Can you still hear me? If you're with me, Fox says it's likely them, Pavel and Margrette. Stay on assignment," Artyom's voice cut in. "Say, 'Help me, Adel!' if you're still with me."

"Help me, Addie!" I cried out. With four big pulls, my head emerged above the snow, elbows propped against the top of the powder overhead.

"My ski! I think it's lodged in the snow," I cried.

"Try to kick it off!" Addie gritted out through her teeth, face flushed and hands gripping my elbows with a confident intensity. She wouldn't let me go. She would hold on until her arms gave out. I could see the fierce promise in her eyes. I nodded.

"I'll try," I promised, jerking my leg.

"Use the toe of your free ski boot and press it against the heel DIN of the binding to eject it!" Addie reminded me. My ski was so immersed in snow powder that the DIN was stuck. I hit the DIN with maximal force over and over, all the while trying to keep my upper body still so that Addie didn't lose grip. Finally, the tension in my ankle released as the ski fell away and Adel's, Pavel's and Margrette's efforts propelled me out of the well and onto the packed snow.

Our pants and ragged breathing filled the quiet wilderness. Our chests heaved like we'd just run a marathon. An electric energy buzzed through, as we understood how narrowly I'd escaped death.

"Thank you," I panted to them. Pavel and Margrette nodded. Addie was shaking, as was I.

"Good," Artyom whispered into my ear. A few moments later, a skier in only a dark turtleneck and dress pants flew past us at the speed of a train. That had to be him.

"Thank you for your help," Addie told the twins. "We—we left our phones in our suite. Would you mind if we used your phone to make a call?" I used the distraction of Pavel's and Margrette's eyes on Addie to pocket my earpiece and straighten my crooked helmet.

Pavel didn't hesitate, not even for a second. He pulled out his phone, punched in the code without even trying to hide it, and handed it right over to Addie.

"Here," he said, still catching his breath.

"Are you okay?" Margrette addressed me. "That was a close one. You were really lucky your friend was with you. We wouldn't have even known you were down there if we hadn't spotted her trying to help you! Here, let's get farther away from that well, just in case," Margrette suggested. I gave her my hand and let her drag me farther from nature's death trap.

"I'm okay—a bit shaken up if I'm honest and my ankle hurts like hell, but I'm okay considering everything," I admitted. "Thank you. You guys helped save my life."

"Your friend did all the heavy lifting—you would have been fine in her hands. Margrette and I just expedited the rescue," Pavel demurred. Addie was still digging around in Pavel's phone. If she was connecting to the spyware, she was doing a good job making it look like she was just having trouble finding service.

"Sorry, the reception is weak out here," Addie explained and raised the phone in the air like she was looking for more bars.

"Pavel and I could ski down to notify ski patrol. You keep

trying to call someone. We'll take the lift back up to see if we can find your other ski and your poles," Margrette offered, looking down at my lonely ski boots. "I'll drop a pin here so that ski patrol can find you more easily, and perhaps they can retrieve the ski you lost in the tree well," she added.

"That would be—" I started.

"That would be very helpful, thank you," Addie interjected. "The cell reception will probably be much better down there," she said. "I'll come with you and try to contact our security team from the bottom of the slopes." Addie unzipped her puffer. "Here, Maria. Wear this for now. I'll be right back. Twenty minutes tops."

"No, keep it on, it's cold," I told her.

"I'm fine, I'll be moving. You're the one perched here like a frozen pigeon," she insisted, wrapping me in the beige puffer still warm from her body heat. "I'll be back. Watch out for the skiers coming around this bend, but don't get too close to those trees."

"I know, Addie." I rolled my eyes at her, playing the part. "You're never gonna let me live this down, are you?"

She grinned at me and took off down the steep slope like an Olympic alpine skier. Pavel and Margrette took off after her.

"Adel, my beautiful friend, I completely had you on that run. You just took the third turn so sharp that you cut my path, and I didn't want to spook you by gunning past." Pavel held Addie's hand and massaged her palm. This was his third excuse as to why she had beaten him down the mountain. The first was that she had a head start and the second was that he wanted to make sure she didn't wipe out.

"You were on my heels the whole time. I saw the effort on your face." Addie smirked, scrunching up her brows and nose as though to mimic him. She was yelling over the loud music pumping in the festive supper club. Pavel chuckled and pulled her in playfully. The place was pretty empty, but the people who were here sure knew how to have a good time. Almost everyone was dancing on the dance floor. Some were standing on their tables. Others waved their dinner napkins in the air.

We were on our fourth round of drinks.

"Well, what can I say? You had my phone! Of course I was on your heels," Pavel said over the music, leaning so far into Addie's personal space that his mouth was mere inches from her ear. He rested his hand on her waist every time he spoke to her. She was stiff from the proximity, her shoulders raised in a subtle expression of discomfort, but her facial gesture suggested she was having a ball.

"I feel like some champagne! Anyone with me?" I called out to Margrette and Pavel.

"Absolutely. Adel? How about you? You interested in some champagne?" Pavel asked her, scooting closer still. She leaned away from him, reaching for her water glass.

"No, thank you, but I would love to take a look at the menu. I'm having a craving for something salty, maybe some caviar if they have anything of quality?"

"They have an exceptional selection," Pavel assured.

"Good idea!" Margrette agreed enthusiastically, bottoming out her fifth martini.

"So, what was it like?"—Pavel turned to me as Addie waved down a waiter to order—"Did you think you were gonna die down there?"

"I didn't really have time to think about it. I was too busy holding onto a branch with one hand and gripping the trunk of the tree with the other hand and my free leg. If I'd realized how bad my situation was, I probably would have panicked," I answered Pavel with all honesty.

"Yeah, I was gonna say, you got lucky that you didn't start

flailing your arms and legs around or you would've been buried in snow and then, you probably would've suffocated to death before we could help you," Pavel commented enthusiastically.

"Nice," I stated flatly. "I feel much better now."

"Armand de Brignac Ace of Spades Silver Blanc de Blancs and the Royal Siberian Osetra, 500 grams should be fine to start," I overheard Addie tell the waiter.

"I'm going to need a card on file," the waiter said, holding his hand out.

"I don't have my wallet with me. Let me call my security—"

"Don't even consider it. You are our guests tonight." Pavel reached for his wallet, which was tucked inside the pocket of his high-collared, finely stitched wool coat. Addie and I watched intently as he pulled the card out, too intently, I realized. I looked back at Margrette and clinked my glass with hers. Addie was closer to Pavel. She would pass his card to the waiter so she'd get a better look than I would anyway.

"On second thought, Marg...you're the big baller, now. Give me your card." Pavel's cheerful tone had shifted into a sarcastic clipped sound of agitation.

"Pavel..." Margrette pronounced with warning in her tone. They had a silent conversation with their eyes—a stand-off. Addie and I made eye contact to mark the awkward exchange.

"What? You don't want to be rude to our guests, do you?" Pavel argued, an edge lingering in his voice. Margrette plastered on a smile.

"Of course not. Here..." She opened her purple clutch and fished out a black card. I squinted to read Credit Suisse printed in the top left corner. Pavel snatched the card from her hand and passed it to the waiter.

"What's wrong?" Margrette asked me after the waiter left. "You're so quiet all of a sudden."

"Oh, it's nothing...I was just thinking."—I scooted closer to her and leaned in to speak—"I was just thinking about how my father has been micromanaging me. A few years back, I don't think he even knew which country I was in half the time. Now, it's like he's itching to install a GPS tracker on me or something," I told Margrette, rubbing the itchy skin on my arm through my long-sleeved blouse over the spot where the Lavidian tracker was installed. "It's so irritating, the way he's been keeping tabs on me. He's always been a private man. I get that, I can understand him and I've always...well...no, well, yeah actually, I've always tried to keep a low profile. I never talk about him, I don't use his last name when introducing myself—"

"Why?" Margrette asked.

"Ummm—I mean you get it. You know how people can be with people like us..." I explained vaguely and she nodded. "My father, he's just always just been really...I dunno, paranoid? His power, his wealth, it makes him a target. Anyone I befriend at school has to be approved through him or his people. Can you imagine? He ran a background check on my roommate, for Christ's sake.

"He told me not to take his phone calls around her. Not like he ever calls me anyway. He even sends a team to my off-campus apartment to scan it for like, surveillance equipment and bugs and stuff. Like, he thinks my roommate could've bugged the place...psychotic. Has your father ever done anything like that?" I asked, hoping to channel a lonely girl looking to be understood.

Margrette ran her painted, electric-blue fingernails through the part of her hair that was side shaved with an X design. I hadn't noticed it earlier, where it was hidden under the rest of her long locks. She stretched out the collar of her multicolor, vintage AC/DC t-shirt with the hook of her thumb. It looked pretty old. I wondered if it was valuable. She was deciding something. Margrette's eyes locked on mine at last and her brows knitted together. Bingo.

"No, I do get it. Like, my dad's been micromanaging my

expenses, too," she complained and I knew I was in. "Well, his accountant has," Margrette said, rolling her eyes in frustration at what she was saying. I leaned in closer still, as to not miss a single word. "Now that Papa transferred most of his assets into my name—not Pavel's because, well...I mean, he's a full-on mess —it's like, every little charge is looked at under a microscope. I wanna say: what are you so paranoid about? It's not like I'd be able to put so much as a ding in his finances, even if, let's say, tomorrow I decided to buy another penthouse on the Upper East Side, Manhattan. But his people go through the charges with a lice comb and I get a weekly interrogation call where I have to explain every single one. It is so annoying and border-line embarrassing, especially when Pavel borrows the card to make one of his insane purchases. Papa gets on my case about it, and what am I supposed to do? Pavel doesn't understand the word 'no.' I've been thinking lately that I have to figure out a way to get my finances in order, and I dunno, get out from under his control. Is that crazy?" Margrette asked, hope sparkling in her eyes.

"No, it isn't. A little independence never hurt anyone, right? You should do it. I'd be down to partner with you on some-thing...I'm really into the idea of opening a bunch of like, women's health clinics, a safe place women can go and just get everything checked out: nutritional deficiency, mental wellbe-ing, restorative meditation, hormonal imbalances, early cancer detection, something like that..."

"I love that. I might have to take you up on that," Margrette beamed, hopeful. A tinge of guilt that I'd actually gotten this girl to trust me left a bitter taste in my mouth.

"Here, let me give you my number." I held my hand out and she unlocked and passed me her phone. "What did you mean about your brother being a full-on mess? Why does your dad not trust him with the assets? Why is it only on you? That seems like a lot of pressure to put you under," I added, in order to remain sympathetic and appear focused on her. I programmed my number in her phone and texted myself. I let my fingers linger over her hand when I passed it back.

"It's a combination of things. The way that Pavel spends and...other things. He gets crazy. Like, no impulse control. He got his last girlfriend a custom-made, diamond-encrusted mint case," Margrette recalled.

I snorted. "A mint case?" I repeated. Margrette nodded. "I'm guessing the girl had a fondness for Altoids?" I joked.

"Yeah, she had a fondness for her little pills, all right, and she got Pavel hooked on the same nasty habit. Papa had to send him to his second rehab over spring break, some coveted holistic program with temple monks." Margrette's words slurred a bit as she shared the tale.

"Wow, that's wild and sort of brilliant," I offered. "Not the part about the drugs, obviously, but the custom diamond mint case...I wonder where he got that. I need to get Addie a birthday gift soon, but what do you get a frickin' Saudi princess who has pretty much everything under the big blue sky at her fingertips? I need it to be super over the top! Something exotic, maybe a pet? Do you know where I could find something like that?" I asked it just as it had been written in my file, word for word. Now, all I had to do was wait.

"Yeah, actually. My older cousin, Lorraine, dated a guy who has access to the craziest shit on the planet. He's probably got a few ideas. I follow him. Let me message him for you. I'll let you know what he says." Margrette got to work on her phone. I did it. Phase two was complete. Adel had installed the bug, I had gotten the in on Margrette, and I had her card information. Now, for the banking information.

"Perfect, thank you so much. Oh...and speaking of spring break..."—I steered the conversation over gently—"I was deliberating whether I should hit up Saint Barth's again this year or go somewhere else. I'm not sure, I love Nikki Beach, Le Ti, all of

it, but honestly, I might be over it...what's your favorite go-to?"
I asked Margrette, lining up my shot with as much verbal preci-
sion as I could muster under the blur of the cocktails.

"Hold on." She reached out to pull a strand of hair off my
lash line. "There..." Her gaze dropped lower and lingered on my
lips for a few moments before she turned her chin up and
looked at the ceiling. "Ummm...well, we don't ever have much
of an option. It's always wherever Papa decides. Like, you think
I'd have chosen Artybash? We're usually in the Alps—most of
our friends are there during the season. But Papa says he has his
reasons for staying in the country. It's all about how it looks,
now. We're being watched, I guess. Papa's become a bit paranoid, too, like yours. But anyways, spring break? I'm usually a
sand crab at Cemetery Beach for a week or two while Papa
drives into George Town all break. You know how it is," she
chuckled and hiccupped.

"Yeah. Trust me, I get it," I bluffed. I had no idea what she
was talking about, but I guessed she wasn't referring to the
Georgetown of Washington, DC. Margrette's gaze roamed over
my blouse, to my neck, and up to my eyes.

"Well, if you're ever on the island...you and Adel, are you
together?" Margrette asked, eyeing Pavel's hand that looked to
be growing far too familiar with Addie's lower back.

"No, we're old friends. Our fathers had mutual business at
some point and that's how we met. Hit it off pretty much
instantly," I said, allowing images of Addie and me to float to the
forefront of my mind. Images that I'd previously crafted and
implanted in my memory.

"You're lucky. Like-minded friends who stick around and
don't annoy you...rare to come by, especially in our circle,"
Margrette remarked.

"I never said she didn't annoy me," I joked. Margrette
smirked at that.

"I hope we keep in touch...foster this fledgling little acquaintanceship of ours?" Margrette moved her hand from her lap onto the seat of the velvet couch between us, the edge of her fingers pressing against mine. A kite fluttered wildly in my belly.

I looked down at our hands and up at her. Her eyes were glazed and serene. I mirrored her mellow smile. "All right," I agreed.

The more Pavel drank, the sloppier he got with his hands. Halfway through the second bottle of Ace of Spades, I pulled Addie away toward the restroom to relieve her from his advances. Because Margrette joined us, Addie and I were not able to talk freely.

"I'm exhausted," I called out to Addie from my stall. "You about ready to head back to our suite?"

"Let's just hang a little bit longer?" Addie asked, surprising me with her response.

"You sure?" I confirmed. "Aren't you beat from everything that happened today?"

"Yeah, I'm a bit tired, but Pavel was in the middle of telling me a really funny story and I wanted to hear the rest before we called it a night," Addie explained. That was code for something. What, I wasn't sure. "You okay with staying a little longer?"

"Sure," I said.

An hour later, Pavel steadied himself by holding onto Addie's shoulders as the four of us made our way down the hall of our hotel. Our suite was on the same floor as theirs, only a bit farther down the hall. His hands roamed closer to Addie's neck and she shrugged her shoulders, giggling, "You're tickling me."

The twins' suite was before ours. Margrette stopped to fish through her purple clutch for her key. "Ahhh, yes!" she exclaimed, waving it around wildly and wobbling over to the side. "All right, Pavel...say good night."

"Good night, Margrette!" Pavel sang to his sister and completely wrapped himself around Addie before rotating her and bear-walking her farther down the corridor. Addie squealed in surprise but didn't fight him off. "Which one is your suite, Princess?" he asked her playfully. I watched him warily, not wanting him anywhere near our suite.

"Come on, Pavel! You'd better have your key on you! I mean it! I don't want you wandering around all night doing whatever it is you do and then waking the entire floor by banging on this door at five in the morning like a lunatic," Margrette called after him. "Can you tell he's done that before?" she asked me.

Pavel ignored her. He and Addie were almost to the door of our suite. I looked at Margrette with worry in my eyes. She stumbled toward her own door.

"All right, I'm doooooone. I'm not feeling so peachy. Good night, Maria." Margrette slurred my name and wobbled into the living room of their massive suite before whipping her head back around. "See you at breakfast?" she asked, her eyelids drooping. I nodded, unable to fully focus on her with Pavel and Addie getting so close to the door of our suite. Margrette saluted me and shut her door with a bang.

I ran to catch up with Addie and Pavel just as he pulled the key card from her purse and let himself into our suite.

"Pavel! Your sister was asking for you. She's not feeling well," I called after him.

"Huh? Margrette?" He spun around, releasing Addie but then swinging a heavy arm around her shoulders. She slouched under his weight and rounded her eyes at me. I nodded to her in assurance.

As I stepped inside after them, the door swung shut with a heavy thunk behind me. The suite was engulfed in darkness apart from the yellow light of a lamp on a side table by the entrance. I was grateful that Pavel was unlikely to spot anything he shouldn't in this darkness.

"Yeah, your sister...Margrette. She said she needs you back

in your suite...immediately," I said more insistently. "You should go."

"Pftttt...yeah, screw that. I'm spending the rest of my night with this beautiful creature and I cannot be bothered to focus on anything else. I absolutely refuse," he purred, holding Addie's chin between his fingers.

"That hurts, Pavel. Your nails are sharp. Please, stop," Addie warned, stepping back from him. "Maybe you should go check on your sister. If she doesn't feel well—"

"Shhh...you're so much prettier when you don't talk—" he cooed and covered her mouth with his palm, chuckling. Addie pushed him off of her. Pavel shoved her back, hard. Addie lost her balance and tripped on the rug, landing in a crouch.

"Don't you dare touch her, Pavel. You need to leave!" I cried. But Pavel lunged for Addie, an ugly scowl marring his face. I was faster. My knife was already in my palm by the time I entered the suite. Before he could reach Addie, I threw him into the table with a kick to his side. Before he could push himself up, my blade was at his throat. "Stop! Or I'll gut you like a fish." The threat sobered him. "Go on, try me," I bit out. I faked punching something into my phone without more than a few glances away from Pavel. "And now, my security team's on the way over here. I suggest you get the hell out of our suite before they arrive," I warned.

"Do you have any idea who the hell you're talking to?" he spat.

I took a step back but kept the blade fisted in my grip, pointed at him, ready to rip into him if he tried anything aggressive. "Yeah, I'm talking to a dead man if you don't get that rage of yours under control. Think about it, Pavel, it isn't unreasonable. You were hurting her and now, we want you gone. Sober up and you can apologize tomorrow," I said. Pavel snorted at that.

"Don't test me—" I warned. I must have a great poker face or maybe he could sense me losing control over my composure, because it worked. He was halfway to the door when he turned back and glared at me, clearly unsatisfied that he'd failed to convince us of his untouchable status. It was at that moment that I recalled the nasty trick I learned after getting attacked in an alley by that degenerate Kiril. I grabbed the blade of my knife, bent my elbow back as though preparing to throw it, and just as I bluffed the throw, Addie cried out, "Maria! Don't!" Pavel turned in a panic and dove out the door, scurrying away like a street mouse running from an alley cat.

"You shouldn't have done that. I could've handled him," Addie muttered, more fear in her eyes now than when Pavel was about to attack her.

"What was I supposed to do? He was gonna hit you—"

I watched him disappear around the corner at the end of the hall and had just bolted the door shut when a muffled voice came from my purse—my com! I retrieved it from my purse where it was tucked away in a hidden compartment, and I brought it to my ear.

Artyom's voice came in through the com, coated in an almost unrecognizable panic. "Maria, answer me! Maria? Do you and Adel need assistance? I can be there in—"

"Artyom! Artyom, we're fine. I-I handled it. He's gone. Pavel...he just left."

There was a telling silence.

"Lark...what did you do?"

Addie and I were packed and on the jet back to Lavidian within the hour. We barely had time to take our cuffs off their chargers and clasp them onto our forearms before Artyom and the other guard, Fox, swept the suite and hustled us out. My heart stopped beating as we passed the twins' suite, but no one jumped out at us as they had in my imagination, and no one ran after us.

I wondered where Pavel went when he disappeared around

the corner of the hall. Did he circle back and return to his suite or was he in hiding in a supply closet somewhere? Or, maybe passed out outside in the snow? *A girl can always hope.* But I was certain that Lavidian was keeping tabs on him to ensure his safety. It would raise suspicion if something unfortunate had happened to him while we were around.

Addie, or I supposed she was Starling again now that the mission was over, tilted her head to rest it against my shoulder sometime after takeoff. I stiffened, surprised by the vulnerable gesture given how angry she'd seemed with me for what I did to protect her.

When she placed her hand in my open palm, my body went completely still. I turned my head slightly to clock Artyom and the other guard's positions. They sat out of our view. To see them, I'd have to turn my head around fully. I faced forward and closed my fingers around hers.

"Starling," I whispered.

"Yes..." her voice was hollow.

"What was the joke you needed to hear from Pavel? I asked you to leave with me and you said you wanted to hear the rest of his joke," I remembered.

"You noticed how many times he went to the men's room during the first half of dinner? He's an addict. Drugs mostly, but gambling, too. He gambled in the privileged circles outside of university and on campus. There were these secret clubs he was part of. He was telling me about it, babbling on and on.

"I couldn't tell you because of Margrette but I needed to go back and get more information out of him. The gambling—he owed his friend over a million and some guys on campus a couple hundred thousand. His father wouldn't cover it, not after his second failed attempt at rehab. I was trying to get names—that's why I let him in our suite..." Starling expressed, her voice trailing off as she returned to her thoughts. I shook my head, thinking of

Pavel, the incomprehensible amount of egotism it took to waste the privilege of his resources, to not even attempt to do something of consequence for the world when given every opportunity.

"Not a great joke," I commented flatly.

"Yeah, it was more a confession than a joke. I told him I was addicted to adrenaline and how close I'd come to death, breaking into the roof of a skyscraper once. Naturally, he had to share his woes—the narcissist he was. Complained he had no one to talk to..."

"Brilliant," I told Starling. "I tried a similar technique with Margrette—"

"Quiet! Or I'll separate you," Fox barked, a warning in his tone.

Starling and I stilled. Silence passed between us for several minutes before either of us moved a muscle.

"Thank you," Starling breathed. It was barely audible.

My heart fluttered in my chest at her unusual softness. She knew I'd be punished for my actions with Pavel. Mikhailov would threaten me with my mother. But I had to do it. In all the universes, there existed no version of my soul that wouldn't have tried to protect her regardless of the pain that she had inflicted on me.

I tilted my head deeper and rested against hers, still on my shoulder. I pressed my eyes shut. I felt Starling squeeze my hand tightly. I hadn't expected any of this from her, and my body didn't know what to do with it. She seemed suddenly to be letting her walls down. Why? Why now? It was throwing me off-kilter. I reciprocated the pressure in her hand as tears pooled and slipped down my face.

As I looked at her hand, I noticed a mark that appeared to be like a brand—a distorted circle with a long vertical line and a shorter horizontal line crossing the middle. I remembered seeing that mark on her when I was down in the cells.

Curiosity got the better of me and I whispered, "What does this mean?"

She whispered back, "It's another set of chains, same as this," while yanking her sleeve up higher to reveal the tracker incision. "It just means no matter what I do or where I go, I'll never be free."

Overcome with a heavy sense of hopelessness and exhaustion, I eventually drifted off into sleep. Oliver appeared in my mind's eye, sitting in the middle of a dim room. The darkness seemed to engulf him. He was very still.

The aching heart, once thought incoherent, when inspired, beats a steady rhythm, he spoke.

Oliver wouldn't say anything like that.

"Oliver?" I uttered, my voice a hollow echo.

The weariness of this road has ground me to nothing. I'm tired. I'm tired of crawling over jagged rock, the voice said once more, but the figure remained still. It wasn't Oliver in the chair anymore. The face had shifted beneath the shadows, features morphing. I was in the center of the dim room, holding a burning candle and looking into a mirror; it was me in the reflection. But it wasn't actually me. It was Lark.

I'll carry us now, Lark vowed in the same hollow echo. Then, the candle went out, plunging everything into darkness.

CHAPTER 31

OLIVER

The hangover hit me the second I awoke. Even with my eyes closed, I could tell something was wrong—I was somewhere I shouldn't have been. My window at home let only the reflection of warm morning light through one side of the room.

I parted my eyelids slightly to take in my surroundings and registered two bodies on a bed across the room. My pulse quickened. I squinted against the aggressive onslaught of morning, winter light in a room where an entire wall appeared to be made of nothing but floor-to-ceiling glass.

It felt like I was in a fishbowl and pesky kids were tapping on the glass. My skull was splitting open and there was a dry spell going on in my mouth to rival the one I endured during my time in Juvie isolation. Water. I needed water.

I rotated onto my side, worried I'd puke. The room went spinning. I refocused on the bodies in the bed. They were nude, whoever they were. I couldn't tell who it was from my position on the couch.

My heart raced and a new worry entered my thoughts. I jumped up despite my protesting headache, and took a closer look at who was in the room with me. Anton was buck naked, lying on his stomach over the sheets. Kiran was beside him but her head was by his feet, a thin sheet barely covering a fourth of her naked body.

My heart hammered more wildly against my chest. I didn't... I wasn't...was I? I looked down at myself. To my relief, I was still fully clothed, but my clothing was wet. Why was I wet? My dress shirt was disheveled, and the top buttons were missing. *What the hell happened last night?*

From the corner of my vision, an animal swept past and I jumped. It was the size of a cat or a small dog but thicker somehow, loping powerfully around the room. Am I losing my mind? I blinked several times, but I was still seeing it. A baby tiger, padding around just inches from me. I froze, trying to stay calm and not make any sudden movements. My eyes fell upon the three empty baby bottles on the coffee table just to the right of the couch. The baby tiger was nearing the chaise at the foot of Anton's bed.

I moved toward the glass doors, hoping to slide them open and get the hell out of this room before the animal paid me any attention, but I heard a groan coming from the bed. and turned to see Anton pushing himself up onto his elbows.

I moved to slide the glass doors open, but he called out and I froze.

"Oy, *wheryuofta*," he vocalized in a voice as rough as gravel.

"Huh?" I asked, turning back to face him but keeping my eye-line strictly above his shoulders.

"There's my beaut, there he is! Look atcha, ya stud." His shoulders shook as he chuckled and quickly fell into a coughing fit. I thought he was talking to me for a second before I realized he was talking to the tiger cub. My memories from last night were shrouded in darkness and that realization was paralyzing. I couldn't remember anything.

To my relief, Anton seemed to be in a strangely good mood. Behind his raspy voice was an almost sing-song intonation. I'd even go so far as saying he sounded happy. I kept my eyes on the tiger. It had somehow managed to climb onto the lounge chair at the foot of the bed and was resting by Anton's feet, licking itself leisurely.

"The...uhh, the tiger—"

"Yeah, he took a liking to you yesterday, didn't he? Thought you were his mama," Anton recalled, nodding at the bottles. I didn't respond for fear of giving away how little I remembered from last night. I hoped he wasn't implying that I bottle-fed the tiger.

A realization hit me like a brick. I patted my damp pockets for it. Empty. I patted my back pockets. Nothing. I crossed back to the couch and scanned the cushions for it, moving the pillows away and checking inside the folds.

"You seen my phone by any chance?" I tried keeping my voice casual while continuing my search, fingers frantic.

Anton released another groan and glanced over his shoulder at Kiran. "Don't you remember? It's in a bowl of rice in the kitchen. You were trying to dry it out," Anton said as he tapped Kiran's backside with his open palm. Her bottom shook from the impact.

"Mhmmm," she moaned in protest. The sound was erotic, accidentally or not. I averted my eyes to the wall behind them where a mauve oil painting hung, but my eyes kept darting down to her so I turned away from the two of them, forcing myself to look at the pool through the glass.

I walked closer to the glass to get a better vantage point of the house. We were somewhere in the hills. The view was over-whelming. In fact, I'd never seen anything like it. The day was clear, and I could see a sliver of the ocean past the city's flat expanse.

Refocusing on the patio just beyond the glass, I took the scene in. It was a hot mess of broken bottles, plastic cups, wrappers, wet towels, clothes scattered about, broken furniture, and something appeared to be in the pool itself. Was that a chair sitting neatly at the bottom of the pool?

I moved to slide the door open.

"Oy, where you off to?" Anton called after me.

"Gonna go get my phone and look for some water," I answered lightly, stifling the outrage I felt at myself for not remembering a damned thing from the night before.

"There's water inside the bar armoire over there," he said, pointing at the dark oak cabinet across the room. "Pour me a glass, too, will you?"

"Yeah...sure," I agreed, reluctantly moving away from the door and crossing the room.

Anton flipped onto his back, making the bed groan beneath him, and exposed his junk to the ceiling. I quickened my steps across the room, resolved to look forward and nowhere else. I strained to remember something from last night, anything.

Had we danced? I vaguely remembered dancing. I remembered watching them dance together. Anton and Kiran. He was touching her. They were looking at...me? I rubbed my aching temple before opening the armoire doors and reaching for a lowball glass.

"So, just out of curiosity, where are we?" I asked him.

He chuckled. This amused him. "La-la-land." I forced a laugh and twisted open the cap of a large glass bottle of water, engraved with a symbol of the sun at the top.

"Are we in Hollywood Hills or Beachwood? I'm not that familiar with LA, yet..." I explained.

"Mount Olympus," he said and I hoped he found his briefs by the time I finished pouring this glass of water.

I vaguely remembered a warning Kiran gave me last night: *Uphold the illusion that you have all the answers.* The memory came back to me in a rush—it was one of the last things I remembered clearly. I'd already blown it by asking where we were. She was probably right. Questions burned my tongue but I swallowed them away.

"Last night was..." I commented, trailing off to allow Anton a chance to finish the sentiment.

"Yes." He nodded, knowingly. "Can't say 'best sex of my life' but top ten, for sure," he went on. My eyes widened and my heart stalled. I tried not to lose my grip on the glass of water as I brought it over to him, my eyes seeking answers in his.

"Was it?" I asked slowly, fighting to remain subdued.

"I've never been watched before," Anton admitted. "When she told you to stay, to sit there. I mean, you heard me...I told her, 'No way in hell.' But she promised it'd be worth it and..." He breathed out through puckered lips, rubbing his beard at the memory. "Clearly, she gets a special kick out of performing for you because last night was...*ahhh,*"—Anton squeezed Kiran's hip, making her release another breathy moan—"she just wouldn't stop. I don't understand how you just sat there and kept it in your pants, but I appreciated that. Would've been tooooooo weird for me otherwise. Anyway, I owe you, my friend. Twice, now," he added lightly, and a tension in my chest uncoiled at his recollection. I didn't realize how uncomfortable I'd felt about what may have happened between us until I learned that it didn't. *As long as it wasn't a menage a trois, I can deal with it,* I told myself.

"Twice?" I asked, returning to the bar cart to pour myself a glass of water. I was itching to get out of the room but this was my way in, my chance to figure out exactly what had happened last night. I hoped I hadn't asked him anything about Mina, because if he gave me answers last night, I'd already forgotten them.

"Yes, twice. The pool…"

"Right—the pool," I agreed slowly. Too slowly.

"When you saved my ass after I hit my head in the pool…"—I blinked at his words, expression blank—"…after Alexei and I fell in when I tackled him…?" Anton detailed, at this point clearly doubting my recollection of last night's events.

"Oh…that…" I lied. "I didn't see what happened that well. I just wanted to help. It was no big deal." I shrugged and downed three consecutive glasses of water.

"No big deal? I cracked my head so hard that I blacked out. They said you jumped in before anyone even realized anything had happened—before my guards even noticed, the ones I pay good money to keep me alive. 'No big deal,'" he scoffed. I grinned at the story, both surprised and in disbelief that I had been able to save anyone while being blackout drunk.

I squinted from the throb in my skull. There was a flash, I couldn't be sure if it was a real memory, but I thought we had ridden back to this place together.

His brother had been there in the car with us, Alexei. *Yeah, I remember him now.* He had watched us carefully, especially me, with a look of distrust. I remember getting the distinct feeling he didn't want us there. But for now, I figured it didn't matter. All that mattered was what Anton thought. Anton did whatever the hell he wanted, that much I knew.

"Wait, what time is it?" I asked.

"I dunno, probably around noon," he guessed.

"Wow, it's late…half the day's over," I noted and moved to leave the room. The tiger pounced onto the floor and began pacing around restlessly. "How old is it?" I asked.

"Bradley Cooper? He's three weeks old. But anyone asks and you never saw this little guy, got it?" he cautioned, his tone devoid of humor. I looked back out the glass doors, hoping that an irate mother tiger was not about to spring into view.

I nodded. "Got it. Bradley Cooper looks like a well-fed house cat to me. Is he hungry?"

"Probably. He gets fed every four hours. *Ey! Ktoto karmil* Bradley Cooper?" Anton yelled to no one in particular. The bedroom door was ajar. I stiffened as a man came to the door and answered something in their language.

"Horosho," Anton said and the man disappeared. "Bradley Cooper has grown rather attached to me. I'd keep him myself but I travel too much and I only own a few penthouses, no acreage. This little guy's gonna need some serious space soon. I have a buyer coming today, actually. Hopefully, she doesn't flake. Alexei's gonna finally get off my case. He's had a stick up his ass since the moment this little guy got here. Then again, that stick might be permanent," Anton chuckled.

"I mean, I kind of get him, though. It might just be a baby, but it's still a wild animal."

"Bradley's harmless; look at him."

"So, if I go out this door, I won't get eaten alive by Bradley Cooper's mother, will I?" I asked, only partially joking.

"Where you trying to go?" Anton asked.

"Wanna grab a ride home, shower—change—shove my head in the freezer."

"My boy!" Anton cried out, crossing the room to embrace me while his junk swung left and right. I held my arm out to keep a distance between our bodies. He patted my back and moved me toward an open door that led to a walk-in closet the size of my bedroom. "Whatever you want today, it's yours, my friend. Choose something that fits. My gift." He clapped my back, once, twice. I held my breath. A third time.

He disappeared into the bathroom. I surveyed the closet. It was mostly empty—it didn't seem like anyone actually lived here. There was a large suitcase in the corner and only a few suits were hung up. I eyed a pair of sweats folded on the shelf and a black V-neck hanging next to the suits. Those should

376 • EMILIA ARES

work. I picked up the sweats and pulled the black V-neck off the brass hanger. I didn't have to check the tag to know every item of clothing in this room was more expensive than my entire outfit, including these sweatpants of his. I checked the tag, yep, designer. Thankfully, when Anton returned, he had a towel wrapped around his hips. Another towel was slung over his shoulder. He tossed it to me.

"Last night, you promised me we'd spar today," he goaded.

"Oh yeah?" I pretended not to recall one of the few things I remembered vividly.

"Yeah. I wanted to last night, but you were whining about my head injury. So honorable. What a guy. Anyways, the gym's downstairs. Let's go a couple of rounds?"

"I'm not exactly in fighting shape right now, Anton." I sniffed myself and wrinkled my nose. But I didn't take too strong of an opposing stance, because this was an opportunity to get closer to him—to get answers.

"Okay, okay. You're in charge. We hit the *banya* and you can have a shower after. Come." He patted me on the shoulder roughly.

"'*Banya*?'" I asked as I followed him back into the bedroom, where Kiran remained fast asleep and the baby tiger was clawing at the pouf by the sofa.

"*Banya* is like a sauna. You said you felt like shit. So, we sweat, get it out of the system. You'll feel better. You'll thank me!" he promised, opening the bedroom door. I followed Anton through the hallway past the open-concept kitchen and living room. I spotted a bowl of rice and hurried over to check it. There was only rice in it. I looked around the kitchen, spotting my phone plugged into a charger by the coffee machine. My heart pounded hard against my chest. *So, maybe it still works after whatever bath it took last night?*

I glanced around the room. Four members of Anton's security team were sitting around the kitchen table by the window, sipping coffee and talking over breakfast. The men grew quiet as Anton passed. One of them nodded at Anton while another greeted him. Anton didn't stop or say anything in return, but just nodded fractionally and that was as good a greeting as he was going to give, I guessed.

I crossed to my phone, hoping there was nothing on the home screen. I touched the screen and it brightened. There were two unread texts from Nyah and seven from Xavi. Blood rushed into my ears as the preview of the last text flashed over the home screen.

XAVI

send ur address should i come or call cops???

"Who plugged my phone in?" I asked, projecting my voice. The men at the breakfast table grew quiet again and turned toward me. I tried to read their expressions. Had they seen Xavi's message? Did they read it? Did they know what it meant?

None of them gave an answer. None of them gave away a thought through their expressions. They just stared blankly. I chose to break the tension myself.

"Thanks for charging it."

The man with the goatee gave a short nod. "You're welcome," he rasped as the rest returned their attention to their meals.

I unlocked my phone to read the full messages from Xavi.

yo all good?

did u find out anything about Mina?

lmk

Oli?

im worried all good?

where r u

I quickly shot him a response.

sri for not getting back earlier, all good hit u up later

"Oy, we'll be downstairs," Anton announced to the men. Then he added something in Russian. All I could catch was Kiran's name.

It was then that I remembered Kiran's security team. "Where's Kiran's guy? Jason?" I asked Anton. He shrugged and smirked before saying something else to his men in Russian.

The same guy nodded in response. He was tall. They all were. He wore a sharp suit. They all did. His hair was neatly combed and gray. The rest of them had buzzcuts. His body language foretold years of training and great potential to dole out pain.

Why does Anton need such an extensive security team? Or are they for Alexei? I nodded at nothing and tucked my phone away, all the while considering any alternative explanations for the size of the Zaharov security detail. Besides the tiger cub, I had yet to spot any merchandise or rare goods around the house.

I followed Anton down to the level below and into one of the most excessive home gyms I'd ever seen. It was stocked with everything a person could possibly need for a workout. There was a training system with pulleys, a boxing bag, pull-up bars, a bench press, even a variety of cardio equipment.

I nodded meaningfully at the soft black gym mat. "Let's go?" I offered, deciding that a sparring match was too good a bonding opportunity to pass up, after all. Anton's face lit up at that. "That is, if you don't mind wrestling me in my damp clothes?" I went on, quirking my brow and wondering what he'd say to that.

"Wouldn't want to soil these," I explained, gesturing at the rolled-up designer sweats and t-shirt in my hand that I was borrowing from him.

"I don't mind. If you don't mind me in my briefs," he joked, thrusting his hips forward. Was he joking? He waggled his eyebrows suggestively. "We have time until Kiran gets her ass down here." I gave him a look of uncertainty. This is getting weird.

"Kiran's...joining us?" God, I hope he wasn't expecting me to watch round two of their boinkfest. Sober, I'd absolutely have to draw the line.

"For the *banya*," he explained.

I still didn't understand.

"Don't worry. You'll like it." But I *was* worried. How far was he going to take this little game of theirs before I had to bail? It was time to get some answers or get the hell out of here.

"All right, let's go," I said curtly, despite meaning to sound enthusiastic about it. I took a sharp breath of air to curtail my nausea. My stomach rolled and I stepped closer to the wall.

"Okay!" he agreed, fully enthused.

I needed to sit but settled for leaning against the wall to stop the world from spinning. I dropped the towel and fresh clothes in the corner on the floor and rubbed my forehead.

"You drink like that all the time?" I asked him as he pulled his towel off and flung it over the press bench.

"Like what? Yesterday? No," he snorted, shaking his head. "I didn't drink much, yesterday. I have a fight coming up. I'm in training," he reasoned.

That wasn't much? I couldn't wrap my head around how he had built such a high tolerance for liquor. Practice, I supposed. He looked fresh as a peach, now that he'd had some time to gain his bearings. He shimmied into his gym shorts jovially.

"That was you taking it easy? We downed most of the bottle between the two of us," I questioned in disbelief, releasing a groan as the room continued to spin, not even bothering to hide my misery.

"Ha! No worries, my man. The *banya* will perform magic on you. You'll feel fresh as a newborn when we're through. Now, come on! I'm eager to see your best moves." He waved me forward, motioning toward the mat.

I let out a heavy breath and ambled over.

I evaluated him, trying to guess how difficult it would be to maneuver him into submission. I didn't know how much jiu-jitsu experience he had under his belt. He was buff, but that didn't matter, not really. His chest was broad, and his overall structure was solid, like a boulder that had suddenly sprouted arms and legs. In essence, he appeared immovable.

He was a few inches shorter than me but far bulkier. That could be used against him. I had been focusing on my plasticity and fluidity of movement in training lately. I was lean and had a natural disposition toward flexibility. It was very useful in maneuvering and manipulating my body in a spar. But did I want to win? That was the real question. Would winning serve my goal or hinder me from getting answers? I'd have to play and see.

"BJJ?" I checked. Anton nodded, his eyes glistening in anticipation. "I usually train in a gi but Master Rig has us grapple no-gi a few times a month. Don't you want to put on a shirt as a rash guard?"

Anton shrugged. "We'll only go a few rounds. Once I feel it burn, I'll tap."

"You just want an excuse to tap out, I gotchya," I teased.

Anton smirked and took position. I mirrored him. We circled, feeling each other out for an attack, a takedown opportunity. I went for a single leg snatch attempt right off the bat to feel him out. He blocked and maintained balance well. His arms over my shoulders had a leaden weight to them but somehow, he managed to move with speed as well. Anton stepped back and attempted his first takedown but because my down block was in place, he couldn't successfully complete the move.

My balance was off, so it took a lot more of my energy than a failed takedown should have, and when I attempted an Uchi-mata, I failed to get his head down, which led to him using the momentum for a takedown. I recovered with a half guard.

"Who is Kiran to you?" Anton asked, before attempting a guard pass and playing with taking his foot to my left hip. I pulled guard and placed my foot on his shoulder. His voice was steady while I strained to answer, but I figured now was a good time to catch him off-guard and feel him out about Kiril and those guys again.

"She's a friend."—I grunted to shift and lift my torso so I could trap his neck under my armpit. It was now or never. "Listen, Anton, you probably know people in...I don't even know what to call it, the Russian underground...circuit?" Anton tucked his chin and slipped through my grip, his neck raw and red. He went for the full mount but without the needed upper body control, he couldn't maintain it. I turned in, started building a base, and began working for a takedown, using my head placement to switch into a full guard pass. I started working for side control.

"How good a friend?" Anton asked through gritted teeth, finally forced to struggle.

"Huh?"

"Kiran. How good a friend?" he repeated, his voice matching the intensity of his attempted underhook.

I blocked and maintained my position. What the hell was I supposed to say? "We have fun," I managed. Was he just going to ignore my question? I wasn't going to let him get off that easy. This was a risk, but I was out of time. "There's this freakish, tall, sort of massive guy. His name is Kiril, I think..." I persisted, feeling him out. He kept fighting to put me back in half guard.

"How long have you two been having fun?" he asked,

ignoring my question yet again and putting more pressure on my shoulder to try once more for the under-hook.

"Not long," I gritted. "This Kiril guy, he's got like, a bowl haircut, Julius Caesar type...big-ass forehead, I think he runs with a powerful group from Russia like I said...They have someone, they took a friend of mine, and I was hoping maybe you'd heard about this group. Maybe you had an idea where they could've taken her—"

Anton released pressure and went limp under me, first suspicion, then anger in his eyes. I could take advantage but I eased my control as well.

"You're asking very specific questions. Questions like that get people hurt. Maybe hurt worse than whoever they took, Oliver." He returned the pressure and rolled under me to flip and complete a takedown of his own. After successfully securing a side control, he began putting pressure on my neck with an under-hook, forming a tight triangle. I tried to tuck my chin but his squeeze was too taut. I tapped out. But Anton didn't release. I tapped again. I tapped the mat, hard and loud. "I don't mess with people like that, Oliver, understand? I deal with the elite of society, the upper class. I make a point not to put my nose into business that isn't mine. Do not ask me about those kinds of people again, Oliver." Anton released me three whole seconds after the last tap. I caught my breath, neck burning from the friction.

"Bravo," Kiran's voice carried from across the room. She had donned a bikini under a sheer cover-up, her curved figure leaning languidly against the doorway. She ran her fingers through Bradley Cooper's fur as the cat moved around unsettled in her arms. As soon as I saw the cub, I got to my feet while Kiran continued her thought, "I can't imagine the urge to roll around on the ground, twisting one's organs into origami, first thing in the morning—"

"You shouldn't have brought the cub down here while we

were sparring; you're going to scare him," I said to Kiran, noticing the tension, the unrest in Bradley Cooper's frantic gaze.

"What are you so afraid of? Look at him," Anton insisted in a gravelly voice, getting to his feet as well.

"He's a wild animal. He has instincts," I stood by my words.

"Anyway..."—Kiran rolled her eyes and placed Bradley Cooper down on the mat. She focused on Anton instead—"Your man upstairs so rudely disturbed my beauty sleep and said you needed me? Said you and Oliver were in dire need of my help in the *banya*? I have to admit I was exceedingly curious about the precise assistance you required." Her smirk widened into a lascivious grin. "But as I came down the stairs, I recalled your particular fascination with *banya* broom whacking, back in New York and how you used to throw those honest-to-God pagan-ritual-looking parties in every posh Russian bathhouse. I was gonna turn right around, but then I figured, you know what? Those were actually fun. Why not? I'm always in the mood for a good arm workout."

"Broom whacking?" I asked, growing wary and somewhat concerned over her enthusiasm. "Anton, can I ask...why tigers? I mean—is the trouble worth the profit?" The question had been bugging me a bit. I looked back at the cub, which was now playing with a foam ball as the three of us made our way through the far-off door toward the large, black-tiled, sleek gym bathroom equipped with a spacious walk-in sauna. *This place is outrageous.* "Is he gonna be okay on his own in there?"

"They're preparing his bottles upstairs," Kiran said.

"Truth is, I love those little guys. The people I sell them to usually have acres for roaming. I don't like them ending up in zoos. Plus, it's done wonders for my reputation. When clients find out I have access to cubs, they think of me...differently. It removes any limits from their requests. They get creative...

freaky, even, and that's when the real fun begins." Anton's eyes lit up, his love for the hustle shining like I'd never seen before.

"Clients? I thought you said they were 'friends,'" I reminded him. Anton's smile broadened. It wasn't a slip. He was showing trust.

Half an hour later, broom whacking had become my new favorite rehabilitative ritual. According to Anton, the *banya* is an East Slavic tradition that dates back to the early 12th century, and broom whacking elevated the experience to a whole new level. Lashing your body with birch branches or eucalyptus in the steam bath is supposed to clear the respiratory system, unblock sinuses, and remove toxins, waste, and dead skin cells from the body.

Kiran had beat us up with a bunch of leaves pretty aggressively while we lay there, whimpering. Well, *I* was whimpering and I may have shoved the bundle of leaves away a few times, purely on instinct. Anton rode through the sensation like it was his favorite feeling on earth, without complaint and with booming laughter.

Had it worked magic on my hangover? I had to admit, I did feel noticeably better when I went outside for some air, leaving Anton with Kiran after she began to spank herself with the bundle of birch leaves.

He and I offered to double-team broom whacking her, but she made another double-teaming suggestion, to which Anton raised a brow and I walked away from. After I gulped down two more small bottles of water, I felt almost like I hadn't blacked out last night at all.

"Listen, forget about it. I can tell you're getting upset again," I was telling Anton. "I just thought—"

"How can I 'forget about it?'" Anton interjected. "This is the third time you ask me about this bullshit."

"I need to know. It's for my friend. Okay? It isn't about me. I'm asking you as a favor. I'm not accusing you of anything. I don't get why you're getting so pissed off. I'd owe you a favor in return,"—I crafted the narrative on the spot, separating my desperation for an answer from my need to ask the question— "It's what I do. I help friends when they need something. I connect people to information. I do favors, build networks…not dissimilar to what you do, right?" *Come on, Anton. Just open up. Trust me.*

Anton raised a brow in disbelief at my persistence. "You don't stop, do you? Why would I know where some Russian pricks would take an abducted girl? Because I speak Russian? Do you know how many people speak Russian in the world, Oliver? Do you know how ignorant you sound? Jesus, give it a rest for a bit. Can we cool off? Have a drink? Break our bloody fast? Take a dip in the pool before plunging into favors and business talk? How 'bout we wait until my overbearing brother's around to micromanage me before bringing this up again? It's his wet dream. Hmm? I'd love to hear *his* thoughts on the matter. Who knows? Maybe he'll have some insight. He lived in Russia longer than I did, after all. So, by your logic, he must know every criminal in the entire country by name," Anton exclaimed sarcastically, exasperated with me.

"Let's do it." I smiled wide at Anton and tossed him a water bottle from the mini-fridge. He caught it, easily. "Let's party. Then, we'll talk." He rolled his eyes but mirrored my grin.

As we moved toward the double-basin sink to wash the sweat from our faces, I realized I had been reading the situation all wrong. Anton was not in charge the way I'd thought he was. Anton was the older brother but clearly, not by much. I should have realized sooner that his brother, Alexei was the one who called the shots, the one who controlled everything. I should have seen it from the start. I was wasting time buttering up the wrong brother and pissing off the one who might have had all the answers, all along. Time was slipping between my fingers, and the panic of losing Mina forever was weighing so heavily on my chest that I felt like I couldn't catch a breath. I had to pivot, quickly—get back upstairs, find Alexei, and salvage things with him. Find common ground.

Anton was scrolling through his phone. "I'll invite some friends over. We'll make an afternoon of it." He glanced back at the sauna, where Kiran remained inside, and he smirked before returning to his phone. This was good—the more people that came through, the more normal it would seem that I was still around. Alexei wouldn't be suspicious. He'd have likely been annoyed seeing me around again this afternoon, maybe even pissed. But, now, I'd be the least of his worries.

"With that pool and that view, I don't blame you. I'd do the same," I encouraged. Anton let out a hoot of excitement and patted my back.

"Now…tell me, what do you like? Peaches? Melons? Curly hair? Dark? Blonde? Tall? Tiny? Curvy? I've got friends in all the right places," he joked, tilting his screen toward me and scrolling through his bikini-clad feed, grinning. The screen was a blur. I couldn't focus on the images. I remembered Mina's hazel eyes, the contour of her cheek illuminated by the morning light, her smile that crinkled her nose, and the floral fragrance of her smooth, dark hair like velvet cascading over white linen. She was the only one I wanted to see. She was the one I may never see again. "What about this one, the legs on her," Anton whistled approvingly.

"I like them all," I remarked with feigned enthusiasm, my voice lacking its usual depth. It's what he wanted to hear. He squeezed my shoulders, getting to work. He typed a message out on his phone, grinning like a madman.

"I promise I haven't screwed them all," he said in a low voice. "But I'm sure you won't mind sharing. You understand, some have trouble moving on from all this." He gestured to himself and flexed his pecs in a dance. I suppressed a laugh. "But one wink from you might be enough of a distraction. All right, check this out." A snort escaped me and Anton mock frowned.

"What's funny?" Kiran had joined us, drenched in sweat, face and neck flushed.

"Just flattering our Oliver, here. But he's taking a piss at my expense," Anton explained. "Oh, and we're throwing a little soirée."

"Oh? I like the sound of that," she commented, perking up.

I offered Kiran a water bottle and opened a fresh towel for her to cover herself with. "Thank you, sweets. As angelic as they get," she purred, patting my cheek before toweling off and shrugging on her robe, not bothering to tie it closed. She walked over and playfully tugged on the towel that I had wrapped around my hips. I chuckled but stepped out of reach and secured the towel. "You've gotten quite fit, sweets. Just look at those abs! I could use your stomach as a washboard for my delicates," she teased. I shifted closer to Anton, who was smiling at his phone.

"Just a lot of sparring and conditioning, lately." I shrugged.

"Not enough sparring, if you ask me," Anton teased.

"Are you posting your address publicly?" I asked over Anton's shoulder, noticing the address he listed on the social media post he was drafting.

"This is not my place. We rent, so it doesn't really matter. Don't quote me on that to Alexei, though," he warned. "At any rate, it's only my 'close friends' list I'm posting this to."

"Your close friends list is like a thousand people," Kiran commented.

"Isn't that average? Either way, that's globally. If we're talking just LA, it shouldn't be more than two hundred, tops. And they won't all be able to make it, obviously. These people are jetsetters. It's the holidays. No one's in LA right now. It'll be a poor turnout, you'll see," he sighed. As he toweled off, his phone was already blowing up with notifications, the sound echoing through the bathroom. He glanced at his notifications and his eyes widened.

"*Pipetz!* Pasha's out of town. You know a good DJ?" he exclaimed, picking up his phone off the bathroom counter.

"Not one I'd particularly like to bring back into my life, no," answered Kiran.

"There's no party without a DJ." Anton scrolled his feed frantically.

I hesitated, then answered, "I know someone."

"Call them," Anton turned to me and said in a pleading tone. "They any good?"

"Yeah, he's great," I promised, hoping I was right. I sent Xavi a screenshot of the pinned location and messaged him.

> wanna DJ a party?

Anton's phone rang, and he answered, "*Da? Let her in!*" He hissed something in his language, slightly irritated. "Down here? Why didn't you call me?" Anton ran his fingers through his hair and adjusted himself through his towel. "*Horosho.*"

He hurried across the bathroom and grabbed the dry sweats and t-shirt that I was supposed to change into. He was halfway into his shirt when he explained, "Buyer's here. Been here a while, apparently. Now she's with Bradley Cooper in the gym."

"Fingers crossed for you, sweetness," Kiran chimed, moving to open the door once Anton pulled his sweats on. With Anton taking the change of clothes I was supposed to wear, I thought about putting my old wet clothes back on, not wanting to walk around the house shirtless, in a towel. Not when Kiran was around. Perhaps I could find a robe somewhere.

"Sorry, Oliver. I didn't bring a change of clothes down for myself. I'll need these. Can't meet the client half-naked. You can head on up and have that shower while I sort this out. Choose anything else you want from my closet. Not damn sweatpants."

"No worries. There are only suits left. I'll just put my stuff in a dryer," I told him, gesturing to the damp clump of clothes I had picked up off the floor.

"They're casual suits. What? You don't like my style?" He waved his hand in the air like I was being ridiculous.

"That's not it. You sure you want me to wear your nice clothes?"

"Oh, come on...you kidding me? You're my guest. Of course!"

"All right," I agreed. I checked that the towel around my hips was secure and moved to follow Kiran, who had opened the door that led back to the gym. She crossed the mats, oblivious that her swimsuit was dripping a wet trail along the floor behind her.

There was a woman crouching in the far-end corner of the room with her back to us. She was watching Bradley Cooper balance on his hind legs and paw at a giant yoga ball. Maybe she was a veterinarian or something.

My phone pinged. It was Xavi.

I'll be there. wat time?

soon as u can

I typed back.

"He's such a sweet cub," Kiran purred as she reached out for him.

"He's gorgeous," the woman agreed. Something about the tone felt eerily familiar.

I tilted my neck to get a better look at the woman; Kiran was blocking most of my view of her. I was curious to see what kind of person would go to someone's house to buy a baby tiger. The woman balanced her weight easily, crouched in dramatic, sharp-toed heels. Her cream coat grazed the floor, a contrast to her silky, auburn hair, which was cut in a perfect slant. A few empty milk bottles lay at her feet. She must have fed him.

Her head turned in my direction as Bradley Cooper ambled toward an eager, open-armed Kiran and my heart stalled, skidding to a crashing stop.

It was Mina.

Mina Arkova was crouched in the corner of the room, a cold, hooded indifference in her eyes that widened microscopically into a bewildered recognition as her gaze met mine. I stood, mouth agape, heart violently hammering against my chest, bare feet rooted to the floor that I couldn't feel anymore.

Mina's gaze flitted between me and Kiran, back to my torso, back to Bradley Cooper, and back to me again. Her brows furrowed minutely, but as her gaze flicked somewhere behind me, the confusion, the daze settled back into the unfazed, neutral indifference she had evinced earlier.

My mouth dropped open as if to explain myself. To ask a million questions. But I could see the warning in Mina's eyes and understood intuitively that I needed to pretend to not know her. I stood frozen in place as my feet urged me to move forward. My arms ached to hold her against me. My heart pleaded with my eyes to never let her out of my sight again, to not even blink lest she disappear.

CHAPTER 32

MINA

bolt of lightning had struck me square in my sternum. Was I dreaming? How could Oliver be here? My Oliver. In this house. He couldn't be here. Had my delusions gotten this vivid? No one had warned me that hallucinations were a side effect of those new anxiety meds that Lavidian had put me on. Did Lavidian know about Oliver? Had they placed him here?

Was this some loyalty test to see if I'd report it?

I tore my eyes away, promising myself he wasn't there. How could he have even gotten here? How had I gotten here, for that matter?

I was missing time again. This happened more and more often when I practiced the advanced meditation technique Artyom had tried to teach me.

That was the last thing I remembered clearly, being with Artyom. When was that? Was that yesterday? No, it couldn't have been...the flight took a whole day, and I had slept in the hotel last night after I arrived. Training with Artyom had to have been days ago, maybe over a week ago, even. *Aghh.* Why couldn't I remember exactly? Mikhailov ordered me to work with Artyom after...after what? I couldn't pinpoint exactly what had prompted the training session. I was missing so much time.

I remembered Artyom and I were standing just outside the combat warehouse. I remembered Artyom walking me through an insanely complex meditation breath technique.

"—it's very effective, but it's unlikely you'll be able to execute it," I remembered him explaining.

"Then what's the point of learning it?" I had asked.

"It's technically basic training for Level 1s and no one ever truly masters it, but if you get close, the results are still power-ful...look, everyone gives in to torture. It isn't a matter of if, it's just a matter of when," he'd told me. "So, all we can attempt to do is to prepare, to anticipate strategies that they'll use. If you're prepared, you'll manage to postpone reaching your pain threshold. The point is teaching you to withstand for as long as possible until the information you carry becomes less valuable."

"You mean, until the batteries on this puppy run out and it shoots kryptonite into my veins?" I remembered shaking my raw, freshly tattooed, Saran-wrapped tracker arm at him.

Artyom crossed his thick, hairy forearms over his chest, ignoring my comment as he continued his lecture—"And even if you don't master the technique, it'll help you get closer to base-line in the middle of a panic attack...which is Gospodin Mikhailov's biggest concern with you at the moment. But we're working on a narrative to add to your backstory, in case you lose control in front of Alexei," he said.

"Why would I need preparation to withstand torture, anyway? I mean who's gonna torture me...besides you guys?" I half-joked and I remembered Artyom frowning at that. "This Alexei Zaharov guy is a liberal politician with a strong moral code. His profile and psych eval suggest he'd never harm me even if he did, let's say, figure out who I really was," I remembered pointing out to Artyom.

"Because he could hand you over to his brother, Anton, to deal with, and we don't know enough about Anton to know what he'd do. He's well-connected, he could outsource...he's a loose cannon," Artyom explained. "So, if you don't mind...shut up, for once, and just listen. Withstanding pain can be accomplished entirely in the mind alone. You have to shut off your mind or remove yourself from where you are to someplace else. When I was in...a dark place, a man once taught me how to create a persona more equipped to endure the torture than myself, and to attempt to swap my mind with that persona for minutes at a time—"

"When you were in...prison?" I remembered asking.

"How do you—? Never mind, I don't care. Just shut up for a second, Jesus. You...what was I saying?"

"When you were in the slammer, a dude taught you to hallucinate—"

"Laugh about it if you want, smart-ass, but if you manage to actually master the technique, it works. In a sense, you are hallucinating, you're going crazy, but in a controlled way. The hard part is going back to yourself when it's over."

It was Artyom who had tattooed the lark on my arm, I suddenly remembered. I looked down at my blazer, itching to lift the sleeve to check for the tattoo, but Anton was fast approaching.

"Ms. Berezova, thank you for your patience. I'm sorry to keep you waiting. I'm afraid we lost track of time in there." Anton Zaharov crossed the room, flashing me a well-rehearsed smile and holding out a hand. Anton was the trouble-making brother of my mark, Alexei Zaharov, aka 'The Young Hope of Russia.' I had expected to run into Alexei down here with his brother, Anton. Instead, I had found Oliver. My Oliver.

I stole a gaze back to the frozen, wide-eyed mirage of him

hovering near the bench press. My eyes darted back to Anton, who furrowed his brows at me ever so slightly.

Anton carried himself with the confidence of someone who was accustomed to getting his way. He fit the profile I'd read in my debriefing so perfectly that I wondered if it could possibly be a front. Even now, I could visualize the breakdown of his life in the files I had studied for so many hours. I pored over his social media account when we gained access to his private profile after he accepted our team's friend request.

I exhaled a breath of relief at the realization that I still remembered it—the file, the assignment, my preparation. Every piece of information and every bit of strategy designed for my current assignment was etched into my mind—not a detail out of place, as far as I knew. Because of that, I could breathe more easily.

I stood from the mat and accepted Anton's outstretched hand. He studied me as he squeezed my hand back lightly, holding on for a moment longer than necessary.

"You can call me Maria." I smiled at him with measured warmth. "Actually, I was glad to have a moment on my own with the cub. He let me feed him." I arched a brow to convey my own surprise but stole another glance at the Oliver mirage, which hadn't moved or disappeared.

"Wonderful!" Anton exclaimed, startling me slightly. He seemed extremely pleased to hear that I'd bonded with the cub. I refocused on a point on Anton's face and slowed my breath. Being this far away from Lavidian made me uneasy. But realizing I was more anxious in this city, my home than I had been at Lavidian made me furious.

This wasn't right. What had they done to me? Was I ever going to feel like Mina again? It had to be unnatural to feel this way. Could the new anxiety meds the nurse put me on have been messing with my head? Everything was blurry, dream-like.

Remaining entirely within my persona of Maria Berezova

required undivided focus and vivid visualization. But this ghost, this mirage of Oliver, his face haunted by uncertainty and fear, was the biggest threat to that focus.

I diverted my gaze to the tiger cub cradled against the voluptuous chest of a gorgeous, half-naked, dark-skinned woman glistening with sweat...who placed her hand on the shoulder of the equally half-naked Oliver. Unless I was dreaming her up as well, people don't generally place their hands on the shoulders of a mirage. He was actually here. Oliver was really in this room with me. The question was, how did he get here?

"Well, I'm off, I'm afraid," the woman announced, drawing my eyes to her full lips. They were faintly stained by the residue of cherry-red lipstick. "That beige, leather pant and silk blouse combo is dynamite," she complimented, scanning me with her honey-colored eyes. She placed the cub back down on the mat, shot me a wink, and cat-walked past me toward the stairs.

"Kiran? What do you mean you're off?" Anton called after her in a British accent similar to hers, but his voice was muffled by the blood rushing to my ears at the sound of that name— Kiran. He had said 'Kiran,' hadn't he?

Could this be her? Was this CJ's wife? Was this the woman who came on to Oliver the night of the rave? I turned to watch her go as an instinctive disdain for the woman surfaced in my gut.

"Aren't you joining us for our afternoon of fun?" Anton called enticingly, but Kiran already had a foot on the first step when she whipped her hair around to look over her shoulder at him.

"I've got Pilates, love. Can't miss it. Anton, I trust you'll take care of my boy, Oli, while I'm out?" she sang as she disappeared up the stairs, not waiting for a response, her hips swinging like a pendulum. *Take care of my boy, Oli.* I ground my teeth. A knot formed deep in my belly and tightened.

Anton bunched his brows and barked out an exaggerated

laugh. "Pilates? Forget bloody Pilates, will you?" he called after her. "Excuse me a moment," he murmured as he brushed past me, but thought better of it and turned back to me, then to Oliver, who remained rooted to the spot, his eyes burning a hole through my skull with the intensity of a thousand laser beams.

Don't speak, Oliver. Don't say a word, I begged internally. Oliver blinked his disbelief away and looked at Anton as though he heard my silent plea. I caught a short, ragged breath of relief.

"I can stay with her if you want..."—he offered to Anton before the other had a chance to ask—"...while you catch up to Kiran before she runs off." His voice was shaky, the first part barely discernible, but Anton didn't seem to notice.

"Thanks, mate—Maria, I apologize. I'll only be a few minutes, unless...well, you know how some women can be," he laughed quietly. I choked down my rebuttal.

"No, I don't know what you mean. But take your time, no worries," I stated blankly, and with a chuckle, he disappeared up the stairs after Kiran.

As soon as he was out of sight, Oliver crossed the room in a few swift strides. He grabbed my face, and I held onto his wrists to stay upright. I looked from one eye to the other rapidly, paralleling my disbelief. He pulled me into his chest, but I cringed back. I spun toward the stairs to make sure we were alone. He reached for me again. His fingers trembled against my jaw. His thumb stroked a soft line across my cheek. I shook my head, turning back toward the stairs, unable to escape the panic rising in my chest—nose stinging and eyes brimmed with tears.His hands were on me. I could feel the pressure of them but I still couldn't believe he was truly here. I had to be imagining this, because if I could have imagined a moment to disappear into forever, this might have been it. It would be Oliver and me, our skin and bones and muscles and organs and souls— the material of us—pixelating into microscopic clumps of cells, spreading, swirling, and merging like a flock in murmuration until we were synonymous, blended, indistinguishably one.

There was one problem: I couldn't be thinking about bird flight formations or clumps of cells when I was on assignment —*the* assignment. Mikhailov had made it all too clear what the price would be this time, if I made another mess of things.

I needed to get eyes on Alexei, not get caught down here crying in Oliver's arms. Alexei was the assignment, the only reason I was here, the only reason I had made an excuse to venture down to this floor of the house. I thought I'd get lucky and bump into him under the guise of looking for the tiger cub.

Back at Lavidian, Artyom and I had drilled multitudes of likely scenarios for days. But we had not prepared for this. Mikhailov and Artyom, who was the senior superior agent on this assignment, were confident that even though this was my hometown, running into someone who knew me as Mina would be highly unlikely in Alexei's circles.

So, although we had drilled hundreds of scenarios, we didn't drill the one where my identity was compromised by someone from my past. A past that now felt decades ago, centuries and lightyears away, though in time it had only been a few scant months.

I was losing perspective. The room was slipping sideways and box breathing—the only technique simple enough to manage at the moment—wasn't working. He was one foot away from me, my Oliver. Except, Oliver wasn't mine, never could be. Not anymore. Not now.

I wouldn't let him fall into this bottomless crevasse with me. Lavidian would expect me to report the incident immediately— to turn, march up the stairs, out of this house, and report it directly to Artyom and the rest of my detail. But I wouldn't do it —I couldn't put Oliver at risk.

I shrugged away from his touch.

"We can't, Oliver—*I* can't," I whispered and hurried over to the staircase to check for company. The steps were clear but a member of Anton's security team was passing by the top of the staircase just as I peered over. I pulled my head back quickly and listened for footsteps. It was quiet.

"Mina, why are you—how are you here? Why are you pretending to be—"

"Shhhh." I covered his mouth, desperate to stop him. "Quiet, please..."—My voice trembled—"...if you don't want to be the reason that they drag me back into that cell and—and if they hurt Mama...listen to me, you—you've never seen me before in your life. We've never met. You don't know me. You understand?" I spoke in fragmented chunks at a time, my words as sharp as shards of glass. I dropped my hand from his mouth and stepped away until we were at arm's length. Oliver's face was drawn in confusion and fury.

"If you think I'd ever let them touch you...you don't understand what it's been like—not knowing where you are, if you were even alive..." His voice faltered. "I'm ready to do anything, anything to keep you safe. I have to pretend that I don't know you? Done. I'll do that and I'll do anything you need. Just tell me what to do—tell me and I'll do it," he urged. "I can't lose you again." He reached his hands up but stopped midway, closed his fingers into fists, and dropped his hands to his sides.

I shook my head and took another step back. "Just this conversation alone is a risk, a threat to my mother's life. Oli, this isn't about me or about keeping me safe. How do you think they've been able to control me all this time? By holding Mama over my head, that's how. Do I want to rot in some room in a basement? No, I don't. But I don't give a shit about myself anymore. They've done so much to her already—I can't let them hurt her again because of *my* actions." I shook my head, failing to convey the fear that lived in me at that thought.

"*They* who?" Oliver asked quietly, looking up at the ceiling. He thought I meant the men in this house.

"*Shhhh*, please, keep your voice down. We can't let them overhear us, Oliver. And no, not them, not Anton. I meant Mikhailov and his group," I whispered, keeping my voice soft.

"Michael-off? That's the guy who took you?" I nodded. "Mina, was he the one in that car that day in the alley—"

"Don't call me that," I warned him sharply, checking the stairway. "I'm Maria, okay? Maria"—I repeated, waiting for it to sink in—"And yes. I think it could have been Mikhailov who was in the car that day when Kiril threatened me. I couldn't see the face of the man who called Kiril back to the car when he tried to confront you. It might have been him, but maybe not," I mused.

I had never asked Mikhailov about it because I didn't want to risk informing him about Oliver having witnessed the incident. It would be a foolish move in case it hadn't been Mikhailov in the car that day. I didn't need to make Lavidian aware of more people I cared about to threaten me with. "It really doesn't matter now," I concluded, verbalizing my thoughts.

"It does matter, Mina," Oliver argued. "Every detail matters. Where have they been keeping you this whole time? I have to know that I'll be able to find you again," he implored.

I shook my head, checking the stairs again. "There's no time. What are you doing with these people, Oliver?"

"Looking for you," he said in astonishment. It was a fact. No uncertainty or hesitation in his voice. I took in a heavy breath as I considered for a moment the massive effort this must have required of him. *How the hell did he find me?*

"You didn't seem like you were looking for me," I whispered.

"And you don't seem like the girl I was looking for either, but things aren't always as they seem, are they?" he whispered back, taking in the sleek new hair, the pantsuit, the heels, the make-up. He was right—I looked nothing like myself. My image was crafted by a team of professionals to reflect the careful sophistication that a woman like Maria Berezova would exude.

"How did you know I'd be here?" I asked him, still not quite understanding how he became so intimately involved with Anton, Alexei's brother.

"I didn't," he admitted. "I was following the only lead I had, which was Anton. It's a long story."

There was so much I needed to say. My hands ached to wrap around his torso, my shoulders twinged to feel the weight of his arms, my nose itched to be buried against the skin of his neck. To distract myself from my rising desire, I looked at the cub, which was pacing between us. I followed its path with my eyes as it prowled back and forth, occasionally stopping to nudge a foam ball with its snout. I met Oliver's gaze once more, unable to keep my eyes off him too long.

It was suddenly impossible to ignore how much he'd changed since I last saw him. He was much thinner. His cheekbones were sharp and his jaw more defined. There was a darkness under his eyes that hadn't been there before. He seemed exhausted, sick, even. His expression nearly broke me. His fear was that potent. I could see how afraid he was for me—his eyes round with panic.

"You said they have your mom? How do you know?"

"That bastard showed me a video they took of her," my voice cracked. "They're keeping her in a bed in one of their medical facilities. I don't know where." I shook my head in quiet exasperation. "The woman that came to the hospital that day, do you remember her?" Oliver nodded, so I went on. "She wasn't a lawyer like I let on. She was CIA."

Oliver's jaw dropped, and I nodded. "I know. She promised they'd put my mom into witness protection under the condition that I went with Mikhailov and his men when they came for me..."—I spoke so softly that Oliver was forced to lean in to make out my words—"...that I wouldn't fight or run, that I'd give in." I could taste the sudden burning in my mouth at the mention of that day, as if molten soot and liquid metal had been funneled in through a breathing tube. The damp concrete. The smell of mold and urine and bleach. I fought for my composure.

There is no Mina. Mina is gone. There is only Lark. Lark. I am Lark. I am Lark. Lark's bones are titanium, her blood is magma. Lark was born of the Bialowieza Forest, raised by wolves. Discomfort is comfort. Pressure is joy. Cold is soothing. Pain is pleasure. I am Lark. Lark feels nothing. I feel nothing.

I repeated the mantra I created under Artyom's guidance, but it wasn't working. My heart rate continued to spike. My chest constricted. *Lark, where are you?* Oliver grabbed my elbows to support me as I hunched forward, gasping for breath, clasping at my own chest.

"What? What's happening? Are you sick? Is it another panic attack? Just breathe, baby. Look at my eyes, breathe with me..."

"Don't. Call. Me. Baby," I managed through strained breaths. But I did as he said. I mirrored his breath. We breathed in counts of four together. It loosened the tightness in my chest but it wouldn't release its grip on me entirely.

I searched the room like Artyom had taught me. "The-the floor-black mat-mirror-tall-tall mirror-two-three-four-five-six-seven-eight tall mirrors—"

"Mina—"

"Window-large window-palm trees-sky-blue sky-sunlight-rays. I'm free-not-in-a-cell. I am cells. I am infinite. I'm free. Free-enough. I'm free enough." I recited my memorized words of reinforcement, ignoring the voice in my head screaming: *Not free! Never going to be free.*

I thought of the forest around Lavidian, the birds, their haunting calls. The Pantone cerulean sky overhead, the same Pantone cerulean of Oliver's eyes—a tone, once a bright and reflective bluish-gray, now dulled by the bloodshot redness veining the whites of his eyes.

Oliver absorbed my state, shaking his head in despair at my fragmented psyche.

"Mina...you need help, baby," he whispered, fingers trembling against my elbows. His hand drifted up to my cheek and cupped it gently.

"Not Mina. Not baby," I chanted, transfixed by the melancholia in his weary regard.

As soon as sensation returned to my fingertips, clarity returned to my thoughts as well. I jerked back. We were running out of time. Someone could come down at any moment. I checked the stairs again before rushing back toward him and blurting my thoughts as quickly and quietly as I could manage.

"She asked me to promise her I'd go—the CIA woman—I told her I'd go with the men if they came for me and I did, I kept my word. She didn't. She promised me that Mama would be taken somewhere safe and that I'd be safe and that someone would always be nearby no matter where they took me. But those were lies. I was supposed to report to my handler about everything that I witnessed after I was taken, but no one ever came. There was no handler; there was no one," I rushed through the story. "I was alone. No one ever tried to reach out to me. So, either she lied—Patricia—either she lied to me or someone did try to find me and failed. Either way, if I ever saw her again, I swear I could strangle her..."

"But, Mina, what if she really c—"

"But nothing, Oliver. At this point, I'd never say a damn thing to her, not a single word. Mikhailov...his organization, I work for them now. That's it. It's that simple. They have Mama. If I do well, they help her. If I mess up, she pays the price. And if they end up killing her, they'll move on to my little cousin. They'll hurt them all, Oliver. They'd hurt you if they knew about you. They're not messing around and if they hurt my mother like they hurt...me"—I was shaking again but I never stopped fighting for breath as I tried to maintain steady fours. I repeatedly uncurled and clenched my fingers, urging sensation to return to them. The numbness of oncoming panic was recurring and spreading up through my arms and into my stomach.

"Mina, please—Mina, come with me now. Let's just run. I'll help you. We'll find her. But first we have to get the hell away from here," he pleaded and it sounded like a dream, like everything I could ever want to hear but that's all it was. It was a dream. "We'll go to the police. They'll help us."

"They can't help us, Oliver. By the time they picked up a pen to take your statement, she'd be dead. You're not listening to me." I took his face into my hands and my gaze bored into him. "I need you to hear me. The greatest danger to me now is you." He flinched, and I let that hard truth sink in.

"There are guards from the organization stationed just outside this house. They're posing as my security team. I am Maria Berezova, daughter of an oligarch named Yuriy Berezov. If you make it seem like I'm anyone else, I'm dead," I whispered, fingers trembling around the frame of his face and expression gravely serious.

"I'll find a way around the guards," he argued. I closed my eyes, losing patience—infuriated with his selfish, blind hope.

"You don't understand. When I say I can't leave, I mean it literally." My hand released his face. I pushed up the sleeve of my blazer and held the inside of my arm to his eye-line. "You see this? This is game over for me. They own me."

"What—" He stared blankly at the inside of my arm. It was nearly indiscernible, the scar beneath the fresh tattoo—especially because the incision was methodically hidden by it. "The bird? They made you get this tattoo? What does it mean?" He moved his hand to touch it. I jerked my arm out of reach. ·

"It's not about the tattoo. The tattoo is nothing, it's just a code name, Lark. Here, feel this lump? It's a tracker. And if I try to remove it, it will kill me—the programming will trigger the release of a neurotoxin," I explained.

Oliver's eyes became impossibly round before his expression contorted into a horrified grimace. The voices upstairs grew louder but to my astonishment and relief, no one seemed to be coming down yet.

"My guards might be carrying the antidote but technically, I have a ticking time bomb under my skin and if the counter toxin isn't administered in time—"

"What happens?" he interjected, eyes wide enough to have already guessed the answer.

"It's lethal. I've been encouraged to trigger the toxin if my cover's blown and someone tries to interrogate information out of me. I wouldn't be surprised if they can trigger it remotely."

"I'm going to mow them off the face of the planet." He seized his head like it might float away. "Jesus, Mina. This is insane. I have to think. We can try something. What if—"

"*Shhhh*, Oliver please, for God's sake. I said no. You don't understand what I've been through. They tortured me...that kind of pain, I-I can't survive it again. I'm on my fourth trial of anxiety meds. This?" I gestured to myself. "This is nothing. This is great—a full-blown vacation away from that hell hole. I have a job to do. I need to focus on my assignment. But they..."—I pointed up toward the second floor—"...can't find out about us, about who I really am. You hear me? You have to leave. Promise me you'll leave. Make up an excuse and go. Get the hell away from here, you understand me?" I hissed, determination and focus returning to me like a savior on a steed. Oliver opened and closed his mouth, clearly losing a battle to his racing thoughts.

"Oliver, listen to me. The people in this house are extremely dangerous. You just need to trust me and leave. Don't come back here...tell your girlfriend, too. Don't tell her why, obviously. Just say you have a bad feeling. Screw that bitch to hell if that's the Kiran that I think it is, but if you care about her, get her away from here." The warning tasted so bitter that I wanted to gargle my mouth clean, but it needed to be said.

"She's not my girlfriend, Mina. I swear to you—"

"It doesn't matter, Oliver," I told him, ignoring the ache in my heart and the tightening knot in my stomach. "If she doesn't listen, forget her. You go. Promise me. Promise me you'll get out of here and you won't come back, please. Oliver?"

Tears were welling up in my eyes again. My whispers were panicked and breathy but I blinked the tears away as fast as they collected, fighting to rein in my pain.

"I'm here looking for you, Mina, it's not what it looks like. They don't even know...I'm not with Kiran, Mina, I swear to you. I'm...she was helping me find you. I came here to get closer to Anton so I could ask about Kiril, about the people who did this to you—"

"Don't. Don't ask about me. Don't tell them that name, Kiril. Are you kidding? Do you want to get me killed? Come on, Oliver! Are you even listening to me? You're playing with things you don't understand. I have work to do. I'm trying to keep my mother alive. Don't you dare get in my way." I moved past him toward the cub but he stopped me by my arm.

"How can I find you if you disappear again?"

"Don't look for me. Forget me. Forget you ever knew me."

"Maria Yuriyevna?" a man I presumed to be one of Anton's men called down from atop the stairs and I fell dead silent. The sound of his slow, heavy footsteps echoed as he descended. I could hear the thumping of my own beating heart pounding in my eardrums.

"Can I offer you a drink in the family room?" he called out.

"Yes, thank you," I called back to the man.

I joined Anton's entourage in the living room without another glance at Oliver. Instead, I forced my focus onto the cub, which was battling pillow tassels. Bradley Cooper was showing off his agility. He released a ferocious little cub growl and goosebumps covered my arms as my instincts sensed the latent predatory potential within him.

When I first read the file on Alexei and came across the Anton tiger cub plan of introduction, I didn't know what to expect. I'd never been around a wild animal quite like this one. I was nervous to make a mistake, afraid that it would sense my anxiety, my fear.

Mikhailov had instructed me to keep in touch with Margrette after Artybash, insisting that the cub was the fastest and easiest in.

"You need to leave a memorable impression," Mikhailov had argued when I suggested a simpler approach.

My conversations with Margrette were supervised but I was encouraged to text her as often as possible. She never mentioned what happened with her brother, so I figured either Pavel had forgotten everything by morning, kept the incident to himself, or Margrette had chosen to ignore it.

Margrette had been intrigued by my Maria persona, that much was clear. She was eager to impress me, to please me, to flaunt her connections. When I asked if she knew anyone with access to exotic animals, she connected me with her cousin's "crazy ex," Anton Zaharov.

MARGRETTE

If anyone knows where to get a baby tiger, it's this guy.

She introduced me to Anton over social media.

Anton just so happened to have recently acquired a baby tiger cub and said he was meeting buyers on his holiday in Los Angeles. We already knew that, of course—Lavidian had the information weeks before I stepped foot in Artybash. I was on a flight to Los Angeles the following day.

Suddenly, everything clicked: Why I had to meet the Mohorenski twins, why I had to mention looking for an exotic gift for my friend, Adel. Why we stopped at the Café de Paris in Minsk in the first place, before we were cleared to go to Artybash. I wouldn't be surprised if Lavidian had already prepared a backup agent in case Anton's brother, Alexei, ended up being unresponsive to me at the bar that day.

As soon as I absorbed the entire file on Alexei Zaharov, everything else began to make sense.

Alexei Zaharov was my true mark, the straight-edged, liberal politician with a strong online presence that had garnered him the admiration of an exponentially expanding pool of young Russian voters. His distaste for the elite and the old regime was well-documented.

Alexei proved to be a difficult man to reach. Our in would be his Achilles' heel, his capricious brother, Anton Zaharov, the eccentric arbitrageur. I'd been told the brothers were an unlikely pair who kept their circles tight. It was my job to weave myself into their lives, most importantly into Alexei's life.

I could still feel Oliver's gaze on me, watching me through the partially closed door he had disappeared behind. I had trained my eyes firmly on the cub when I heard the clicking of dress shoes on tile. I turned toward the sound.

Alexei, the man of the hour, at last strolled into view, dressed in a familiar navy suit, quite similar to the one he donned at that bar in Minsk at the Café de Paris. The initial release at the anxiety of finally seeing him lasted just a few seconds—because his presence meant it was showtime.

Alexei glanced at me.

"You..." Alexei trailed off, clearly at a loss for words. He stood entirely still, unblinking, staring at me with an appraising look. He held the refrigerator door ajar, still watching me as I sat on the couch.

"Me," I mirrored with an added tone of detachment, half expecting his surprise, half wondering if he remembered exactly where he'd seen me before. As recognition sparked in his eyes, delight filled mine. The corners of my mouth quirked up.

"We've met before, yes? Minsk? Café de Paris?" he asked, his tone indicating he found it hard to believe. "The escort?" he teased, the corner of his lips inching up just the slightest. *This again.*

"The grouch?" I countered, not bothering to correct him.

"You remembered!" He sounded pleased.

"Couldn't forget it if I tried, Plato," I remarked, dryly.

"What are you doing in my living room? Did Anton hire you—"

"Hire *her*? This woman could own both our asses in the blink of an eye, you git," Anton's voice filled the living space as he blew through the front door. "Do you know who the hell you're speaking to, Alexei? This is Maria Berezova—"

"Watch your tone," Alexei warned him flatly.

"You watch yourself, kid," Anton bit back with a cool chuckle.

Alexei regarded me as though my name meant diddly squat to him and shrugged. "So, you're the buyer." It was more of a statement than a question.

"Potential buyer," I corrected. My gaze briefly met Oliver's, who was still watching through the door gap from the other room.

As Anton and Alexei volleyed verbal jabs at one another, Oliver and I stole a moment, a moment of weakness—a moment that I would stretch into a lifetime if I could. I tried to memorize the lines of his face so I'd never forget him, but I had to divert my gaze before anyone else noticed. I returned my attention to the cub.

"You two look perfect together," Anton complimented, startling me out of my hypnotic state. I was forced to return my attention to Anton and Alexei. Anton effortlessly transfigured his frustration into the well-rehearsed smile from earlier, as he beamed at the cub and me on the couch. Alexei, whose opinion of me seemed to have somehow plummeted into the abyss, bit into his bagel and scowled at me from behind the kitchen counter.

Anton, clearly intent on the sale of the cub, insisted I stay for his party. I was growing more anxious with every passing minute as Oliver had chosen to ignore my warning by remaining in the house. He kept his distance from me, at least.

I was nursing a wine glass by a high-top on the patio under an umbrella when Alexei joined me. I looked up, surprised. He regarded me with careful calculation, and after a moment, I returned my attention to the view.

"Why are you really here?" he probed, without a hint of subtlety. I was thrown off by the accusation, but at the same time I'd been prepared for this grilling. We anticipated that he'd be suspicious after meeting me in Minsk.

Mikhailov had stood by his insistence that Minsk was a necessary test of interest before proceeding with me as agent on this assignment. Based on our brief encounter, Alexei demonstrated a satisfactory level of raw intrigue based solely on Artyom's observational report. As it turned out, even Café de Paris was a test.

"I would think that's obvious," I said coolly, gesturing toward the cub with my wine glass. "I am here for the tiger." Bradley Cooper was wrestling an inflated duck a few feet away.

"Of course you are...how do you know Anton?"

"I don't. He's a friend of a friend."

"What friend?" he asked. I deliberately bristled at the question.

"Margrette..."

"Margrette who?" he quizzed.

"Mohorenski."

"Hmmm," he considered. I held back an eyeroll and maintained neutrality. "And what do you need an animal like that for?"

"Excuse me?" I raised a brow.

"What on Earth are you going to do with a tiger?" he pushed.

"Haven't you heard? Tiger cubs are the new rage," I answered with levity in my tone, hoping to steer away from his intense line of questions.

He didn't ease up his intensity—he just folded his forearms to display his cross disposition with me, as though my mere presence vexed him, somehow.

"I'm not gonna eat it...if that's what you're worried about," I joked. "I'm flying into Las Vegas tonight, to celebrate the birthday of an old friend, so—"

"Old friend," he mocked, clearly unconvinced how old of a friend I could possibly have. *This isn't good.* This meant he probably considered me too young...too young for him.

I *was* too young for him. The problem was, for this assignment to work, he needed to be interested enough in me to at least get me to phase 3 and it was becoming clear that he wasn't.

Whoever had come up with this tiger idea was an idiot—there were a thousand better ways to have met him. I had unwittingly had better luck with him on my own at the Café de Paris than abiding by the script of this moronic plan.

"I'd like to surprise my friend with a special gift, a token of our unique friendship," I tried, improvising a bit. "You might remember my good friend, Adel? She and I were together that day in Minsk," I reminded him. He nodded along, not entirely convinced but listening.

"She loves tigers, grew up around them since she was a child. This one might be a bit plain for her tastes—hers were always quite rare in color and breed, but it's the thought that counts."

Alexei ran his eyes over me, cataloging me with such leisurely meticulousness that a chill ran down my spine. "She mentioned once that she missed it...raising a cub. She was right. They're exceptional, aren't they?" I declared with forced assuredness to make up for the brief stutter.

"You're not afraid?" he surveyed.

"Of what?" I asked.

Alexei nodded toward the tiger.

"Afraid of Bradley Cooper? He's harmless. Besides, very little frightens me," I affirmed, at last, mastering the steady delivery of the Maria Berezova I had so carefully crafted.

"Why is that?" Again, there was a challenge in his tone, as though every word from my lips revealed some fault of mine.

"Do not fear death but rather the unlived life," I tried, attempting to soften him up, to redirect the conversation, like, maybe this could be our thing: throwing quotes out as a challenge.

He took the bait. "Naruto?" he guessed, taking me completely off-guard to the point of laughter.

"No, it's Natalie Babbitt," I clarified. *"Tuck Everlasting...*you probably wouldn't know it; it's romantic. Wait...you know manga?"

"It's a classic. And Naruto was romantic enough." Alexei shrugged. His brows furrowed that same way they had when he had been upset with the news reporting. Then, his worry lines smoothed out.

"Take him," he blurted.

"Take him? After that ominous little warning of yours?" I teased.

"I can see from that stubborn look in your eyes that my warning was of little consequence to you. I want him out of my house. I'll make Anton give you a bargain, a good price," Alexei pronounced, a promise in his eyes. It was funny that this was the famous younger brother, this wound-up, testy man who looked like he slept in a navy suit and showered in one, too. As though he could read my thoughts, he glanced toward his older brother, Anton, who was laughing, lost in conversation with Oliver and some new guy who had joined them.

The new guy was about our age. He was tall and muscular, with skin a russet, reddish brown that was slightly darker in tone than Oliver's.

As I clocked their body language, I observed how close this new guy was to Oli, how familiar they must have been with one another. Oliver allowed this guy to touch him, to grip his shoulders, to tap his back with his open palm without flinching or visibly tensing the way he often would when he was startled. They must have built up some trust, a sort of special friendship that had quickly blossomed while I'd been...away.

My heart squeezed at that realization, relieved that Oli wasn't alone, that he had someone. Of course, he did. Of course, he would. He was wonderful. *One day, he'll be surrounded by plenty of good people, people who will become like family. And me, I'll probably be a hazy memory—that one girl he knew back in the day.* Maybe one day he'd wonder whatever happened to me.

"Am I boring you?" Alexei reminded me of his presence. I had almost entirely forgotten he was there. I scolded myself and renewed my efforts, focusing entirely on the grumpy, dimple-chinned man before me who clearly had a bone to pick.

"Thank you for the offer but it isn't about money. It's about the cub's temperament. I need to know if he's right for Adel."

"The cub's temperament...he's a wild animal, for Christ's sake! Ridiculous," Alexei scoffed. "Listen, I'm against this lunacy. I don't want trouble. I swear, Anton pulls this crap just to spite me. That is a wild animal. It belongs in the wild. It's illegal to have it here."

"But it's not illegal in Nevada," I mused.

"You think you're clever, don't you?" he jeered.

"I don't think about it that much, to be honest. It's just sort of a fact that I live with, like the absence of sound in space."

"You think you're above the rules?" he challenged. I was trying to figure him out—crack the code to his vault—but as we volleyed back and forth, I couldn't pinpoint his precise motivation with me. What was it about my persona that irritated him so deeply?

Levity wasn't working and this whole tiger thing had gotten me in the door but was pissing him off to no end. He was growing more and more agitated. I needed to figure out how to lower the heat to a simmer and quickly.

"No, I'm not above the rules, but finding my way around them can be fun." There, that was neutral. How could he find fault in that?

"It isn't about money, huh? Let me guess, Miss Berezova... daughter of an oligarch? Raised in privilege but thinks she's somehow superior to the rest of the egocentric bloodsuckers..." He carried such inherent disdain for me that it dripped from every word he uttered. How was I supposed to salvage this? I itched to throw his words about privilege back in his face, but he wasn't meant to realize how much I already knew about him.

"What makes you say that?" I deflected.

"My brother said you could own us...him...maybe, but no amount of money could ever buy *me*. What else? Your English, for one...it's too good, too fluent to be learned in Russia. That nearly perfect accent is typical of boarding school in the States. Your watch, a replica of the early nineteen hundreds antique, only the very wealthy have replicas of their collections made that well. The perfection, the shine gives it away—it's over a hundred years old and carries no signs of aging," he listed.

"There's only one Berezov that I've heard of who is well-enough connected to send a child to the States for boarding school, who could afford to own the original of that watch, who could raise a daughter with the absurd idea that a tiger is a suitable gift for a friend without a thought to the consequences of gifting such a thing.

"That alone says so much about her habit of having problems solved for her,"—he went on, seething—"Only one Berezov whose daughter could have a friend with a large enough acreage and equally insane upbringing to possibly accept such a gift— and that man is Yuriy Berezov, the media giant so private that the world knows nothing of his personal life or that he even has any children."

"So what? Those facts are surface. Anyone who's anyone knows them. That's not who I am. You don't know shit," I claimed with blatant rebellion echoing through my outrage.

"Did your father send you here to catch my eye?"

All right, let's try another approach. I let out a haughty laugh and retorted, "Why would my father do that? What exactly makes you so special? I told you, I'm here for a tiger. I don't do my father's bidding. It's enough that I have to stomach seeing him every year for the holidays. I've spent my life keeping my distance from that man and his suffocating money." This hits him in the right place. His face softens just the slightest. "I've made my own money," I go on with renewed hope. "It isn't billions, but it's mine and I can do what I please with it. I happen to want to buy my best friend a meaningful gift. She happens to love tigers. Your brother's selling. I'm buying. End of story."

"Perfect. Be my guest. Get it the hell out of here." This man was insufferable. "You know something funny? I'll be flying into Las Vegas tonight, as well. Had the trip planned for weeks and suddenly, my, my, how our schedules have aligned. One can't help but wonder if by fate or design." He looked for the surprise in my eyes. I made sure it was there. He pretended he believed it.

"I don't understand what you're insinuating, but you're the

one who waltzed over here to have this tedious conversation," I snapped and turned my back to him, taking a few steps closer to the tiger cub, which came to my side and rubbed against my leg. I knelt to run my fingers along its fur.

"That little guy's grown attached, probably can smell the caviar on your breath." Alexei's voice was softer, now—almost teasing. I had him. Turned out, he needed the push. I was deeply relieved I had read him right.

"Why do you insist on speaking to me when I clearly anger you? Do you think I want to be near someone so void of happiness that he sucks the joy out of anything within a two-meter radius of himself?" I asked, deliberately pushing harder this time. Worry filled me, knotting my gut with the fear that perhaps I'd pushed too far.

I hadn't expected him to be so resistant—hesitant and suspicious, perhaps, but not antagonistic to this degree.

He took a step back, away from me. "Feeling happier?" he asked. He took a step farther away. "How about now?" He smirked.

"Much better." I smiled at the first joke he'd made. Now, for the moment of deliberation. I held my breath. Alexei's hard mouth broke into a grin, like a chisel cracking into a block of ice. *I'm in!* I had him. My shoulders softened in relief.

Past Alexei, Oliver stood in the doorway to the living room between his friend and Anton. He watched me carefully, acute pain visible in his eyes, clenched fists at his sides. My heart rose to my throat. I swallowed it back down with effort.

"You were right. The little guy has indeed grown attached. Tell your brother I'll wire him. Have him reach out with an amount. He needs to arrange delivery to my jet in a few hours." I patted Bradley Cooper and stood from my haunches.

"Enjoy Las Vegas," I told Alexei without looking up at him. I finished the last of my wine and placed the empty glass in Alexei's open hand as I walked away.

CHAPTER 35

OLIVER

"Oliver! Why haven't you been picking up? I've called you like a million times...were you talking to Lily?" Nyah's frantic voice came in through the phone.

"Lily? No, how would I have talked to Lily? I wrote, saying I saw Mina, not Lily—"

"Oliver, no, Oliver, I found Lily! She's been trying to reach you," Nyah declared, breathless. My brain was spiraling inside my skull. Were we talking about the same Lily—Mina's mother?

"What do you mean you 'found Lily?'" I thought I might hurl in the bushes.

I had texted Nyah about five minutes after I got back upstairs.

Mina's here, she's at Anton's but it's complicated, she's going by another name and she can't leave with me...they have her working for them and they have Lily locked up somewhere.

I couldn't risk being overheard, so I didn't pick up Nyah's calls, plus I was afraid to take my eyes off of Mina.

When I realized that Mina had left, Xavi and I made up an excuse. We ran out the front door to look for her but she was already gone. There was no trace of her. My heart was racing like mad, and Xavi was the only reason I didn't fall to the ground when my knees gave out after I finally stopped running down the street.

"I still don't know exactly what went down with Lily," Nyah explained. "But she was desperate to talk to you, Oliver. She kept asking about Mina. I gave her your number."

"It could be a setup, Nyah. They could have had a gun to her head...we don't know. Maybe you shouldn't have said anything. They could be using her to fish for information or to see if Mina's been loyal to them. Mina said she saw a video of her mom being held in some kind of facility," I muttered quietly into the phone, walking back up the street toward Anton's place with Xavi by my side.

"Are you kidding, Oliver? Lily would die rather than ever, ever be complicit in something like that. I don't care what threat they used. It's just not possible. She'd protect Mina at the cost of her own life," Nyah corrected. She was right. I wasn't thinking straight.

"You're right. I'm—I didn't think."

"Anyway, Lily says she's been in witness protection this whole time. It doesn't sound like she was in danger at any point after leaving the hospital from what she says. She was transferred to some physical therapy facility in Ohio. She did say that they lied to her—they told her that Mina was also safe and in hiding."

"That doesn't make any sense. Wait, how did you manage to reach her in the first place?" I asked, disoriented by doubt.

"I remembered how Lily, a few years back, had set up this social media account under a fake name and some random profile picture. She had friend requested both Mina and me to find out what we really got up to over the summer. She didn't know that we knew it was really her. She thought she was being clever but Mina figured it out pretty early on. I remembered that account and I figured…well, it was a long shot, but I thought, what if I sent her a message through there? It was probably linked with her email or something. What if she saw it, somehow? You know…why not try? So, I did. I messaged the account—a shot in the dark."

"What did you say?"

"I asked her, 'Ms. Arkova, are you in danger? Where are you?' I ummm…I told her, 'Mina's missing. Those men drugged me and took her. We don't know where she is but Oliver's never stopped looking for her. Call me if you ever see this' and I sent her my number."

"And…" I asked.

"And nothing. She never responded, she never called. I could see she read it, though, because it was marked as read. That's why when you texted me about seeing Mina, I didn't hesitate to message the fake account again. I wrote, 'Oliver saw Mina. She's at a house here in LA. It belongs to this guy Oliver's been trying to meet, Anton. Mina told Oliver that they're keeping you somewhere. Can you get word to us on where you are? We'll try to send help.' Not even a minute later, she called me," Nyah rambled in her usual thousand-words-per-minute-without-breathing style of speaking.

"What did she say when she called?" I urged, still skeptical.

"She said she had a bad feeling the entire time she was in recovery, a bad feeling about Mina. At one point, she got desperate enough to check her emails and her social media accounts in case Mina had tried to send word. As soon as she saw my message, she realized they weren't telling her the truth about Mina and she reached out to her husband—well, her ex, Mina's dad. She told him what had happened. He promised her that he was doing everything he could to find Mina and to appease those people. He helped Lily get out of Ohio. That's all I know—"

"Why didn't she write back or call when she first saw your message?"

"She said she wanted to keep me out of it, that it was dangerous to be involved in any capacity."

"Nyah, you said Lily called me?" I scrolled through my missed calls; there were several from an international number.

"Yes, I gave her your number. I told her you found Mina—"

"Mina's gone, Nyah! She was here but now she's gone. I lost her. I-I thought she was in the bathroom but she must have left through the front and I missed her—" The burning sensation of impending doom was returning. I pounded my chest with my fist to fight through it, as though it was a physical thing when I knew damn well that it was my head playing its games with me.

"I gotchyu, brother." Xavi patted my back and squeezed my shoulders. "We'll find her. You'll see. Don't worry, Anton's got her number. We have a lead this time," Xavi soothed.

"Oliver—" Nyah's voice came through the phone.

"Nyah, I have to call Lily," I pressed.

"Yes, okay, but call me back."

After she hung up, I took a long, deep breath and dialed the international number listed in my missed calls. An unusual international dial tone was emitted and after several rings, a muffled voice emerged at the other end. The familiar rasp sent a shiver down my spine.

"Oliver? Where is she? Oliver?"

"Lily, where are *you*? Are you okay? Tell me you're safe," I blurted in a rush.

"Yes, I been fine but sick with worry. You are with Mina?" Her voice was panicked but hopeful.

"No, Lily...she isn't here," I declared, still unsure about how much was safe to say over the phone.

"Nyah telling me she is a there with you! That you seen her. What you mean?" Lily cried out.

"She isn't here anymore, Ms. Arkova."

"So...you *did* see her. What happened?" Lily asked, a tremor in her voice.

"Yes, she was here. She seemed okay. She wasn't injured as far as I could tell. But I don't know where she went. She refused to tell me. What about you, Ms. Arkova? Do you need help? Anything you need, anything at all...just ask. I can help you. Maybe you can't say anything right now, maybe someone's next to you making it hard to speak freely? I'm here. You can count on me. We can negotiate something with them. What do they want? Money? I can help —" I promised. My lower lip tore as I chewed on the skin. I sucked on the blood from the tear and licked my lip to try to seal it.

"I am safe, Oliver. I'm here with Nikolai. He helped to bring me out of Ohio and keeping me and my parents safe for now," she explained.

"Nikolai's there? Can I talk to him?" I insisted.

"*Shto on hochette?*" a deep, masculine voice sounded over the phone.

"Is that him? Is that Nikolai or someone else?"

"This is Nikolai next to me, yes," Lily reported.

"Nikolai, can you hear me? Nikolai, who are the people who took your daughter? Can you tell me exactly what happened? They told Mina that you did something to cause them to go after your family. Is that true?" I demanded.

"Oliver, bro." Xavi shook his head, indicating with his hands for me to calm down.

"*S kem razgovarivayesh', mal'chik na pobegushkakh?* Huh? Errand boy, who you speaking to in this tone? This none your business, just answer to Lilia question. Where you see my daughter? When? And is she okay?" the man urged.

"What did you do, Nikolai?" I persisted. "Who are these

people? There's Kiril, some guy...Michael-off, I think and...who else?" Anger was blazing through me, unbearable and out of control.

"Listen to me—" he tried.

"No, *you* listen. I was there in the alley. I saw them cut into her face. I know what they're capable of,"—I enlightened him because clearly he hadn't even heard of me before—"She told me they sent you videos of her being tortured—" I added in a hushed tone.

"Nikolai?" Lily's cry broke through the line. She didn't know. He hadn't told her. He mumbled something to her that I couldn't understand and she answered with anger and hurt in her voice.

I went on, "So, no. I'm not your errand boy. I haven't been able to sleep for the past two months. I've been looking for Mina day and night, scavenging for crumbs of information, for anything, a name...a city...You know who's doing this. Tell me something...you—" I cut myself off. *You piece of shit!* I screamed in my head.

"Just calm down, Oliver, and tell to me where was this place you saw her and where do you think she can be now? Please, just tell to me the truth," Lily's gentle plea came through the line and I let go of the rage I was clutching onto.

"She was at this house that I'm at right now—"

"Was she scared? Where is this house?" Lily urged.

"She's been through a lot, but she seemed...okay. She's so strong," I assured her gently, leaving out the part about the anxiety attack. "It's a friend's house. Well...he's not a friend of mine; he's an old friend of the wife of my business acquaintance. It's a long story." I kept my voice low. I looked around us to make sure there were no surveillance cameras that could catch our conversation now that Xavi and I were nearing Anton's house again. I continued in a soft whisper, "He deals with luxury goods, like rare goods, I guess. He's trying to sell her a baby tiger of all things, if you'll believe it—"

"A tiger—"

"A tiger cub. She's pretending to be someone else, Marina—no, Maria...Breaze-ova, something like that, pretending to be the daughter of some wealthy guy." I rubbed my forehead, trying to remember exactly what she'd said.

"Why? Why she's there pretending this?"

"I don't know. They're making her, I think. She said she works for the men who threatened her in the alley, Kiril and the others, the ones who hurt you and took her. Who are these people, Lily?"

"Oliver...let me talk to her," Lily begged.

"*Net*," I heard the deep, masculine voice interrupt Lily. He said something quickly and quietly to her in Russian.

"*Horosho*," Lily told him. "Oliver, Nikolai saying is not good idea for me to talk to her. If she working for them, we cannot disturb her. *You* must not disturb her or try to intrude. It will becoming very dangerous if her identity will be compromised in front of them in any way."

"Lily, she isn't here anymore, that's what I'm—that's what I was saying," I admitted, a fracture breaking my voice. "She must have quietly slipped out. I was on the patio, and she was there, too. She went into the house. I—I thought she went inside to use the restroom. I followed her inside as soon as I could. I was trying not to be obvious. I stood outside the locked bathroom door for a while. When I knocked, someone else came out—it wasn't her. She must have left through the front door. Anton knows her number. I'm going to ask him for it—"

"Be careful what you will say to him about her, Oliver"—Lily warned and added something in her language to Nikolai—"We don't want to make a bad situation worse. Maybe is better you leave this place? Forget about these people? Me and Nikolai will finding her?"

"Lily—no, Lily, we need to work together," I urged, hesitating in a moment of deliberation. "She thinks you're a prisoner. She said she saw a video of you in one of their facilities. That's why she's working for them. They're threatening her with her cousin's life, Nyah's life, *your* life. She's afraid if she messes up this job or whatever this thing is that they have her doing, that they'll hurt you and it'll be her fault."

"Oh, God," Lily breathed. "Nikolai, we have to bring the rest of my family here," I heard her say, panic evident in her voice.

"I don't understand...what footage could they have shown her that convinced her that they had you?" My mind reeled with thousands of possibilities, each one more unsettling than the last.

"Could been anything," Nikolai cut in. "Maybe they hack facility cameras where Lilia was in rehabilitation but...unlikely. More likely, the footage is doctored like a deep fake. When they brought me footage of Mina, I, at first, thinking...hoping that it must be a fake..."—Nikolai uttered in a low voice riddled with hesitation—"...but then, I heard her voice and I just thinking even if there is chance it could be real, I must do what they need. So, I did. Now, I know it was real," he concluded, shame lacing his admission. He added something indiscernible to Lily in a quiet voice.

"Nikolai, have you ever done what Mina is doing for these people? Have you worked for them that way?" My question was met with silence. I dropped the phone to my side and growled my frustration to the sky before lifting it to my ear again. "Lily, you're one-hundred percent sure you were never under their control?" I pushed.

"I was not. The agent transferred me to a live-in physical therapy center in Ohio, gave me the new name, but they lying to me from a beginning about Mina safety with promise she completely safe in another city, same like me. They say we will be reunite as soon as is safe. But I understand my instinct on that whole bullshit just totally correct, it would never be safe, so when will I see my daughter? Was I to live my life without her? Impossible. And then, I read Nyah's message. I, right away, reaching out to Nikolai. Oliver, what is the name of a man which this house belonging to?"

"It's a rental, I'm pretty sure, but his name is Anton Zaharov. But it seems like she's really here for his brother, Alexei," I whispered, pacing farther away from the house again. An uneasy silence filled the line. Neither Lily nor Nikolai spoke a word. "You know those names—that's why you're not saying anything. Are you guys going to tell me anything about these people? Who are we dealing with here? How deep does this run? We need to work together, combine intel…"

More silence followed before Lily finally spoke.

"Is better the less you know, Oliver," Lily said softly. "Safer for you. Nikolai and I, we will looking for way to free Mina. You must promise me to stay away from these dangerous pe—"

"Okay, well, if you're not gonna tell me anything, I gotta go. I gotta talk to someone who will. Time's running out. When you change your mind, you know how to reach me."

"Oliver—" Lily tried but I hung up the call and turned the ringer to silent.

"Where you been? I thought you fell in the bog," Anton declared cheerfully as Xavi and I joined him out by the pool deck. I shrugged with a grin I hoped didn't look as fake as it felt. Xavi and I went back to his makeshift DJ booth and he switched the track as Anton followed us over.

"Ey, say your farewells to Bradley Cooper. Berezova's taking him to Nevada with her," Anton declared triumphantly, shimmying in a celebratory dance.

"Nevada?" I asked, keeping my tone casual.

"Yeah, she's jetting to Vegas in an hour or so—it's a friend's birthday, and Bradley Cooper's the gift, apparently."

"Vegas...nice. She coming by soon to pick up Bradley or what?" I asked, hopeful.

"No, I gotta deliver him. I'm trying to get my brother to do it since he's flying out later today anyway. He could've easily popped by the private airport in Van Nuys before his flight in Burbank with the common folks, bless his humble heart. I told him she might even give him a lift on her jet if he asked nicely. But he's being a proper git, told me to take a walk. Surprising, too. I've never seen him say more than one word to someone his team hasn't vetted, but you saw him having a good, long talk with Berezova like they were old buddies. At first, I figured he fancied her...but I guess not."

I ground my teeth, recalling the intense frustration I'd felt watching Mina and Alexei engage in a poolside conversation that appeared far from casual. Clearly, Alexei was part of her job here, but his interest in her had been blatant, even from a distance. To say I didn't like it was a colossal understatement. It had taken everything, every ounce of control I could muster, not to interrupt them, not to cross that patio and hold her in my arms. To throw her over my shoulder like some caveman and get her the hell away from here, away from everything.

"We can do it," Xavi jumped in with the offer, casual as ever, and I beamed at him. *Brilliant.*

"Do what? Deliver Bradley Cooper?" Anton asked robotically as he typed something into his phone.

"Yeah, why not? You can't leave your own party," he noted, shrugging.

"Naw, mate, you're here to DJ. You *are* the party. The energy dropped as soon as you walked away for a few minutes. Did you find what you went looking for in your car?" Anton asked Xavi.

"No, must have left the cable at home...it's all right, it's just a backup. I thought this one was faulty but it's working fine now," Xavi covered.

"I can deliver Bradley if you want," I offered, picking up off Xavi's cue.

"Naw, mate, it's no worries. I'll get one of the boys to go," Anton swatted away the offer.

"Bradley likes me. I don't mind, honestly," I threw back quickly, trying to think on my feet. "And, I gotta admit, she's pretty fine. I wouldn't mind seeing her again. I was actually gonna ask you for her number."

"*You* are interested in Maria Berezova?" Anton challenged with a particularly loud amusement in his tone.

Had I taken the wrong approach? Was I supposed to still be faking an interest in Kiran? "Don't say anything to Kiran," I added, trying to cover my bases.

"Ohhh," he snorted, and mimed zipping his lips before throwing away the key. Then, to emphasize that he was in an especially playful mood, he felt around for the key, picked it up, and partially unzipped the corner of his mouth to comment, "Your secret is safe, my friend. Funny enough, I was connected to her through my ex...my ex's cousin actually met Berezova at a ski resort, I believe. Listen to me, mate, I wouldn't want you to waste your time." He threw his hands in the air and shrugged.

"Why do you say that?" I challenged.

"A woman like that? You know who she is?" he asked while typing on his phone again.

I shook my head. "What? She's rich or something like that?"

"Rich," he snorted. "If only it was that, mate." He looked up from his phone and lowered his voice like he was letting me in on a secret. "She's the daughter of one of the most powerful, most reclusive oligarchs of them all. I mean no one even knew he had a kid, that's how careful this guy is. He doesn't like his picture taken, keeps his name out of the press at all costs. He's the majority owner of one of the biggest telecom companies in Asia."

I realized then that men like Anton luxuriated in rarities. He got off on knowing special people and making them out to be bigger than life, just like he got off on being this master curator of rare goods.

"Wow, that's interesting," I commented, my tone indicating I was brushing it off like it wasn't important—a speed bump in my life.

"Yeah—so, naturally, my brother's pissed at me that she was here. You heard him yelling."

"Why was he pissed?"

"I mean, to be fair, he wasn't too thrilled about having you and Kiran here, either. Gave me so much shit about it last night, well, first about the tiger, then about the two of you. That one's always been strung a bit too tight but lately it's becoming unbearable—" he answered without really answering, a forte of his. I let it go, deciding it didn't matter.

"So, you want me to deliver Bradley Cooper for you or what?" I offered with a smirk, fighting to stay on topic.

"Look at you," he laughed and patted my shoulder. I stiffened but shrugged through it, staying light.

"What can I say? I wanna see her again." I grinned.

"*Haha*, wow! You're showing all of your cards, lover boy. You wear your heart right on your polyester sleeve, don't you?"

"What's wrong with polyester?" I asked. "This is your shirt, by the way."

"Clearly, this is one hundred percent organic cotton and please, keep it. I was talking about the fashion crime you committed last night. Look at this, your skin is finally breathing," he teased, pulling on the hem of the shirt. I chuckled at his proclivity to stray off topic by noticing details of the smallest consequence.

"Don't you worry about my skin," I assured. "My skin's made

of the toughest stuff. So...spontaneous trip to Vegas? What do you think? You down?"

He let out a belly laugh and clapped my back. "I like you. You go after what you want. Alexei's heading there, too, for business. He won't want me around."

"It's a big place—we can stay out of his way," I reasoned. "Wait, what are you so happy about?" I asked, noting his wide grin.

"I always feel better knowing someone wants something from me. It's wholesome. I can trust a person who openly wants something from me. I didn't quite understand what the hell you were doing here before. At first, I thought maybe you lost a bad bet with Kiran and agreed to be her bitch for a while. Which, I admit, amused me but also made me uncomfortable, to be perfectly transparent with you. Then, all those questions about those people...as though, because I spoke Russian I somehow knew every Russian on the planet, which is ridiculous, to be frank. Didn't like it. Rubbed me the wrong way. But this? This is something I can do. A desire—that's what I do, Oliver. I deal in desires. I can make unlikely things a possibility."

"You can?" I challenged.

"I can give you her number. I can put in a word or two." His smile widened. "If...if you give me something in return," he added.

"Something like what?" I asked, tentatively.

"I'm sure you can come up with something—if you're as clever as Kiran claims."

"Don't you owe *me*?" I reminded him.

He met my eye, a recognition in his gaze—fellow hustler. "That's right," was all he said.

My phone vibrated in my pocket. I pulled it out, checked the caller ID, and picked up, stepping away from Anton and Xavi.

"CJ?" I answered quietly, cupping my hand over my mouth.

"You watched him screw my wife?" CJ's voice was so hollow,

I froze as though he was right in front of me. "Yes or no, Oliver?"

I opened my mouth. No sound came out. The call ended.

We made our way toward the SUV parked beside the jet that was fueled and ready to go, waiting on the tarmac of the private airport. We approached quickly, silent as a pack of wolves. I led the charge, flanked by Anton's men on both sides. I held Bradley Cooper, who was asleep in a dog carrier.

The sound of CJ's cold anger hadn't left my mind but I'd have done anything to get to Mina. I'd make things right with CJ later, when I could. I typed a message out on my phone, highlighting the entire text so that I could delete it with one tap of my screen if I needed to.

> Lily's safe, she called me, they were lying they don't have her. she's with your father. your grandparents are there. I warned them that your cousin's in danger

Mina peeked her head out the jet door and descended the ladder to meet me. My breath hitched as she approached. Her skin radiated under the golden light of the sunset, her dark and glossy hair complementing her sophisticated and sleek attire. However, what truly stood out was her unique walk. In an instant, she transformed into the same girl who once exited her dance studio and confidently approached me next to my bike – her hips swaying, her gaze lowered with the grace of a jungle predator. Had she looked this dangerous then? It was unquestionable, she was different—sharper around the edges—but the softness from before was hidden somewhere behind those hazel eyes, I was sure of it.

I moistened my dry mouth, then swallowed. We came to a stop, leaving an easy-to-close gap between us.

"Miss Berezova," I pronounced, drinking her in, allowing myself the luxury of putting all of my uncertainties and fears aside by simply being across from her. Mina was here. She was okay and for this brief moment in time, that had to be enough.

But Mina was not at ease, nor was she feigning to be. Her eyes darted around as if she was searching, looking for someone. Who? Anton? Alexei? Was she hoping for someone else? Did she need someone else to be here?

"Something wrong?" I asked quietly so that Anton's men were unlikely to overhear.

"Not at all...I just wasn't expecting you," she explained, a slight tremble in her voice.

"Disappointed or pleasantly surprised?"

"Surprised," she played along, eyeing my security detail.

"You guys mind giving us some space?" I asked the fellas flanking me. They grunted their bored indifference. Surprising me with their cooperation, Anton's men approached the flight crew with the duffle bags that were filled with necessities for Bradley Cooper, then they stepped several feet away from us. I returned my full attention to the girl I'd turn the whole world over to find.

I stepped forward and bent down to place the carrier holding Bradley at her feet. I slowly straightened, meeting her gaze, closer now than before. She lost a long breath at our proximity. I watched for every flutter of her lashes, every small change in her expression as I pressed my fingers against her palm.

"Before you go," I breathed, lifting my phone and placing it in her hand. She looked down at the message I'd typed out, then back up at me, her eyes wide with questions. "I really enjoyed talking to you earlier today, Maria," I emphasized her name. "I feel like we have something special between us, a connection. If you maybe...feel it, too, perhaps we could keep in touch?" I rasped.

"Are you sure about this?" she asked, referring to the message but making it sound like a response to my proposal.

"Absolutely," I answered without wavering.

Her eyes flickered between mine, brimming with emotion—desire, sadness, a simultaneous hope and hopelessness that mirrored my own.

She licked her caramel-colored lips—the lips I dreamed of—and took a step closer to type something into my phone.

I closed my eyes and inhaled her. Under the scent of sweet perfume was the essence of her, of the girl who loved my ugly and called it my resilience. And she'd been right, it had taken everything in me to escape that hell. Just as it would take everything in me to get her out of this one. And I would. Nothing would stop me. That's who I was. That's who I always would be. I was relentless. I was a force. I deserved to be here.

A jolting screech tore through the air, along with the rising sounds of the jet engine. I spun to find four gray vehicles on approach. Two had arrived and two more were joining.

"FBI!" I turned toward the familiar voice. At the front, wedged between the open door and body of a gray jeep, wearing full FBI gear and gun trained on me, was CJ.

I covered Mina and Bradley with my body. I threw my hands in the air.

"On the ground! Now!"

Anton's men were already in their car and peeling off, smashing through the gates. No one followed.

My eyes were wide on CJ, disbelief flooding me. How had I missed this? What the hell was CJ doing? The world felt like it was crashing over my head as it dawned on me. Did I play right into his hands? Did this psychopath and his batshit crazy wife really just set me up? What was he playing at?

"CJ—"

"On the ground!" the other Fed shouted. My world spun as I dropped to my knees. "You too, ma'am."

I was flat on my belly when Mina dropped to her knees on the ground beside me. She turned to me and there was a moment—before Mina's eyes widened and she looked at her tattoo, before the metal cuffs bit into skin, before CJ boomed into my ear that I was under arrest for wildlife trafficking, before they hauled us off in separate vehicles—this impossibly peaceful moment, this tiny moment, an eclipse of a moment when the sun and the moon crossed and I knew that nothing could erase this link between Mina and me.

We happened.

"Always," whispered the universe.

PLEASE REVIEW MY BOOK

I sincerely hope you enjoyed reading this book as much as I enjoyed writing it. If you did, I would greatly appreciate a short review on Amazon or your favorite book website. Reviews are crucial for any author, and even just a line or two can make a huge difference.

WHERE YOU CAN LEAVE A REVIEW:
GOODREADS
STORYGRAPH
FABLE
BOOKMORY
LIBRARY THING
B&N
INDIEBOUND
AUDIBLE
SCRIBD
LIBRO
AMAZON (AFTER OCT 15)
AND MORE...

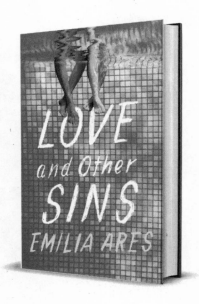

Dying to know how Mina and Oliver's paths *first* crossed?
Check out the acclaimed first installment of the
LOVE AND OTHER SINS SERIES.
AVAILABLE IN
PRINT - AUDIOBOOK - EBOOK

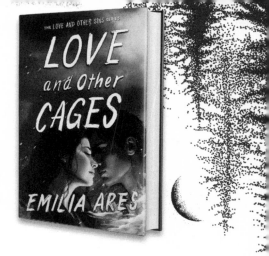

ACKNOWLEDGMENTS

Every creation is a product of a creator's unique life experiences. Years ago, during an eight-hour drive to a film location, the Love and Other Sins series began taking shape in my mind. It has come a long way since then, and I'm profoundly grateful to the readers who hold Mina and Oliver's journey as close to their hearts as I do.

Storytelling is not just an inherent part of the human experience; it's a powerful tool connecting us to one another and our ancestors. With Love and Other Sins, I aimed to shine a light on the foster care system's flaws and draw attention to the stigmas immigrant families face. Most importantly, I wanted to uplift people, advocate for those often overlooked in our community, convey a message of hope, and reaffirm the possibility of healing. The arts, especially storytelling, are a powerful tool for fostering empathy toward one another.

I want to express my heartfelt gratitude to everyone who contributed to making this novel possible: My grandfather, Arkadiy, a brilliant and gentle man with a beautiful heart and mind, who passed down the remarkable survival stories of our Armenian ancestors and taught me to communicate with passion and purpose. My incomparable grandmother, Svetlana, whose love and unwavering conviction sustained me throughout my upbringing and helped me flourish into the woman I am today. My mother, Lioudmila, strong, selfless, loving, and wise, who taught me to see beyond the surface and to believe in myself despite any obstacle. My father, Ares, funny, generous, kind and caring, who instilled in me a belief in the goodness of people. My delightful sister, the heart of my existence, who infuses life with her brilliant sparkle, who championed this work from the very beginning, who happens to be the wildly talented singer/songwriter SOZI, who composed and produced the breathtaking theme music for the Love and Other Cages audiobook intro/outro. My husband, Slava, my best friend, who understands me without words, grounds me, challenges me, inspires me and makes me better. Thank you for your unwavering, unconditional support. Sebastian, my kind, brilliant, humorous, clever, creative, and loving child. Vivienne, my joy, my cuddle bug, my fierce, brave, and fiery girl. I love you both to the farthest star and back infinity times, my babies.

My brother, Grigor, for employing minimal teasing when answering my questions regarding his medical knowledge. My fantastic friend, Adam, for abundant cheer and the outrageous billboard. Thank you to Lina, Yurik, Lee, Sonya and my family and friends. All those who pre-ordered my debut novel and helped spread the word, I acknowledge each of you and hold you very dear in my heart. The incredible women of Coastal Grandmas Book Club, Alix, Andrea, Elyse, Joey, Julie, Kelly, Paula, Rosalie, Rose, Terresa, and my good friend Cassie, thank you for your encouragement and camaraderie.

My editor, Beth Cody Kimmel, for an invaluable, enlightening and delightful collaboration. My proofreader, Mike Waitz, for his sharp eye and exceptional attention to detail. Miblart for the gorgeous cover. SERA Press for spreading the word.

And finally, to you, yes, you, reading these words right now, my cherished reader. I want to express a massive, wholehearted "Thank you" to you for embarking on Oliver and Mina's journey, for loving them, and for breathing life into the *Love and Other Sins* series. Your support and patience as I brought Love and Other Cages into existence mean the world to me. I am deeply grateful and excited to have you along for this ride.

Until next time.